An Everyday Savior

An Everyday Savior

A NOVEL

Kathryn Larrabee

FOUR WALLS EIGHT WINDOWS
NEW YORK / LONDON
2002

Published in the United States by
Four Walls Eight Windows
39 West 14th Street, room 503
New York, NY 10011
http://www.4w8w.com

The author can be reached at www.kathrynlarrabee.com

ISBN: 1-56858-225-0
Cataloging-in-Publication data for this book
has been filed with the Library of Congress.

10   9   8   7   6   5   4   3   2   1

For Janet Desaulniers,
who started me on this path,

and for Michael Brothers,
who kept me on it.

An Everyday Savior

T HE LIGHTS FROM THE AMBULANCE BARN across the street cut through Sonia's lace curtains, sending flowery shadows over the bed. The drivers wait until they're on the highway to sound the siren, but I'm a light sleeper and the lights are enough. Sonia mumbles in her sleep, what sounds like random words in English and Russian. Sometimes she paints, mumbling the names of colors, and her fingers twitch, brushing against my back. Tonight she says "green" over and over, and sighs.

I fold back the quilt that was a wedding gift from my mother. She bought it from the Mennonite women who sell them at a farm market every Saturday. The floor is cold, but Sonia insisted on leaving the hardwood bare. I walk over to the window and push back the curtain. The ambulance pulls out onto the main road and speeds away. It's been snowing the last few hours, and the only tracks are the ambulance's.

Sonia rolls over onto her side, edging her back toward the middle of the mattress. In her sleep, she's looking for me; when she discovers I'm not there, she'll wake up. We've been married six months, and already our bodies have developed this relationship, this rhythm that makes it hard to sleep alone.

I check the clock on the nightstand: three more hours before the alarm sounds. I slip under the covers and nudge my hip against Sonia's back. Her skin is warm in her flannel nightgown. The house is cold at night, so she bought three of them at the local department store. The store is a tourist attraction; I took Sonia there to show her the pulley system used to make change, the small wooden cups speeding across the ceiling to a central cage with a cashier, then speeding back to the salesperson at the counter.

Sometimes I think I can smell the Russianness on her skin: the food, the vodka, her brother-in-law's cigars. Her hair is thick and glossy; it lies in heavy clumps on the pillow. She brings eggs and beer and vinegar with her into the shower, working them into frothy combinations, and she brushes it hard every night, a hundred strokes from the roots to the tips that settle against her shoulderblades.

I fit myself against her back and touch her lightly on the shoulder. She stirs, but doesn't wake. Her arms are muscular from painting, her back strong from sitting for hours in front of her easel. She says when she's painting she forgets where she is, that the sun might set without her noticing.

She's taped an art postcard to her vanity mirror. It's a Kandinsky painting she says reminds her of me, of what I looked like to her the first time we met. A man and woman on horseback ride past a floating city. They're fairy tale characters, Ivan Tsarevitch and the beautiful Jelena, riding home after capturing the firebird. Jelena has dark hair and eyes like Sonia's, the color of smoke.

"Harley?" she says, turning toward me.

She rolls over to face me, and I touch her side. "It's all right," I say, and she closes her eyes again, drifting off to sleep.

I lean back against the pillows and wonder about the ambulance being sent out so early in the morning. The drivers are volunteers; they all have to work other jobs, so they rotate the overnight shifts to keep from losing too much sleep. There must have been only one or two on call so late, nodding off over their desks. I imagine the startling ring of the phone, the rush to put on coats and gloves while the police dispatcher gave the address. There are fishing and hunting cabins so deep in the woods that the owners have to register a map with the police.

"Green," Sonia says, her voice muffled by the pillow, and I feel myself sliding back to sleep. I remember, as a child, my mother bowing her head every time we saw an ambulance pass, and so I say my own prayer now, for the ambulance drivers and the person they're racing to save. I ask God to keep them safe, and then, while I'm at it, before I've completely drifted off, I ask Him to save Sonia and me, too.

❦

The alarm is on my side of the bed, but this morning Sonia hears it first. I wake up with her leaning across my stomach, slapping at the button on the clock radio. The slogan for the local radio station is: "WQRT: All the hits from Glenn Miller to Barry Manilow." This morning, it's Percy Faith and his Orchestra, playing "Theme from a Summer Place."

"Wake up, sleepyhead," Sonia says, digging her elbow into my chest.

I reach out and turn off the radio. "Where'd you learn 'sleepyhead?'" I ask her.

She shrugs and kisses me, smiling, so that her lips tickle against mine.

"You watch too much TV."

"How else do I learn?" she asks, leaning to kiss me again, resting her weight on my chest. When we met, her English was good, but she likes to watch TV for the slang. The other morning I caught her watching an exercise show that she said was good practice for her numbers.

"Sonia," I say, "you're hurting me," and she rolls off me onto her own side of the bed.

"When do we pick up Mama?" She wrestles her flannel nightgown from where it's tangled in the sheets, kicking the covers down to the foot of the bed.

"I said we'd be there between nine and ten." I know my mother hates the way Sonia calls her "Mama," but it's too late to tell Sonia. I walk over to the bathroom, pulling at the seat of my sweatpants; I can't get used to sleeping in clothes, but the house is cold at night, and heat costs a fortune.

I've got my T-shirt on backwards, and my hair's sticking up all over. I run my hands through it, raise the toilet seat and pee. Sonia's been making me take vitamins, and besides the taste, they turn my pee bright green. Sonia walks in before I'm finished, glances in my direction and starts brushing her teeth. I don't like her walking in on me like this, but I can't think of a way to tell her that wouldn't embarrass me. I finish and flush, and she walks around me, hikes up her nightgown and sits down, holding her toothbrush between her teeth and absently brushing again, up and down, while she pees. She looks tiny, like a child, with her toes curled against the bathroom tile, in her flannel nightgown and with her toothbrush handle jutting out of her mouth.

"Don't flush," I tell her, turning on the water in the shower. I pull off my T-shirt and sweatpants, waiting for the water to heat up. Sonia smiles and puts the toilet lid down.

She leans close to the mirror and pokes at the skin under her eyes, dabs some cream and pulls her hair back into a tight ponytail. Sonia cuts her own hair, and the ends are even and thick, swinging from her rubber band. She turns so easily from grown woman to little girl that some-

times I can imagine her as she must have been, with a
bundle of books and falling kneesocks. She would have
been a serious-looking girl, too young for a face that
would later be beautiful.

Steam from the shower rises toward the ceiling. I turn
the heat down and step under the spray. The men in my
mother's family all lost their hair young, so I worry about
mine. I buy the expensive shampoo and pay attention to
how much hair winds up in the drain. Sonia doesn't wear
perfume, but she uses a soap that smells like flowers. I
keep forgetting to buy a bar of something bland for
myself, so I use hers and hope nobody notices.

When I get out of the shower, Sonia's already dressed,
wearing a turtleneck, a navy blue sweater, tights and the
denim skirt I bought for her on our honeymoon. I kept
telling her to choose whatever she wanted, a fancy dress,
but she only wanted the American denim that was so
expensive in St. Petersburg.

She comes up behind me and pats my rear. "You have a
good body," she says.

I show her the roll of fat beginning at my middle. "I
have to work on this," I say.

She shrugs.

I pull on some jeans, a T-shirt and flannel shirt. I take a
pair of sneakers out of the closet, the ones Sonia's always
giving me a hard time about. She wants to know why I
wear basketball sneakers if I'm not a basketball player.

Sonia takes the quilt off the bed and straightens the
sheets. I tie my sneakers and go to help her. We pull a
wrinkled top sheet up from the bottom of the bed, press it
with our hands and tuck the corners under the mattress.
Sonia smiles at me across the bed, then climbs onto the

mattress and reaches for me, walking across the sheets on her knees.

"Hey," I say, "You're ruining it," but she pulls me down onto the bed with her, tugging at the collar of my shirt. She's got her face close to mine, her eyes brilliant, breath tickling my cheek.

"Let's not get Mama," she says. "Let's stay home and make love."

"Sonie,' I say.

She kisses me hard. "You love me," she says with a commanding tone.

"It's already after nine."

She sighs and pats the front of my shirt. "Why does Mama come to live with us?"

I've explained it a million times. "Because she broke her leg, and they won't let her stay at the retirement center if she can't get around by herself."

She sighs again and lifts herself up from the bed.

"You agreed to it, Sonia," I say.

"I know," she says. She walks to the doorway, acts as if she might say something, argue with me about the nursing home, but she knows it's no use. On the day I went to check it out, the halls smelled like urine from dirty bedclothes and someone was screaming, calling for Charlie over and over again in a room with a flickering television. Instead, Sonia looks at me and changes her mind, says, "We go soon."

I follow her downstairs to the kitchen. Sonia opens the refrigerator and reaches into the crisper. She takes two green apples from the fridge and drops them into her purse. She eats all the time, mostly fruits and vegetables. She says she can't believe how easy they are to get here, how cheap.

"You want one, Harley?" she asks, looking at me over the top of the refrigerator door.

"I thought we'd get something later, with Mama."

She nods, walks to the door and pulls her coat off its peg on the wall. It's the same one with the fake fur collar and missing button that she wore in Russia. I've been saving a little from my paycheck each week to buy her a new one for her birthday. I have about a hundred and fifty dollars saved, but now I'll have to find a way to drive to the city without Sonia knowing. There's only the one department store in town, and it doesn't carry the latest styles.

Sonia climbs into the truck while I raise the garage door. I'd like to get an automatic one, but we don't have the money, and it seems lazy in a town where so few people even have a garage. I start the truck, waiting for it to warm up. Sonia's chewing on her apple, holding a piece of paper towel to her chin. I reach for the apple, and she hands it to me. It's tart, not quite ripe, so my teeth ache a little with the sweetness, but Sonia likes them this way. She likes anything sweet.

"You'll get fat eating so much, Sonia," I say, though it isn't true. If anything, the hollows under her eyes have filled in a bit, making her look a little less tired, a little less small and frightened.

Sonia slouches in the seat, pushing her belly out from the waistband of her skirt. "I will be a fat Russian peasant woman," she says.

"Never," I say. "You're much too pretty," and she smiles and straightens in the seat. We turn onto the main road and head through the middle of town. It's Sunday, and the church parking lots are full, but nothing else is open.

Pulling onto the lake road, we swerve a little, and I touch her leg in case she's afraid. "Not enough salt on these roads," I say, pointing to the floor of the truck. The engine noise is so loud that I'm almost shouting at her. I keep meaning to slide underneath and have a look at the muffler.

She checks her watch. "We are hurrying?" This is her way of telling me I drive too fast. I ignore the question, but slow down a little and turn on the radio. It's a country station, so I put on a southern accent and sing loud, raising my chin like a coyote howling. Sonia laughs, and we glide past the summer houses overlooking the lake.

The houses are empty. The snow is fresh, the driveways unplowed, inches of snow lie balanced on the mailboxes. These are the show places owned by "summer people." The townies put up with them because of the money they spend on antique furniture and wine from the local vine- yards. Every year, you can tell when summer's coming, because prices go up at the grocery store.

I sing "Your cheatin' heart...will tell on you," and Sonia scans the hills, the giant houses full of windows, with cathedral ceilings and fancy alarm systems. She knows we'll never be able to afford one, but she studies them in a way that makes me uncomfortable. In Russia, she must have thought I was rich. Now, she's starting to know better.

"Stop," she says suddenly. She says it in Russian, too flustered to translate. "Stop now."

I pull to a stop, and the back of the truck coasts, then catches hold again before sliding into the ditch. I smack the steering wheel hard with my fist. "What? What is it?"

She opens the passenger door and steps out into the snow. "Sonia?" I ask. "Sonie?"

She walks partway up the hill, stops and whistles loudly, two fingers between her teeth. Then I see it, a dark spot against the snow, up near the porch of the next house over.

She whistles again, and the dark spot becomes a dog, white with a black nose and what looks like a black smudge above its tail. The dog crosses over to the yard above where Sonia's standing and stops, panting, with its tongue hanging and its mouth open in a grin.

Sonia must know the dog doesn't belong here. The surrounding houses are empty, no smoke rising from the chimneys, no tracks in the snow except the dog's. Sonia whistles one more time and climbs the rest of the hill. The dog sees her coming and playfully circles away, then runs toward her, stopping about ten feet away from her. "Sonia," I yell from the truck, but she either ignores me or doesn't hear, stepping carefully through the deepening snow. Her new shoes will be ruined, but she keeps walking toward the dog, clapping her hands and shouting, "Here, puppy. Here, puppy."

The dog runs another wide circle, stops a few feet short of her and sniffs. She steps closer and holds out her hands, and the dog moves in a few more steps. She bends her knees and reaches her hands toward the dog. It wags its tail tentatively and approaches her, gently sniffs her fingers. "Come," she says, patting her leg, and begins to walk back toward the truck. She turns, looking to see if the dog will follow, but it stands still, watching her. "Come now," she says and starts walking, and this time the dog bounds ahead of her, turns and circles back before running off again.

At the bottom of the hill, the dog stops to lift his leg against a snowdrift, then crawls over the top of it, stands sniffing the air before lowering his head and rolling onto his side, kicking his legs until his coat is covered with snow. He stands and does it again, rolling onto his other side and kicking with all four paws. Then he stands, shakes and waits for Sonia to pick her way carefully down the hill. She climbs over the snowdrift to where the truck is waiting, opens the door and calls to him. He runs toward her and jumps into the cab of the truck, spraying snow all over the seat.

"Sonia," I say. "What do you think you're doing?"

She climbs into the truck, and the dog turns to lick her face. "He's cold."

"He's got a collar. He belongs to somebody."

The dog sits, panting. He has large brown eyes, a black nose, terrible breath. He lifts a paw and swats Sonia with it, wanting her to pet him. "Good dog," she says.

"Sonia," I say and reach for the dog's collar to read the tag. It looks hand–lettered, just "Hale" and a phone number.

"Hale," I say. "I went to school with Doug Hale. He lives on a farm a couple of miles from here."

"Miles?" she says and rubs the dog's ears, gives him a kiss on the nose.

"Must have run off. He'll find his way home." I have a mental picture of my mother waiting for us in her wheelchair, with her coat on and her purse balanced on her lap. I reach for the door handle to let the dog out.

"No," Sonia says. "We will take him."

I'm surprised. It's the first time she's directly contradicted me. "Sonia," I say, "we're late as it is."

"Later, then," she says. "After Mama."

I'm about to argue with her, but instead put the truck into gear. Sonia's holding the dog's ears, making kissing noises, and she has the same look she had when she saw the shoes she's wearing in a store window. They're blue ballerina slippers, leather with little bows on the front, a fancy Italian brand. They were eighty–five dollars on sale, but the look on her face was enough to make me buy them and be happy about it. I'd have paid anything for the power to put that look on her face.

The wheels spin and catch hold, and we lurch onto the highway. I turn off the radio, letting quiet settle inside the truck, and listen to wet snow spraying against the wheel wells, the dog's breathing, Sonia shifting her weight on the seat.

"You like dogs?" I ask after a while. The dog stands on the seat between us, staring through the windshield and sniffing at the heat vents.

She nods. "When I am small, I had one."

"What happened?" I'm concentrating on the road, trying to stay inside the tracks left by other cars.

She shrugs. "It dies."

I don't know what to do when she says something like this. She abbreviates her sadness, keeps it hidden from me, from fear or mistrust, I don't know. I glance in her direction, but the dog is in the way, and I can't see her expression.

"We could get a dog," I say finally.

She pulls the dog onto her lap, tugging at his paws, then cradles him and scratches his stomach. The dog is nervous at first, but relaxes when she speaks to him softly in Russian. She looks at me then and smiles, showing the two metal caps in the back of her mouth. Her smiling like this is a way to measure her happiness. She's self-conscious about the caps and usually tries to hide them, but when she's really happy, she forgets.

༈

We pull into the retirement center fifteen minutes late. I park by the door and tell the dog to stay, pointing my finger in his face. I feel stupid, not knowing whether he even understands the word, but he seems willing to sit in the truck while Sonia and I get out and shut the doors. He watches Sonia walk to the retirement center entrance and barks once before she goes inside. She turns around and waves at him, motioning for him to lie down on the seat.

I take a deep breath before walking through the automatic doors, bracing myself for the smell of rubbing alcohol and old age that hits me once I'm inside. My mother's room is off the main hallway, past the TV room and the cafeteria. Three old women are smoking in the TV room, completely ignoring the blare of the television. In the cafeteria, they're already cooking lunch, something with beef. They feed the residents here early; otherwise, they complain.

Someone's taped paper flowers on the doors to the rooms with pictures of each room's resident glued to the center. It's as much for the residents as it is for visitors. The halls all look alike, and the old people whose minds wander have trouble remembering where they belong. This isn't my mother's problem. Her mind is sharp, even if her bones are brittle as toothpicks. In the picture of her on her door, she has her hat and gloves on, she's holding the collar of her coat closed at the throat, and her hair's been blown around her face. They must have caught her by surprise; I can see from her expression that she's startled and irritated.

Sonia waits next to my mother's door, and I knock lightly, two knuckles against the wood grain. Mom won't answer, but I want her to be warned I'm coming in. I open the door, and she's sitting with her coat on, facing the window that looks out onto a small patio. There's no telling how long she's been sitting like that. Now, when we take her outside, she'll complain about the cold.

"Take me to the bathroom, Harley," she says.

I look at Sonia and start to say something, but Mom interrupts me.

"She can't lift me in this thing," she says, pointing to the cast that reaches from above her knee to her foot.

"She'll have to while I'm at work, Ma," I say.

"I am strong," Sonia says. She grabs the back of Mom's chair and wheels her toward the bathroom.

"You should put me in a home," Mom says over her shoulder.

"You don't want that, Mama," Sonia says softly, half pushing and half lifting the chair onto the bathroom tile.

"Easier on everybody," Mom says as Sonia closes the bathroom door.

I look at the photos on my mother's dresser. Me in my Little League uniform. Me in tights in the high school musical, me at my college graduation. Mom had a new gray suit, a pink blouse and matching pink shoes. She insisted that she and Dad stay at a hotel they couldn't afford because it was close to the gymnasium and she didn't want to ruin the shoes. My father had on the dark blue suit he wore to weddings and funerals.

When I was a kid, I wanted more than anything to be in a farm family, eight or ten kids in a huge house surrounded by fields. I wanted people to say, "He's one of those Jenkins kids" or "one of the Watts boys." I wanted to come to school in shirts worn at the elbow that one brother wore the year before and another one would wear the year after. I liked the way farm kids always had someone to eat lunch with, someone to talk to in gym class and sit with on the bleachers at football games. They walked around in noisy packs in the hallways or on the school bus. They played touch football in the fields behind their house and basketball in the driveway. My own house was quiet, only a ticking clock and the sound of the porch swing creaking while my mother read Victorian novels and my father smoked his pipe and read *Field & Stream* cover to cover all Sunday afternoon. My mother was forty-two when she found herself pregnant, an embarrassment she never quite got over. My father was fifty; he retired from the mill when I was fifteen, died when I was twenty-one.

My mother sold the house a few years after my father died and moved into a condo by the college. She loved the house, but it was like her to make tough decisions quickly; she'd call it "being practical" and never look back, never mention it again. I tried to help her keep the house up, but it was going downhill, peeling stucco and a roof that needed expensive repairs. I drive by it sometimes, park by the curb and sit in my truck. The new owners make improvements I try not to hate, a mud room where my mother's rose bushes used to be, a new driveway over the one I helped my father pave, azaleas where we buried the cat. Sometimes I think if I ever had the money, I'd buy the house back and tear it all down.

Sonia wheels Mom out of the bathroom, and I pick up one of the boxes with Mom's things. Mom winces when the cast bumps against the doorjamb on the way out, but she doesn't say anything. I fold up the quilt on her bed; it's a twin bed and the quilt brushes the floor at the sides. I put it carefully on top of the box with her night creams and medicine bottles.

My mother doesn't wave or speak to anyone on the way out, just nods slightly, the same way to all of them, nurses and patients. One of the nurses comes over and kisses her cheek. Mom doesn't see her coming and recoils at being touched, but the nurse ignores her, shouts, "Goodbye, Mrs. Cookson. Take care now," and hurries off down the hall. Mom wipes her cheek absently with her gloved hand.

Sonia passes through the automatic doors, and we all stop short in front of the truck. "We forget the dog," Sonia says softly, tugging at the sleeve of my jacket.

"Where'd that dog come from?" Mom asks.

"I will hold him," Sonia says, gesturing toward her lap. She's afraid I'll leave him here in the cold, miles from where he belongs.

I load the box in the truck bed, setting it on top of an old blanket to keep it from sliding around.

"I never liked dogs," Mom says. "Dumb and dirty."

I walk over to the passenger side door and open it. The dog moves to the edge of the seat and sniffs my jacket. "Get back," I say, motioning for him to move backward, "back."

Sonia wheels Mom behind me. "Get back," I say again, but the dog just stares at me, sniffing.

"You'll have to get in first," I say to Sonia. She comes around from behind me and climbs onto the seat, pushing the dog with her body so that the dog stands behind the steering wheel.

"Your turn, Ma," I say, and lean toward her. She reaches her arms around my neck like a child, and I lift her, straining with the weight of the cast, and drop her sideways onto the seat, so that her cast is wedged diagonally under the dashboard. She winces when her foot knocks against the dash, then smooths the fabric of her skirt where her slip is showing. I feel sorry for her, having to be hoisted like that, but it's the best I can do.

"You are okay?" Sonia asks my mother, touching her hand lightly to Mom's skirt.

Mom looks at her as if deciding whether or not to answer, then turns toward the window, clears her throat and says, "Fine."

I walk around the back of the truck, lift the wheelchair into the bed and open the driver's side door. Sonia pulls the dog onto her lap, and I climb into the truck. The dog goes willingly enough, but tries to keep his balance by digging his toenails into her leg. She frowns and moves her legs apart, bumping against my thigh, then shifts the dog's weight so that his paws rest on the truck seat.

"The Hales'll be looking for their dog," I say.

"We can take him first," Sonia says.

"I don't know if Mom's eaten yet," I say quietly, but Mom overhears me.

"I ate," she says, "hours ago."

I start the truck and back out of the parking lot, then take a left heading away from town. The Hales' farm is some-where on Temperance Road, if I remember right. Doug Hale inherited it from his dad. He and his wife, Lynette, and their kids live in the main house, and another brother and his wife live in the nearby trailer. I haven't talked to Doug or Lynette since I moved back to town. I saw them once at the movie theater at the plaza, but I don't think they recognized me. I might not have recognized Doug either, all these years since high school, but he looked too much like his dad, and his brother has darker hair.

I concentrate on the road, watching for patches of black ice. These country roads don't get plowed very often. The county doesn't have the money for more trucks. Some of the farmers have plows they hitch to the front of their pickups, and they take a drive by when they can, but it's a drop in the bucket with the kind of snow we get.

Sonia remembers the apple in her purse and offers it to the dog. He sniffs at it and turns away.

"I'll take that," Mom says, and Sonia hands it to her. Mom opens her mouth wide, showing the gold dental work at her gum line, and bites down. She chews quickly and takes another bite, leaving red lipstick smudges on the white fruit.

The dog shifts his weight, balancing his elbows on Sonia's thigh so he can lie down with his front paws out-stretched. She moves to give him more room, and he lowers his head onto my lap.

"Good boy," I say, patting him. He's not a bad-looking dog for a mutt. Around here, only the tourists have fancy dogs with breed names. Most of the others are combinations of dogs from neighboring farms and the strays that wander into warm barns in the winter. In the spring, the strays disappear, leaving behind litters of puppies. The local humane society's always getting on people to fix their dogs, but the farmers mostly just put signs by the road advertising free puppies, and families take them in. We're probably one of a handful of families on our street without a dog; most have two or three.

Mom finishes the apple, rolls her window down a few inches and throws out the core. It bumps against the side of the truck before landing next to the road.

We follow the main rural route to the end, and I turn right on Temperance, a steep gravel road. The dog raises his head and stands up, clawing Sonia in the leg. He stares out the windshield and whimpers.

"Look," Mom says, pointing a finger at the dog. "He knows where he lives."

I'm not sure exactly where the farm is, and Temperance is a long road, so I slow down, occasionally kicking up gravel against the truck's belly. About halfway down a steep slope on the left-hand side, I spot a black mailbox with white, faded lettering, "HALE." Someone has wound plastic flowers around the mailbox post and left them to fade in the sun. From this far away, even in the snow, they look real, fluttering in the wind.

I turn into the driveway, and the dog strains toward the windshield, whimpering and barking. I stop the truck, and the dog climbs over my lap to be first out the door. He runs into the yard and pees against one of the small bushes lining the porch, then disappears around the back of the house. It's a cedar shingle house, an old one, leaning a little with cracked wood on one side and a crooked porch railing.

A woman opens the front door and steps out onto the porch. She's wearing a cardigan sweater that she pulls as far as she can around the baby balanced on her hip. It's Lynette Wilson Hale, though she doesn't for a minute look like a girl I'd recognize from high school.

"We brought your dog back," I say, walking quickly across her yard. The wind's kicked up, it's cold, and I'm hoping that maybe if she doesn't recognize me, this won't take long.

"Where was he?" She shifts the baby, reaches two fingers into her mouth and whistles. The dog comes trotting from around the back of the house and stands next to Sonia in the yard.

"On the lake road."

"What's his name?" Sonia asks, reaching to pat the dog's back. She pulls off a mitten and scratches him gently with her fingers.

"Whitey." Lynette steps forward, walks down the porch steps toward Sonia and the dog. The baby fusses, acts as though it might cry, but Lynette rocks it gently on her hip, and it goes quiet, nestling against her side. Lynette's careful in the snow, wearing slippersocks, wool sewn to leather soles. She comes toward me, stepping into the glare of the sun on the snow, revealing the hint of a bruise over her left eye. She looks in my direction but doesn't make eye contact.

The dog, Whitey, begins to play with Sonia, growling and leaping away from her when she reaches her hands toward him. He takes her hand in his mouth, nipping at her but not biting her, and she grabs his snout, jerks it from side to side.

Lynette walks toward Sonia, reaching for Whitey. "C'mere," she says and hooks a finger under his collar, then pulls him toward the house. He barks in protest, but lets her drag him to the porch. She reaches the door and has to let go of the dog long enough to open it. She orders Whitey into the house and turns, still balancing the baby, who's restless again, squirming in her arms and snuffling, ready to cry. "Thank you," Lynette says, looking first at me and then at Sonia. I nod and Lynette goes inside, letting the screen door bang shut, then closing the heavy wooden door. The baby cries from inside the house, a sudden wail that goes quieter as Sonia and I walk back toward the truck.

Sonia's new shoes are marked with salt trails. I wait for her to walk toward me and when she reaches me, I bend to kiss her cheek. "Harley?" she asks, but I smile and pat her lightly on the back, walk to the driver's side of the truck where my mother's waiting, eyes forward, hugging herself for warmth.

I have to start the ignition twice before the engine turns over. Sonia sits in the middle between Mom and me, hold-ing her mittens over her mouth to blow warm air on them.

The engine starts, but before I can begin to back up, the door to Lynette's house opens, and she comes quickly down the porch steps, jogging toward my side of the truck. She knocks on the window, and I can still hear the baby crying, louder now with the front door open. I can see the bruise over her eye and another mark, crescent-shaped and yellowing, on her cheek. "Harley," she says, still not looking at me, but staring into the truck, at Sonia's red mittens. "Thanks," she says and turns away, walks quickly back toward the house.

ॐ

"Was that the Wilson girl?" my mother asks.

"Yeah, Ma," I say. "Lynette Wilson."

"You know her, Harley?" Sonia turns toward me, her face flushed with the cold.

"I dated her in high school." I concentrate on the road, avoiding Sonia's gaze, feeling as though I should have told her about Lynette, but not sure exactly why. She doesn't talk about her old boyfriends; I don't know how many she's had, and I don't particularly want to.

"Then you help her," she says. Sonia clutches my arm, her red mitten against my dark jacket. She points to her eye, the same place as Lynette's bruise. "Someone hurts her."

ॐ

"That bruise could've been anything." I take the hill a little too fast and have to slow down when the truck fishtails. My mother grabs the dashboard, but doesn't say anything. "The baby could've kicked her, she could've tripped and hit her head, the dog could've knocked into her...."

Sonia shakes her head. "No. I don't think so."

Her nose is running just a little, a drop at the tip that her skin is too cold to feel. I want to reach into my pocket for my handkerchief and wipe it for her, but for some reason, I leave it alone.

"How do you know?"

Sonia looks at me and shrugs. Then she pulls off her mitten, runs her finger over the knuckles of her hand and mimics fitting those knuckles to the bruise on Lynette's face.

"What am I supposed to do about it?" I turn off Temperance, slowing a little, but trying to keep my foot off the brake. My mother's wheelchair knocks against the side of the truck bed.

"Nothing," my mother says. "You can't do anything about it." She says this looking straight ahead, her breath blowing clouds toward the windshield. "This is a small town," she says. "You can't afford to accuse people of things you're not sure of."

꙼

CHAPTER II

WHAT I REMEMBER ABOUT LYNETTE is the smell of apples. Her father's orchard was high on a hill overlooking the lake; we'd climb in second gear up the gravel drive with the headlights out so we wouldn't wake her parents, past the shop where her mother sold applesauce and cider, past her parents' house with the apple-shaped cutouts in the shutters. We'd park in the back rows of MacIntosh higher up the hill, facing out toward the lake. Through the leaves, I could just make out the shimmer of light on the black surface of the water. In fall, the ground under the trees would be littered with rotting fruit, and the air, when I leaned to kiss her and, with my thumb and forefinger, pinch open the buttons of her blouse, smelled of sweat and sugar, fruity and strong enough to stay on my clothes the next day.

Lynette was a runner. Every morning she ran the five miles from her father's orchard to the girls' locker room at the high school. I would see her sometimes, in shorts and a T-shirt, with a ponytail in her hair, her face red and dripping with sweat, her strides long and even. I honked, but she never waved; she was concentrating, pumping her arms close to her chest, breathing evenly, the laces of her sneakers tied in double loops she wouldn't trip over. In the school locker room, she put her head under the faucet, then she dried her hair with paper towels and left it loose to drip down her back. In first-period English, I watched the patterns that formed on the back of her T-shirt, I saw how her skin was clear and flushed, I saw the muscle in her back and along her collarbone and thought how strange and remote she was from me, how perfect she was, how lucky I was that she let me pick her up in my car and take her places, let me sit in the front seat, kissing and touching her, in the far reaches of her father's orchard.

$\backsim$

"Here we go," I say, reaching for my mother. I hesitate before sliding my hand underneath her, not wanting to touch her there, but she doesn't say anything, just turns her head. I lift her, smelling her perfume, noticing the pearl earrings dangling from her tiny earlobes, feeling how light she is, like a child, until I slide her off the seat and the weight of the cast hits me.

"We'll have to put a ramp in," I tell Sonia over my shoulder.

Sonia manages to lift the wheelchair down from the truck bed and carry it up the steps behind me. "How much is it costing?" She's worried about money. With my job at the electric plant, we barely make the mortgage payments, and even if Sonia could get a job, somebody has to stay home with Ma.

"I'll build it myself," I say. "Something simple to fit over the steps. Shouldn't be too difficult." I say this without any idea how to do it, but something in me wants Sonia to think I'm handy.

Sonia sets the wheelchair down to open the door. She lays it on its side, wheels spinning. Mom leans a little in the direction of the wheelchair and says, quietly, too quietly for Sonia to hear, "Don't scratch it."

While Sonia holds the door open, I carry Mom over to the couch. I can't bend my knees far enough to set her down gently; I have to drop her from about six inches above the couch. She falls against the cushions, then smooths her skirt and slowly maneuvers the cast, balancing it on the edge of the coffee table. "Harley," she says, "I'm cold."

"The heat is up to sixty-eight," Sonia says behind me.

"It's all right," I say, and go to the thermostat, turn it up to seventy.

Sonia walks over to my mother, leans close to her ear and says loudly, "I will get a sweater for you, Mama." She goes out the front door, letting it slam shut behind her and comes back with a box of my mother's things. She sets it down on the floor next to the couch and rummages through it for the white cardigan my mother wears, the one with buttons big enough for her arthritic fingers. Mom takes the sweater from Sonia but doesn't put it on. Instead, she folds her arms over it and sits shivering and staring at Sonia's paintings.

"Can I get you something, Ma?" I ask.

She looks up at me, her eyes watery and vague, then at Sonia, opens her mouth but doesn't say anything. I can see that she's lost and afraid, that she doesn't remember who we are or where she is, and I tell myself she's tired and under a lot of stress, but I know this is probably the beginning of something.

"I'll get you some tea," I say.

Sonia looks at me; she's worried about Ma. The lines around her eyes have deepened, her cheeks are flushed, and her mouth is set in a thin, straight line. She has no idea, and there's no way I can tell her, that this is how she's most beautiful to me, with this sadness and worry in her face.

"Milk?" I ask. "Sugar, Ma?" When she only looks at me, I lean away from her toward the kitchen, wanting to break the silence by doing something. But then I feel her hand on my arm, surprisingly strong, holding me. "No," my mother says, almost whispering, so that I have to lean close to her mouth to hear. "Don't leave me," she says, and so I sit on the couch next to her, holding her hand, while Sonia gets the tea.

و

My mother joined the church choir when I was thirteen. "She's terrible, but they're low on altos," my father said in the kitchen, clipping a tie to my shirt collar. I had a blue suit so tight across the shoulders that I couldn't lift my arms, shiny shoes and a pair of dress socks I kept in a ball at the back of my underwear drawer. My father wore a suit with the pants twice as worn as the jacket; at work, he left the jacket in his locker, rolled up his sleeves, loosened his tie until the knot dangled at his sternum. He wasn't ordinarily a church–going man, but we went whenever my mother sang.

My mother practiced Sunday mornings, stretching her mouth in strange directions, repeating vowel sounds, "may, me, my, mo, moo," sipping at hot tea that she said kept her vocal chords loose. She wore a ruffled blouse that showed under the collar of her robe, and white gloves that she kept folded in her purse during the service, then put on again before shaking hands with our Presbyterian minister at the church doors. "It's proper," she said, when I asked why she wore the gloves, "and the Reverend sweats."

In our town, there were church families and what my father called "C and E people," people who got religion on

Christmas and Easter. Church families had a place they usually sat. They looked smug during the hymns; they knew where the page numbers were listed on the wall, and they marked the pages ahead of time. They sang harmony, and they always got the verse right. They recited the prayers in a loud, clear voice, instead of burying their head in a prayer book, and they were the first ones out the door at the end of the service. My father and I were "C and E people," we stumbled through the service, mumbling hymns, garbling prayers. We were the last ones out of our pew, and we waited nervously by the door, shuffling our feet and getting in the way, waiting for my mother to hang up her robe and come out front to meet us.

"Got a minute, Frank?" Mr. Gilmartin, the choir director and music teacher at the middle school asked my father one Sunday when my mother was more than typically late. Dwight Gilmartin was a bald man with just a few patches of blond hair behind his ears. In winter, the crown of his head turned a spotted pink, and the tops of his ears chapped.

"Wait for your mother," my father said, walking toward the coat closet at the back of the church. He had his hands in his pockets, and the backs of his shoes were worn uneven from scuffing his feet.

I could see them through the open doorway, Mr. Gilmartin gesturing with his hands and my father looking at the floor and nodding in a rhythm that said he was listening and he understood. Mr. Gilmartin came out first, said "See you in school, Harley," and sprinted toward the door. My father followed him and clapped a hand on my shoulder, frowning and rocking on the heels of his shoes.

"What'd you think of that second hymn, Frank?" my mother asked. Her face was flushed as she fastened the pearl buttons on her gloves and shrugged her shoulders

into the wool coat my father had bought for her three
Christmases ago.

"A doozie," my father said, pushing the heavy church
door open and holding it for her.

"I couldn't master that harmony for the life of me," she
said, "so I sang the soprano part an octave lower." She had
her hand on my back, steering me toward the car. "Watch
your fingers, Harley," she said. She slid carefully onto the
passenger side of the front seat, smoothing her skirt over
her knees, then flipping the sun visor down to check her
lipstick in the mirror attached to its underside. "I don't think
anyone noticed," she said. "No one said anything, anyway."

"Dwight Gilmartin said hello," my father said, edging
onto Main Street, turning the wheel with both hands. The
station wagon had no power steering; in order to make a
turn, the driver would have to throw his shoulders into it,
pulling hand over hand. My mother rarely drove.

"Did he?" my mother asked, nervousness beginning to
edge into her voice. Dwight Gilmartin and my father had
little more than a passing acquaintance; if Mr. Gilmartin
spoke to him, it would have to be business.

"He says you've been working very hard," my father
said carefully. "He says you've been putting in a lot of
hours practicing, that you might like a vacation."

"A vacation?" my mother asked, straightening in the seat.
She glanced in the rearview mirror as if to check whether
Dwight Gilmartin was still in the church parking lot.

"Dwight says that what with the shortage of altos,
they've been depending an awful lot on you." He slowed
for a Mennonite wagon, pulling over to the other side of
the road where the gravel wouldn't bother the horse.
"With Mrs. Martinson back, you could take a break."

"Oh," my mother said. "Well." She leaned toward the visor mirror, took her glove off and reached a pinkie to the corner of her mouth, wiping at stray lipstick, then leaned back against the seat, exhaling slowly. "Well," she said, looking absently out her window, "that might not be such a bad idea." She crossed her arms over the front of her coat. "Yes," she said, her voice tightening. "That's just fine."

My mother stopped attending choir practice, and our family stopped going to church. I rolled my clip-on tie in a ball with my dress socks and left them in the back of my drawer. My mother put away her gloves, and my father took to wearing slippers and white athletic socks on Sundays. At Christmastime every year, my mother still collected our old clothes, bought extra cans of soup and beans and asked me to donate the games I didn't play with, but now I had to go with her to the church. She'd park by the door, and I would carry in our bundles and drop them in a heap by the Reverend's office with a note in my mother's spidery lettering: "Charity donations, Margaret L. Cookson."

౪

I wheel my mother over to the kitchen table, angling the wheelchair so that the leg with the cast extends diagonally under the table. She has a sock pulled over the tip of her cast, covering her toes. It's a white sock with a small yellow pom-pon on the back, and I can't imagine where it came from. I've never seen my mother in anything but pantyhose.

Sonia brings a stack of my mother's china to the table, and I pass around the plates and salad bowls. The china has a floral pattern around the rim; the pinks and reds of the flowers have faded, and the white background is turning yellow. Mom picks up a butter plate and runs her finger over it. "Chipped," she says, wistfully.

"They were yours, Ma," I say. "You gave them to us."

"I know," she says, setting the plate back down on the table. "You don't have to shout."

Sonia looks at me and shrugs. "They are lovely plates, Mama."

My mother cringes at the word "Mama," but only unfolds a paper napkin and drops it onto her lap.

Sonia's made macaroni and cheese from a mix, along with a green salad. I help my mother with the hot bowl of macaroni, and she digs a fork into the salad, saying, "I thought there were tomatoes in here."

"At the bottom, Ma."

Sonia loves rich foods, cheese and meat and thick bread she buys at the bakery in town. She smiles while she eats, and once, when I tried talking to her during dinner, she held up a finger to shush me.

The doorbell rings, which means it must be a stranger; everyone else knocks on the back door and walks in. I get up from the table, bracing myself for some kid selling candy bars or magazine subscriptions. I fumble for the switch to the light over the front door—I'm still not sure exactly where the switches are on the walls in this house—and then, when I look up, I see Lynette Hale standing outside with her dog.

"Lynette?" I say. "Have you been crying?" Her eyes shine as though damp, and the skin underneath looks swollen.

"No," she says, and laughs a little. "My eyes run from the cold." She takes a brown cotton glove off and reaches into her pocket for a Kleenex, blows her nose and stuffs it back into her pocket. She's wearing one of those down coats that make any woman look heavy, and a knitted scarf, the kind sold at church bazaars.

"Harley," she says, "it was good of you to bring my dog back." She looks behind her at the road, at a car going past, and then down at the dog. He's restless, but she holds tight to the piece of rope she has tied to his collar.

"Your wife was so nice," she says, looking but not staring into the hall, at our furniture, the painting Sonia hung at the bottom of the stairs and the huge antique dresser we haven't figured out how to carry up the stairs. "I thought she might want to keep him," she says. She holds out the piece of rope tied to the dog, and when I look surprised, she says, "Doug doesn't much like dogs."

I take the piece of rope from her, only because she's holding it out to me, and because she looks as though she might cry. The base of her nose is red and rough-looking, and a strand of hair has blown across her mouth. I can see her truck parked at the curb, and I wonder where the baby is, if she's left it home with Doug, or if that's the reason she keeps turning back and looking at the street, if the baby's there, strapped into a carseat.

"Lynette," I say, "are you all right?"

She turns around again, and I can see how cold the wind is, that the tears in her lashes are hardening toward ice. "Sure," she says, with a tone of voice that tells me to mind my own business, "fine." She smiles then, slowly, in a way I suddenly remember from high school, so that I almost might recognize her, even in that cheap down jacket. "So," she says, "you want him?" She looks down at Whitey, then back up at me. "If not…" she says and lets her voice trail off.

I'm already holding the piece of rope; it's as if I've already agreed to it. "I guess so. Sure."

She smiles again, then leans toward the dog and pats him twice on the back. "Whitey," she says, "be good," and she turns, walks quickly down the porch steps, across the lawn to her truck. She's quick to put the truck in gear; I can see her brake lights before I'm even sure she's all the way inside, and then, after a minute, she's gone.

～

"Whitey," I say, "you hungry?" He wags his tail at the sound of his name and hops, lifting his front two paws off the floor. I let go of the rope and let him follow me into the kitchen. He nudges me with his snout at the back of my knees, tripping over my heels.

Sonia sees Whitey and holds out her hands. He sniffs them and sits, begging for the melted cheese he smelled on her fingers. She scoops some macaroni off her plate with her hand and offers it to him. He leans forward and takes it from her, dropping the macaroni on the floor. When he's done, he rises to a sitting position again and gently licks her fingers.

"Good puppy," she says to him. She smiles; I can see how good his tongue must feel against her skin, but when she turns to me, the smile is gone.

"What happens?" she asks.

"She gave him to us."

She scoops more macaroni onto her fingers and offers it to Whitey. "Why?" She watches him carefully while he licks her hands, then pats him once lightly on the head.

"What's the matter with him?" my mother asks. She has cheese smeared across her bottom lip; she glides her tongue across it, then wipes her mouth with her napkin. "Does he poop in the house?"

"She says her husband doesn't like dogs."

"You know him?" Sonia asks, her voice hushed. She curls her fingers and scratches Whitey under the chin. His tail sweeps the floor. "You know this husband?"

"I used to."

"Oh," she says and sighs, then rests her chin on Whitey's head, nuzzling him with her cheek. "Oh, Harley," she says.

❧

A picture of our senior year football team still hangs at the town hall. They were all–state champions. The quarterback and tailback went on to be college stars and eventually made it to the NFL. Every five years, my class holds a reunion, and they make a big deal out of inviting Swensen and Melovich; they put together slide shows full of them pouring coolers of Gatorade over each other's heads, blow up the team photo a hundred times and paper the gym with it. So far, neither one has shown.

Doug Hale was a linebacker, and he was good. On any other team, or in any other year, he might have been a star. He's in the front row of the team photo, third from the left, smiling, with his arm around Melovich. He's missing a tooth on the right side, his hair's cut short and spikes in the front, and he's squinting, staring into the sun, so that his expression looks vague and unfocused.

Lynette and I went to all the home games and whichever away games were within a two- or three-hour drive. The heater in my car was broken, so we brought coffee in a thermos and passed it back and forth. We had the same stadium blanket we used in the orchard all summer; during the game, we spread it over the two of us and some–

times I slipped one hand underneath her sweatshirt and brushed against her bra.

I mentioned once that Doug was a good linebacker, and I remember that Lynette agreed with me, but that was it. She didn't know much about football; she mostly commented on the cheerleaders or the band or who was at the game and who wasn't. She wore knitted gloves and a hat with the name of our team on it that she slid on over the ponytail at the back of her head. If it was cold, she pulled the hat down until it reached her eyebrows and zipped her ski jacket up to her chin.

I had played junior varsity football my freshman year and I liked it, running with the ball in my hand, hitting the ground hard, coming home muddy and sweaty, still breathing hard when I walked in the door. I liked being outside in the fall, with the smell of burning leaves and burning seaweed down on the beaches. But by the next year, I was smaller than half the other guys, and I started to be afraid of getting hurt. When the coach cut me, I was relieved.

Doug was a year ahead of me in school, but he was kept back my sophomore year because of grades. He wasn't stupid, at least I never heard anyone say so, but he had a mother who was dying of cancer, and he stayed home a lot, taking care of her while his father worked the farm.

During our senior year, Doug had a girlfriend from the next town over. She had mousy brown hair she wore hanging straight, with just a little bit of it tacked in a plain, drugstore barrette at the back of her head. She sat alone at the games on one of the bottom bleachers, screaming at the top of her lungs for Doug's plays. At parties later, we saw Doug with his arm around her, wiping hair out of her eyes and whispering things that made her giggle and squirm.

I never heard him yell at her, never saw him hit her, never saw a bruise on her, though I'm not sure why I should be trying so hard just now to remember. It's as if my mind is playing tricks on me, jumping so far ahead of what it knows, suspecting things of somebody I've known or at least been acquainted with all my life, a regular, hard-working guy with a tough job and a family to support, like every other guy I know in this town.

༈

My mother tries to help with the dishes, but her hands are shaky, and I tell her to go sit down by the TV.

"Harley," Sonia says, "be gentle."

"I was trying to save the dishes."

Sonia touches me on the shoulder. "She gives them to us."

I like her hand on my shoulder, but I'm not sure how long I should leave it there. Sonia wants me to do something about Lynette and her husband and her dog. She believes, with a certainty that unnerves me, that she knows exactly what's happening in that cedar shingle house, and she's already imagining Ivan Tsarevitch capturing the firebird. She thinks I can fix anything.

I step away from her, carry the dishes to the sink, dunk my hands in near-boiling water and start scrubbing at them with a sponge. Sonia doesn't say anything, but she brings the rest of the dishes over and sets them next to me on the counter.

"Here, puppy," Sonia says, reaching for Whitey, but he flinches and backs away.

"Careful, Sonia," I say, clearing my throat. "He doesn't know us real well."

She reaches her hand out to him, and he growls softly, lowers his head.

"Here, puppy," she says, dropping to her knees on the floor and holding her hands out to him. He seems to relax a little, still watching her hands.

"Good boy," she says, "good puppy," but this time when she reaches for him, he growls and snaps at her, so quickly that I hear the sound without seeing him move. Sonia pulls back her hand in surprise, then rubs at it where his teeth grazed the skin.

"No," I say, not yelling but firm, and shake my finger at the dog. Whitey looks at me, his ears flatten against the sides of his head, and he skirts past me, down the stairs to the basement.

"Are you all right?" I ask Sonia, wiping my hands with a dish towel.

She nods, rubbing at her hand. She looks more frightened than hurt. I take her hand and hold it, turn it over in mine. The skin is broken, but she's not bleeding.

I breathe out slowly, blowing air from my cheeks. "I'll take him back tomorrow."

"No," she says softly, shaking her head. "No, Harley."

"We can't have a vicious dog in the house."

Sonia's hands are small, veined to show her age, but childlike, too, with stubby fingers and nails she bites close to the quick. I keep hold of her hand, squeeze lightly.

"He is not vicious, Harley," she says, pulling her hand away. "I think he is afraid."

"He bit you."

She looks closely at her hand, at the broken skin along the outer edge of her palm.

"I don't think so," she says. She walks to the top of the basement stairs, turns on the light and looks for the dog.

"Can you see him?"

She shakes her head. "He wants to stop me," she says. "He thinks I will hit him."

I walk over to her, touch her on the back and crane my neck to see down the basement stairs. All I see at the bottom are shadows and a stack of lumber. The lumber's been there since we bought the house. The previous owner made birdhouses from scraps.

I start down the steps, calling to Whitey, bending to see into the corners. I catch sight of what looks like a patch of white next to the furnace. I call to him again, but I can't see his face, only that he's curled tightly into a ball and his legs are shaking. "Okay," I say softly, "okay."

I walk heavily back up the basement steps to Sonia. "How do you know that about the dog?"

She holds her hand up in front of my face. "Because he doesn't hurt me," she says. "If he wants to, he can." She walks past me down the stairs, and I can hear her at the bottom, calling softly to Whitey, "Good puppy. Good boy."

کی

My mother's asleep in front of the TV, still in her wheelchair, with her head dipped down toward her chest. The sound from the TV is just loud enough to be uncomfortable. I walk over to her and touch her on the shoulder. She's startled and her head snaps back; it takes her a few seconds to realize where she is. "The dog peed," she says, pointing to a spot on the floor, but when I walk behind her, ready to wheel her into her bedroom, I can see a dark stain on the back of the wheelchair, and I smell urine when I lean close to release the brake.

"It's all right, Ma," I say.

I wheel her into the small bedroom in the back of the house. It's painted peach, even the ceiling, and we haven't had time to repaint, but it's on the ground floor and Mom can't make it up the stairs. I tried to open the window yesterday, but it was painted shut. Sonia put clean towels in the bathroom and a rubber mattress pad on the bed.

"Do you need help changing?" I ask, knowing she's wet down the back of her skirt.

Mom shakes her head no. "Get *her*," she says.

"Sonia?"

She nods.

I go out to the kitchen and call to Sonia down the basement stairs.

"He doesn't come," Sonia says. She's sitting on the bottom step, rocking herself and talking softly to the dog.

"Mom needs help."

She looks once quickly at the dog before climbing back up the stairs.

"Talk to him," she says. "Harley, tell him you are not angry."

"He didn't bite *me*," I say. I smell vinegar on her hair as she walks past me.

"You yell at him," she says. "He is afraid."

I turn on the light to the basement, pulling on a chain attached to the lightbulb over the top of the stairs. The chain feels sticky, from cobwebs and WD-40. I walk as quietly as I can to the foot of the stairs and sit down in Sonia's place. I can see him next to the furnace, still curled in a ball, but facing me now. He's not shaking, but his ears are close to his head.

"Hey, buddy," I say. He watches me, eyes on my hands, waiting for me to do something. I put my hands in my pockets, and he seems to relax.

I lower my voice in case Sonia comes back. "Listen," I say, "I can't let you bite Sonia." I know he doesn't understand, but it makes me feel better to say it out loud. "No biting Sonia."

Sonia calls me, and I go upstairs. I find her in the bathroom with my mother perched on the toilet lid. The wheelchair is out of sight, folded and stowed behind the door.

"Harley? Help me lift her to bed." She's looking at me carefully, pleading with me not to mention the wheelchair or ask where it is. I nod and reach for my mother, waiting for her to put her arms around my neck so I can bend my knees and lift her into bed.

"Scoot me down," my mother says. She tries to push herself toward the foot of the bed, but she can't do it with the weight of the cast.

"Stop, Ma," I say, and grab her feet, pulling as gently as I can. The foot without the cast is so small, the skin so white I can see the veins pulsing. I hold her ankle and reach one hand under the cast, pull her down to the middle of the bed, take an extra pillow from the headboard and stuff it under the plaster.

"Okay, Ma?" I lean to kiss her, and she's warm, sweating a little. She reaches a hand to my face and slaps me lightly on the cheek.

"You're a good boy, Harley," she says.

﹏

"Harley?" Sonia says. "You will keep the door open?" She has on a long flannel nightgown, the one with the blue flowers, and orange socks. "For Whitey."

"He won't come all the way up here."

"Maybe." She climbs into bed with her socks still on and

pulls the covers up to her chin. I turned the heat back down as soon as Mom went to bed.

I walk into the bathroom, flip on the light and sigh when I run my fingers through my hair. I have soft pouches under my eyes that don't go away, my gut is soft and there's a permanent crease in my forehead. I brush my teeth, leaning over the sink, wipe my chin with the towel on the back of the door.

I change into a pair of old sweats that don't quite reach my ankles and turn the TV on low, Mary Tyler Moore on cable.

"You are watching TV?" Sonia asks.

"It's too early to sleep." I pull back the covers, turn the light on next to my side of the bed. We bought a baby monitor for my mother, in case she wakes up in the middle of the night. I keep it in the drawer, where I can hear her snoring through the wood.

Sonia turns toward me and kisses the side of my face.

"What'd you do with the wheelchair?"

She leans back, rolling away from me. "I take the cover off to wash." She frowns a little and touches my thigh. "Why, Harley?"

"I don't know."

She reaches toward me and touches my thigh again, patting me, moving her hand back and forth. "You are upset why?"

"What?" I know she's touching me, but I can't concentrate on it, can't will myself to notice.

"For Mama or your friend?"

"You mean Lynette?" The sound is too low to hear, but I think I remember this episode, about Rhoda and a beauty contest.

"Lynette," she says and pulls closer to me, hooks her leg over mine.

"I don't *know* anything."

"But you think" she says and leans her head on my chest.

"I don't know."

She raises her head and nods. "I know you will help her," she says, touching her hand to the side of my face. "Yes," she says and smiles, "you will."

CHAPTER III

ﺯ

I N DREAMS, SOMETIMES, I hear the splash of water against the sides of a boat. The dream is so real that I can feel the side-to-side dip and lean, the inch of water seeping into my shoes. I can smell perfume and flowers, hear the rustle of the girls' dresses, the clink of empty beer bottles in the cooler. I wake up in near total darkness, and it's a minute before my eyes adjust, before my heart takes back its normal rhythm and I stop feeling it in my chest, my throat, my ears. Sonia says I've woken her in the middle of the night, waving my arms like I'm swimming.

Lynette and I were in the back. She faced me, and I could see Gordon and Diane in front, facing away. Gordon had an arm around Diane; with the other, he dipped a hand into the water and splashed her, so that she squealed and pushed against his chest. He took his wet hand and touched her bare shoulder, then let his hand drop to her chest, to the skin above the wide pink ruffle that covered her breasts.

I was drunk and pretending not to be, but not as drunk as I thought I might need. For months, the two of us in Lynette's father's orchard, she let me pull her hips toward me, let me press an erection I thought might kill me against her, let me plant one leg between hers and grind myself against her, but later, after I'd unsnapped her bra and let my hand hover above the zipper to her jeans, she'd push me, lightly, almost but not accidentally, away. In another few months I'd be leaving for college, where I imagined everyone else would know more, would smell virgin on me like a sickness. That night I'd spent forty bucks on a tux rental, another forty on dinner, thirty for the prom tickets, seven on a corsage. I danced with her for hours in the gym, sweaty and uncomfortable in a jacket that kept riding up in back, catching on the buckles for the cummerbund. I thought, not that this entitled me to anything, that I'd proven the specialness of the evening, that I had treated her well, and that she might feel romantic, or at least adventurous, in return.

Behind Lynette, I could see Gordon feeding Diane beer, tipping the can to her mouth, at the same time pulling at the elastic ruffle, so that for a quick second I saw her white breast and the nipple, a pink one unlike Lynette's. I had my hand on Lynette's foot, kneading the skin. She had taken her shoes off hours ago, saying they rubbed the backs of her heels raw. She'd been barefoot since then, through the parking lot to my car, to Gordie's parents' dock, onto his father's fishing boat, where she dipped her toes into the water in the bottom, showing where she'd painted her toe-nails red, and kicked water up against the cuffs of my tuxedo pants.

She was leaning back, looking and pointing at the stars, letting her hair drag dangerously close to the floor of the boat, and I reached my hand a little higher, letting my thumb graze the flower design woven above the ankle of her pantyhose. She flinched as though she'd been tickled, but didn't say anything, so I slowly reached higher, leaning in closer to her, careful not to rock the boat. I was standing in the boat with my knees bent, leaning toward her, run-ning my hand up to the back of her knee and then higher, to the inside of her thigh, and I could see Gordon licking

Diane's throat while she laughed uncontrollably, slapping at the back of his tuxedo jacket.

Lynette raised her head and looked at me in a way that told me she wasn't drunk, then said softly, "No, Harley," but I was balanced in the bottom of the boat, leaning too far forward, so that when the boat rocked, I clutched at her, at the hem of her underpants and she said again, louder, "No, Harley."

"Okay," I said, but she didn't hear, and I was falling backward when my fingers tangled in the fabric of her dress.

"No," she said, really yelling now, and kicking at me, pushing me back with her foot.

I fell onto the seat, smacking my tailbone hard enough against the metal edge to make my eyes water, but she was screaming and kicking, rising toward me.

"I said no," she said, "you jerk." She had shaken some of her hair loose from the twist at the back of her head, and her face was wet, the makeup smeared under her eyes.

I reached up, trying to apologize. She was standing, keeping her balance, but when I tried to stand, she moved backward, the boat rocked, and the next thing I knew, I was flailing in cold water.

We weren't far from shore. We had rowed out onto the lake, because we were afraid to use the motor. The lake cops were out, and we were underage. But I came up under the boat and was terrified until I reached a hand up and felt the metal hull. I held my breath and swam, coming up again feet from the boat, where I could see Gordie and Diane. He was a summer lifeguard at the park, and he had his arm across her neck, swimming backward, leading her to the shore and completely ignoring the fact that her dress had fallen open to her waist.

I was treading water, and Lynette found me first.

"Harley," she said and pulled me with her to shore, her arm like a stone around me. She was so strong that I let her pull on me until my feet touched bottom, and I crawled out of the water with her standing behind me, untangling her sodden dress from the seaweed at her feet.

"I'm sorry," I said, first to her and then looking at Gordie and Diane, sputtering on the beach.

"I'm sorry," I said again, walking over to the two of them. I had lost my shoes in the lake, and I wondered what I'd say to the man at the store, how much I'd have to pay.

Gordie looked up at me. "What the hell happened?" Diane was crying and shivering, holding her dress up with two hands. She didn't look at me, but nestled against Gordie's sopping jacket.

I looked at Lynette. She was bent over, trying to shake loose the pins in her hair. She glanced up and saw me watching, but didn't smile or say anything.

"Lost my balance," I said, shrugged and walked away, up the beach toward Gordie's, before they could ask me anything else.

༨

I hear my name called like something from a dream. It's my mother's voice, weaker and with static. I roll over, reaching for the nightstand, but my legs are caught in the sheets, and I have to kick them loose. I turn on the light, open the drawer to the nightstand. "Harley," I hear. "Harley's in the well." I hold the baby monitor to my ear and listen to my mother calling for my father. "Frank, Frank, Harley's in the well."

I swing my feet over to the cold hardwood, take a few breaths before rising. Sonia mumbles and rolls away from the light. She has both hands curled under her chin, clutching the covers. She must be cold. I pull the quilt up from the foot of the bed and drape it over her shoulders. She burrows under the covers, hiding half of her face.

I step out into the hall and grope for the stair railing, waiting for my eyes to adjust, hanging onto the rail and feeling with my feet for the grooves where the stairs are worn in the middle and the wood's been polished smooth. I stop a minute on the landing, look outside at the streetlight on the corner, the snow flurries that drift in circles around it. At the bottom of the stairs, a draft from the front door grazes my ankles. The clock in the hall—the one that's always broken—chimes three times, grinds its gears and stops.

In the room Sonia uses as her studio, she's been getting ready for an art fair in Pennsylvania. She has boxes full of five-by-seven-inch paintings with gilded frames, tiny landscapes, troika horses and ice skaters. She fusses with them for days, correcting flaws too small to notice, and I keep telling her she either has to stop working so hard or raise her prices. She charges twenty bucks apiece in the morning, then goes to fifteen by three or four in the afternoon.

The bay window lets in the light from the ambulance barn parking lot; the spotlights on the corners of the building cast strange shadows over her paintings. I don't know anything about art, but I think they must be good, because I keep wanting to look at them, and because they remind me of Russia, even the parts of it I haven't seen.

I open the door to my mother's room carefully. I don't know if she's awake or asleep, or if she'll even recognize me in the dark. She's still calling for my father, asleep with her head buried in the pillow, but when I step closer, I see another pair of eyes. It's Whitey, asleep at the foot of my mother's bed, nestled against her with all four paws in the air.

"Ma?" I say, touching her on the shoulder. Her skin feels cool, and I wonder if I should bring in a space heater. "Ma?"

She's startled and tries to sit up, but it's hard for her to move with the cast on her leg and the dog wedged against her. She knocks Whitey in the head with her cast; he stands, shakes and jumps off the bed.

"Ma? It's Harley," I say, helping with the pillows.

"Frank?" she asks, her voice frightened and childlike.

"No, Ma, it's Harley."

"Oh, Harley," she says, patting my hand, "turn on the light."

I switched on the light next to the bed. She looks up at me, with her eyes a blue that's almost crystalline and her white hair plastered close to her head.

"You okay, Ma?" I ask.

"My leg," she says, frowning, and then, touching the cast, she remembers. "Oh," she says, "yes."

She reaches a hand up and brushes the hair off her forehead. "I was dreaming," she says.

"I heard you calling me."

"I was remembering when you were three or four." She raises the covers to her chest, smoothing them flat with one hand. "We were visiting friends in the country." She hesitates. "The Thompsons," she says, pointing a finger. "No, the Tomkins." She smiles and reaches for my hand, holds it loosely. "They had a well, and you were playing outside. We went to look for you and couldn't find you." She squeezes my hand. "I thought you fell down the well." She lets go of my hand and covers her mouth with her own, as if to show how afraid she was.

"I didn't, though."

"No," she says, slowly turning her head. "You were pooping in the bushes."

She looks at me then, and we both laugh, startled at the sudden mood shift. She shakes her head, as if to say how crazy life is, how unpredictable.

"Think you can sleep now?"

"Harley," she says, "I've been waking up and going to bed on my own power the last seventy-eight years."

I lean to kiss her, take in the smell of talcum powder and cologne. On my way out, I pat Whitey a couple times on the head, and he follows me upstairs and to bed with Sonia, settling against the backs of her legs.

ॐ

The snow came early this morning; by six, a sheet of it over the front lawn and falling quick like sifted flour. Already this year we've had more snow than the last two combined. It reminds me of winters during my childhood, when snowdrifts reached over my head and school closings were a gift from God. In years when the lake froze, my father took a broom to the ice and cleared a skating rink. My mother didn't skate; she was afraid, but she stood on the shore with a thermos of cocoa and cheered when my father skated backwards or on one leg.

I had weak ankles and skated on double runners until I was seven or eight. After that, I concentrated on speed, leaning forward, hurtling across the ice too fast to fall. My mother screamed at me to be careful, but she was only a blur I skated past in tight circles, letting the shore and the house and the color of her jacket fly past me in dizzying streaks of color.

Later, my eyelashes, the hair on my face and in my nose

would be frozen, and I'd be breathing hard, exhilarated and overheated in the layers of clothing she made me wear. In the distance, my father would be skating slowly, arms behind his back, legs moving in long, even strokes. If I listened carefully, I could hear his skate blades scrape the ice, a sound as steady as skips in the pavement.

Whitey is asleep beside Sonia, nestled against her legs. The two of them breathe in and out of sync, snoring a little. I don't know what pulled me out of bed so early, if one of them bumped me or if it's a sign of age. I have the feeling I've been dreaming, but I can't remember what about. I touch the window, trying to feel how cold it is. The snow in the ambulance barn driveway is fresh, no new disasters, and I'm glad for that, at least.

"Harley?" Sonia asks, sitting up in bed.

The dog stands and shakes, jumps off the bed.

"It's all right," I say. "Go back to sleep."

"Are you sick, Harley?" Her hair has caught static from her flannel nightgown. Strands of it hover near her ears and lift off from her scalp.

"No," I say, "go back to bed," and she curls herself under the covers again, sliding one hand under her pillow.

"Harley," she says, her face against the pillow, "you take Whitey out?"

Whitey hears his name and comes toward me, rises up onto his back legs so he can swat me on the ass.

"Just a minute," I say, pointing a finger at him, but he only stares and follows me to the bathroom. He waits for me to pee, but jumps against me before I get my sweatpants pulled up. His toenails scrape my thigh, leaving a scratch. My skin's dry in the winter, and I scratch easily. Sonia's always trying to put a lotion on me that smells like perfume, but I usually manage to push her away.

Whitey follows me downstairs, nudging me in the back of the legs with his snout. He seems happy, trotting at my heels. At the foot of the stairs, a loose board creaks under my step, and he jumps again, nearly knocking me off balance.

I lead him to the back door, where the fence will keep him in the yard. He looks at me before going outside, as if to ask whether I'm coming. It's cold, so I close the door behind him and go to the kitchen to make coffee. I might still go back to sleep, but I doubt it. More and more, once I'm up, I'm up.

I wait a few minutes, staring at the digital clock on the coffee maker, before I go back out onto the sunroom to get Whitey. The metal screen door is freezing cold and sticks when I try to open it, but I can see Whitey, peeing against the side of the fence. He stops and sniffs, digging in the snow with his nose, then I see him flop over on his side, rolling in the snow first on one side, then flipping over to the other. He stands and shakes, catches sight of me and stands in the middle of the yard, panting.

I jam my fist a couple of times against the button to release the door until it finally opens, then walk outside for a second and stand at the top of the stairs. I'm barefoot in the snow, freezing, and I look over the top of our fence at the neighbors' yards, the apartment house behind us, the road and the fields in the distance. The road's empty, the apartment house quiet, the neighbors' windows dark.

Whitey comes back up the stairs, grinning and panting, and brushes against my leg, his back wet with snow. I bend to pet him, but after last night, I'm careful, coming at him slowly, trying not to scare him. He moves past me, nudging open the door with his head, and starts sniffing around the floor for food. When I touch him I can feel his ribs, and I wonder if Lynette's been feeding him enough.

I lead Whitey into the kitchen and stand over the heating grate in the floor, letting the metal edges of the grate leave imprints on the soles of my feet and wondering what I was doing out there, barefoot in the snow. I've taken to doing strange things lately, things that surprise even me. I shake my head and marvel at my standing on the porch landing, gauging how easy it would be to skate away—to leave Lynette, Whitey, Sonia and my mother to their own devices, to put my arms behind my back and vanish in the distance, my steps as sure and steady as blades on ice.

ॐ

"Harley?" Sonia asks. "You are awake so early." She has on the flannel bathrobe my mother gave me for Christmas and socks with treads; her hair is flat on one side, high in the middle.

"Couldn't sleep." I pour another cup of coffee and root in the fridge for the little doughnuts from the bakery in town. I pull one out of the bag that looks like it's been chewed around the edges. Sonia picks at them, pulling pieces off with her fingers. Whitey comes out from under the kitchen table and sits in front of me, begging for food.

"I will fry some eggs," she says. She walks over to the fridge and pulls out another doughnut for herself. She takes a bite and uses her fingers to brush the crumbs from her mouth.

"No," I say, shaking my head. "This is fine." I hand a tiny piece of doughnut to the dog; I can't stand him staring at me.

"Mama will want eggs?" She fusses at the side where her hair is flattened, pushing it away from her face. I don't answer, but stand and go to my mother's room, pushing the door open, turning the glass doorknob as quietly as I can. She's sleeping on her side with the covers wrapped around her, so that I can see how much she's shrunk, not just in stature, but in actual size.

"Ma," I say, touching her shoulder, and the snoring stops so abruptly that for a second I'm afraid she's stopped breathing.

"My leg," she says, trying to roll onto her back. She's trapped; her cast is caught in the sheets.

"It's the cast, Ma. Your leg is broken."

She looks up at me, her eyes searching my face. "Yes," she says, "of course," but her voice is unsure. She smiles and reaches a hand out, touches my arm.

I slowly fold back the covers and lift her cast from the tangled sheets. She looks down at the cast and finally remembers, patting at the plaster with her hand.

"I'll take you to the bathroom, Ma," I say. I bend to lift her, see the stain on the mattress, catch the smell.

"Oh," she says, softly when I put my arms around her, "I'm wet." It's not that she's surprised, but she wants to pretend she doesn't know how it happened. I turn my head, bend and cup her with my arms, carry her to the toilet and drop her carefully on the seat. I'll need Sonia to change her clothes. I turn back toward Ma to tell her where I'm going; she looks and smiles, but there are tears in her eyes.

"They won't take me back," she says.

"What, Ma?"

"The retirement center," she says. "If you wet, they send you to the nursing home." She's really crying now, tears gathering in the wrinkled skin under her eyes, sliding toward her nose.

I'm standing in the doorway. I know what Sonia probably thinks, that it would be best for all of us to send Ma away. She has the right to think it; we've only been married six months, and she wants some privacy. She doesn't know my mother. She doesn't understand my mother's pride, her white gloves and a hat at weddings, black gloves and a veil at funerals. She wouldn't understand my mother's need to keep things in the family.

"Then you'll stay here, Ma."

My mother nods and sniffles, relieved, and I go upstairs to find Sonia.

༄

"My mother needs some help," I say, pulling the sweatpants down quickly, feeling the shock of cold air, and sliding on a pair of jeans.

"She is okay?" She's brushing her hair with the heavy wooden-handled brush she's had since childhood, bending her neck so that her hair falls forward and she can brush it from underneath.

I reach for the coffee mug she's brought upstairs and drink from it. The coffee's lukewarm and she's put in too much cream. "She wet herself."

Sonia straightens, letting her hair fall back into place, and nods; I don't look directly at her, but I can see from the corner of my eye. I'm waiting for her to say something about the nursing home, and I can't tell her yet what I've promised my mother.

"I will do laundry," she says. "You have some whites?"

I take another sip of coffee and shake my head. "I'll do it myself."

She touches my back. "I think I will do it anyway," she says.

"Okay." I turn and squeeze her arm, kiss her quickly on the cheek. "In the hamper."

"Harley," she says and reaches for me.

"I have to get to work," I say, and kiss her again.

She nods and lets me walk out of the bedroom, follows me downstairs to the kitchen, and holds the door open while I walk through it to the garage. I turn and she's watching me. "Be careful," she said, "on the roads," and she raises her hand in a wave before shutting the door and disappearing inside.

It's cold, I can see my breath, and I start the truck before raising the garage door. Sonia hates it when I do that, but it's only for a minute, and there's no way this old garage is airtight.

Sonia will close the garage door after me, so I leave it open and back out of the driveway, heading around the side of the house toward the main road. At the corner, I stop at the light and look back toward the porch; it's starting to sag in the middle, and I keep wondering how much it'll cost to fix.

Next to the door, I see something, a large box, open at the top, with what looks like a blanket or rug sticking out of it. I pull over and stop the truck with the motor running, hop out, climb onto the porch. I can't see Sonia through the window; she must be in the back of the house with my mother. I bend and rummage through the box, find a piece of old rug, a half bag of dog food, a steel-bristle brush and flea shampoo, an old tennis ball and squeaky toys and two bags of jerky treats. I don't know how late or how early Lynette was here, leaving this box on the porch, or why she didn't just ring the bell. I pick up the mini football, the rubber pull toy, the plastic pork chop, and I have to wonder what Lynette wants from me, what she thinks I can do to help.

CHAPTER IV

ॐ

I T WAS JULY, and Lynette and I had been dating for seven months. My mother sat with her legs crossed on the bedspread, picking at loose threads on one of the seams. She looked up and gave a tight-lipped smile, moved her legs so that I could sit next to her. I had never found her alone in my room before. I knew she cleaned; I found piles of clean laundry on the bed, but I had never seen her sitting alone in my room, waiting.

"Ma?"

"I came in to clean," she said, "and I found these." She picked the box of condoms up off the bedspread and handed it to me. It was open; I had taken one out to practice. I opened the drawer of my nightstand and put the box back where I had left it.

"Did you buy those in town?"

I shook my head.

"In the city?"

"Gordie and I drove up last Saturday."

She nodded and slowly got up. She had on navy pumps with thick, stacked heels and a matching navy sailor dress. My father would be home from work in half an hour; she always dressed for him, did her hair and put on makeup. She told me once that she did it because of the secretaries at the mill; she didn't want my father to think she was any less glamorous.

"Harley," she said on her way out the door, "be careful. Make sure there aren't any holes."

༄

On my way to work I keep watch on the sky, looking for snow clouds or wind in the trees. I lied on my job application and said I wasn't afraid of heights. I'm mostly over it, but on windy days, when the pole shifts while I'm climbing and I can feel it drift against my thigh, I still get queasy. I try not to look down, only at the tools in my hands and out over the hills surrounding the lake, at the curls of chimney smoke from cabins deep in the woods and the crows that glide and settle on rooftops.

I turn the radio on low, Waylon Jennings in a soft murmur. The sky is clear, but it's cold; it'll be even colder twenty feet up where the phone lines are installed. I have an extra hat and liners for my work gloves in my locker, and there might be a thermos somewhere I can fill with coffee and carry in the truck.

I pull into the gravel parking lot, park in the back. I'm on time, but the lot's full. Most people in town keep farmer's hours: up by six, in bed by ten. Stores close at about 5:30; after that there isn't much to do besides city council meetings and bridge clubs. Except for the teenagers who drag race on country roads, people get in the habit of being home by dark.

I find my boss in the bathroom. He's in a stall, but the cigar smoke drifting toward the fan in the ceiling gives him away. Bernie's a widower in his fifties who chain-smokes like a guy with a death wish. His wife died fifteen years ago; she had an asthma attack during a car trip and drove into a tree. Bernie's never gotten over the fact that

Sharon died young, when the whole time he was the one with the dangerous job.

I take the stall next to Bernie and sit down. I don't have to go, but I try anyway. I don't want to discover I have to go when I'm ten feet up a pole, carrying a load of heavy equipment. Some guys go in the ditches, but I have a shy bladder; I can't go if I think somebody might be watching.

"How's the wife?" Bernie asks me at the sinks, after I've given up. He holds the cigar between his teeth while he washes his hands. His fingernails are yellow and cracked.

"Good," I say, "real good."

Bernie nods. "Cute accent," he says, mumbling.

"You got some service orders for me?" There's a hand dryer next to the sinks, but it takes forever, so I duck into a stall, pull some toilet paper off the roll and use that.

"Yeah," he says, "on my desk." He shakes his hands in the air, then wipes them on his pants, leaving wet streaks. "Your mom good?"

"Well," I say, "getting older."

"Yeah," he says, "ain't we all," and laughs, a deep guttural laugh that slides fast into a cough. He curls his fist over his mouth to hold back the phlegm, but he looks at me to show me he's still at least partly laughing.

"I knew your Ma," he says when he's done. "When I was a kid, I delivered her paper." He turns back toward the mirror and runs a hand over his slicked hair.

"That so?"

"Yeah," he says. He leans close to the mirror, picks an ash flake from the front of his teeth and drops it in the sink. "Nice lady."

"I'll tell her you said hello."

"Nah," he says and waves me away. "She wouldn't

remember. I was a pimply-faced kid then," he says, gesturing to his face, the pockmarks on his cheeks.

I put my hand on the door, ready to push it open. "You know a guy named Hale?" I ask. "Doug Hale?"

Bernie thinks a minute, puffs on his cigar. "Don't think so."

I push on the door, so that it swings wide into the hallway, and step through.

"Wait a minute," Bernie says.

I catch the door, hold it open from the other side.

"Big guy, blond? Farmer?"

I nod.

Bernie shrugs. "We drink at the same bar. Comes in smelling like manure, couple of beers and he heads out. Never says much." Bernie leans over the sink and flicks ashes. "Seems all right."

I nod.

"Any special reason you want to know?" Bernie's not a gossip, but he lives alone and he's bored.

I shrug. "Saw him the other day." I loosen my hold on the door, and Bernie grabs it, lets it swing in toward the bathroom. "We were in school together."

Bernie nods, blows smoke through his nose. "Old ghosts," he says, smiling. "Town's full of 'em."

ॐ

I pull a job replacing some lines along the lake road, up near Lynette's father's orchard. I park the supply truck at the bottom of the hill, climb the gravel drive up past the shop, the house, her father's tool shed. It's quiet, boarded up; I can hear my boots on the snow and gravel, my breathing a little too hard. From this far away, the lines I'm up here to replace look like black licorice, dangling between the wooden poles. The sky is clear; I look down toward the lake, steel blue and barely moving, and out, over the hills. I must be thinking of Whitey; I keep looking, instinctively, for loose animals, but there's nothing, no one out here but me.

I wait a minute before climbing, to catch my breath. I used to be able to run up this hill. I could sprint from the bottom up into the orchard, chasing Lynette between rows of trees. We'd take our shoes off and run barefoot through wet grass, trying not to slip and fall on tree roots or the cores of rotten apples. We weren't drunk; we hardly ever drank, and even then only beer. We were young and horny and caught up in each other. But still, it wasn't until after I caught her, grabbing at the back of her jeans, land– ing hard on a couple of knotty tree roots and pulling her on top of me, when I was kissing her and smelling sweat and talcum powder and lip gloss, kissing her face and neck and getting strands of her hair caught in my mouth, that I thought of sex. I mean, it felt like love to me that I didn't want her until then, that the whole time I was chasing her, laughing and listening to her laughing and running, I wasn't thinking of anything but being with her, of being next to her. I didn't know any other girls that well, but I was still pretty sure that with any other girl, it might not be the same.

In a couple of months I'd be leaving for school, and she'd be going to a small college in Pennsylvania whose name I can't remember. We went to the movies week after week, smuggling in hot dogs from the stand that was only open in the summer. We couldn't think of anything else to do, so we saw one movie after another, two or three a weekend, what–

ever they were showing, from kids' movies to action flicks to the very occasional art film that bored us both. She liked the action films if the hero was good-looking, animated kids' films and anything romantic. I liked horror, where she leaned against me, digging her head into my shoulder, and screamed when something jumped out from the screen.

After the movie, we walked around town, waiting for her parents to go to bed at 10:30. We bought ice cream if I could afford it; otherwise, we looked in store windows and talked about college. She said she couldn't wait to leave town, but we all said that. We wanted to get away from a place where everyone knew our parents and we were always being watched.

I strap on the belt 'n hooks, and climb slowly, making sure the two-inch hooks take hold in the wooden pole. A guy on another crew fell last year and wound up in the hospital with a broken back. The doctors say he may never walk again.

Lynette was a fast runner; she could outdistance me if she wanted to, but she stayed a few yards in front of me, jogging in place, waiting for me to catch up, then sprinting off again when I got too close. When she finally got tired and let me tackle her, wrapping an arm around her waist and butting her with my shoulder, turning aside just in time so that I wouldn't land on her and hurt her, she'd be breathing hard, laughing a little, and reaching to kiss me. "I love you," she said once, quietly, not watching me but looking up at the sky, so that I wasn't entirely sure she was talking to me.

I didn't say anything; she didn't seem to expect it. She let her fingers drop to my waist and started pulling at the hem of my shirt where it was tucked into my jeans. She wasn't laughing. I could feel the quiet; I strained to hear something, thought I could make out waves on the lake.

This time of year, there's a cracking and groaning, slabs of ice knocking against each other. I'm too far away to hear it now, but from the top of the pole, I can see the different colors of the ice, white in the middle where it's thick, gray closer to shore. In winter, my father called the lake "old man." "Quit your complaining, old man," he'd say. "Spring's coming." He'd sit on the porch, drinking coffee, listening to the lake and driving my mother crazy, wondering what he was doing out there in the middle of winter.

I've never been to the orchard in winter. By the time winter came around, Lynette was seeing Doug. Now, snow outlines the tree limbs; a blanket of it makes the ground look smooth and even, seamless.

Lynette's hands were cold; she had bad circulation. She held her hands on my back, tapping lightly with her fingers. We were kissing, mouths open, and I pulled on her T-shirt, slipping it out of her jeans and farther up along her rib cage. I kissed her and kept tugging, hoping she would get the hint and help me pull her T-shirt over her head. She leaned back and looked at me; her face was serious, she was almost frowning, then she reached for the hem of the T-shirt, pulled it off, looked at me again and unclasped the front hook of her bra.

I work slowly, my hands stiff in work gloves, my ears aching under the knit hat. I get a couple of earaches every winter from being in the cold. I swab my ears with alcohol, take a lot of aspirin. Occasionally, I get an infection and end up in the emergency room. They give me antibiotics and tell me to stay home from work. I can't afford more than a few days off, so I go anyway and try to be careful, afraid the infection will make me lose my balance.

Lynette's breasts were beautiful, smallish and round, glaringly white in the moonlight. It was still a shock to see them that way, so bare and unhidden. I was used to slowly peeling back her shirt and bra, kissing her nipples and letting the cloth fall back on top of them. I reached for her and let her rest her weight on top of me, wanting to press my body against her and wanting her to feel the hardness underneath.

I pulled at her jeans, let myself rock against her slightly. She pulled back, and I thought she might say something to stop me and walk away, but she stood and took off her jeans, still frowning, and stepped out of her underwear. I had never seen her so clearly, so completely naked. I was embarrassed and quickly glanced up at her, then pulled my own jeans down to my ankles. I still had on my underwear; I was in no hurry to show her my erection, I wasn't sure she'd seen one before.

I kneeled and hugged her legs. It was dark, but that's when I saw the marks on her thighs, dark smudges wide as a finger.

"What are these?" I asked and traced them with my hand.

She pushed me away. "Nothing."

"Are you hurt?"

"I fell, running."

I didn't think I believed her, but I nodded as if I did. I was relieved, I think, that she wasn't going to tell me something I might not want to know. I looked up, took both of her hands and tried to pull her toward me.

"No," she said quietly.

"What?" I was beginning to get cold in my underwear, and I pulled again on her hands. Whatever it was that she wasn't going to tell me wouldn't matter so much, I thought, if I just held onto her a while.

"Stop it, Harley." She snatched her hands away and bent to pick up her clothes. She was dressing fast, stuffing her

T-shirt into her jeans, sliding her bra into her back pocket.

"Wait, what's going on?"

"Changed my mind," she mumbled, buttoning the fly of her jeans with hands that looked like they were shaking.

"Hey," I said, not moving and not understanding why she suddenly didn't want to be near me, "wait a minute."

"Go home," she said, turning toward me just long enough for me to see her face, her eyes fierce and focused somewhere above my head. Then she was walking fast, marching down the hill to her parents' house.

ॐ

I decide on drive-thru for lunch; Sonia loves McDonald's. I figure I'll order a Big Mac for myself, a Quarter Pounder with cheese for Sonia, grilled chicken for my mother, some fries and a diet soda. I don't like the artificial sweetener, but I figure I should start cutting back a little, get rid of this gut.

I shout into the speaker and pull the truck around. It's about one o'clock and the parking lot's full of high school kids. They can walk here, but they climb into cars, six or eight of them at a time. The kid driving the rusted-out F-150 behind me keeps revving his motor. Another boy and two girls crowd next to him on the seat. The girls are singing along to something on the radio. They're singing loud; I don't know the song.

The girl at the window looks familiar, but I don't recognize the name on her uniform tag: Dierdre. She has oily skin; she's covered with acne around her mouth and chin, and when she turns to get the sodas, I see that she's pregnant, wearing a special maternity uniform. She doesn't look much older than the kids in the truck behind me, maybe only a year or two.

"When's the baby due?" I ask her when she hands me the cardboard drink carrier.

"Month and a half," she says, looking like she only gets asked that question a million times a day. "Fries'll be a minute."

"You want me to pull over there?" I ask, pointing to the parking lot.

She leans out of the window, shades her eyes with her hand and takes a look at the F–150, where the kid driving is still revving the motor.

"Nah," she says. "It'll just be a minute." She pulls back inside the window, scraping her stomach on the ledge.

"You get a lot of kids this time of day?"

She rolls her eyes, resting her arms on the window ledge. "Don't I know it." She's dabbed a little powder over the acne around her mouth, but it still looks red and sore.

One of the machines in back goes off, and she turns away from the window. The kid behind me taps his horn twice, but stops when I lean out the window and check my side mirror.

Dierdre comes back with the food. "Fries are hot," she says, handing me the bag. "Ketchup? Salt?"

"Just napkins."

She nods, reaches under the cash register, pulls out a wad of napkins three inches thick and hands it to me.

"Okay?" she asks.

"Yeah."

The kid taps his horn again. Dierdre leans out the window, shoots him a look.

I pull a few fries from the bag, make sure the drink carrier is wedged against the seat back. "Take care of the baby," I say. "Don't work too hard."

She laughs, snorting through her nose. "Don't worry."

৵

Sonia's in the kitchen when I get home. "Oh, good," she says and claps her hands together when she sees the food. "You bring McDonald's."

I carry the bag over to the table. Sonia follows me and pulls the hamburgers from the bag.

"The chicken's for Mom," I say.

She nods and hands me the Big Mac. She unwraps her own cheeseburger and takes a bite out of it, grinning.

Whitey smells the food and comes running, his toenails clicking on the hardwood. He walks over to the table, raises his front two paws on the seat of a chair and sniffs with his nose at the table edge. I push the food away, toward the middle of the table.

"Where's Mom?" I ask, and Sonia points to the living room, her mouth full of cheeseburger.

Mom's asleep in her wheelchair, listening to the stereo with my headphones on. She's sleeping lightly, not snoring but just breathing heavy with her chin on her chest.

"She listens so loud, Harley," Sonia says, standing in the doorway with her cheeseburger.

"It's all right," I say, and tap my mother on the shoulder. She doesn't wake up, so I shake her a little until she jerks herself awake.

"Harley," she says and smiles slowly. "Are you done with work?"

I pull the headphones from her ears and set them on top of the stereo receiver. "No, Ma. I came home for lunch."

She reaches for my hand and squeezes it in hers. Her fingers are ice cold.

"Warm enough, Ma?" I ask.

She nods. "It's cold."

I take the sweater from the back of her chair and drop it over her shoulders.

"I brought you a sandwich. Chicken."

She smiles again, and looks up at me. "I am hungry," she says, "come to think of it." It's something she said all the time when I was a kid, as if her hunger came as some kind of surprise.

Sonia brings the chicken sandwich from the kitchen and hands it to my mother. Whitey follows her in and puts his head in my mother's lap, sniffing at the sandwich. Mom unwraps her chicken and takes a bite, and Whitey lifts a paw and swats Mom in the leg.

"This is mine," she says, shaking a finger at him. "Not for you."

Whitey looks at her, sees that she's paying attention to him and gives her another swat in the leg.

"Oh," she says, "for crying out loud." She pulls a piece of chicken from her sandwich and hands it to Whitey. He takes it from her and eats it in one bite, then swats her again. She opens the bun of her sandwich and tries to pull another piece of chicken from it, but then she drops the whole thing, chicken and bun, on the floor.

Whitey hunkers down over the sandwich and starts eating, ripping the chicken apart with his teeth. The sandwich is gone, but I figure the mayonnaise and tomato can't be good for dogs, so I reach down to pull the rest away from him, but before I even touch the sandwich, Whitey latches onto my wrist with his teeth and gives a low growl.

The pain is surprising, crushing, and I'm afraid he might actually break my wrist.

"No," I say, my voice low and calm, but he ignores me and keeps growling.

"Whitey," Sonia says softly, "go lie down." She points to the far corner of the living room. "You are good boy. It's okay."

Whitey looks at her, blinks and lets go of me, then slinks over to the corner, tail between his legs.

"Mercy," my mother says.

"That's it," I say, rubbing at the tooth marks on my hand. "I'm taking him back."

"You can't, Harley," Sonia says.

"I sure as hell can." Whitey cowers in the corner, panting and watching me. The skin isn't broken, but my hand aches, and I realize I'm afraid of him, that he can hurt me if he wants to.

"You want me to get you another sandwich, Ma?" I ask. Sonia looks like she might say something, but I ignore her and concentrate on my mother.

"Oh," she says. "Fine."

I wheel my mother into the kitchen and Whitey follows, but stays out of hitting range, sidling along the walls.

"He thinks you will take food from him," Sonia says. She walks over to the refrigerator, pulls out some lunch meat to make a sandwich for my mother.

"I never hurt him," I say.

She shrugs with her back to me, finishes the sandwich, salami and cheese with mustard on both slices of bread, and brings it over to my mother. Mom takes it from her but doesn't say anything, just looks from Sonia to me and back again.

I pick up the Big Mac and take a few bites. The fries are

cold, but I dump a handful onto the table and eat them anyway.

Sonia stands over the table, holding her Quarter Pounder with cheese and taking small bites. "Harley," she says. "I find a box on the porch."

"I saw it."

She raises her head and looks at me. "She leaves it for you."

I pick through a pile of fries, looking for the over-cooked, crunchy ones. "You mean she left it for Whitey."

Whitey hears his name, but doesn't move, just stays where he is, curled up with his head facing the wall and his ears rotating in my direction.

My mother chews her sandwich and stares out the window. She ignores the soda I bought her and sips at a cold cup of coffee left on the table from this morning.

Sonia sets the rest of her cheeseburger down. She walks over to the broom closet, opens the door and reaches inside for Whitey's box. She takes out the rubber pork chop and a squeaky toy in the shape of a purple dinosaur. "Look, Harley," she says, holding them up to show me. "Your friend pays money for these. She loves Whitey."

Whitey raises his head at the sound of his name this time, walks gingerly over to Sonia and sits in front of her. She offers him the plastic pork chop, but he ignores it.

"Then why'd she give him to us?"

"Because we will care for him." Sonia drops the toys back in the box and shuts the broom closet door. She reaches carefully for Whitey, pats him on the head, then sits down at the table and finishes her lunch.

Three weeks before Lynette was supposed to leave for school, her father had a heart attack and fell from the tree he'd been spraying for bugs. Lynette's mother found him on a pile of rotten apples, barely breathing, holding his chest and grimacing with pain. She called the ambulance; the call went out over the police scanners, and six or seven neighbors met them at the hospital. I heard about it at the coffee shop where I worked the grill during the lunch shift: hamburgers, patty melts, fried egg sandwiches. I left to pick up Lynette at the mall in the city, where she was shopping for school clothes. I found her car in the parking lot and waited next to it for an hour until she came out.

"Harley?" she said, walking toward me with two shopping bags, one from the jeans store and the other from the department store with the best prices.

"Your dad's had an accident."

She set the bags down next to her car, slowly unlocked the door and slid the bags inside, onto the passenger seat.

"What kind?" she said, whispering, then cleared her throat and asked again, louder.

"He had a heart attack. He fell out of a tree."

She walked around the back of her car and came toward me, stood directly in front of me and shaded her eyes with her hand.

"Is he dead?"

"No," I said, shaking my head. "They took him to the hospital. That's all I know."

She lowered her hand and looked at me, made eye contact before she turned away, nodding. Something was wrong; she wasn't upset, at least not in the way I'd expected her to be.

"Why don't I drive you?"

She nodded, walked over to the passenger side of my car and waited for me to unlock the door from the inside. "Are you all right?" I asked, pulling out of the parking lot. I didn't look at her; I was busy driving. "Don't worry," she said, her voice just a little shaky. "I'm better," and when I looked at her then, she had started to cry, softly, barely making a sound.

_{~}

I should head back to work, but I turn the wrong way off Main Street and head out into the country, pretending I don't know where I'm going, but making the turns automatically.

I park across the street, like a peeping Tom or a lovesick boyfriend, and stare at the house, the empty driveway, the plastic flowers on the mailbox post. Birds circle what must be loose grain in the field to my right. The barn door is empty; I can see Doug's tractor, a new John Deere, parked inside.

The house is quiet. I roll down my window, but can't hear anything: music, TV, a crying baby. The wind is cold, and I'm late back from lunch, but I just sit, staring. I look as far as I can in each direction, but can't see another house, only a flash of light on the metal siding of the trailer where Doug's brother and sister-in-law live. It's parked deep in the woods behind the house, with nothing but a dirt track leading up to it, a wooden mailbox at the side of the road.

The road is empty; a small, private airplane buzzes in the distance, a chipmunk or woodchuck scurries from the ditch into the field.

I can imagine Lynette running, doing stretches in the

driveway and then heading out on this road, careful to stay in the dirt furrows where traffic has separated the gravel. I can imagine it, even though I'm sure she doesn't run anymore, not with a baby and not with the work she must do keeping house, taking care of the farm. But there's something I like about the idea of it, of her out here in the wind, sweating and concentrating.

I start up the truck and pull slowly into the road, gravel crackling under the wheels. I don't know if Lynette's seen me, or if she's even home. I could pull into the driveway, knock on the door, ask if she's all right, but instead I step on the gas and pull away.

⌇

Most of the town showed up for the funeral. The Methodist church was full of flowers, mostly lilies and carnations; it smelled sickeningly sweet, like cotton candy, with too many flowers and too many brands of perfume.

Lynette's mother sat in the third pew from the front, the first one that had people in it. She had on a black short-sleeved dress with little bows on the sleeves, and she cried, sobbing and gulping in the arms of the woman who worked in the orchard shop with her, a fat woman with a tight permanent wave. Lynette sat on the other side of her mother, eyes front, like she was paying attention to every word the minister said, like her mother wasn't crying next to her.

I tried talking to Lynette after the funeral, but she was surrounded by teachers and friends of her parents. Her hair looked stringy, she had a smudge of lipstick on her cheek, and she kept lifting her heels out of her shoes like they were hurting her.

My mother wore a black dress that smelled like cedar

from the closet where she stored it and black gloves that fastened at the wrists with small white pearls. I had on a gray suit too short in the sleeves but that my mother said would be all right so long as I kept my arms crossed. I borrowed a tie from my father, gray with maroon stripes.

Afterward, my mother and I drove over to the Wilsons' with a strawberry torte it took her hours to make. Mrs. Wilson had gone up to her bedroom to rest; the woman who worked with her served coffee and cake to droves of neighbors crowded together on the furniture in front of TV trays or perched uncomfortably on the arms of the couch. They talked about Mr. Wilson as a good neighbor, a hard worker, a church-going man, until the conversation gradually drifted to other topics: high school football scores, bowling team lineups, lake levels, crop damage. I looked for Lynette but couldn't find her, just the droves of neighbors and some girl cousins fooling in the corner with Barbies.

I went outside, let the screen door slam behind me and headed out into the orchard. It was warm, and I took my suit jacket off, hung it on a tree limb. I wasn't looking for Lynette, just kicking at tree roots and apple cores, walking, listening to the murmur of people talking inside the house.

"Looking for me?" Her voice was soft and a little rough; she cleared her throat, letting me know where she was. I walked over to the tree where she was sitting, saw her shoes where she'd left them at the base.

"Why aren't you inside?" She had torn her pantyhose climbing into the tree; one leg had a run from her foot to somewhere along her shin.

"Wanna come up?" She motioned to the tree limb next to her.

I shook my head. "Won't hold me."

She nodded and started climbing down, jumped when

she got close enough to the ground. She landed on her feet, bending her knees and straightening.

"What are you doing out here?"

I shrugged. "Walking around."

The grass was wet, but she sat down and pulled off her pantyhose, wadded them into a ball and threw them into a tree. She stood up and looked at me, squinted like she was deciding something. She'd been crying; her makeup was smeared under her eyes.

"Are you okay?"

"Come with me," she said, and pulled on my wrist, led me away from the house, toward the farthest row of trees.

"Where are we going?" I didn't like her tugging on me, and I pulled back my arm.

She wheeled around on me so fast that I almost bumped into her. "You still want it?" she asked.

"What?"

"It," she said, and started unbuttoning her blouse, letting it hang open. "Me."

"What are you doing?" I asked, but I was rooted to the ground.

"I'm giving it to you." She bent and reached under her skirt, pulled her panties down to her ankles and stepped out of them. She looked at me.

"Knock it off," I said, stepping backwards, then thought again. "You okay?"

She unzipped the back of her skirt and started pushing it over her hips. "You wanted it before." She was crying again, but in a strange way; her shoulders were still, her breathing was no different, but her eyes leaked onto her cheeks.

"I'm sorry." I was almost whispering.

She looked at me again through her tears and finished

taking off her skirt. I tried to look down, away from her hands, but my eyes rested on her thighs, on the marks I could barely make out.

"Cut it out," I said. "You're just upset."

She raised her head, looked me in the eye and pulled her blouse off her shoulders. "No," she said and wiped her blouse, still fastened at the sleeve, roughly over her eyes. "No, I'm celebrating."

I stood there, staring. I didn't like the way she was talking; I couldn't tell if she was being sarcastic. I took a few steps toward her, but stopped. I wanted to help, but she was scaring me.

"Lynette," I said, "put your clothes on."

She cried harder, her shoulder shaking. "You wanted it," she said.

"I'm sorry." I moved toward her and leaned down for her clothes, handed her the skirt. She pulled the skirt on and zipped it, lifted the blouse back onto her shoulders.

She stood with her blouse open, her hair loose and frowzy. "I'm so tired," she said, and held up her hands, let them drop at her sides.

I walked toward her and wrapped my arms around her, felt how she trembled with cold. I let go, slowly buttoned the front of her blouse and led her back inside.

꒰

I pour a cup of coffee and check Bernie's desk for messages. He's taken one from Sonia, something about my mother needing pens or pins. Bernie's handwriting is terrible: small and square with a backward slant that makes the letters run together. He's on the phone with another line installer, so I sit on the edge of his desk and wait.

"You take this?" I ask, waving the pink message slip.

"Yeah."

I take a look at his hands; his fingers are like sausage links attached to huge, beefy palms.

"What'd she say?"

"Oh," he says, and points to the message slip in my hands. "Your mom needs some pills refilled. You gotta pick 'em up after work."

"Did she say which pills?"

"Yeah," he says. He picks up a pencil, taps it on the desk. "Blood pressure," he says, "something like that."

I fold the message slip and put it in my pocket. "You want to go for a drink later?"

"Thought you had to go to the drug store."

"I can do that first."

He looks at me, tilting his head. "What about the little woman?"

"I can call, tell her I'll be late."

He nods, then laughs, a little uncomfortable. "Jesus," he says. "It's Monday night. Even I don't drink on Monday night."

"Couple of beers."

He shrugs. "Sure." He holds out a stack of work orders but doesn't let go when I try to take them from him. "Troubles at home?"

"No," I say, "nothing like that."

"Okay," he says and holds his hands up, "it's none of my business."

"I was hoping to run into somebody."

"Yeah?"

"A guy I used to know."

Bernie nods. "Your farmer friend?"

"I know his wife. They're having problems."

Bernie sits back in his chair, looks relieved to find out it's nothing to do with Sonia and me. "Well," he says, "times are tough. There's a lot of that going around."

CHAPTER V

ॐ

I LEFT FOR COLLEGE three weeks after the funeral. I
hadn't talked to or seen Lynette. She was easy to avoid;
the day after the funeral, she left to visit her grandpar-
ents for a week. After that, I scheduled extra shifts at work,
saving money for school, and if I saw her on the street, I
waved and pretended to be on my way somewhere else.

She sent me a postcard in September from the country
club. She was working there, serving Friday night fish fry
to old people who spent the other half of the year in
Florida. She wrote on the back that she'd decided to work
a year before going to school. Her mom was having a hard
time, and Lynette didn't want to leave her alone. Lynette
had an older sister, Caroline, but she moved to Colorado
after high school and never came home to visit. She was
some kind of nurse in a hospital out there. Lynette said
she'd reapply for college in a year, ask them to hold over
her scholarship.

I never wrote back to her. By then, I'd lost my virginity
to a girl in my anthropology elective, and I was embarrassed about it. I didn't know if Lynette was still my girlfriend or if it should be this new girl, the one I'd slept with.

Her name was Amanda. She wore filmy Indian-print
skirts in green or brown; she said the colors ran when she
washed them in the machine at her dorm. She braided her
hair so tight that I could see white patches between the six
or seven thin braids scattered all over her head. She asked

me to study with her, which I thought was strange, since she was the better student. She raised her hand a lot and asked questions I didn't understand, and I sat behind her, imagining a tiny car driving the jagged lines of bare scalp.

I went over to her dorm, buzzed her from the lobby. Her roommate walked past me on her way out; I knew her from class, where she sat next to Amanda. Cathy was a tall blonde with glasses and pink sweaters, at least three that I remembered from class. Her half of the room was decorated with weeping ceramic masks and pictures of ballet dancers. Amanda's half had tribal masks, fuzzy wall hangings and fertility statues with pointy breasts. She had lit candles; they dripped all over her desk and made the room smell like wax.

Amanda poured wine into plastic cups and we split a bag of Frito's. We pretended to study, leaning together over her book, where she'd written questions in the margins. I was embarrassed to show her mine, because the friend I sat next to rated the girls sitting near us on a scale from one to ten. Amanda had gotten a seven and a half, because she was "hot, but weird."

I waited, with her braids swinging against my face every time she moved her head, until the Frito's were gone to kiss her; her lips were salty, her breath smelled like corn. She pulled the braids back from her face and tilted toward me, kissed me with her mouth open.

We kissed a while, and she kept scooting closer to me, leaning against me, so that after a while, we were lying on the floor. The carpet was worn and grainy, like no one ever vacuumed, and I rolled on top of her so that her braids wouldn't slap me in the face, feeling crumbs under my shirt.

She wasn't wearing a bra, but something like an undershirt with a blouse over it that looked like it was made from scarves. When she pulled off her blouse, I flashed for a minute on how much my mother would hate her. She took off the undershirt, too; she was flat-chested with hard, brown nipples, and her ribs showed above the elastic waistband of her skirt.

I kneaded her chest with my hands but concentrated on not getting too hard. I was waiting for her to stop me. I was so used to Lynette pushing me away that I hesitated before tugging on her skirt, knowing it'd be over soon and I'd have to slink out of her room and go home. But instead, she stood up and said flatly, cheerfully, "Let's get on the bed." She sat on the bottom bunk and waited for me, laughed when I stumbled getting up from the floor.

I cleared my throat, still tasting Frito's and wine. "You sure?"

She nodded. "I'm on the pill."

I walked over to her, kicked my sneakers off and got onto her mattress. I pulled off my shirt, let it drop on the floor next to the bed, thought better about it and picked it up, threw it onto her desk. I was still thinking maybe she'd stop me. I started unzipping my jeans, looking at her. She laughed lightly and said, "Any day."

I took my jeans off and practically dove under her comforter. It was yellow with blue flowers, department-store expensive. She wrapped her legs around me and started kissing me again. I kissed her a while, her shoulders and chest, wiggled out of my underwear and left it at the bottom of the mattress.

I hugged her and jammed myself against her, reached under the covers and touched her, felt where she was wet. She picked up her hips and guided me into her. I moved, felt a rush of blood, went a little lightheaded. She made a sound, a yelp that made me wonder if I'd hurt her, then a slow sigh. She looked at me and laughed again, lightly, then started moving, bumping against me. I moved too, pumping a little, but I couldn't get the rhythm right. We were bumping against each other, but I started to panic that nothing else was happening. I thought she'd say something about it, but instead she started swearing, saying, "Oh God, oh shit," in a way that worried me until she opened her eyes for a second and smiled. Then the rhythm was suddenly right for about thirty seconds and I came. It surprised me how much of it there was, how long it took, how sensitive I was after. I pulled away from her, and she smiled again and said, "That was good."

I thought she was lying, but it was nice of her, and I was too tired to care much. I rummaged around for my underwear, pulled it on, got up off her mattress. She lay still with her arms behind her head, her breasts pulled almost flat and her ribs showing. I thought I should say something. I had expected sex to make me feel closer to a girl, but somehow I was standing there, staring at her, feeling farther away.

"I should go," I said, and she nodded, looking at the clock radio on the milk crate next to her bed.

"My roommate'll be home soon."

I picked up my jeans, put them on. I pulled my shirt off her desk.

"Thanks."

She looked at me and laughed. "Yeah," she said, "no problem."

She pulled the comforter up to her chin before I opened the door. The hallway was full of smoke; people were smoking in the lounge across from her room.

"See you Monday," I said.

She waved, and I walked out.

Bernie's favorite bar is on the south end of town, across from the mill. If my father'd been a drinking man, this would have been his place, but he rarely took more than a glass of wine at dinner. He said drinking made him act in a way he didn't like, but I always wondered if maybe it was my mother who didn't like it. She never offered to refill his glass, never once asked him if he wanted more. She had a way of silent disapproval, a look she could send across the table that kept me from extra gravy or second helpings.

The bar is full of mill workers; I can smell the factory on their clothing, see the buckwheat dust in their hair. Most of them are too young to have worked with my father, but I scan the faces of the older ones, trying to remember from the funeral.

Bernie leads me over to a table, takes his jacket off and drops it on the seat next to him. We're close enough to the door that I can feel a draft every time it opens, so I keep mine on. Bernie waves to the girl behind the bar. She nods, writes something down on a slip of paper she leaves at the cash register, then walks over to us.

"Bernie," she says. She's young, in a T-shirt with a daisy on it, a khaki miniskirt and a short red apron. She's got straight, dust-colored hair halfway between blond and brown, held back from her face with two pink barrettes. She's been growing out her bangs, and the parts that fall loose from the barrettes brush against her eyes.

"Pitcher," Bernie says. He turns to me. "Miller Lite?"

I nod, and the waitress writes "ML" down on her order pad and draws a circle around it.

"Hey," Bernie says to me and holds a hand out to the

waitress, asking her to wait. "You hungry? You wanna split a pizza?"

"Yeah," I say, "sure."

"Large," Bernie says. "Pepperoni, extra cheese."

The waitress doesn't bother to write this down, just taps her pencil against the order pad and walks back to the kitchen.

"Food's good here," Bernie says. "They got a new chef. She makes the dough herself and freezes it for later."

"You mean her?" I ask, pointing in the direction of the waitress.

Bernie shakes his head. "Her mother."

The waitress walks out of the kitchen, over to the bar. She fills a pitcher of beer and sets it on the bar counter, waiting for the foam to collapse. She wipes a damp rag over the countertop, sticks out her bottom lip and blows upward, lifting the bangs out of her eyes.

"Is she twenty-one?"

Bernie shrugs. "Never asked."

Doug's not here yet, but it's early. It'd take him a while to drive into town. I excuse myself to Bernie and walk to the phone. Somebody's punched "Achy Breaky Heart" on the jukebox, and I have to jam a finger in my ear to hear the phone ring.

"Cookson residence," Sonia says, but she has a lot of trouble with "residence."

"Sonia," I say, "I'm going to be a little late."

"For dinner, Harley?"

"Bernie ordered a pizza."

"Oh," she says and pauses. "You will have extra?"

"I'll bring you a slice."

"Good," she says. "Two slices, Harley?"

"Whatever's left over."

I can see the door from where I'm standing. Doug Hale walks in alone, goes to the bar, leans over the counter to give his order. His jeans are clean, but he's wearing his work boots; there's dried dirt and manure along the soles.

"Harley," Sonia says, "you will get Mama's pills?"

"I'll bring them home with me. How's she doing?"

Doug takes a shot and a beer from the bartender and sits down alone at a booth by the wall.

"Sleeping."

"Okay," I say. "I'll be home soon."

A guy, tall, in a flannel shirt, jeans and cowboy boots comes out of the bathroom, walks over to the jukebox and dumps in three quarters.

"Harley?" Sonia asks.

The guy hunches over the jukebox and runs his finger over song titles, choosing.

"Yeah, honey?"

"Come home." Her voice is soft, sexy, but I can tell she's worried. This is the first night I've been late coming home. Usually, I can't wait to walk in the door and put my hands on her. A few nights, I've embarrassed myself by attacking her in the foyer, and we made love on her mother's Russian area–rugs.

"Soon," I say. "I'll bring you some food."

An old Willie Nelson tune, "Blue Eyes Crying in the Rain," comes on while I'm walking back to the table. Bernie's pouring his second beer. He smiles at me. "Everything okay?"

"Sure."

He cocks his head in the direction of Doug's table. "That the guy?"

I nod, trying not to look directly at Doug. He's smoking; I can see out of the corner of my eye his hand lifting the cigarette, the frayed cuff of his shirt.

"Gonna go talk to him?"

"No."

Bernie laughs softly, shakes his head. "Then what are we doing here?"

A short woman with dyed-red hair, in a cook's uniform that strains across huge breasts comes out of the kitchen with a pizza, walks to our table and sets it down. She pulls two small plates out of the deep pocket across the front of her uniform and puts one in front of each of us. "How's it going?" she asks. She crosses her arms over her stomach, showing the rings she wears, silver or cheap gold with tiny glass stones, on every finger except pinkies and thumbs.

Bernie looks up at her, grinning. "Keeping busy," he says.

"That right?" She gives him a sly smile and lets her eyes linger over his face.

"Yeah," he says and looks down at his beer. "You working hard?"

"Not every night," she says. She waits for Bernie to raise his head and look at her. When he does, she laughs, turns and walks slowly back to the kitchen. She takes another look at him, still chuckling, before she walks through the swinging doors.

"She's joking around," Bernie says, flustered and blushing.

"Didn't look like it."

"Yeah," he says, and gives a short, surprised laugh, "right."

The waitress with the barrettes walks over to Doug's table. She's wearing dirty white canvas sneakers, and while he gives his order, she rolls first one ankle, then the other, letting the sides of her sneakers touch the floor.

"So," Bernie says, "what are we doing here?" He pulls a slice of pizza from the pan, grabs the cheese string with his fingers and pinches it off.

I take a slice of pizza myself, drop it onto my plate. "Eating," I say, and take a sip of my beer.

꒰ꜜ

I left school right after my last fall semester exam, handed in my blue book, got in the car and headed for the thruway. The roads were bad, and my eyes burned; I'd fallen asleep wearing my contacts, had to pry them off early that morning and wore glasses I'd had since junior high. December twenty–second, and it'd already snowed a couple of times, enough to stick. The exam was in basic Russian: Kak vas zavut (what is your name)? Minya zavut Harley (I am called Harley).

I passed the cemetery at a little after nine. The light was low over the lake; birds gathered in the trees where the groundskeeper had hung pine cones coated with peanut butter and bird seed. I wondered, idly, where Lynette's father's tombstone might be, looked for a grave that might have been dug recently. I turned right at the four corners; the car drifted sideways on the turn, and I let it glide a couple of seconds, feeling reckless, before turning into the skid. A few miles out of town, a truck passed on the right, startling me and spraying slush against the passenger–side door.

I skidded to a stop at the bottom of the hill and flipped on the hazard lights. The hill had been plowed, but not for hours. I could see lights on at the house, downstairs and in a bedroom that wasn't Lynette's. It had started to snow, and the light was golden. I thought for a second I could go and see Lynette, just walk up the hill and knock on the door, but I wasn't the kind of person who could go where he might not be welcome. I just didn't have the nerve.

The orchard would have been quiet at that time of year

anyway, but Mrs. Wilson had closed the shop, and no one knew if it would open again. My mother told me she'd heard the Wilsons were deep in debt, that Mr. Wilson didn't carry much life insurance. All the money was sunk into the orchard, and now there was no one to work it.

Snow collected on the windshield, the flakes getting bigger and wetter. I hadn't spoken or written to Lynette since that last night in the orchard, and I wondered what I should do: call her and pretend everything was the same, that she didn't dare me to have sex with her and I didn't stand there like a jerk, like someone who didn't give a damn about her—or do nothing and pretend not to see her when I ran into her in town.

I had slept with Amanda once more after a party at my dorm. When I walked in, she was dancing alone in the middle of the floor, arms flailing, windmill–like, knees churning. There was something liquid in her movements— I wouldn't know until later that it was because of the dope she'd been smoking in somebody's dorm room—and I wasn't the only one watching.

She had her eyes closed and managed to smack me in the mouth with the back of her hand before noticing me standing in front of her. She saw me and stopped dancing, a liquid smile spreading across her face, and I took the hand she had smacked me with and led her off the floor. It seemed, I don't know, bigger than life—like a scene from a movie—and on my way out the door, I nodded at the boys who were still watching, just a quick dip of the head that said I knew what they were doing and it was fine with me.

She'd worn a red T-shirt with thin straps and a red mini-skirt that barely covered her ass. The whole thing looked like it had been white once and then dyed; the color was uneven on the T-shirt straps and the skirt pockets. I walked behind her up to the second floor, catching glimpses of her white underpants through the open grillwork of the stairs.

Amanda smelled like incense and dope and the sweat that had settled into a "v" in the middle of her T-shirt. She hummed and pressed herself against me, then suddenly twirled away, as if part of some dance step our parents might have done, and I pulled her to me and thought how much easier it was to be with a girl like Amanda, who didn't need so much conversation.

With Amanda, I thought, I could really discover what the whole sex thing was about. She was as free with her body as any boy, and she didn't require the kind of negotiation my friends had with their girlfriends: you can touch me here, but not there. This was the way it was supposed to be, I thought, with her naked and laughing and saucer-eyed beneath me.

Afterward, we slept for a while, back to back on my tiny mattress, and then later she got up and dressed, and I heard she went back down for the tail end of the party. I didn't wake up until five, when my roommate pounded on the door, and I had to get up to unlock it.

It wasn't that I never thought about Lynette while I was away at school. I did. I thought about how smart she was and how much she deserved to be at college, instead of serving fried fish to senior citizens. Her grades were better than mine and she had earned it more. But there was nothing I could do about that.

Even with the engine running, it was too cold to sit for long in the car. I turned the wipers back on, checked for traffic behind me. I decided I'd call Lynette, ask her if she wanted to go to a movie. I didn't know how she'd react. I knew I'd done something wrong that night in the orchard, but I'd never been able to figure out exactly what I should have said or done that would have been right.

Still, I thought I owed it to her to call her again, and I wanted to. I wanted to sit in a dark theater and smell apples. I had condoms in my suitcase, but I knew I probably wouldn't use them. I was beginning to think Amanda and Lynette were two different kinds of girls that had nothing to do with each other, and maybe that was what made it okay, being with both of them, wanting to be with them both. I pulled into the road, made a U-turn and headed back toward home.

ᘐ

I walk out of the bar with Sonia's two slices wrapped in a couple of napkins. Bernie's still in the bar, half in the bag but drinking coffee now and waiting for the cook's shift to end. Doug left half an hour ago, after three shots and three beers. He drank alone, paid in cash, left a two-buck tip.

The sky's clear, full of stars; I take a deep breath, feel cold air hit my lungs, nose, the sharp ache in my chest and my nose hairs bristling. I look both ways, cross over to my car. In another hour, the streetlights will change to flashing red. The street's quiet—no traffic—and I can barely make out the words to Patsy Cline's "Crazy" coming from the bar.

I get in the truck, slam the door, start it up and head into town, but at the four corners I stop for the light and switch on my blinker, making the turn out into the country. Sonia will be waiting for me; she's probably worried by now, but I step on the gas and head for Temperance Road anyway. The truck's headlights cast uneven shadows over the road, lighting up pieces of gravel, darkening the potholes. Without streetlights, I can only see a few feet in front of me; I can feel the rise of the hill, the summit and the downward slope, without seeing the change.

The headlights pass over a reflective stripe on the side of Doug Hale's mailbox. I slow the truck to a stop and turn off the lights, but keep the engine running. I roll down my window and listen to wind in the trees. A light goes on upstairs, then a shadow passes over the window. Smoke rises through the trees from Doug's brother's trailer, and light falls unevenly on the surrounding tree trunks.

Doug's truck is parked next to the barn, not flush to the side of it but roughly perpendicular. The barn door is closed, an orange plastic sled leans against the steps to the porch. A light from the back of the house probably comes from the kitchen. A shadow passes again, slowly, over the upstairs window, and a few minutes later, the light goes out. Everything looks exactly like it should.

CHAPTER VI

ॐ

MY FATHER WAS BUSY MAKING COFFEE when I walked into the kitchen with my bags. He had on the sweatshirt I'd sent him from college, an old pair of corduroys with an elastic waistband and the leather slippers he wore in the house. My mother complained about him drinking coffee at night; she said it kept him up, but he claimed nothing else tasted right in winter. He plugged in the percolator they'd had as long as I could remember, slipped in the filter. He wore half-glasses on a chain around his neck, raised them to his eyes when he wanted to measure the coffee.

"Just get in?" he asked. He wasn't sick yet—at least, we didn't know about it then—but he looked older and tired, his skin and hair drained of some of their color.

I nodded. "Mom up?"

"In bed, reading." He drummed his fingers on the counter, like he might wait there until the coffee brewed.

"So why are you still up?"

He smiled and rubbed the back of his neck with his hand. "Trouble sleeping," he said.

"So you're drinking coffee?"

"Yup," he said. "Retirement." He looked at the percolator, checked the plug, walked over to the kitchen table and sat down. "Thirty years, I get up at six every morning. Now I'm like a kid on summer vacation. I stay up, sleep in." He grabbed a pack of playing cards from my mother's lazy

Susan, started dealing for solitaire. "You want in?" he asked. "Play double?"

I shook my head, walked over to the refrigerator, stared inside at the fruit salad and deviled eggs my mother made because she knew I liked them.

"Your mother thinks I'm crazy," he said. "Still gets up at six."

"Maybe you are," I said, "crazy."

He laughed. "Yeah." He slapped a red three on a black four and shuffled the pile. "Crazy working thirty years for the same company, waiting to retire." He smiled and shook his head. "Then it happens. You can't sleep, eat too much, watch too much TV."

He flipped over the third card, looked for a place to put it, shuffled and flipped again. "You want something to eat?"

I shook my head. "You guys fighting?" On second thought, I got up, pulled a couple of deviled eggs out of the fridge with my fingers, popped them one at a time into my mouth and swallowed them whole.

"That's not for you to worry about," he said, his voice sharp, but then he sighed and put the pile of cards down on the table. "You've got enough to worry about with school."

"I'm doing okay."

"The job okay?" he asked. "You got enough money?"

I'd taken a second job at night, washing floors in class buildings. In the morning, I tracked dirt over my own work. "Sure," I said. "All set."

He nodded, moved over a king. "Got a girl?"

I shrugged and got up for the coffee, poured us both a cup. "I see somebody."

"What does that mean?"

I poured the coffee and brought it to him. "I go out with a girl. Nothing serious."

"Okay," he said. "I guess that's good." He took a sip of coffee, put it down on the table, on the edge of his ace of spades. "No hurry," he said. "Get a job first, a career. Get the hell out of this town."

"I thought you liked it here."

He had to move his coffee mug to put a two down on the ace. "Sure," he said and shrugged. "Yeah, I like it fine. But you need something bigger."

"Bigger? You mean a city?"

He turned over a red six, held it in his hand while he searched for a place to put it, shook his head. "A bigger life."

I pulled a napkin off the lazy Susan and wiped deviled egg from the corner of my mouth. "I don't know, Dad. I think your life looks pretty good."

"Yeah," he said and nodded vigorously. "Yeah, it's good for me. It's a good life." He nodded and looked down at his cards. "But it's not enough for you," he said. "You'll do something more."

꒰

I park the truck in the garage, and Whitey meets me at the back door. He sniffs my hands, looking for the pizza, then gives me a small lick across the knuckles. I pat his head and walk into the kitchen, where Sonia's pouring a glass of milk. I reach my arms around her, smell the vinegar in her hair.

"Where's Mom?" I ask, kissing the back of her head.

"Sleeping." Sonia's tired; her voice is soft, her accent thicker. She sets the milk down and turns, leans against me with her head on my shoulder.

Whitey gives up on looking for pizza, curls up on the dining room rug and sighs.

"You are smoky," Sonia says and rubs at her nose.

"I went to a bar with Bernie."

"Drinking?" She knows I don't drink much. There are three six-packs in the fridge left over from Labor Day.

"Doug Hale drinks there."

"Oh," she says, nodding against my shoulder. "Spying."

I don't know what I thought I was doing, but I didn't think it was spying: keeping a lookout maybe, doing a favor for a friend.

"You bring Mama's pills?"

I wince. "Geez, Sonia, I forgot."

Her hair is down, twisting around her neck from the ponytail she had it in this morning. I reach a hand to the back of her head and stroke the hair with my fingers.

"The Wal-Mart in Glennville is open all night. We could get the pills later."

"Okay," she says and yawns against the front of my shirt where my coat's open, so that I can feel her warm breath through the cloth.

"You bring the pizza, Harley?" she asks, pulling away from my hand when it snags in her hair.

"I left it in the truck." I turn and open the door, and Whitey squeezes out the opening with me, follows me to the truck. He acts excited, like maybe we're going for a ride, hops in when I open the door.

He has the pizza before I even think about reaching for it, eating through the napkins wrapped around it, tearing the white paper to shreds, then swallowing large chunks of crust, sauce, cheese and pepperoni together. He eats quickly but carefully, his head bent over the pizza, tail pulled close to his body.

I have my hand out to reach for the pizza, but then he raises his head and growls at me, a long, low growl meant as a warning, and I back up slowly without even dropping my arm, without even thinking about lowering it but acting on instinct, wanting him to see I'm not a threat.

I don't know what to do. I can't take the pizza away from him. He doesn't follow orders, and I'm afraid to touch him.

He eats all the pizza, both slices, while I stand there watching. Then he moves to the edge of the seat and looks at me, wags his tail a couple times. My hands are still shaky, but I motion toward the house, wait for him to jump off the seat so I can close the door and follow him into the kitchen.

"He ate your pizza," I tell Sonia. I have the few shreds of wet paper towel Whitey left on the truck seat, and I show them to her before throwing them away.

Sonia looks at me and at Whitey, who's sitting at her feet, begging for more food. "Oh," she says, "I will make some eggs," and turns to the refrigerator.

"We have to get rid of him."

Sonia takes the eggs from the refrigerator. "Your friend has enough trouble." She pulls a pan from the drawer at the bottom of the stove and sets it on top, adds some butter and cracks two eggs.

Whitey sniffs around the edges of the counters, but gives up when he doesn't find anything and lowers himself to the floor, drops his head on his paws and sighs.

I reach from behind Sonia and put my arms around her, feel the front buttons on her sweater and stretch my fingers up to her nipples. I brush against them, and she flinches, pushes my hands away. "Harley," she says. "I am cooking."

The eggs start bubbling, and she puts the lid over the frying pan. I kiss her neck and she stops for a second, leans against me.

"We have to get rid of him," I say again, softly, in her ear.

"Harley, I told you..." she says and stops herself.

"We could have him put down."

"No." She turns off the stove burner and moves the pan of eggs to the back of the stove, takes my hands and kisses them, holds them to her chest.

"If he's vicious...."

"He's not."

"If he hurt you...."

"I don't think so." She lets go of my hands, reaches into the cupboard for a plate and slides the eggs onto it, pushing at the yolk a little with her finger.

I reach for her again, wrap my arms around her. "I can't let you get hurt."

She leans against me, her hair brushing against my chin, tickling, and sighs. "Harley," she says, "let me eat the eggs."

I take my hands away, kiss her on the shoulder where her sweater and neck meet up, smell wool and flowered soap.

"I will come to you later," she says, turns and kisses me, slowly, on the lips. Her breath smells like chocolate; she must have snuck a cookie while I was in the garage. She likes the ones with marshmallow inside.

Whitey shifts on the floor, rolling over onto his side.

"What are we going to do about him?"

She looks at Whitey and back at me and shrugs. "He doesn't mean it."

I step around Whitey and into the living room, look out onto the street, where the flashing red stoplight on our corner reflects off the windows of parked cars. Too quickly, I start thinking about Lynette, wondering what she's doing, if she's lying hurt somewhere. I don't like these thoughts of her sneaking in, at any time and for no reason, sliding under the doors, slipping between window panes, rising up from cracks in the floor. I don't want her here with Sonia and me.

Sonia walks up behind me and touches me on the shoulder. "Harley?" she asks softly. "Why do you spy?" She leans forward, letting her head rest between my shoulderblades. "Why you don't *ask*, Harley?" she says, her voice muffled against my coat. "*Ask* if you can help her?"

 ༈

I waited until after lunch, when my mother was washing dishes and my father scooped a second helping of tuna casserole left over from the night before onto his plate, before going upstairs to use the phone in their bedroom. The sun was out, dazzling on the snow, and inside, dust motes drifted from the ceiling, the clock on the dresser ticked and the bed springs squeaked when I sat on the mattress. I dialed and waited for the ring, blowing air through my cheeks. She picked up after the third ring, sounded a little out of breath, like she'd been running, when she said hello.

"It's me," I said.

"Harley?" she asked, like maybe she wasn't sure.

"Yeah."

"You home?"

"Yeah, I'm home."

"Well," she said, "that's good."

I sat back against the headboard. "How have you been?"

"Oh," she said, like she was thinking about it, how to sum up the time since I'd seen her, "good."

"How's your mom?"

"A little better," she said. "How're your parents?"

"Good," I said. "You want to go out? See a movie or something?"

There was a pause. I heard the clock ticking, saw the small hand shake and jerk forward, marking the minute. "Oh," she said, "not really. I mean I can't."

"You can't?"

"I'm kind of involved." She waited, like she was expecting me to ask another question, and cleared her throat. "With Doug Hale," she said.

I waited for a question to form in my mind, saw that it was snowing again, wet snow mixed with rain.

"How long has that been going on?"

"Not long," she said. "About a month."

If I concentrated, I could almost hear the snow on the windows, falling against the glass and sliding down toward the sill.

"I would've told you," she said. "I didn't hear from you for so long, I thought maybe…" She let her voice drift off, and I wondered what the tail end of that sentence might be, if she was going to say she thought I was dating somebody, or she thought I was mad about the last time I saw her, or maybe she just thought I didn't want to see her.

"You like him? He's nice to you?"

"Yeah," she said, "sure."

There was a smudge on the comforter from my sneaker. I reached down and brushed the dirt off. I knew she'd hang up soon, and I was buying time. I thought about Amanda, wondered what it'd be like to really care about her, if that was what I was supposed to do now.

"Hey," I said, "did you take him to the orchard?"

She waited a minute; I could hear her breathing. Finally, she said, "I'm sorry, Harley, but that's none of your business."

ꝏ

Sonia walks up behind me in the bathroom and leans against my back, sniffs. She kisses me between the shoulder blades, walks to the toilet and sits down. I let the water run, not wanting to listen to her pee. I brush my teeth and spit, watch from the corner of my eye as she wipes herself and flushes. I run the toothbrush under the faucet and she touches me again on the shoulder, lets her hand brush across my back as she walks out, into the bedroom.

She's bent over a dresser drawer, fumbling for a nightgown, her back bare, spine showing, all ridges and dents. I rest my hand flat against the middle of her back, and she straightens but doesn't turn. I let go and pull her toward me, my hands on the knobs of her shoulders, until her body leans into mine, my knees bent slightly, cupping her. Only then do I touch her breast with one hand, gently lifting the soft weight of it in my hand, and massage her nipple until it hardens and I can feel every small imperfection, the tiny bumps of glands around the hardened center.

She bends, so that her breast pulls away from my hand, and reaches for the waistband to her leggings, pulling it and her underwear down over her hips. I step away and let her undress. I pull my own shirt over my head, kick my sneakers off and open the fly of my jeans.

She slips naked into bed and waits for me, shivering. The room is cold, and I have to concentrate, willing myself not to go soft. The sheets are icy when I climb under the quilt, and I grab for Sonia, wanting her warmth as much for itself as her body. But then she wraps her legs around me, and I want that, too.

჻

I drove to the movie theater three nights in a row before I saw Doug's truck. I'd parked in front of the drugstore, and I waited for them to cross the parking lot. I thought for a minute Lynette might have seen me, but she didn't say anything or turn her head. Doug had his hand at the base of her neck, guiding her. He took long strides; she had to take twice as many to keep up.

They bought popcorn; I could see them at the counter, but I recognized the girl in the ticket booth and didn't follow them inside. She'd have seen Lynette, and if she saw me alone, she'd put two and two together.

I could see them at the candy counter, and when they walked away, Doug was still steering her like that, with his hand on her neck. The thing was, she didn't seem to mind. She was laughing, and she looked happy.

჻

I stare at the ceiling, at the drywall seams showing through the paint, and wonder if I shouldn't have disguised them somehow, maybe patched them with plaster. Sonia's beside me with her hip wedged against my thigh, and I find myself matching my breaths to hers, holding them just a second longer so that we can breathe in and out together. The baby monitor crackles in the nightstand drawer—we forgot to turn it off and I'm afraid my mother's heard the two of us—but then there's nothing, just static.

"Oh no," Sonia says, "the pills." She raises the back of her arm over her eyes, and I can see the soft fuzz under her arms.

"What?" I tickle her, wanting her to move her arm so I can see her face.

"Mama's pills," she says, "you are supposed to get them."

༉

Sonia stands up and starts looking for her socks under the bed. She's beautiful, bending like that, with her hair covering her face, her skin so smooth, even where it curves over her ass and along her thighs.

"Shouldn't somebody stay here with Ma?"

She walks barefoot over to the nightstand, pulls the monitor out of the drawer and holds it to her ear. She turns it toward me and holds it out. I listen, but don't hear anything, and she holds it to her ear again, then snorts, imitating my mother's snoring.

"Stop that," I say, and she shrugs, walks over to her dresser and starts shuffling around for a pair of jeans and a sweater.

I pull on sweatpants, the T-shirt and flannel shirt I was wearing earlier. I find a new pair of socks and run my fingers through my hair, trip over my sneakers in the middle of the floor.

"She needs those pills tonight?" I ask.

Sonia pulls the sweater over her head and, gesturing with her arm, says, "Blood pressure...."

Whitey's standing at the bottom of the stairs, light reflecting eerily from his eyes. I grab my coat from the closet and try not to make eye contact with him. I'm not sure I want to bring him along.

Sonia comes downstairs in stocking feet, steps past me to the closet and roots around on the floor for her boots.

Whitey walks over to her, jumps up on his back legs and pushes against her, pleading for a ride. She looks at me.

"You want to take him, Harley?"

I shrug. "He can stay."

Whitey jumps against her again, panting and wagging his tail.

"He wants to come," she says. She bends down toward Whitey. "Okay," she says, "you come. Okay." He jumps against her, and when she stands, he nudges her toward the door.

The truck is slow to start up, and Sonia blows on her hands, holding her curled fists to her mouth. Whitey stands on the seat, breathing foggy circles on the windshield.

It's brittle cold, too cold for snow. The air burns a little in my lungs, and the sky's full of stars. We pull onto the highway that'll take us north of town, toward Glenville and the 24-hour Wal-Mart. There was a protest before they built it and a petition I might have signed; a newspaper editorial called for a boycott, but it's impossible not to shop there when the prices and the hours are better than anything in town. I'm mostly glad they didn't build it any closer to home.

I pull around a tractor-trailer making its way up the hill on Route 32A and keep my eyes peeled for loose dogs or deer. Last year, a woman was killed when she hit a deer and a hoof came through the windshield. She had a husband and a six-month-old. The Council of Churches put on a spaghetti dinner and the Lions Club auxiliary raffled off a quilt to help with the funeral costs.

"It's cold," Sonia says, rubbing her hands together.

"It'll warm up in a minute."

She nods and smiles, puts her hand on my leg. I feel

myself go suddenly shy, seeing how small her hand is on my leg, and remembering what we were up to half an hour ago.

"How many pills does she take a day?" I ask.

Sonia counts on her fingers. "Five," she says, "six?"

There are no streetlights, and most of the farmhouses are dark already; I have to concentrate to make out curves in the road. "Why does she sleep so much? Why is she tired all the time?"

Sonia looks at me, turns away and shrugs. "Old age."

I pass the old cobblestone house with broken windows some nuns have bought and are planning to fix up. An article in the paper said they were refinishing the woodwork by hand. "Those doctors must have her all doped up."

"No," she says and sighs, stares out her window like she's tired or tired of me. "The pills, they help her."

"She shouldn't be sleeping so much."

"Okay," she says and reaches up to scratch Whitey's back. "You talk to the doctors."

I pull into the lot and park next to a rusty yellow Escort full of teenagers. The windows are foggy, but I can make out a girl in the back seat with ratted hair and a ring on every finger of the hand she holds out the window, tapping ashes. Whitey barks at the rap music they're playing. Sonia shushes him, but he keeps barking and tries to crawl over her to the window. She turns her back to him, still shushing, opens the door and steps down to the pavement. I climb out my side and follow her into the store.

It's eerily quiet and bright as a hospital inside. One of the cashiers, a girl who looks like she could be a friend of the kids in the car, reads a Judith Krantz novel, one leg up on a shelf under the register, popping gum and flicking at her peeling black nail polish.

Sonia will want to buy things. We don't come here often, but when we do, she's like a child, picking things up she'll never need because of the pretty colors or fancy packaging, so I say, "We'll be quick. We can get the pills and go home."

She ignores me and stops short, lets her hand glide across a sweater made from some kind of fleecy fabric.

"Do you need sweaters?" I ask.

"No," she says, her voice small, and starts walking again to the pharmacy. I hate myself when she does this, hate the part of me that even hesitates to give her whatever she wants.

"They're only $19.99. You can have one."

She smiles and pats my arm. "I am not needing anything."

The pharmacist is balding; the hair at his forehead and the back of his skull is wispy, almost transparent, so that what's left is like two parentheses at the sides.

Sonia hands him the prescription and Ma's Medicaid card, and he takes it, barely glancing at her. He looks tired and pale, but I realize it's only the fluorescent light that's turned his skin sallow. When Sonia looks at me, I see the shadows under her eyes, the lines around her mouth.

We sit on plastic chairs next to the pharmacy desk and listen to Kenny G over the intercom. Sonia pats me on the leg, stands and wanders down the health-and-beauty aisles, fingering foot powders and acne medications. She walks over to me, holds out her wrist for me to smell. She's sprayed on something strong and flowery that makes me sneeze. "Nice," I say, and she laughs because of the sneeze.

A woman in a plaid wool coat with a baby asleep on her shoulder comes to the counter with children's aspirin, diapers, tampons and baby shampoo. She has to lean to one side to pull the wallet out of her purse without waking the baby. The baby's wearing a snowsuit, but a few fingers have worked their way outside the mittens. They're wrinkled and so tiny, peeking out between the layers of fleece, delicate as spiders' legs or butterfly wings.

The pharmacist calls Ma's order, and Sonia and I have to shell out sixty dollars that Medicaid may or may not reimburse. I find myself almost saying something to the pharmacist, about how every month they figure out how not to cover something else, but I look at him, see how tired he looks with the lines on his forehead and at the corners of his eyes, and stop. I figure he's got a wife and kids waiting at home for him to get off his shift at three or four in the morning, and he'll get maybe four hours of sleep before somebody accidently wakes him, and he hears all the time how some guy thinks his prescription costs too much, he probably hears it a million times a night, and what can he possibly say that'll make it any different? So I just take the bag he hands me and shuffle back toward Sonia.

We're on our way out when Sonia stops and pulls me over to the deodorants. "Your friend," she says, pointing a finger in the direction of Lynette and her husband, coming down the main aisle to the pharmacy. Lynette's coat is draped over her shoulder, left open in the front, and I wonder why she hasn't buttoned it on such a cold night, but then I see her arm underneath, wrapped in a cast and tied across her chest.

"Her arm's broken," I say, though Sonia has eyes.

Sonia nods and looks at me, worried.

"I gotta say something." I move away from the deodorants, into the aisle.

"No," Sonia whispers behind me.

I step into the aisle and walk toward them. Lynette's

seen me, but she pretends she hasn't, ducking her head and avoiding eye contact. He's steering her with his hand on her neck, and it makes me crazy.

"Lynette," I say, too loud.

"No, Harley," Sonia says, hardly above a whisper.

Lynette stops and turns, gives a nervous smile.

"Who is this guy?" Doug asks, mumbling.

"Harley Cookson, Doug Hale."

I step close enough to shake his hand. It's not as big as I thought, but the skin is rough, calloused.

"Do I know you?" he asks, less like a challenge than because he's really curious.

"I don't know."

"We go to school together?"

"Yes, we did."

Sonia tugs on the back of my jacket, and I pull her toward me, put an arm around her and run my hand over the back of her hair. "My wife, Sonia."

"Nice to meet you," Doug says, gives a quick half-nod and starts off toward the pharmacy counter.

"Yes," Sonia says, and I've already got an arm out, pulling at the sleeve of Lynette's coat. It slides off her shoulder. I grab at the fabric, but she moves away. She looks me once quickly in the eye and says, "Don't," too quiet for Doug to hear.

"Harley," Sonia says and tugs on my jacket, starts walking me toward the door.

"Damn."

"We can go now," Sonia says, walking fast.

"Damn," I say, rushing past the checkout stands through the automatic doors, out into the freezing air.

CHAPTER VII

M Y MOTHER COLLECTED Christmas ornaments
she bought one or two at a time in antique stores:
glass balls, icicles and stars, blown glass roses and
fish and tiny musical instruments. She had my father string
colored lights over every branch, criticizing when he
missed one, so that the tree and the ornaments, all the
combinations of colored light and colored glass, dazzled.
Then, for the rest of the season, the two or three weeks she
kept the tree up until New Year's, she fidgeted and fussed,
shifting ornaments from one limb to another, slipping
lights over the tips of branches, frowning and stepping
backward, tilting her head and stepping back again.

She bought five or six rolls of wrapping paper, even
though there were usually just the three of us, and she
sometimes used two or three colors of ribbon on one
package, curling the edges or leaving them straight, making loops or bows or curlicues. My father and I covered the
things we bought for her with paper, using a box if we had
one, once using rubber cement when we ran out of tape,
but neither one of us knew what to do with a piece of ribbon. I found her once crying in the kitchen, after a Christmas dinner my father and I both said was perfect, but that
she claimed was dry and overcooked. "It's my own fault,"
she said and laughed, dabbing at her eyes with a corner of
dry dishtowel, "for wanting too much."

That year, my freshman year in college, when Lynette

left me for Doug Hale, my mother gave my father a plaid bathrobe to replace the one with the elbows worn through, and he gave her a sweater she'd picked out herself and put on hold. The two of them gave me two pairs of jeans, a pair of sneakers, three plaid shirts and an envelope with enough cash to keep me from taking a third job that semester. I bought my father a hooded sweatshirt for working in the garage and my mother a book about wildflowers.

I had gone to the bookstore in the student union and bought a Christmas ornament for Lynette, a small bear in a jogging suit and sweatbands. I'd wrapped it in some of the paper my mother had left over, red with little green Christmas trees, and the night before Christmas, I drove to her house and left it in the mailbox at the foot of the driveway. I didn't leave a note. Maybe she'd think it was stupid, maybe Doug would take credit for it, or maybe she'd know it was from me and throw it away, but anyway, I didn't want it, and I couldn't imagine giving it to anyone else.

⨞

The ambulance lights come on a little after four, flashing over the bed, tinting Whitey's fur and the sheets pink. I nudge him off my feet, swing my legs over the side. Sonia's been leaving the humidifier on at night, gurgling next to her nightstand, and she's mumbling in Russian, "red, yellow...house, green."

I poke a finger at the blinds to separate them. They're dusty; Sonia once said something about cleaning them, but never got around to it. The lights are rhythmic and blinding as the ambulance pulls carefully out of the garage, especially against the dark street, nothing but the traffic light at the corner, flashing too, and the one light at the house kitty–

corner to ours. It's a hall light Mrs. Turner leaves on. She's a widow and lives alone, worries about burglars or rapists. She's always cutting back the bushes that block her front porch, locking her doors in the middle of the day.

Once out of the garage, the ambulance speeds up, fishtailing at the corner before heading out of town; whoever it is must be in bad shape. I sit on the edge of the mattress and wish we had a police scanner, so I might not be wondering now about my friends and their health problems, Bernie's angina, my lawyer who's diabetic, my tax man Marty's blood pressure and his mother's recent stroke.

Whitey stretches and rolls onto his side, his paws butting up against my leg. I'll have trouble getting back into bed now. If I try to move him, he'll growl.

Sonia's dreams make her fingers twitch, tickling my rear. I pull the nightstand drawer open and listen for my mother's breathing, but I hear her voice instead, "Frank," she says. "Cold, Frank. It's cold."

It's cold in the house at night, but every time I call the furnace guy to fix the forced air system in our basement, it costs me two hundred bucks, and the benefits are temporary. Sonia claims the house is dusty in winter from the warm air blowing through dirty vents. I'd never say so, but it's as much because she's a lousy housekeeper.

"Cold, Frank," my mother says, and I pull away from Sonia's fingertips, pad downstairs in my socks, not bothering to turn on the lights. The urine smell hits me in the doorway to her room, and I know she's lying there shivering.

"Frank?" my mother says when I turn on the lights, the hair on top of her head thin enough to see her scalp through, eyes cloudy, hands shaking when she reaches toward me, a shadow in the doorway.

"No, Ma. It's Harley."

"Harley?" she says. "I saw Frank. I talked to him."

"You were dreaming," I say, looking for the wheelchair so I can lift her into it.

"It's cold," she says. "I'm cold, Harley."

"I know, Ma." I pick her up slowly, try not to notice how cold and wet she is down the back of her nightgown, drop her into the wheelchair. I pull another nightgown out of the dresser, ask her to put up her arms, try not to look at her breasts, the belly round like a child's, but with skin papery and wrinkled.

"He was so handsome," she says, holding her arms over her head while I fit them into the clean nightgown, pushing the sleeves over her hands. "I forgot how handsome he was."

"You need to pee, Ma?"

"The cancer," she says, "turned him into a ghost." She looks up and shakes her head in answer to my question. "So fast," she says.

I wheel her as close to the toilet as I can, hand her a warm, damp washcloth and the bottle of lotion Sonia keeps in the bathroom. She leans toward me, and I hold her by the shoulders, so she can wipe herself and smooth on the lotion. Her hands and shoulders are stiff, and she can't reach behind herself very well, but we have an unspoken understanding that I won't touch her there, and I'll pretend not to notice when she touches herself.

"I ironed his shirts," she says, handing me back the washcloth. "Every day, a freshly ironed shirt, a clean tie."

I wheel her back into the bedroom, park her next to the bed and reach under her to lift her into it. She grimaces when I drop her from a little too high above the mattress.

"I put creases in his sleeves," she says, "and he rolled them up." She touches her elbow, as if to show me where. "He loosened his tie and let it dangle," she says, and lays her head on the pillow. "He spilled coffee on his shirts. I had to scrub them in the sink."

I touch my hand to her forehead as if checking for fever, feel how clammy her skin is and pull another blanket from the foot of the bed.

"I was embarrassed," she says. "He embarrassed me."

"That's okay, Ma." I smooth the hair on her forehead away from her face, petting her.

"No," she says, shaking her head, rolling it from side to side on the pillow. "I should have known better." She coughs, I keep petting, and she slowly closes her eyes.

⌁

I sat next to Amanda in class, watched her doodle obscenities about the professor in her notebook, listened to her crack gum. I tried to think of her as a girlfriend, someone I could care about, and I did a little, I thought. I let my arm brush up against her, felt how warm she was in a scratchy brown sweater that looked like a man's. I could see where she missed a little with the eyeliner around her eyes, the place where her hand skipped and the line dropped a little too far below her lashes. I saw that she had nice skin where the "v" of her sweater and the "v" of her T-shirt met up to show a little chest, and she had long, straight fingers and straight white teeth her parents must've paid for, and I could see that she was a smart and complicated girl, and I liked that about her. These are the details of a person I could like, I thought, and I reached over and touched her left hand with my fingers, let my hand settle there. She turned to face me, smirked and crossed her eyes, but she waited a little before she pulled her hand away.

No one made coffee, so I search around in the cabinets for filters, don't find one and pull yesterday's out of the trash. It's cold and windy, windy enough for the trees to sway, and I'm a little afraid, like I sometimes am on windy mornings, to get up on that pole. If I said something, I know Bernie would laugh it off, squint out the window and tell me to stay inside, but I can't imagine doing it, actually saying something to him. I stand and think about it, but I can't imagine doing it.

"Did you hear?" he asks, walking over with his empty coffee mug. He glances at the trickle of coffee dripping into the pot and stands rocking on his heels. He's the kind of man whose shoes wear unevenly, sloping at the outer edges, because of how heavily he walks, and so he always seems to be balancing, trying to keep his feet from rolling underneath him.

I turn toward him with raised eyebrows, still thinking about the wind and swaying trees, wondering how cold it will be and how to keep the pole from moving while I'm on it.

"Doug Hale got himself killed last night."

He actually looks excited when he says this, like he's been looking forward to telling me, and I think I'll have to forgive him later for enjoying it so much.

"How's that?" I ask, though I heard him the first time.

"Doug Hale's dead," he says.

"You sure?"

"Heard it on the scanner. Damn thing crackled on at four this morning."

I hear voices in the hall, two of the secretaries walking

toward us, so I ask under my breath, leaning close enough to Bernie to smell the smoke on his clothes, "How?"

"Drowned," he says. He's trying to whisper, but it comes out a soft growl. "Ice fishing."

"He fell in?"

He nods and looks somewhere over my shoulder. "That's what the wife said."

"She was there?"

The secretaries walk past: Janice and the new one with a funny name, Clarice or Felice or something. Janice has on a sweater and plaid leggings that make her look heavier than she is. Clarice or Felice is more dressed up in a short skirt and silk blouse. One of them is wearing a lot of perfume, something spicy, just this side of medicinal.

Bernie watches them until they're out of sight down the hall before he turns toward me. "Yeah," he says. "She was fishing with him."

"She was fishing?"

"That's what they said. They took her to the hospital." He bends at the waist, checking the coffee pot. "Her arms were wet," he says, gesturing at his shoulders, barely meeting my eyes, "like she tried to pull him out."

I pull the coffee pot, even though it's still dripping a little. Coffee sputters on the burner. I fill Bernie's mug and my own before putting the pot back, setting it on top of the hissing coffee.

"Bernie," I say, "I might need some time."

"Take whatever you need," he says. He cranes his neck forward to take a sip of coffee. "You gonna tell me where you're going?"

"Personal time," I say and start walking away from him, back toward the office.

"That's what I figured," he says and stays where he is, rocking on his heels.

⟿

I drive back to town, put the blinker on to head home and tell Sonia, but then, before the light turns, I click it off and make a left, out past the Tastee–Freeze, the used car lot, the dry cleaner and the cemetery up on the hill. I turn slowly onto the Lake Road, trying not to fishtail where the road's still icy, gaining some speed and then slowing again before the turn into the orchard, up the steep gravel driveway, where I can feel the tires slipping underneath me, the motor grinding and wheezing, gravel crunching where the road is dry.

I know Lynette's not here anymore, hasn't lived here or probably been here for years, but before I go home and hear the gossip about her, about what kind of marriage she had and how much she might have wished or prayed for something like this to happen, before I even listen to Sonia tell me Lynette's husband was beating her, it seems important to sit here and remember something about her, about how she was before.

She was so strong, and there were times, in the orchard at night, when I was afraid she'd outrun me, leave me panting at the bottom of the hill while she hid somewhere in the trees. I'd call to her softly, listening to my feet scrape gravel as I climbed slowly, listening for her. I kept calling, a little louder each time, until she appeared in front of me, shushing. It wasn't just the humiliation I was afraid of, her being stronger than me, but the possibility that she would leave me behind, that we would somehow stay that way forever, one of us lost and the other one looking.

I think I should go to her. I should tell her how sorry I am, sorry for her husband's death and the rest of it—Whitey and her children and her big, ugly coat. But I hesitate. I think: She might not need me or even expect me, she might need me and want something from me, or she might not even remember or think of that time or me at all.

Halfway up the hill, the truck stalls. I turn off the motor, listen to the wind and, far away, the ice creaking. I start it up again, try to move forward and stall. This time, the quiet lasts longer. I sit, slapping my thighs, watching tree limbs quake a little in the wind, listening for the sound of it.

Finally, I start the ignition again, pop the truck into reverse and slide slowly down the hill. It's like walking away backwards, like saying goodbye.

CHAPTER VIII

ᘓ

M Y PARENTS got a Winter Family Weekend flier in the mail and took it as a summons. They never told me they were coming; they assumed, since all parents were expected, there was no need to mention it. They called me from a thruway rest stop to tell me they were making good time, and I raced around the room picking up beer cans and pizza boxes, stashing my baggie of pot.

My mother sat hugging her purse, the top of her hat, a knitted beret, brushing against the upper bunk. The hat was made of something soft like angora, and the tiny fibers drifted against the metal rail. Snow melted off the short plastic boots she wore snapped together over her shoes. My father stood and stared out the window or into my closet, looking at nothing and itching to smoke. He had quit after the first shadowy X-ray, had stopped cold turkey, but his fingers twitched with wanting.

"Your grades okay?" he asked for the second or third time since they arrived.

I nodded. "You thirsty?" I asked. "I could get you both a soda from the machine."

My father shook his head. "Job?" he asked suddenly.

"Dad?"

"Job going okay?"

"Sure, Dad."

My mother cleared her throat, stood and started unbuttoning her coat. The room was small and, with the three of us in it together, it had gone from warm to stifling. She pulled the coat off her shoulders, glanced toward my closet and lay the coat next to her on the bed.

I cleared my throat. "Will you excuse me for a second?" and jabbed my thumb in the direction of the hallway.

My father nodded, and my mother said, "Of course, dear," smoothing her skirt over her knees. I walked to the end of the hall, bent over with my hands on my knees to clear my head, then started running. I ran down the two flights of stairs to the lobby, out the door, over to Amanda's dorm. I called her on the phone in the lobby, waited for her to buzz me in, then ran up the stairs to her room. Amanda's roommate took one look at me standing in the doorway and walked out, saying she was going to the library.

"What's wrong?" Amanda sat in a chair in front of the full-length mirror she had leaned against her desk. She was fresh out of the shower, in a long, tie-dyed T-shirt with blue and purple bullseye designs, clipping her wet hair into sections for braiding.

"I thought you might want to meet my parents."

She released a clip from the back, bowing her head forward and reaching for the strands of hair. "Okay," she said, working her fingers in a pattern, not having to look at what she was doing.

I was still breathing hard, and my body was still trying to decide if it was warm or cold after I'd run across campus without a coat. "So you'll come?"

"What?" she asked, raising her head. "Now?"

"Yes," I said, noticing the stuffed animals on her roommate's bed, the smell of sandalwood and shampoo, the way Amanda's T-shirt rode up along her thigh. "Well," I said, "a half hour, an hour, whatever...it's okay."

"Jesus, Harley," she said. "How about a little notice?" But

she got dressed in a pair of jeans and a navy blue sweater, undid the three or four braids she had finished and instead put all of her hair in one long braid at the back. She didn't wear makeup, just left her face smooth and clean, and she looked good. I told her so.

On the way back to my dorm, she held my hand, shivering because of her wet hair, standing close to me for warmth. "Just tell me," she said as we passed the library, and let go of my hand. "You weren't going to invite me," she said, and it wasn't exactly a question.

She wore the fake leopard-skin car coat she must have bought at the Salvation Army store in town. I reached for her hand and started to lie; she let me hold her hand but, while I stammered out a lie, she just stood there shaking her head, looking off somewhere over my shoulder.

"You were afraid," she said and her eyes dropped to my face, and I was sorry for everything I hadn't said or done for her, "of being alone with them."

"That's crazy. I've always been alone with them," but I was talking too loud, the way I did when I knew I was wrong. I was afraid of my parents. I was afraid of how little we already had in common now, and how it was only going to get worse. I wanted Amanda there, because I wanted the three of us to have someone to talk to, and, after she went home that night, someone to talk about. It wasn't fair to her or to them, but that's what I wanted.

"Okay," she said, and we walked together into my dorm.

༃

We ordered a pizza with half mushrooms and olives, because Amanda was a vegetarian. My mother asked how exactly that worked, if she had to cook her own food, and

Amanda said no, the dorm usually had either salad or cereal on hand.

"Breakfast cereal?" my mother asked.

Amanda nodded. "Wheaties," she said, holding her arm up to make a muscle.

"Do you have a kitchen you could use," Mom asked, "if I sent you some things? Vegetable spaghetti sauce? Bean salad? Ambrosia?"

"Sure," Amanda said, "but you don't need to...."

"You can't eat cereal for dinner," my mother said in a way that made Amanda shut her mouth and smile.

My father and I split the meat half of the pizza, and my mother had half from each side, so at the end of dinner, Dad asked the waitress to box up the rest and slid it across the table to Amanda.

He lagged behind Mom and Amanda at the door, gave me a quick shove with his shoulder. "So," he said, "this is the one you're seeing."

I coughed and nodded. "Yup."

"Nice girl," he said and let me walk ahead of him a few steps. "Bad coat."

వి

The wind has died down, but I can feel the cold in my ears, a piercing pain in the eardrum that makes me wonder if I'll hear the same, and I think of Doug Hale, gasping for air in icy water, looking for the hole, the patch of light where the ice is broken and Lynette's reaching, wet to the shoulders.

I watch the sky, blue–gray with clouds flattening toward the horizon, and wonder how long she knelt on the ice with her arms in the water, how long with her fingers and feet and knees so cold and then so numb, before she ran for help. Or if she even ran for help. Maybe she was still there, kneeling like that, when they found her.

The wind freezes tears in my eyes and eyelashes, and I keep blinking, feeling the weight of them. I grab for tools, pick them up and put them back in my belt, each movement a little off, a little strange. I take another look at the lines and start climbing down, checking each movement twice; I have to be this careful because I'm looking off in the distance, searching for ice between the trees.

CHAPTER IX

ॐ

T HEN MY FATHER GOT SICK; the chemotherapy turned his hair to sawdust and made him so tired he spent the whole day on the porch, dozing on the glider. He wore elastic-waisted pants with paint splatters on them, the sweatshirt I'd sent him from college and leather scuff slippers that flapped when he walked. My mother said nothing, not even when he drove downtown and sat in the diner in those clothes, his hand shaking while he held a cup of coffee. She didn't mention when he forgot to comb his hair. She let him drag her good quilts out onto the porch and sleep on the pillowcases she embroidered as a girl. When he came into the house with a quilt wrapped around him, she only picked up the end of it that trailed on the ground, like a bridesmaid carrying his train.

I was patient, too. I spent most of my spring break sitting with him on the porch, listening while he tried to tell me important things. He fiddled with fishing lures, running the tips of his fingers over the hooks, and stammered about love and life and his childhood dreams.

He told me he had wanted to be a teacher, but that his parents couldn't afford college for him or his brother. Instead, he left school at sixteen to work his uncle's dairy farm. "Things happen," he said, quietly rocking, letting his slippers drag slowly across the porch floorboards. "Things change." He stopped a minute, staring at the waves. "It's all right," he said. "Most times, it works out all right."

He met my mother at a VFW dance after the Korean War. He didn't talk about the war, except to say he'd been in the motor pool, and he learned a thing or two about engines and taking orders. He decided if he was ever a boss, he'd listen to his workers, let them know what they knew and stay out of their way unless it was important. It made him a good boss, one the men at the mill respected and were willing to work hard for.

My mother arrived at the dance with a corporal named Grady Fitzpatrick. She'd gone to high school with Grady in Bradenton, about thirty miles west of here. They'd been on a double date with a buddy of Grady's from the supply corps, who'd gotten a job at the mill. That was before my dad worked there. Grady's friend dated someone my mother knew from the semester of nursing school she attended before my grandfather died and she had to stay home and help support her mother.

My father always mentioned how classy she looked, how elegant in a straight wool skirt, a wine–colored sweater set and matching pumps. "The exact same shade," he said, "like she bought them to go together."

She was blond and held her cigarette delicately between two fingers, like a girl from the city. He walked up to the table and asked her to dance, something he knew he'd have to pay for later, getting punched by her date in the parking lot, but somehow he didn't mind. That way, she might at least feel sorry enough to dance with him the next time. And he had a feeling he'd see her again.

"Lilacs and hairspray and Ivory soap," he said. "She dabbed lilac perfume behind her ears." He raised a glass of water to his lips and stared at the fog hanging over the lake. "She smelled clean."

"Did he punch you?"

"What was that?" he asked, staring at the lake.

"Did her date punch you?"

"Oh, sure," he said, leaning his head against the back of the chair. "Knocked me flat." He raised a fist in the air and made a punching motion, then he started laughing and had to drink more water when he started to choke.

My father and I almost never touched when I was growing up. He sometimes ruffled my hair or punched my shoulder, but we didn't hug or reach for each other. When I started high school, we shook hands and touched even less.

That spring, though, he might be sitting next to me in that rocking chair and suddenly reach his arm out sideways, clasping my forearm in his hand. Or I might be making a sandwich in the kitchen and he'd walk up behind me and lay a hand on my shoulder. Once, he leaned over me from behind the couch and placed a light, feathery kiss on my forehead. I closed my eyes and tried hard to remember what it felt like, to let his touch leave some kind of imprint on me.

I was in my senior year of college when he went into the hospital for the last time. About a week later, I got a package in the mail with twenty-nine fishing lures.

⤳

When I come in through the kitchen door, Sonia's washing my mother's hair at the sink. The wheelchair's backed up against the counter, and Ma's balanced on a pair of phone books so that she can rest her neck against a towel on the counter edge. She's got the cast propped on the seat of a dinning room chair; Sonia's washed and bleached the pom-pon sock stretched over the end.

Sonia looks up and smiles, cupping her hand to pour

warm water over the back of Ma's head. Ma has her eyes closed and seems to be sleeping, her eyelids flickering with dreams. With her hair wet, her scalp is laid bare, thin and delicate, veined like a bird's egg.

I walk carefully behind Sonia, trying not to wake Ma, and touch the back of her head, let my fingers settle in her hair, and when she turns her head, kiss her gently on the lips.

"Where's Whitey?" I ask.

"Oh," she says and looks around the edges of the room, where he might be sleeping or hiding, "upstairs, maybe."

"I have some news," I say. "Have you heard anything?" I unbutton my coat and drape it over the back of a chair.

Sonia shuts off the water and gently touches my mother's shoulder, but my mother doesn't stir. She raises her eyes and looks at me, shaking her head.

"Lynette's husband died."

Sonia's picked up the towel from the kitchen counter and she stops with it in her hand, looks at me again, watching my face. "Died?" she says.

"A fishing accident." Saying it like that makes it seem so ordinary.

"Fishing?" she asks. "In winter?"

"Ice fishing on the lake. He went through the ice."

Sonia touches my mother again, who starts, murmurs something and raises her head. Sonia covers it with the towel and starts kneading, like bread, then pulls off the towel, smiles at my mother and hands her a comb.

"Harley," Ma says, "you're home" and smiles as if genuinely pleased to see me.

"Yeah, Ma."

"Good," she says, her eyes bright, "we can eat soon."

Sonia walks to the chair, holding up my mother's cast and gestures for me to help her. I lift the cast and hold it while she pulls the chair away and raises the footrest from the wheelchair. I set the cast down gently, and Sonia moves to the back of the wheelchair, pushing it away from the sink.

My mother pats me on the arm and leans toward me, and when I lean closer to see what she wants, she kisses me on the cheek.

"An accident, Harley?" Sonia asks quietly, guiding the wheelchair in the direction of the downstairs bedroom.

I nod and she smiles, nodding herself.

"Well," she says and sighs, "now we know he doesn't hurt her."

ॐ

"Harley," Amanda said, sniffing at the bunk bed mattress, "this place reeks." She rolled onto her back and lifted an arm to play with the springs under my roommate's bunk. "Jesus, it wouldn't kill you to do some laundry once in a while."

"I do laundry. Scott never takes a bath." Scott left his dirty T-shirts on the floor, then, after a few days, figured they'd aired out enough to be clean again.

Amanda grabbed at one of the bunk bed's crossbars and acted as though she might pull herself out of bed, then let go and dropped back against the mattress. "You could change the sheets."

"Okay," I said, and pushed my bare foot against her hip, "get out of here and I will." I pushed at her playfully, letting her know I might actually kick her out of bed.

"Okay, okay," she said, lifting the covers and sitting up with her feet on the floor. She had wide shoulders for a girl; her back was thin and angular. "I'm gone. I'm outta here." She put her hands down flat on the edge of the mattress and hoisted herself up, so that she was standing with her head above Scott's bunk, and I couldn't see her face.

She'd thrown her clothes on my desk, and she walked over to them, picked up her underwear and pulled it over her hips. I was always surprised by the scars on her legs from nicks and scratches she said she got as a little girl, when she was still a tomboy and spent most of her time climbing trees or building things she and the boys in her neighborhood would later set on fire. She pulled on the undershirt with thin straps she wore instead of a bra and the striped T-shirt she wore over it, then the mini-skirt and strappy sandals with heels that were thick and wooden and made a Clydesdale clomping sound on the sidewalks around campus.

I turned on my side to face her, held myself up on one elbow. "Horse shoes," I said and giggled a little, the effects of a joint we'd smoked earlier that morning.

"What?" she asked.

"Nothing." I shook my head, noticing how greasy and thick my skin felt.

"So," she said, "see you later." She picked up her book bag but didn't strap it over her shoulder, just swung it to the ground and held it down near her feet.

"Okay," I said.

"Okay, what?"

I lay back against the mattress. "Okay, I'll see you later."

She stood for possibly a full minute, staring out the window, before she said, "You know, Harley, you could treat me like a girl sometimes. You could act like you love me or something."

"What?" I asked not because I didn't hear her, but because I wanted to give myself a minute before answering. I slid to the edge of the mattress, so that I could lean up and see her face. "What?"

She was standing with the book bag perched on top of her sandals, squinting like she did when she was angry, the braids random as weeds along her scalp.

"You heard me," she said, but then she opened her mouth to speak as though she wasn't completely sure I did.

"I do love you," I said, not because I'd planned to say it, but because, watching her face and how angry and hurt it was about to look, I couldn't not say it.

"You do?" she asked, a little surprised.

"Sure," I said, and she moved the book bag aside and dropped suddenly to her knees, banging her knee caps against the floor, crawled over and kissed me hard on the mouth.

૪

Lynette's house is dark, except for her porch light and a light in an upstairs bedroom. The trailer is dark, too, and I wonder if they've all gone somewhere, maybe to stay with another relative, but then, quickly, I see a shadow cross one of the bedroom windows.

I turn off the engine and open the window a crack, listening. Faintly, I hear crying, rhythmic and steady; it must have been going on a while now, with the baby red-faced and gasping for air.

I left Sonia half-asleep on the couch, her feet in heavy wool socks, tucked between the sofa cushions. We'd been watching a World War II documentary, and they'd just started liberating the camps when I got up, brushed tortilla chip crumbs off my pants and walked into the kitchen for my coat.

"Harley?" she said and turned her head, her hair fanning out across the sofa pillow she'd balled up against her cheek. "You will not be long?"

I walked to her, grabbed the back of the couch and bent to kiss her cheek. It wasn't something we did; we weren't the kind of married couple that habitually, dutifully, kissed goodbye and hello. Her cheek was soft and smelled like her soap. She turned away from me, back to face the TV, her hair sliding forward over the side of her face, and I checked for the truck keys in my pocket and walked away from her and out the front door.

Again, the shadow crosses behind the bedroom curtains. The side of my face aches from the cold, but I keep my window rolled down, listening for the baby. Something small and clumsy, a woodchuck, moves into the drainage ditch, its body liquid as it slides among the weeds.

Then the crying stops—I'm sure of it—and I can just barely make out the sound of Lynette's wind chimes on the porch, a tinny tinkling sound that carries because of how high it's pitched.

The moon is somewhere over my shoulder. I can't see it, but I know from my walks with Whitey the last few nights that it's there, high over the horizon, at about three-quarters full.

When I look again, the curtains are still, but I know she's standing in front of the window. I can't clearly see her, but I can feel her there, watching. I reach for my car keys, dangling from the ignition, and think I'll start the truck now and drive home, but when my hand closes over them, I leave it there without turning the one in the ignition.

It's deathly quiet, and I wait, counting the seconds, letting the wind blow icy against the side of my face, ruffling my hair. The light in her window changes in such a way that I know she's stepped away from it, slowly, and I think everything will be all right, now that she knows I'm here watching for her, and that that's enough.

But still, I don't move. The digital clock on the dashboard flips the minute from four to five, the keys leave jagged imprints against my palm, cold air blows against my scalp, and I shift my weight in the seat, settling deeper into the upholstery.

The front door opens then, and she steps from the dark hallway into the light on the porch. She waits, looks to both sides as if checking to see who else might be waiting for her, then turns and walks toward me across the yard, holding a sweater tight across the front of her with the hand that's still in a cast, letting go only to brush the hair out of her face when she reaches the road.

She looks both ways again, even though there's no traffic on the road, as if she wants to give me a chance to see her coming.

"Harley," she says, without tapping on the window this time, and she smiles, raising her broken arm to brush the hair from her face and clutching the sweater I can now see is green and hand-knitted, with a lopsided sunflower on the pocket that rests against her hip.

"I thought you might come," she says. "I saw you out here before."

I let go of the keys and roll the window all the way down, so she won't have to hear me through the glass. "I was just checking."

She nods as if this is something she understands, my coming out here to check on her without her ever asking me to. "I know." She looks up toward the moon behind me and back toward the house. "Nice night," she says. She places her left hand, the one without the cast, on the window ledge and taps it lightly. "Would you like to come inside? I could make coffee."

I shake my head. "I should go." I turn the key this time and hear the engine start up, too loud: definitely a hole in the muffler.

"Lynette," I say, "I'm sorry," and she nods as though she understands that what I'm sorry about is the death of her husband, not my being out here alone, spying on her from the road.

"Me too," she says, still nodding, and when she takes her hand away from the window ledge, I can see the skin where the sleeve of her sweater pulls back, bluish-white where it must have been nearly frozen, and the jagged cut on her palm, not deep but long, and most likely painful. She takes two big steps backward, as if part of some dance, giving me room to pull out onto the road, and when I do, she raises her other arm to wave, the white cast like a flag against the sky.

꒳

Amanda and I moved into an apartment off campus our senior year; it was an old, converted hotel, close to the highway and cheap. We listened to semis rumbling past at night, downshifting at the corner, trailers rattling over cracks in the pavement, and kids younger than us in cars with loud stereos, heading out of town to a bar that wouldn't question their fake IDs.

We lived in one big room with a bathroom so small you could sit on the toilet and turn the water on for the shower, and a kitchenette with a stove where the burners bumped. Amanda painted the walls blue, and when I mumbled something about the security deposit, she said she'd paint them again before we left. She made curtains for the windows, one to section off the kitchenette and another to section off the bed. She borrowed her mother's sewing machine, and, while she was at it, made a table-cloth and a skirt for herself from the same material. It was yellow with red and blue and pink tulips; they were sup-posed to be in straight rows with the buds pointing up toward the sun, but Amanda made a mistake, and on the curtain by the bed they were upside–down.

That winter, she started applying for teaching jobs for the next year; she bought a navy blue suit with two or three different silk blouses and a pair of blue pumps. She started wearing her hair in a single braid, like she'd worn it for my parents, and she practiced in the bathroom with makeup, rubbing it onto her eyelids and wiping it off again.

We drove home every other weekend to visit my father, and when I could I skipped a class and went home during the week. My father told me Amanda sometimes went by herself on the weekends I worked. He liked her company, he said. She saved jokes to tell him or she told him stories about her family. "Did she tell you that one about her uncle and the vacuum cleaner salesman?" he asked and smiled, remembering. He didn't laugh much anymore; he occasionally chuckled, but he couldn't get enough air for a full–throated, open–mouthed guffaw.

On one of those visits, Amanda stopped calling him Mr. Cookson and started calling him Frank. The next Saturday, when she walked in the door, trailing incense, and said, "Hi, Frank," both my mother and I turned our heads. She wore the skirt she'd made of the same material as our cur-tains and a red short–sleeved sweater cropped at the waist. She had on the wooden–heeled sandals; she was bare-legged, and she'd painted her toenails bright red. I realized then that when she sat on our bed the night before, painting her toenails, she'd been doing it for my father, and from the look on his face, I could see that he liked it, her cheer and the way she seemed to bring the world in with her. He was smiling; his eyes still swam in pain, but his lips were curled in a noticeable smile.

My mother and I, I saw then, had for months been playing our part as the grieving family; she had on a gray pantsuit that wouldn't wrinkle when she fell asleep later, sitting in a chair pulled next to his bed, and I had on the torn jeans and faded T-shirt I'd put on because for the last month I'd been spending my weekends at the hospital and hadn't done laundry.

She pulled the one empty chair next to the bed and raised her foot where he could see it. "What do you think?" she asked, pointing her toes. "Pretty wild, huh?"

I could have been sitting closer than I was, I realized then. Instead of sitting at the foot of the bed, I could have been where she was.

"Sure," he said, "wild," and she dropped her foot, letting the heel of her sandal smack against the floor.

"Loud, too," he said quietly.

My mother stood up from the chair where she'd been doing needlepoint, something she'd taken up again when he first went into the hospital. Later, she would make couch pillows people would admire but that neither one of us liked much, because they reminded us of his death. After a few months, my mother took them off the couch and sent them as a gift to her sister in Ohio.

"Do you need anything, Frank?" she asked. "Water? A blanket?" She had her purse clutched to her chest, which meant she'd be going to the cafeteria.

"Pills," he said, whispering, so that she had to lean close to make out the word.

She looked at her watch and patted his hand. "It's not time yet," she said, her voice low, too, so that we could all pretend Amanda and I hadn't heard.

My mother turned toward me, still clutching her purse. "Harley?" she asked. "Amanda? Can I get you a soda?"

I shook my head, but Amanda said yes, she'd like a soda, and when she said it, her eyes, like my mother's, had tears in them.

My father watched my mother walk out of the room, and when the door closed behind her, he turned his head toward Amanda and said, "She used to paint her toenails, too."

⌇

The back porch stairs are iced over because of a bad gutter that drips, and I have to grab a coffee can full of rock salt from the garage, pepper the steps with it. Whitey hovers near my feet, and I'm afraid he might jostle me, send me skidding down the stairs. I've got my sneakers on, unlaced over bare feet, and I'm thinking about the high deductible on my health insurance and wondering if there's disability in place if I break my back.

Whitey manages to make it down the stairs and into the yard, and I go back inside, double-checking each footstep, shivering from the cold air on my ankles. The overhead kitchen light is too bright, forcing my eyes to dilate and making the brown and gold pattern in the linoleum undulate under my feet. I plug in the coffee maker and fish under the sink for my thermos; it smells a little funny, but I'm hoping the hot coffee will boil off any bacteria.

On mornings like these, I wish Sonia would wake up

early, make eggs and oatmeal, fill the room with conversation. She sings, sometimes, when she cooks, Russian lullabies or American TV jingles, all of it in the same quiet, singsongy voice just under her breath. When she catches me listening, she smiles and stops, and no matter how many times I tell her I like it, she doesn't start up again.

When the coffee's ready, I pour two mugs and carry one upstairs to Sonia, leave it on the doily on her nightstand. I open the drawer and listen to Ma's monitor for a few seconds, hear that she's snoring and turn it off, close the drawer.

"Sonia," I say and touch her shoulder, the hard muscle under her collarbone. "I brought you coffee."

"Where do you go?" she asks, rolling over to face me, her nightgown twisted tightly around her and her cheek creased from the pillow.

"Making coffee."

"No," she says and shakes her head as if clearing it. "Last night."

I pull two pairs of socks from the dresser and sit on the bed to put them on. "I went to check on her."

"Your friend," she says.

"Lynette."

Sonia sighs and throws the covers back. "She is okay?"

I pull on the thick, cotton gym socks I wear because I'm allergic to the wool pair that will keep my feet warm. "I think so."

She sits up, dangling her feet over the side of the mattress. "You went," she says carefully, "a long time."

I have an urge to correct her, to say, "I was gone a long time," but I stop myself and say only, "I'm sorry."

"Do you talk to her?"

I pull on the second pair of socks and stand, testing to

see if I can feel the cold floorboards. Sonia looks at me over her shoulder, frown lines beginning.

"No," I say. "I just looked." It's the first time I've lied to her.

She nods and stands, rubbing the back of her head where her hair has tangled. She opens her dresser drawer and pulls out a pair of panties, holds them in her hand as if weighing them and slides them on under her nightgown. "Now," she says, "you will not go to her again. Right, Harley?"

"No," I say and notice again how large her eyes really are, how much of her face they occupy and how startling it is when they fasten on me. "Right."

❧

"I'm not going to ask you where you went yesterday," Bernie says, handing me a cup of coffee. I'm sorting through work orders, looking for the ones that make the most geographical sense, that can be grouped together into a day's work.

"Thanks."

"Yup," he says and rocks on his heels.

"Is this County Road 6 here?" I ask, pointing to a work order. I take a sip of the coffee; it's only lukewarm, as if he's been standing around waiting for me to show up.

"Yeah," he says, "that's right." He scratches his scalp, then tries to smooth his hair down where it's sticking up in back. He looks as though he wants to say something to me, and I only hope he's not going to grill me for information about Lynette.

"So listen," he says, "you know that cook? At the bar?"

I have to think for a second. "The one with the pizza?"

"Yeah," he says. "She makes her own dough."

"Sure." I set the coffee down on the desk. When he leaves, I'll dump it out and pour another cup.

"So," he says and leans toward me so suddenly that I automatically take a step backward, "you think she wants me to ask her out? A movie or something?"

"Sure," I say, relieved this has nothing to do with Lynette. "Why not?"

He stays where he is, leaning forward at the waist, so that I wonder who else might be seeing this. "You think that'd be good?" he asks. "A movie?"

"Well, I don't know, Bernie. You'd have to ask her."

I suddenly remember the name of the new secretary when she walks past: Cherise. She has what looks like a long gold necklace wrapped twice around her waist, with little gold bells that make a tinkling sound when she walks.

"Yeah," he says, "right." He looks down at his hand and picks at the dirt under one of his nails. "I could go down to the bar and ask her. You think that'd be all right, or do you think I should go to her house?"

"Have you been to her house?"

"Well no," he says, "but I know where she lives."

I stack the sorted work orders together and knock them on the desk, straightening the edges. "I think you better ask her at the bar."

"Or I could call her," he says. "You think I should call her?"

I pick up the mug again and turn in the direction of the coffee maker. "You know the number?"

He checks his nails again and then stuffs his fist in his pocket. "She's in the book."

I take another small sip of the coffee and move to step around him. "You should probably go to the bar."

He turns so that I can fit past him. "Yeah," he says. "Okay." He takes his hand out of his pocket and picks up his own coffee mug. "You want to come with me?"

"Huh?" I've dropped one of the work orders, and Bernie bends to pick it up.

"Bernie, you don't need me there."

The hair is still sticking up along the back of his head; I can see it when he picks up the order. "Right," he says. "You're right."

"Just go talk to her."

"Yup," he says. "I can do that." He hands me the work order and stands, nodding and staring at the floor. "I'm probably going to have to order a pizza," he says and looks up. "You know, so I'll have time to get comfortable." He rocks on his heels, looks at the work order in my hands. "It'd be a lot of food for one person."

"Okay, Bernie," I say. "Leave at six?"

"Okay," he says, still nodding. "Six." He's got both hands in his pockets, and when he turns to go, he nearly knocks a stack of papers off his own desk.

"So," he says, "any particular movie I should ask her to?"

꒰

My father's funeral was held in the church he rarely attended; mention was made of his and my mother's long-time membership, their regular contributions to charity drives. The mill was closed for the day, and mill workers filled the pews; they sat shoulder to shoulder in wrinkled suits, reeking of Old Spice. Most wore Brylcreem in their hair; from the front of the church, they looked like a herd of seals.

My mother was stone-faced, but she clenched her teeth, working the muscles of her jaw, so that, as I watched her, her cheeks flattened and drew inward, her cheekbones disappearing and reappearing.

The church wasn't air-conditioned; parishioners folded the program in half and fanned themselves with it. When I offered to do the same for my mother, she frowned and turned away. While the mill owner spoke of my father's dedication to the company, I watched the sweat circles under his arms, the way he kept poking his middle finger at the bridge of his glasses.

After what seemed like an incredibly long service, during which Jesus' name was mentioned more often than my father's, we stood at the back of the church and men from the mill filed past us, pressing sweaty envelopes stuffed with twenty-dollar bills into my palm. The total amounted to a few hundred dollars; my mother used it to pay the minister's fee.

Back at the house, my mother opened the front door, leaving only the screen, so that the mill workers' wives could enter with their hands full of Jell-O salad or tuna casserole, scalloped potatoes and buttermilk biscuits, some of them with raisins, making them "scones." My mother stood leaning in the doorway to the dining room, directing traffic, her eyes focused somewhere above the heads of the mill workers' wives, my father's poker bodies, members of her bridge club.

Amanda missed the funeral because of a chemistry test, but she turned up later at the house and stood holding my hand, clasping it and letting it go, nervously twisting my fingers in hers. She had on her blue interview suit, and her hair curled over her sweaty forehead. I told her to take the suit jacket off, but she said the blouse underneath was sleeveless and she was afraid her bra straps would show. I was touched that, as a gesture of respect for my father, she had taken the trouble to wear a bra.

Lynette arrived late, after most of the others had gone,

because she had worked the lunch shift at the country club. She had taken off the black bow tie but was still wearing the rest of her waitressing outfit, the black skirt and white tuxedo blouse, and she'd neglected to wipe a dab of mustard off the heel of her shoe.

"Harley," she said and shook my hand, something she'd never done before. Touching her in that way was distracting, and I had trouble keeping track of what she was saying, though it was something along the lines of what everyone else said, about how much she liked my dad and how sorry she was. "Sorry for your loss," she said in the same stilted, rehearsed way other people used the phrase, as if trying to avoid using my father's actual name.

"Thank you," I said. Her hair was lighter, sun-bleached, and I wondered if she'd been working outside, either in the vineyards for extra money or maybe even trying to reclaim her father's orchard.

"I thought I should come," she said. "You were so good to me when my father..."

I felt Amanda shifting next to me, and I turned to see how carefully she was studying Lynette's face. I tried to remember what I'd told her about Lynette, possibly only that I'd had a girlfriend back home, but that it ended when I went away to school.

"I'd like you to meet Amanda," I said. "Gibson."

"Nice to meet you," Lynette said and thrust out her hand again, catching Amanda off guard. Shaking hands was more something grown women did; girls their age usually nodded and smiled. The two of them shook hands, and Amanda let go and brushed a piece of lint off my suit.

"Harley," Lynette said, "it's nice to see you, even if..." She let the rest of the sentence fade away and smiled instead. She wore silver earrings, vaguely Indian-looking, the kind they sold at the craft market on Saturdays. I didn't remember her wearing earrings before; at least, I'd never noticed them on her.

"Yes," I said, "you too."

"Are you staying home this summer?"

"No." I felt Amanda leaning slightly against me. "I have a job up at school."

"Well," she said and looked at Amanda, "I guess that's good. There aren't many jobs here."

"You're still at the country club?" I asked, though I knew she was.

She nodded. "It's not too bad," she said. "The tips are decent."

"Is Doug working?" Amanda turned suddenly at the sound of his name, but Lynette only nodded.

"His father pays him to work the farm."

"Right," I said. "Of course."

Someone had told a funny story about my father, the kind of anecdote people save up for occasions like this, and a group of five or six people laughed at the punchline, something about my father telling a man that the next time he wore a tie on the line, either the machines would strangle him or my father would himself.

"Well," Lynette said, "take care, Harley," and she quickly looked away, out the window to where her car would be parked. She nodded at Amanda and started walking toward the door. "Your father," she said and had to raise her voice a little, to be heard over the people who were still shaking their heads and chuckling. "I'll miss him." She gave a small wave at my mother, which my mother didn't see, and left the room.

"She's pretty," Amanda said and lifted the handkerchief I'd handed her to her forehead. "Is she as pretty as when you dated?" She dabbed at the sweat on her forehead and above her lip.

I held out my hand and took the handkerchief from her, put it back in my pocket. Someone began stacking my mother's wooden folding chairs against the wall; a stack of three or four of them slid out of place and clattered to the floor. My mother was talking to the minister and one of our neighbors, and she excused herself and started walking toward the chairs.

I took Amanda's hand again, pressed her warm, smooth palm to mine, "I don't remember," I said and squeezed her hand to my side.

༈

When the last car had pulled out of the driveway, my mother stepped out of her shoes, wrapped her good quilt over her shoulders and walked out onto the porch.

"It must be ninety-five degrees," I said. Amanda had started doing dishes. She had taken her own shoes off and ducked into the bathroom to take off her bra. Her shoes and the bra, a pinkish-purple color, were in a small pile next to the door.

"It's for the smell," she said, pointing to a glass left on the far end of the counter and gesturing for me to hand it to her. "It smells like your father."

I walked into the living room, stood next to the window and watched my mother in the rocking chair, letting her stocking feet drag across the rough floorboards, with the quilt held between her cheek and the back of the chair. She ignored the lake and closed her eyes, let her cheek drift against the fabric. She was unaware of me at the window, and I thought I should look away, but I also knew it was something I might never see again, my mother at a moment like this, so completely unguarded.

Amanda waited a few minutes before coming to get me and touching me on the shoulder. "Give her a while," she said.

I pulled the dirty tablecloth off the dining room table and carried it into the kitchen.

"I never knew."

She shut off the water, took the tablecloth from me and wiped her hands on it. She looked at me, patiently, waiting for me to finish the thought.

"That she loved him so much."

She nodded, handed the tablecloth back to me and shrugged.

"It was between them."

ॐ

It's warmer today, and the roads have gone slushy; turning onto the lake road, it sounds as if the truck is being pelted with handfuls of sand. It's just beginning to rain, and I flip on the wipers, wondering how long before it freezes and turns to sleet. The metal gutters on the house sound like drum beats in a hard rain. They're old and coming loose already, sagging where they've been dented by hail or falling tree limbs. We'll be lucky if they make it through the winter.

I park on the lake road, next to the old fire hall, and wait to see if the rain will stop. The new, two–million–dollar fire hall in town replaced this one, but I've heard they still hold AA meetings here and use it as rehearsal space for the ama-teur theater company that performs in the high school auditorium. My mother designed costumes one year for *A*

Midsummer Night's Dream. Her fairies' wings had seed pearls that gave them an iridescent sparkle.

The rain is heavier now, and I turn off the engine and the wipers, let the rain wash over the windshield, leaving icy trails now where the glass is cold. I open the thermos of coffee at my feet, pour a cup that I hold in both gloved hands. I could turn on the radio but don't, just sit and listen to the rain and the occasional tractor-trailer rumbling past.

I could go to them now. I could sit in my truck, across from Lynette's driveway, and stare at her windows. I could even walk up to her door and knock and let her show me inside. Or I could go home to Sonia and tell her not to worry about the sound of our creaking gutters or the rush of cold air from under our front door. I could stand in the doorway to my mother's bedroom and listen to her breathe.

But I don't do any of those things. I sit and hold the plastic cap of the thermos to my lips, sip my coffee, watch the rain turn to sleet and let thoughts of them quietly come to me and just as quietly slip away.

᙮

CHAPTER X

I'VE FORGOTTEN ABOUT BERNIE and going to the bar, but at six o'clock, he walks over to me with my coat in his hand and slaps me on the back. "Ready?" he asks.

He's put on some kind of cologne and wet-combed his hair so that it swirls unnaturally around his ears.

"You sure you need me?" I ask, and he takes his hand off me, ready to be disappointed.

"Well, no," he says, disappointed. "I guess not."

"Okay," I say. "Just let me call Sonia."

Sonia answers, out of breath, on the fourth ring. I've told her she needs to be louder on the phone, that it's difficult to hear, but she says she has trouble, sometimes, understanding voices on the phone, and it makes her shy.

"I'm going to be a little late. Bernie needs me for something."

"Working?" she asks, and I consider telling her the truth, but decide it's simpler to agree.

"Yes," I say, "working."

"Okay." I can hear the television in the background, some children's show on cable.

"Harley," she says, her voice hushed, as though she's about to tell me a secret. "I am painting."

"Good," I say. "That's good."

"I am painting," she says, "on the wall."

"What're you painting?" I'm trying to imagine what the

neighbors would think of a nine-foot nude in our living room.

"No," she says, "you will like it."

"Okay. Where's Ma?"

"Mama," she says, her voice still playful with the surprise, "is sleeping."

"Did you feed her?"

"Yes," she says. "I feeded her spaghetti."

"Okay. I'll be home soon."

"Okay, Harley," she says and hangs up the phone.

Bernie keeps his parka wadded in a desk drawer, so it stays wet and wrinkled and hangs unevenly at the hem. He tries smoothing it with his hand but gives up when we reach the stairwell. "You want to ride along or follow me?" he asks, walking ahead of me down the stairs, with the inside-out hood of his jacket bobbing along at the back of his head.

"I'll follow."

"Okay," he says, holding the door open at the bottom of the stairs. "I thought *Armageddon*, maybe," he says, and I pass through the door, and when I look at him, he adds, "for the movie."

"Or you could let her choose."

He turns and looks at me, nods his head. "Or I could let her choose." He heads toward his car, slips a little on the sidewalk, but catches himself before falling.

Bernie makes turns without signaling, but I know where we're going. I follow behind him, see how he holds his hand in front of his mouth at the stoplight, checking his breath. When we get to the bar, he's out of his car fast and walking over to the truck before I've turned off the engine.

"Okay," he says, blowing air through his cheeks. "Okay."

My mother called a few months after the funeral and asked Amanda and me to drive up and have dinner with her. It was a strange request. My parents were never much for eating in restaurants, and it wasn't like my mother to call and ask me to come and see her without having another reason: celebrating a holiday or birthday, cleaning the gutters or resealing the driveway.

She drove us to the Land Lubber in the old station wagon. When she turned the wheel to pull out of the driveway, two gold bracelets on her wrist jangled and flashed in the light from the street. She wore lipstick she checked in the rearview mirror and a sleeveless pale blue dress with a matching jacket. Her hair was stiff and tightly curled, and the lace edge of her slip showed when her skirt rode up on the car seat.

Amanda sat by herself in the back, rhythmically kicking my seat with the toe of her sandal. I turned and stared at her, but she only made a face.

"The scallops here are good," my mother said, pulling into the parking lot, "and the codfish."

"Did you come here with Dad?"

"Oh," she said, "not for years."

"So how do you know?"

"Harley," Amanda said in a warning voice before she opened her door and stepped out of the car. My mother got out, too, brushing off the back of her skirt with her hands.

"What's that, Harley?" She slammed the car door and walked over to Amanda. She glanced down at Amanda's skirt and fingered the fabric, admiring it. "That's lovely, dear."

"Thank you," Amanda mumbled, blushing.

"Have you been here lately, Ma?" I asked, walking ahead of the two of them so I could hold the door.

"Harley," Amanda said. "It's none of your business."

"Oh," my mother said and looked from Amanda to me. "Well. Yes." She walked into the restaurant and stood in front of the specials board. "A few times. With some women friends."

"Women friends?" I didn't remember my mother having many friends. She had a sister a few years older who lived in Ohio and there were a few couples my parents played bridge with, but she wasn't the kind of woman who talked to other women on the phone or sat in the kitchen with them, gossiping. My parents mostly kept to themselves. My father belonged to the Rotary but quit after a few years. My mother collected donations for the Cancer Society and volunteered a few days a month in the hospital gift shop, but she had left the church and she had stopped going to PTA meetings after my graduation.

My mother requested a table by the window, so we could look out at the lights on the lake. I pulled out a chair for her and one for Amanda, with my mother smiling at my manners, and took the seat that faced away from the window.

"I never get sick of that view," my mother told Amanda. "I always wanted to live on the water."

"It's beautiful," Amanda said, laying the cloth napkin across her lap. She looked a little nervous, holding her elbows in tight to her body.

"Women friends?" I asked. "You have women friends?"

"Harley," Amanda said softly and looked as though she might kick me under the table.

"Yes, honey," my mother said. "Just some other widows. Like me." She picked up her fork and seemed to check it for spots. "We take day trips, sometimes," she said to Amanda. "Niagara Falls. Cooperstown."

"That sounds nice," Amanda said and looked over in my direction, frowning.

"Where'd you meet them?"

She smiled and put down her fork, placing it carefully next to the plate. The two bracelets slid over her hand, and she pushed them back and laid her palm against the back of her hand. "There's a group of us," she said. "We meet at the church."

"You went back to the church?"

Amanda did kick me then, rapping me hard on the shin with the wooden sole of her sandal. "What's wrong with you?" she snarled, just loud enough for me to hear.

"Well," my mother said and sighed in a way that suggested all the effort it took her to prepare for this evening, to curl her hair and spray it in place, to pick out the right clothes and iron them and put them on, to choose lipstick and eye shadow and put on fresh stockings and high-heeled shoes, to get used to driving the station wagon by herself again, to choose this restaurant, to call and invite us. "I needed something."

ॐ

Bernie and I walk into the bar in time for the tail end of "Are You Lonesome Tonight" and the beginning of "Blue Christmas." He fiddles with his jacket and wipes his feet too many times on the mat inside the door.

"I don't see her," he says.

"She's probably in the kitchen."

"Yup," he says, nodding and smoothing his jacket, "right."

"You could go talk to her while I get a table."

"Oh no," he says, turning to me, eyes wide. "They don't let people in the kitchen."

"Okay," I say and walk ahead of him to a table. He follows, stumbling on the carpet edge, and sits down across from me. I glance, automatically, over at the booth where Doug Hale sat. Two mill workers are smoking and listening to the music, not saying much. One keeps flipping a packet of matches over on the table, using only his thumbnail.

"Pepperoni?" Bernie asks, seeing that the waitress is walking toward us. She trips on the same carpet edge as Bernie and skips a little, looking back over her shoulder. "Cocksucker," she mutters, walking toward us.

"Hey, Bernie," she says.

"Hey," he says, ducking his head. He has all ten fingers lined up along the table edge, and he keeps glancing at them as if counting.

She taps her pencil on her waitress pad and looks from Bernie to me.

"Large pepperoni," Bernie says, looking at her from underneath his eyebrows.

"Okay," she says. "Miller Lite?"

"Pitcher," he says.

She seems a little disappointed that we didn't order something more exotic. She doesn't write the order down, but turns and walks back toward the kitchen, carefully stepping around the bump in the carpet.

"Pammy," Bernie says. "Her name is Pammy."

"What's her mother's name?"

"Bernice."

"The lovely Bernice."

"Yeah," he says, blushing, "something like that."

The jukebox goes quiet, then starts up again with "Love

Me Tender." A woman at the bar, thirty-five or thirty-six, in a sweater she wears pulled down firmly over her wide rear end, laughs too loudly at something the bartender says and rubs a cocktail napkin under her eyes.

"So what was it," Bernie asks, "you were trying to head off between that farmer and his wife?"

"I thought he was hitting her."

"Jesus," Bernie says and shakes his head. "Too much of that going around."

Pammy comes back with the pitcher and two mugs, sets the mugs down on the table and pours. I try to ignore the hand she lets rest on the rim of my mug while she pours for Bernie. She has a braided leather band on her left wrist, much too big for her. Her T-shirt is a plain blue one, the kind that come in packs of three at the drug store; it's tight and shows the outline of her bra. Her khaki miniskirt rests mid-thigh, and her legs are bare, despite the weather. She must change here in the bathroom before her shift starts.

"Did the wife tell you he was hitting her?"

"No."

"So what made you think...?"

"She had bruises."

"Geez," he says and blows air through his cheeks. "Lucky for her..." he says and doesn't finish the thought.

The doors to the kitchen swing open and Bernie turns suddenly, but it's only Pammy, heading toward one of the other tables with two huge baskets of wings.

"But she never said anything."

"No."

"And he died before you could find out."

"That's right."

Pammy's chatting with the two mill workers. She picks

up her right foot and, with the toe of her sneaker, scratches
at the back of her left leg.

"Wow," he says.

"Yeah."

"That's some coincidence."

"I guess." I take a sip of lukewarm beer and wonder
when our pizza's coming. "Hound Dog" starts up, and the
bartender slides a margarita to the woman at the bar. She
takes it and smiles, tips the glass and sips from it, wipes
her mouth with the cocktail napkin. She catches me looking and smiles again.

Bernie leans toward me. "You ever think it could be
more than coincidence?"

"No."

"Okay," he says. "You know her better than I do."

"Right."

"Yeah," he says. "I mean, you don't even know for sure
he was hitting her."

"Right."

"So even if he was," he says, "it would take a certain
kind of person to do something about it."

"Bernie, she didn't do anything," I say firmly.

"Right," he says. "Like I said, you're the one who knows
her."

Elvis sings "You ain't never caught a rabbit," and Pammy
walks toward us with a pizza on a tray held high over her
shoulder. She bends almost to the floor and slides it onto
the table, then gets up and starts cutting. She puts slices on
two plates and sets them in front of us.

Bernie clears his throat. "Will you tell Bernice I'm here?"

Pammy steps back from the table. "She knows." She raises
a hand to push hair behind her ears, and the leather bracelet
slides to her elbow. "She's busy. She'll be out in a minute."

She looks down at the floor, fiddles with the waitress pad in her apron, fanning the pages with her fingers. "More beer?" she asks.

Bernie looks at me, but I shake my head no. "Sonia's expecting me."

"How's it going?" Bernie asks Pammy, not quite looking at her.

She shrugs. "Okay."

"You and your mom busy?"

"She's doing payroll."

"Who's cooking?"

"Me." She glances over her shoulder at the kitchen. "I should probably get back there," she says and starts walking away from the table.

"Talkative girl," I say.

Bernie laughs. "She's a good kid. Hard worker." He picks up a slice of pizza, squeezing the cheese string between his fingers. "Hey," he says, turning to me suddenly. "I'm sorry about what I said."

"No sweat."

"I'm just an old guy with nothing to do but think crazy thoughts."

"It's okay, Bernie."

"Been watching too many movies."

"Really, Bernie, it's okay."

"Okay," he says. "Sorry."

Bernice walks toward us, wiping her hands on her cook's uniform. She's done something with her hair, dyed it a funny orangy–blond color that no one's ever born with. "Bernie," she says boisterously. "Come to ask me on a date?"

"Thought I might," he says, mumbling.

"Really?" She seems genuinely surprised.

Bernie clears his throat. "I thought we could see a movie."

"Is he coming, too?" she asks, looking at me.

"Harley Cookson," I say. "I'm here for moral support."

"Bernice Clark," she says and shakes my hand roughly.

She turns to Bernie, acts as though she's giving him the once-over. "Sure, Bernie," she says. "When?"

"Friday?"

"Okay," she says. "Seven?"

"I thought *Armageddon*, maybe."

"What's that?"

"For the movie," he says, looking at her.

"Oh," she says. "Sure." She looks over toward the juke-box and shakes her head. "I can tell you one thing," she says. "I wish that damn Elvis fanatic would leave my juke-box alone."

"Should I pick you up?" he asks.

"Pick me up?"

"Friday."

She turns back to Bernie and smiles. "Sure," she says. "You can pick me up here if you want to." She looks up and catches a guy in the corner, wearing a John Deere cap and sunglasses, heading toward the jukebox with a roll of quarters. "Hey," she shouts and starts jogging toward him. "Knock that off."

༄

After graduation, Amanda got a job at a daycare center, where she said she spent a good part of each day escorting three-year-olds to the bathroom. She learned songs about bunnies that she sang in the shower, and she had the hair around her face cut short after she discovered a wad of gum in it. She talked about the kids, too: Bradley, whose mom was pregnant and who walked around every day with a stuffed animal under his T-shirt; Meghan, who punched boys; and Danitra, whose parents were divorced and who drew pictures only in black.

I got a job assistant managing a Blimpie's and wondered why I ever bothered going to college. I worked from five to closing, five or six nights a week, with a Puerto Rican kid named Javier who wore his hair net pulled low over his forehead and named his Thunderbird "Carmela" after his mother. Frances, who worked split shifts with Javier, had eczema on her face, which she scratched until it turned bloody; I had to remind her not to pick the scabs in front of customers.

Still, there was a comfort factor with the job that I liked. The manager worked days, so I was the man in charge from five to closing, and I liked Javier and even sometimes went drinking with him after work. I could do the job with my eyes closed, and I could choose the radio station. Some nights, when it was quiet, I read a book or called Amanda and talked dirty to her, mumbling with my hand over the receiver. I kept a copy of *Moby Dick* under the counter, and sometimes Javier asked me to read part of it to him, because he was convinced by the word "dick" and the presence of sailors, that one of these days we'd get to the part where they all go on shore leave and have sex with prostitutes.

Amanda usually came in for half a veggie sub at about ten; it was the only way we got a chance to see each other. She liked extra hot peppers and brown mustard, and she sat at a table by the window and read magazines: *Vegetarian Monthly, Cosmopolitan, Atlantic Monthly, Elle.* She ripped out perfume samples that she rubbed over her chest and neck, along with recipes she taped to the refrigerator but never actually used for cooking. Twice at the end of my shift, we had sex in my car in the back of the parking lot, and when I kissed her and rubbed my face between her breasts, my nose tingled from the mixture of scents. Amanda nuzzled my hair and complained that I smelled like meat.

At the end of the year, she invited me to the graduation ceremony at the daycare center. She handed out diplomas with ducks and frogs on them, hugging each child to her, carefully disentangling her braids from the fists of infants and toddlers. She laughed and held out her arms, and when Bradley stepped into them, she pulled him close and stood, lifting him into the air, twirling, her skirt rising like a cloud around her legs. Bradley laughed crazily, and she leaned her head back, still twirling, with her braids lifting off her shoulders and her laughter echoing, her face all lips and teeth. She was happy in a way I'd never seen before, and full of light, a tall and suddenly, shockingly beautiful girl.

꒛

I'm careful this time with the leftover pizza, stuffing it into my jacket pocket before walking into the house. Sonia's in the living room, squatting on a huge drop cloth, painting the bottom edge of a mural. It's drawn in pencil, but looks to be a landscape, hills and trees and tiny houses in the distance. She's wearing an old sweatshirt of mine with bleach stains and the sweatpants I've been sleeping in, rolled up at the ankles.

"That's nice," I say and bend to kiss her, and Whitey comes trotting out from my mother's room, sniffs at my jacket pocket and whines.

"I brought you pizza," I say. "Pepperoni."

She pulls the tip of her paintbrush from the wall and

drops it into a jar of water at her feet, then wipes her hands across the stomach of my sweatshirt.

"Hey," I say, "I like that sweatshirt without the paint."

She stands, bending her knees and flexing her ankles to work out the stiffness. "It is ruined first," she says, pointing to the bleach stain under her arm. "Harley?" she says. "You bring me two slices?"

Whitey pokes at me with his nose and sits whining, so I step away from him, carrying the pizza into the kitchen, where I drop it into the refrigerator and notice that Sonia's been picking again at the edges of the doughnuts. "Two slices," I call to her.

Whitey sees me close the refrigerator door, but waits a minute, his butt on the ground and tail wagging, in case I decide to bring out more food. I turn to read the front page of the local paper where Sonia's left it on the coun-tertop, and he stays where he is, still waiting.

"Only two?" Sonia calls to me.

There's more snow expected by the end of the week, and the high school kid who's president of the local chap-ter of Future Farmers of America has won a full scholar-ship to ag. school. His father said he used some kind of fancy computer program to design a better way to feed lambs. "What's that?" I ask.

"Only two slices?" She's standing in the doorway and wiping her hands across her stomach, grinning.

"That's all you asked for," I say, noticing the paint on her fingers and the dab of it on her cheek. "And you've been eating doughnuts."

Her face reddens, and she stands with her mouth open in mock horror. "Who, me?" she asks and folds her hands as if praying, to show me what an angel she is.

"You," I say, and open the refrigerator door, pointing to

the shelf where the doughnuts are kept. Whitey sees the door open and quivers on his haunches on the linoleum.

Sonia brushes past me, reaching for a glass. "I am starving artist," she says and carries the glass to the refrigerator.

"You'll get fat."

She pulls the milk from the refrigerator and carries it and the glass over to the counter next to me. "Yes," she says and sighs dramatically, "and then you will be leaving me."

I turn the page for the list of movies at the local cinema; maybe next weekend we could take Mom to a matinee. "Right," I say, "for a supermodel."

She pours the glass of milk, sets the carton on the counter and sighs. "And the divorce judge," she says carefully, "he will be so sorry for the poor, Russian, fat woman, he will give me all your money," and she looks at me and bats her eyelashes, before turning to take the milk back to the refrigerator.

I gather up the unread sports section and reach toward her, swatting her in the rear with it, and she yelps, surprised, but then, before either of us has seen him move, Whitey is standing at my side, growling and baring his teeth. I stand frozen, and Sonia looks quickly at me and says "be still" in Russian.

She squats close to the floor. Whitey sees her but doesn't turn; he's still gowling at me, and I'm afraid to make eye contact with him, afraid he'll see it as a threat.

"Good dog," she says, "good puppy, good dog, good puppy," her voice soft and sing-songy, and he doesn't move but stops baring his teeth, only growling now.

She stands and moves toward me a few steps, and I say, whispering, "Sonia...."

"He protects me," she says, slowly, and she comes

toward me again, and Whitey sees her but doesn't turn toward her. "He thinks you are hurting me."

She's standing directly in front of me now, and when Whitey doesn't move, she makes sure he's watching, then reaches her arms to my neck and hugs me. I hold her with both hands on her back where Whitey can see them, and he stops growling and stands for a few seconds, watching, before he runs to the basement stairs.

"Oh, Harley," Sonia says, breathing into my neck, "it is so much sadness."

౨

One night after my Blimpie's shift, Amanda and I groped each other in the back seat of my Volkswagen while raccoons scrabbled in the dumpster. I leaned into her neck, smelled her skin, kissed her neck and ears, and she held my head, grasping hard at my hair, and let go.

I massaged her nipple through her T-shirt and she said "Harley," softly, so that I thought it was part of the foreplay.

Then, "Harley," she said, "Harley," and moved away from my hand so that her back was flat against the window.

"What?" I moved both hands around to her back and tried to pull her closer.

"This is crap."

I let go, dropping my hands in my lap. "What is?"

She was sweating; a thin film of it on her forehead and under her nose. "Acting like teenagers. Making out in cars."

"We can go home," I said. "I thought you liked it here."

She bent her neck, so that I could see the ragged pony-tail she'd made with a rubber band, binding her braids together. "Sure," she said. "The Paris Hilton."

"Okay," I said. "Fine." I reached behind me and opened

the door, got out of the car. I stood there a second before slamming the door, saw that she was watching me and waiting to see what I'd do next.

Garbage had spilled out of the dumpster; I stepped in a puddle of chocolate milkshake without realizing it, slid on the pavement. I opened the driver's side door, fell onto the seat and wiped my feet on the already filthy floormats.

Amanda waited for me to start the engine before climbing into the front passenger seat. I moved over to give her room and, when she bent forward, saw the outline of her spine against the thin cloth of her T-shirt.

"Let's go home," I said and put the car in first, easing across the parking lot.

"I didn't mean that." She turned away from me, staring out the passenger-side window. "I meant we should act like people, you know, who give a shit about each other."

"I thought we did." I turned a little too fast around the outer edge of the building and landed square in a pothole I usually tried to avoid. Amanda grabbed the armrest on her door but didn't say anything. "This isn't the movies," I said.

"You've got that right." She had a tone in her voice I'd only recently started to notice.

I hit the far edge of the parking lot and waited at the light. Across the street, the McDonald's crew had turned off the sign but were still inside mopping floors. "I never asked you to come here," I said slowly, watching for the light to change. "I never said...."

"Gordie and Diane are getting married."

I flashed, like I did whenever I thought of them, on the sight of them on the beach after prom, Diane trying to pull her dress up from around her waist and Gordie talking softly to her and pouring water out of his shoes.

"What? When?"

"April."

"Who told you that?"

"Diane."

"Is she pregnant?"

Amanda turned her whole body to face me, suddenly furious. "Jesus, Harley, why do you have to be so fucking cynical?"

"Put your seatbelt on." I had never heard a woman use the word "fucking" before. I had never heard my mother swear. The light changed and I surged forward, letting the needle hit sixty-five before slowing to the speed limit.

"What if they happen to love each other, Harley?" she asked. "What about that?"

"Okay, okay, so they love each other and she's pregnant." I was beginning not to like the sound of my own voice, but I wasn't ready to let my guard down; Amanda could turn mean in a heartbeat.

"So what about us?"

"You want to be pregnant?" We hadn't had sex, but the car smelled sweaty; I rolled down my window and leaned into the wind a second. When I looked back at Amanda, she was staring at me instead of answering.

"I don't know what you want," I said.

"Why don't you ever say it first?"

"Say what?" I rolled through a stop sign, looked at her again, and again she didn't bother to answer.

"I do say it. I say 'I love you' all the time."

"I want to be in love like them."

"You want to get married."

"No," she said, and something like uncertainty crept into her voice. "Not necessarily. Not right away." She looked out her window, and I didn't say anything, didn't answer. I parallel parked in a space on the street next to our apartment building, and she waited with her hands in her lap. I turned off the engine and glanced at her, and she was try- ing to read the expression on my face.

"I'm not ready yet," I said, and the tone in my voice was gone now that I genuinely felt sorry for her.

"Okay," she said, turned and opened her door.

ᓵ

Amanda and I both got a couple of days off at the end of August, so we drove to meet her parents at rented cabins on Waneta Lake. Amanda had bought a silver bikini that flashed in the sun like it was made of metal. I had stopped bothering to cut my hair and wore it long under my father's old fishing hat. Amanda smoked pot in the car on the way there and talked about all the petty things her parents would do to make her feel worthless, but I imag- ined sunlight and beaches, three days away from my job— no customers, no cash register, no hair net.

I had met her parents once before. Mr. Gibson wore polo shirts with the collar flipped up and had a tan all year long. Mrs. Gibson had a hairdo frothy as whipped egg whites and smelled like hair spray when she leaned to give me a dry kiss on the cheek. When Amanda told them my name, Mr. Gibson said "like the motorcycle" with what sounded like new appreciation.

"No, sir," I said. "After my great uncle."

"Well," he said. "That's fine." It was a favorite phrase of his, something he said whenever he didn't know what else to say, but which Amanda claimed meant that deep down, he thought he should have to give his approval to every- one and everything.

Amanda and I had our own cabin next to her parents',

with two single beds Amanda made as much noise as possible pushing together. We spread the blanket we usually kept in my car—reeking of pot, motor oil and mosquito repellant—over the two beds and slept naked underneath it. Amanda initiated sex by giving me nightly blowjobs I didn't exactly refuse; twice I had to put my hand over her mouth to keep her from screaming, and I had nightmares about her father rushing into our cabin with a loaded gun.

In the afternoons, Mrs. Gibson would wrap a scarf over her head, and she and Amanda would drive into town together in Mr. Gibson's Mustang convertible to shop for birdhouses and homemade jam. With the two of them gone, Mr. Gibson made gin and tonics in tall iced glasses he kept in the freezer, and Amanda's fourteen-year-old brother, Pierce, sat in weeds on the far side of the cabin, where he carefully, studiously, went about setting things on fire. I lay on a towel on the boat dock and pretended to fish; most often, I fell asleep and dreamed of fishing trips with my father. In them, I remembered the sound of his voice and his face when I was young enough for him to tower over me, to seem both frightening and kind. At the Seafood Shoppe in town, Mrs. Gibson bought shrimp or clams that we ate for dinner. No one ever seemed to expect me to catch a fish. Amanda and Pierce both stopped pretending to be vegetarians; Pierce was allowed beer, and Amanda and I were given gin and tonics, although there were rarely enough frosted glasses to go around.

At nightfall, we built a bonfire on the beach and roasted marshmallows only Pierce was willing to eat. I sat on a log and Amanda leaned against my knees, and we were happy, ignoring Mr. Gibson's rambling stories about his childhood in New Hampshire, both of us too warm in our proximity to the fire but too lazy and comfortable to move.

I thought of my mother alone in a house that was much too big for one person, sitting in front of the television she said she kept on "for the noise." She had recently become addicted to gritty, violent cop shows. I made the mistake of phoning her in the middle of one, and she asked me to call again another night.

This was life, I thought: real life that stretched out like a flat road for fifty or sixty more years, and you were lucky, damn lucky, to have someone to sit it out with, to work all day at your boring job and then come home to have dinner with, to wash dishes and recline in matching Barcaloungers with until it was time for bed.

Because then, when it was over, after you'd raised your kids and left your job after forty years with a decent retirement plan, after mind-altering sickness and death, you were alone again in front of the TV set, trying to remember all the dreams and plans you'd been so hot for in your twenties, the heroic things you thought you'd accomplish, the recipes for future fame and glory.

It was a sign of my maturity, I thought, that I had such low expectations, that I imagined myself working long and hard at a job I didn't hate, living with a woman I cared about who was willing to spend the next fifty years of her life with me, sleeping in my bed, raising my kids. I would be happy, I thought. I would never look back on the rest of my life with regret. Because I had no plans for greatness, I would never be disappointed by what I had failed to become.

I would marry Amanda and be happy.

᠔

Sonia's scrubbed her face and changed into her night-gown; the fresh layer of skin across her cheeks glistens while she bends over Whitey's body, curled next to her on the bed. "Good puppy," she says, "sweet puppy," and she strokes the fur on his belly, barely touching but gliding her hand over it, and his eyelids slowly close and then open, still keeping guard.

"Be careful, Sonia," I say, barely above a whisper, and clear my throat, coughing into my hand.

Whitey lifts his head at the sound of my voice, and Sonia pulls her hand away, but then he lowers his head to the quilt, and she keeps stroking.

I kick off my shoes and sit on the bed, take my flannel shirt off and pull my T-shirt over my head. Whitey growls softly, but Sonia keeps petting his belly. I unfasten my jeans and stand to take them off, and he lifts his head, watching me.

I take my T-shirt and jeans into the bathroom and drop them in the hamper, pull out the sweatshirt and sweatpants with Sonia's paint on them and put them on. When I walk back toward the bed, Whitey growls, louder now, and Sonia pulls her hand away.

"Hush now," she says softly, still not touching him. "Hush, puppy," and has no idea she's saying something strange, the name of a brand of shoes.

He's growling, louder and deeper, and watching me, and I stand frozen next to the bed.

"Turn, Harley," Sonia says, whispering.

"What?" My fingers are tingling, anticipating his teeth on my wrist.

"Turn," she says and holds her hand in the air, making a circle with her index finger.

I slowly turn with my back to Whitey, and the growling softens and stops. "Now what?"

"Come to bed."

From the corner of my eye, I can see that she's folding back the covers, making a place for me to lie down.

"Are you crazy?"

She pulls the covers back a little farther and says, whispering, "You show him your back. You show you don't hurt me."

I begin to lower my body, slowly, by inches, to the mattress, the whole time waiting to feel his teeth on me, until I'm surprised by the feel of the mattress underneath me, and I'm sitting with my back to Sonia and him.

"He protects me," Sonia says, and I lower myself onto my side, letting my body fall by inches, until I'm lying on the mattress, facing away from the middle of the bed, and Sonia drops the covers back over me.

She waits until I'm settled with my head on the pillow before she turns and shuts off the lamp next to her side of the bed. I can feel Whitey's foot, on top of the covers, barely grazing my ass, and Sonia says softly in the darkness, "He loves me, I think."

꒱

Bernie's written out directions for me to find a downed line in a patch of privately owned woods. I can just make out in his backwards scrawl that I should climb about a quarter mile straight up from the speed limit sign at the bottom of the turnoff to the old state highway. The snow's crusted over with last night's freezing rain; my boots randomly glide over the surface and break through, jarring my ankles each time, so that I begin to imagine myself on crutches. I can feel the climb in my chest and the backs of my legs, the burning in my hamstrings, hear the sound of my breathing and measure it against my heartbeat, and I think for maybe the tenth time this season that even in this town, there must be an easier way to make a living.

The land's posted every couple of feet with "no trespassing" signs, but I can see a couple of pairs of footprints ahead of me up the hill. The owner used to be the chief financial officer at the mill; if it's the same man, he used to hunt his own land for deer. I remember he invited my father one year, along with the mill owner and the lawyer who handled the mill's taxes.

I take a rest somewhere near the top of the hill, careful to lean against a tree. I could set down my tool belt, but then I'd have to work with my tools wet, and I don't like taking those kinds of chances around a possible downed electric line. I'm warm in my jacket, but not warm enough to take it off, so I stand and kick at the frozen snow at the edge of my footprint, glancing off to my left, where prints from something small, a rabbit maybe, lead off in a line toward a pile of brush and disappear.

My heartbeat slows a little, I arch my back and flex my fingers, beginning to feel the snow seep between the leather uppers and soles of my boots, and I remember that the mill owner took his son hunting with them that day, and that I'd wanted to go along, too, to be with the men in the woods, but that my father never asked me. So instead I stayed in the kitchen with my mother, working on an overdue English paper and going to the window every half hour or so, watching for their truck, waiting for them to appear.

My mother was simmering stew, absent-mindedly chopping carrots and onions and adding them to the pot that would sit all day on the stove. She kept the radio on, turned to a murmur so it wouldn't disturb me, and she glanced often at the phone.

At mid-afternoon, I saw the truck coming down the

road, watched as it pulled into our driveway. The mill owner's son hopped down from the truck bed, and he was still carrying his gun, standing in the driveway with the barrel pointed down.

The other men got out of the truck, and I could see that there was something big resting on a plastic tarp in the truck bed. If I squinted, I could just make out what looked like a hoof leaning against the truck's tailgate.

"They're here," I said, and my mother tilted the cutting board toward the stew pot, sliding in a pile of chopped onion and celery.

She set the cutting board on the counter and wiped her hands on her apron. "Is your father with them?"

They were all wearing orange camouflage jackets, and I had to wait until they came close enough to make out his face. "He's fine," I said, because I knew she'd been worrying.

She nodded, said, "good," and sighed. She stood looking into the pot, then went to the refrigerator for more carrots. "Every year," she said, not looking at me, but pulling a few more carrots from the bunch, "someone has a heart attack or falls out of a tree."

"He's fine." I watched from the window as the men talked and shook hands in the driveway, and my father handed over the rifle he'd borrowed from the mill owner.

"They bagged one. A doe, I think."

My mother switched off the radio, and the kitchen was silent except for the hissing of the stove burner where she'd spilled some water. "Oh dear," she said softly and came to the window behind me, put her arm around my shoulder and pressed her lips to the back of my head. "Your father will be heartsick."

࿋

CHAPTER XI

I KNOCK THE SNOW OFF MY BOOTS by banging them against the supports to the porch steps; it usually sends Whitey into a frenzy of barking, but this time, nothing. I unlock the front door and step inside, and still nothing.

"Where's Whitey?" I ask Sonia, stepping over to her across old newspapers and margarine containers with different colors of paint.

"Gone," she says.

"What's that?" I'm glancing through the mail she forgot to bring in from the box: the electric bill, a few paint catalogs, and, amazingly, we keep qualifying for an American Express card.

She turns, holding a paintbrush with green paint. She has paint on her face, on her hands and on the rolled-up sleeves of my sweatshirt. "Your friend takes him."

"Lynette took him?"

"Yes." She nods and turns back to her painting, dabbing at what looks to be a row of small green bushes.

"When?" I drop the mail on the coffee table. Already I must be adjusting to the fact that Whitey's gone; with him here, I'd never leave anything like the electric bill where he might suddenly decide to chew it to shreds.

She puts down the margarine container with green paint and stands, flexing her knees and wrists. "Early," she says. "After you go to work."

"Why didn't you stop her? Why didn't you call me?"

"I think you want him to go," she says. "You say he is dangerous."

"He is."

Sonia stands with her arms straight at her sides, dripping paint onto the drop cloth at her feet. She looks away, toward the kitchen. "I don't know why you are angry," she says quietly.

"He'll hurt someone," I say, lowering my voice. "She has small kids."

Sonia turns to me, frowning, and I'm struck again by how big her eyes are, how much of her face they occupy. "She wants him. She asks me for him." She gestures with both palms raised to the ceiling and drops her arms to her sides.

"I can't let her do it." I know I won't bother to take my jacket off, so I pick up the paint catalogs from the coffee table and hand them to her.

"Harley?"

"She can't have that dog in her house."

"Maybe he doesn't," she says and glances at the names on the catalogs. "Maybe he doesn't hurt them."

I jiggle the keys in my pocket, take a quick look to see if my mother is somewhere nearby or sleeping in her room. The back of the house is dark; she must be asleep, and I think of telling Sonia she shouldn't let Ma go to bed so early, but I'm afraid she might cry, and then I would have to stay here with her instead of driving to Lynette's.

"Maybe he is only afraid with us."

"He could hurt her," I say flatly, trying to sound like the last word. "He could hurt the baby."

Sonia doesn't say anything, but she follows me out the front door. She almost trips on the sweatpants she's rolled over two or three times, but she keeps following me, leaving the door open with only the screen.

"I'll be back soon," I say, and keep walking fast to the garage. I raise the garage door, and she steps underneath it and stands with her arms crossed next to the truck.

"Harley," she says, "listen, Harley." The garage is dark, and I can't tell from her voice if she's more angry or frustrated. "She asks us to help her, and we do," she says slowly, as if instructing me. "Then we are finished helping, and she asks for Whitey, and we must give him to her."

I start the truck, listen to it idle, and she stands there waiting for me to say something, but when I don't say anything and the truck inches backward, she waits until I'm out of the garage and lowers the door herself, the sweatshirt lifting enough to show bare skin. She turns toward the sidewalk, and the glare from the headlights washes the color from her face, making her look angry or fearful. She doesn't wait for me to back out of the driveway, but steps quickly up the sidewalk and back into the house.

༉

A dead deer by the side of the road makes me slow the truck and flash my brights, looking for more of them in the woods that line sections of Temperance Road. The carcass is mangled; at least one of the legs is broken, and the neck hangs at a crooked angle. The Fish and Wildlife workers will have to come out and bury it or the scavengers that come out to feed will line the roadway, too.

I roll the window all the way down; I want to be clearheaded, and I think the cold air will do it. I slow to a crawl near her driveway, trying to get a handle on things, on what I might say. The light on the porch is out, but one of the bedrooms is lit, and there's a light somewhere downstairs. I pull into the driveway slowly and ease toward the house; I'm afraid I might scare her, and I want to give her time to recognize the truck.

I get out, slam the door and go stand in the middle of her yard, kicking snow off the soles of my sneakers, looking toward the windows but not seeing any movement. I step onto the porch, and Whitey goes off like a gun blast. I knock, but don't expect her to hear over the sound of the barking.

She opens the door slowly, with the metal chain across. "Harley," she says softly. She bends down and hooks the fingers of the hand still covered in a cast in Whitey's collar, showing the streaks of gray in the hair she keeps in a ponytail and a ballpoint pen that somehow stays in place just underneath the rubber band. She shushes Whitey, who stops barking and growls softly, not seeing me in the doorway, before she unhooks the chain on the door.

She opens the door just enough so that I can see her whole face while she leans against the doorjamb. She has on a long flannel shirt that reaches mid-thigh—it must be Doug's—a T-shirt like the kind Pammy wore at the bar but not as tight, a pair of jeans, slippersocks. She crosses her feet, holding one on top of the other, like a ballet move learned at a younger age.

"I thought you might come," she says, her voice softer, huskier than I remember.

"Tonight?"

She shakes her head. "Sometime."

I've suddenly run out of things to say, and I turn away from her and stare out across the road to the farm machinery left rusting in the fields, in jagged outline against the sky.

"Are you all right, Harley?" she asks, and I turn toward her and answer quickly, because the question unnerves me. "Fine."

"You could come in this time," she says and smiles, as if the fact that I'm her stalker, her own personal peeping Tom, has become a joke between us.

Whitey edges his way around her and pushes out the door. He sniffs my jeans and the tips of my fingers and decides I'm not a threat, then stands at the edge of the porch and stares at the sky a few seconds before sauntering off into the yard.

"I came about Whitey."

Lynette steps back from the doorway, allowing me into the house. She leads me through the front hallway without turning on any lights and into the kitchen, where the lamp over the formica table, a large glass bulb with a wicker basket–like cover, is turned low with a dimmer switch, and cream–colored thank you cards lie scattered over the tabletop.

"I was thanking people," she says, "for the sympathy cards." She motions with her hand as though waving them away. "Some of them gave us money."

"I'm sorry I wasn't there," I say, wondering for a second if I shouldn't reach into my wallet right now and give her a twenty. I make a motion and stop short, not having a clue how to pull a thing like that off.

She sees my hand move toward my wallet and holds a hand out to stop me. "It was pretty small," she says. "Mostly just family." She groups the cards into one big pile and motions at the seat across from where she's been sitting.

"Coffee?" she asks, and I shake my head, noticing the half-finished glass of red wine on the table.

"There's more wine," she says.

"Please."

She walks over to the kitchen cupboards, shuffling a little in her slippers, opens a cabinet that seems to be full of paper bags and the kind of plastic cups toddlers can't spill from, and rummages in it until she finds another wine glass somewhere toward the back. She looks at it in the light, checking that it's clean, and sets it on the counter, pulls the bottle of wine from a small wooden wine rack. "So," she says, "you came about Whitey."

"I don't think..." I say. "I'm not sure...."

She pours the glass of wine and, instead of handing it to me, sets it on the table in front of me, as if setting a plate in front of a child. She sits across from me and holds her hands in her lap, patiently waiting.

"It could be dangerous," I say, "to have him here."

She frowns and picks up the wine glass, but doesn't drink from it. "Did he hurt someone?"

"Oh," I say. "No. Not really."

"Not really?"

"He grazed Sonia's hand." I run my fingers along the side of my hand to show her. "He broke the skin a little."

"Oh." She seems to take notice of the wine glass in her hand and sips from it before setting it back down on the table. "I'm sorry about that." She wipes at a smudge on the table with her hand, then slowly starts picking at it with her fingernail. "He must have been afraid," she says, "in a new place."

"He never hurt you?"

"No," she says. "He'd never hurt me." She gets up suddenly and walks over to the sink, rinses a sponge with water and carries it back to the table. "He's a good dog," she says and starts wiping, working her shoulder into it so that the table legs rattle against the linoleum. "Doug was rough with him."

"He hurt Doug?"

"Well," she says and shakes her head as if shaking off the question. "Nothing he didn't deserve."

"What if he hurts the kids?" I ask and notice for possibly the first time how quiet the house is.

"He won't," she says and stands with the sponge in her hand. "He's always looked out for the kids, protected them."

"I just think...."

"Listen, Harley," she says and pats me on the shoulder. "I appreciate what you're saying. I appreciate what you did for me." She carries the sponge back over to the sink, rinses it and sets it next to the faucet. "But he's my dog and I know him better than you do."

"Okay," I say. "I just don't want you taking any chances."

She grins suddenly. "Same old Harley."

"What's that supposed to mean?"

"Nothing," she says and shrugs. "Just that you've always been so...steadfast, so dependable."

"Anything wrong with that?" I empty my glass and set it on the freshly wiped table.

"Of course not," she says. "I didn't mean anything."

"I want you to be careful."

She nods. "I know."

"Okay."

"Okay," she says, still nodding.

I get up and slowly push my chair in, making sure it's perfectly aligned with the table. "I didn't mean anything either," I say.

"I know."

I walk into the dark hallway, feeling the way with my hands, trying not to knock down any pictures.

She steps around me and opens the door. "Harley," she says and touches me lightly on the arm, so that I stop on the porch and turn toward her. "It's just that on a night like this, alone in the house with the kids at my mom's, he's the best protection I've got."

"Okay," I say and start navigating my way down her porch steps in the dark.

"But thank you," she says, "for coming over."

"Sure." I step down onto the gravel walkway, trying to avoid the wet patches of snow.

"Harley?" she says, calling to me. "Thanks," she says, "for your help."

⇛

It was the first Christmas after my father died, but I tried not to think about that, about any connection that might have to my asking Amanda to marry me. Instead, I sat her down in front of the fake, revolving Christmas tree she had bought at the drugstore for six bucks and handed her an old TV box with eight more boxes wrapped inside, down to the smallest one holding a quarter-carat diamond necklace, because I couldn't afford a ring.

The Christmas tree started up with a plunky music-box arrangement of "White Christmas," and Amanda opened the first box, saw another one inside and said, "ooooh, sneaky."

After the second box, she said, "I wonder what *this* can be," and her smile began to look a little rehearsed, unnaturally wide and showing a lot of teeth. When she came to the smallest box, she held it in her hand, pausing for effect. The light from the Christmas tree reflected in her eyes and her smile widened even more. She was wearing the white cashmere scarf from her grandmother over a pair of men's flannel pajamas, and she fingered the fringe at her throat.

"It may not be exactly what you think," I said slowly.

She opened the box, and her smile, in the seconds before she said anything, was steady as a rock. "It's beautiful," she said and looked at me with tears in her eyes. "It's just beautiful, Harley."

"I couldn't afford a ring," I said. "I wanted to ask you to marry me, but I couldn't afford a thousand dollars for a ring. I thought this might be okay for now."

"That's okay," she said, and she was trying so hard to look happy. "Yes. I mean yes, I'll marry you."

༕

The next day, we drove to my mother's, with Amanda sitting next to me in the passenger seat, fingering the necklace at her throat and making sure the diamond faced front.

We found my mother in the kitchen, wrapping packets of cookies in cellophane and placing them in metal tins with old-fashioned Santas on the front. She had flour on the front of the apron that buttoned over her sweater and a dab of dough on her neck, near her ear, when she came over to kiss me.

"You caught me," she said. "I should have finished this days ago."

She hugged Amanda and kissed her cheek, and when the two of them separated, they looked flushed and happy.

The buzzer on the stove went off; my mother picked up a pot holder and bent to pull a cookie sheet out of the oven. "This is the last batch," she said, setting the cookie sheet on the stovetop burners and banging the oven door closed with her foot. "Thumbprints," she said. "They're not very fancy, but they're my favorite, and Harley's always liked them."

This was my cue, and I stepped forward and lifted three

cookies from the sheet, offering one to Amanda. My mother laughed and warned me not to ruin my dinner.

I took Amanda's coat and hung it and my own in the downstairs coat closet in the hall. Mom had painted the hallway a light tan and put up some old photos, mostly of my father. There was one of him in his Army uniform, standing in the snow with the sun in his eyes, and another of the two of them at their wedding: a picture of them dancing, with my father's arm bent at the elbow, holding Mom's veil up off the floor of the VFW hall. He'd gotten his hair cut for the wedding; it looked as though the top of his ear had been nicked with the clippers. He stared into my mother's eyes, and it was clear he'd just been laughing; his smile was natural and easy, not the crooked, forced smile that usually appeared in photographs. He had one hand on the back of her gown, barely touching; he was not a delicate man, and yet he held her so carefully, as if she were fragile to him, something he valued as both rare and expensive.

I walked back into the kitchen and stood with my hands in my pockets. Amanda had already settled at the kitchen table with a cup of coffee. My mother held up a package of cookies and twisted it, turning it in the air, then wrapped a pink ribbon around the top. "You must be tired, Harley," she said, dropping the cookies into a metal tin and tamping them down with her hands to make the lid fit. "Why don't you take your bags upstairs? I've been sewing in your room," she said, setting the tin with the cookies aside and starting in on the next package. "You two can stay in the front bedroom."

I glanced quickly at Amanda and saw that she hadn't noticed the uniqueness of the offer, that my mother had decided not to keep us in separate rooms. It embarrassed me, and I picked up the bags without looking at my mother, who seemed to be busy concentrating on what she was doing at the stove.

I set the suitcases down inside the doorway and didn't bother to turn on the light, but just stood next to the bed, staring out the window, where flurries had begun drifting down onto the beach. I could feel how the house had grown quieter, older, so that I now heard every creak of the wind in the eaves, each barely audible sigh of snowflakes on the roof. My father had never been a loud man, but his absence, in that house, was deafening.

When I came back into the kitchen, Amanda and my mother were filling the last two tins.

"Harley," Mom said, turning to me. "Amanda's told me your news." She wiped her hands, brushing them quickly across the lap of her apron, and reached with one hand to cup the side of my face. "I'm so happy to hear it."

"I'm sorry, Harley," Amanda said. "I couldn't wait."

I watched my mother carefully, studying her expression, looking for some hint of worry or doubt, but she was stacking cookie tins, counting them softly under her breath.

"We thought maybe August," I said, "or September."

"Well," she said and turned toward me, "that sounds lovely." She pulled a list out of her apron pocket and handed it to me. "Harley," she said, "if you wouldn't mind too much, can you deliver these?" She wiped the side of her hand, still with a light dusting of flour, across her forehead and tilted her head in the direction of the stacked cookie tins.

I looked down at the list in my hand, the names of neighbors and friends of my parents, the minister and the mill owner and the man she had hired to shovel the driveway.

"I just don't think I could stand it," she said, "all that sympathy."

∽

That evening, my mother put on an old Bing Crosby album, and we sat in front of the artificial tree she'd bought at a garage sale the summer before. "I do miss the smell," she said, "but it's too much trouble for one person."

She'd bought me two flannel shirts and a pair of jeans, and she gave Amanda a small notebook full of vegetarian recipes she had copied out by hand. Amanda jumped up off the floor and hugged her hard.

"Goodness," Mom said. "I'm glad you like it."

I had paid forty dollars for an orangy-brown sweater that, according to the salesgirl, was "the new color," but that, the minute my mother held it up to herself, looked like it was made for someone else.

"I left the receipt in the box," I said, and she shook her head and said, "No, Harley, it's lovely," but the tone in her voice told me how hard she was trying to put a good face on things.

She bent to pick the wrapping paper up off the floor, crumpling it in her hands, and said thoughtfully, "I have something else for you, Harley." She walked into the kitchen, where I could hear her putting the wrapping paper in the garbage, then slamming the kitchen door behind her.

"Do you think she liked the sweater?" I asked.

Amanda shrugged. "She said she did."

My mother came back with a large cardboard box and handed it to me, standing with her arms crossed to warm her hands. Inside were the brown leather ice skates my father had worn, with the blades sharpened, the leather oiled and the laces replaced.

"I found them," she said. "You wear about the same size. I thought you might want to go out on the lake." She turned toward Amanda. "If we don't have any skates here to fit you, we can go buy some in town."

My mother looked down at the skates in my hand, then out through the window to the lake. "I used to love to watch the two of you," she said, "out on the ice."

⌁

I asked Amanda if she wanted to go skating with me the day after Christmas, but she said no; she was busy flipping through the pages of *Anna Karenina*, which she was supposed to have read for her "Women in Lit" class the year before.

I took a push broom from the basement and carried it down to the shore. I wore a pair of galoshes I found by the back door; I didn't recognize them as my father's but couldn't think of anyone else who might have owned them. There was almost no wind, but it was cold and the air smelled like woodsmoke. Amanda had loaned me her cashmere scarf; it was soft and, when I tied it over my mouth and nose, smelled like her grandmother's perfume.

I stepped carefully onto the ice and started sweeping sections of it clear. I thought I'd make a smallish circle; I didn't think I'd be out long—just enough to get the feel of it again, to remember what it was like. But the snow was dry and light, and I kept sweeping, developing a rhythm in my shoulders and arms and enjoying the quiet, just my own breath and heartbeat and the mechanical whir of a snow blower off in the distance.

Before long, I looked up and saw that I'd swept a few hundred feet out from the shore and maybe a hundred feet across. I walked back to shore, sliding a little on the cleared ice, and sat on the ground, feeling wetness seep through the seat of my jeans.

I opened the box with my father's skates, took my gloves off and touched the leather, which was soft yet cracked with age. I unbuckled the galoshes and fit my feet inside the skates; with wool socks, they were a little small, but I still didn't think I'd stay out very long. I tied them up, flexing my fingers to keep them from getting stiff, and stood balancing on the pebbles that made up the beachfront.

I stepped onto the ice and immediately pushed forward, feeling myself let go, giving myself up to gliding, rather than walking. I reached the first turn without falling and kept going, faster now and more sure of myself. I turned again and faced the shore, saw my mother at the window, sipping from a coffee cup and waving, looking happy. I came full circle and this time turned so that I was gliding backward, feeling how well my body remembered doing this.

I turned again, came directly back toward shore, stopped, digging the sides of my blades into the ice, waved back at my mother, turned and skated out toward the lake, smoothly moving past bumps and grooves in the surface of the ice. I leaned forward, put my arms behind my back, and gave myself up to the rhythm of skating, the sound of each blade set carefully down, one at a time on the ice. It was all right, this feeling. I shared my father's memory and my own, and it was all right.

჻

Sonia opens the door while I'm still looking for my key. She's taken a shower and left her hair wet, and her feet are bare under the flannel bathrobe my mother gave me a few Christmases back.

"Sonia," I say, staring at her bare feet on the linoleum. "You'll catch cold."

She shakes her head slowly and presses herself against me, kisses my cheek and my lips.

"What's wrong, Sonia?" I ask, wrapping my arms around her and carrying her forward into the kitchen so I can close the door behind me.

"Harley," she says. "Let's make love."

She's kissing me, open-mouthed, and I have to lean away from her to answer. "Okay," I say, "okay. Just give me a minute." It's not like her to be so aggressive, and I wonder, suddenly, if this is what she's been wanting from me all along, something rougher. It unnerves me a little.

"I'll meet you upstairs," I say.

"No, Harley," she says, nuzzling my cheek. "Now."

She lets go of me and steps back, and without looking me in the eye, she opens the front of her robe. She's naked and shivering, and she lets the robe fall open with the belt dropping to the floor.

I wish I knew what prompted this change, and whether or not it's permanent. Because even while my body responds to it, to the sight of her naked body and to her desire for me, I'm not sure this change is something I want between us.

"Sonia," I say and reach for her, take her breast in my hand. "Slow down a little." I'm kneading her breast with one hand and with the other, I pull her closer to me and bend to kiss her. "Just give me a second," I say, but with her body leaning against me, she knows I'm aroused.

"Come with me," she says and leads me by the hand to the front hallway, where she kneels on her mother's rug and begins to unfasten my jeans.

"Where's Ma?" I ask, my voice rough.

"Sleeping," she says and tugs at my jeans, letting me know she wants me to slide them over my hips.

"Sonia," I say, pulling away from her hands. "No, Sonia." I lower myself to the rug and slowly begin untying my work boots. Once they're off I stand, lean toward her and kiss her, gently, on her lips and neck, before pushing the robe from her shoulders and letting it fall. I undress then and make love to her, slowly, reverently, in the way that's habitual for us, and afterward, I lie next to her, breathing in the scent of her skin, and worry about a stain on the rug.

"Oh, Sonia," I say, and reach for her hand, making our fingers intertwine.

"Harley," she says softly, "you are finished now? You are finished with her?" and it's as though I've entered the conversation too late, as if I'd been daydreaming in class and missed a crucial piece of information.

"Yes," I say, bending to kiss her, to feel her lips soft and fluttery with mine, and it's good, I could get lost in it, but a part of me knows I'm stalling, avoiding those eyes. "Yes," I say again, finally, "I'm finished."

꒰ ꒱

"So," Bernie says in the coffee room. "It's Friday."

"Yup." I take the mug of coffee he hands me. The mug says I'M A NATURAL BLONDE. PLEASE SPEAK SLOWLY. It belongs to one of the receptionists.

"T.G.I.F.," he says.

"Yup," I say. "Thank God."

"Big plans for the weekend?" He's wearing an alpine sweater over a shirt and tie. The sweater has reindeer knitted into the pattern and a collar that makes the tie bunch at his throat.

"Not really." I take a sip of coffee; it's a little strong for my taste, so I add a little creamer, trying not to wonder how long it's been left sitting out on the counter.

"So," he says, "I've been thinking about *Armageddon*."

"The movie?"

He laughs. "I hope just the movie."

"Is that tonight?"

"Yeah," he says. "We said Friday."

"Is that what you're going to wear?" I ask, pointing to the sweater.

"You don't like it?"

"No, Bernie," I say. "It's good." The coffee's still terrible; Bernie must not wash out the pot. I dump in a packet of sugar. "Don't spill your coffee on it."

"Oh, geez, you're right," he says. "I better be careful. Being nervous and all." He sets his coffee mug down on the counter.

"Just take it easy," I say. "You've got about nine-and-a-half hours to go."

"Right," he says, "right. It's just—I put this sweater on because I lost a button." He lifts up the cuff of his shirt and shows me where it's missing. "It'd be nice to have somebody, you know, to sew stuff back on."

"You don't sew your own buttons?"

"Well, I could," he says, staring at his shirt cuff, "but I was afraid I might ruin the shirt."

"Don't worry," I tell him. "With that sweater over it, she won't notice."

"That's what I was hoping." He picks up his coffee mug

and takes a sip, with his arm held out about a foot from his body and his neck craning toward the mug. "Well," he says, and smiles, "it's not all I was hoping."

"Okay, but don't get too far ahead of yourself."

"I was just thinking," he says, "how nice it would be to have a daughter." He stuffs his hands into the pockets of his corduroys. "Sharon and I never had a chance to have kids."

"Bernie," I say. "It's just a date. You'll scare her if you start talking like that."

"Yeah," he says and starts rocking on his heels. "I know you're right. It's just..."

"You never know," I say. "You might even decide you don't like her so much."

"Oh," he says, "I doubt that." He takes a hand out of his pocket and reaches up to scratch the back of his head. "She's a kind woman," he says, "a good, kind woman." He glances down at his coffee mug, picks it up and sets it down, decides against the risk of taking another sip.

"Then I hope she's your dream girl," I say.

"Oh, she is," he says, nodding and rocking on his heels. "I don't ask for much."

꒒

The day before the wedding, I walked to the corner liquor store and called Lynette from the pay phone. Her mother answered the phone; I took on the tone of voice of a magazine salesman and asked for a Miss Lynette Wilson.

"You mean Lynette Hale," her mother said.

"What?"

"She's married now," Mrs. Wilson said. "Lynette Hale, and she's not at this number anymore."

"Can you tell me where she is?"

"Harley?" her mother asked suddenly. "Is that you?"

"No," I said and hung up the phone.

⌇

I pull into the McDonald's drive-thru behind an Explorer with the name of a real estate agency on its doors. I recognize the name of the agency; it specializes in mansions that overlook the lake, architectural nightmares in steel and glass bordering acres of vineyard. They're the summer homes of New York City doctors and lawyers, minor sports figures, the occasional has-been entertainer; an autographed photo of a minor soap opera star hangs over the customer service desk at the PriceBuster market.

I order a Big Mac, fries and a soda and pull up to the second window. Dierdre sticks her hand out the window and takes my money, then turns and notices me for the first time when she hands me my change. "Hey," she says.

"How're things?"

She laughs and points to her belly. "Things are big."

"How much longer?"

She shrugs. "Couple weeks, but, you know, it could be any day." She jams a paper cup against the soda dispenser and stands waiting for it to fill. "My mom was early with her first." She puts a lid on my soda and hands it out the window to me.

"Hey," I say, pointing to the gold band on her finger. "You got married."

"Yeah, well," she says, "it seemed like a good idea."

"Congratulations."

"Don't bother," she says. "He's no prize."

I stab the plastic lid of my soda with the straw and

hand back the wrapper. She takes it and walks away to get my Big Mac.

"Still, it's got to be better for the baby...."

"Yeah," she says, handing me the bag with my food. "Plus, I sort of love the jerk."

"Well," I say. "Good luck." I take a peek inside the bag just to make sure she got the order right. "Let me know how it all turns out."

"Yeah," she says and laughs again, snorting through her nose. "Sure thing."

ॐ

The sun's out, and the roads are slushy. If the temperature dips below freezing, the roads will ice over and be treacherous tomorrow. I balance the Big Mac wrapper on my lap, pull fries out of the bag on the seat while I drive. I should eat better, I keep thinking. I should eat better, floss more, exercise, swear less, go to church.

I pull into her driveway, crumpling the wrapper in my fist and throwing it on the floor of the truck. I wonder if I could fix her porch in a weekend, buy some cement blocks and prop it up on the side where it sags. In the spring, she could put out a porch rocker and sit with the baby.

Doug's truck is back, parked next to the barn, and there's a crazy second or two when I think they might have fished him out of the lake alive. But of course that's ridiculous. They've just brought back the truck.

I park and get out, my legs a little shaky, step onto her porch, noticing the slope, and knock on her door.

"Harley," she says, "what are you doing here?" She has her hand, the one with a cast, resting on the head of a blond toddler in a T-shirt and diaper. The child squirms but doesn't step out from under the weight of the cast.

I don't have an answer, so I look down at the child fidgeting under her hand. "Yours?"

"Timmy's two," she says. She ruffles the hair at the back of his head. "He needs a haircut."

She looks up and into my face, frowns a little, lines forming around her eyes, and I can see how much time has passed. "Why don't you come in?" she asks. "We were about to have lunch."

"I've eaten," I say, but I step around her to the hallway. Her kids have been playing with wooden blocks; they're spread all over the floor. I pick one up, and it's smooth and shiny, varnished, with a semi-circle cut out of one side to suggest a porthole or the top of a rounded window.

"Doug made those," she says and takes it from me, turning it over in her hands. "When I was pregnant with Matthew." She drops the block, clattering, to the floor. "Matty's four. He's shopping with my mother. Picking out his birthday present."

"Three kids," I say.

"Yup," she says, nodding. "A lot of time gone by."

She walks ahead of me into the kitchen, where the baby sits in a highchair, banging her hands against the tray. What little hair she has is gathered into a pink barrette on top of her head. Lynette walks over to the counter, opens a package of Saltines, breaks a Saltine in half and hands it to the baby. She leans to kiss her lightly on the head before asking if she can make me a bologna sandwich.

"No, thanks," I say. "I've eaten."

"Right," she says. "You told me that."

The baby leans back her head and screeches like her throat's being cut. Lynette ignores her, spreading mayonnaise on two slices of bread, and the baby discovers the Saltine in her hand and shoves a piece of it in her mouth, gumming the corner.

"Wow," I say. "Are my ears bleeding?"

"It's a phase," she says. "You get used to it."

Lynette cuts a bologna sandwich in half and puts it on a paper plate. She helps Timmy onto a chair with a booster seat and sets the sandwich in front of him. Then she brings over her own sandwich and places it on the table without a napkin. She walks to the refrigerator, pulls out two Diet Cokes and a spill-proof cup with what looks like milk, puts the latter in front of Timmy and hands me one of the cans, setting the other next to her sandwich.

"So," she says and tips her Diet Coke toward me as if toasting. "Old friends."

I open my soda and imitate the gesture. I take a sip and get a mouthful of fizz and Aspartame.

Timmy chews on his sandwich and watches me carefully, his eyes following my hand as it lifts the soda can and sets it back down. He chews around the crust, letting it drop back onto the plate. "Done," he says.

Lynette glances at his plate. "Three more bites."

"Done," he says, louder, in a way that suggests he's gearing up to scream.

She reaches over and pulls the crust off the other half, points to it on his plate. "This much more," she says.

"No," he says, but he picks up the sandwich and takes another bite. "Done," he says again.

"A little more," she says and chews her own sandwich.

"Done," he says. "Done, done, done," and now he really is screaming. The baby starts to fuss, and Lynette sighs and puts down her sandwich.

"Okay," she says. "Go play." She stands up and pulls out

his chair, helps him down. He runs into the hall, where more blocks are sent clattering to the floor. Lynette picks up her sandwich, smiles at me and continues eating.

"Timmy's a handful," she says. "Middle child."

I shake my head. "I wouldn't know."

She nods and looks as if she might ask me why I don't have kids, but decides against it. She takes a swig of her soda and turns her head, listening to the sounds from the hallway. The clock on the wall behind me has a pendulum with a noticeable squeak, and I can feel the seconds passing, as if marked with a metronome.

Lynette finishes her soda and sets the empty can on the table. It falls onto its side and rolls toward me a couple of inches.

"How did he die?" I ask.

"Doug?"

I nod, and she smiles, as if to let me know she's aware it was a stupid question.

"Don't you know?"

"Ice fishing. That's all I know."

She nods slowly, looking me straight in the eye. "But you need to know exactly."

"Yes."

"I could ask why," she says, but when I open my mouth to tell her I don't know, she shakes her head, silencing me.

"It was stupid," she says and sighs, lifts the cast and sets it on the table. "He went out on the point, because it was quiet and no one else would be there. We'd been arguing. I told him not to fish there, the ice was weak, but he ignored me because we'd been arguing." She raises her eyes, glances at me and then out the window, where a haze that looks like rain is forming along the horizon.

"Anybody who's ever been ice fishing around here

knows not to fish there. The current changes, and the ice shifts. It can be hard on top, weak underneath." She lifts the cast and holds her other hand under it, showing me hard layers on top of weak ones. "But Doug wouldn't admit he didn't know what he was doing. I went along to try and keep him out of trouble." She smirks and drops her hands to the table, the cast making a hollow sound against the tabletop.

"He used an axe, made the hole way too big. The ice was weak. He fell in. I couldn't pull him out." She turns over the palm of her good hand and shows me the cut where she tried.

I clear my throat and stare at the puckered skin on her hand, the scab that reaches from her wrist to the base of her middle finger, criss-crossing her life line. "It was an accident," I say and clear my throat again, let it develop into a cough, covering my mouth with a curled fist.

She sighs and turns her hand over. "Yes." She turns to the window again, watching as the sky along the horizon darkens with sheets of rain that seem to be moving toward us, slowly, by inches. "Is that what you came here to ask?"

I can't quite meet her eyes, so I stare again at her hands, the short, unpolished nails and the thin gold band on her wedding finger. The veins on the back of the hand without a cast are prominent, blue, crossing over the tendons. "I don't know." I raise my eyes then and see that she's not angry and that there's something else there: kindness, patience, possibly even amusement.

"Well," she says and slowly takes another bite of sandwich, "since we're asking questions—"

Her expression changes, hardening, and I can see that whatever amusement there might have been a minute ago has vanished.

"Does your wife know you've been spying on me?"

"Not spying. Checking."

"Does she know?"

The baby's hands are covered with moist cracker crumbs; she shoves three fingers in her mouth and sucks.

"She doesn't mind."

"Well," she says, and I know from her tone that she doesn't believe me, "she must be very understanding."

"She was worried about you," I say, "with the dog," and as soon as I say the word, I wonder where he is and start looking for him, scanning the corners of the room.

"He's outside," she says and stands, pushes aside a peach-colored curtain to show me where Whitey's tied to a tree with a long rope. He's staring at something in the distance, probably birds or squirrels, with his legs straight, chin raised.

"That's very kind of her," she says, "to worry."

"Yes." I stand too, resting my knuckles on the tabletop. I see myself stepping toward her and pulling her to me, her crying against my shoulder. Then I imagine simply nodding and walking away, out through her hallway, her front door and away from her forever. And in both cases, I try to imagine what I might say now to convince her of my good intentions, the purity of my concern.

"You could tell me anything," I say.

She nods. "Right," she says and looks me in the eye. "If there was anything to tell."

"Exactly," I say. "Yes," and I choose the second option, lifting my hand from the table, using it to finger the keys in my front pocket, walking—so that it feels like racing—into her hall, stepping over her child on the floor with a tower of blocks and out the door, believing I may choose never to see or talk to her again.

CHAPTER XII

꒰

I STOOD AT THE FRONT OF THE CHURCH near the flowers, looked down at the floor and saw that Mr. Gibson's shoes were tassled and newly polished. I stood flexing my hands, which had suddenly gone numb, and breathing slowly in and out, and I kept telling myself that nobody knew what might happen forty or fifty years down the road, but that the point was to try, to work hard and keep working hard and put up with each other way past the moment when you'd stop putting up with anyone else.

Then the music started—not the wedding march, but something else classical and vaguely familiar—and it was a couple of seconds before people realized that Diane, who was eight-and-a-half months pregnant, was waddling toward the front of the church, where she made a sort of half-curtsy aimed at the altar and immediately had to sit down.

By the time Diane was settled, Amanda, who'd insisted on walking herself down the aisle, was coming toward me, her hair in a single French braid, wearing a simple satin gown without lace or fancy beading, because, in the end, she'd won that battle with her mother, too. And, carrying an armload of roses, she truly was beautiful, and I knew that years later, I'd be pleasantly surprised to see from the photographs how lovely she'd been.

꒰

At the reception, I danced with my mother, who laughed when I stepped on her toes and said, "Just like your father. A regular Fred Astaire."

"He taught me how to dip," I said and began leaning forward.

"Don't you dare." She let go of my shoulder to swat me with the beaded clutch purse she held in her hand.

"He would have liked dancing with Amanda," I said, watching her dance with her father, the two of them twirling under each other's arms until they knotted up and bumped torsos, then standing forehead to forehead and doing something bunny hoppish with their feet.

"Yes," she said and laughed. "He liked her style."

I made a sudden move, turning my mother so that she faced the bandstand, she said, "Ooooh," and we continued box-stepping while Amanda and her father separated and did a Charleston move with their hands over their knees.

I kept box-stepping, trying not to count out loud or look at my feet, and my mother touched her gloved hand to my cheek. "I think he would have been glad," she said, deftly moving her left foot to the side, where my shoes wouldn't find it, "to know you're not alone."

~

Amanda and I spent our honeymoon at the same cabin her parents had rented on Waneta Lake; we had barely enough money left over for the beer and pizza we practically lived on for two weeks. But I liked the click of my wedding ring against a can of beer, liked how it kept me from getting carded in the fisherman's bar where we ate fried catfish and Amanda put her foot in my lap under the table. I liked the way middle-aged men stared at my bra-less wife with hooded eyes and tipped their fisherman's hats to her while they held the door. And I liked the gentle break of waves on the shore while I rocked the wooden headboard of our bed against the cabin wall.

Once, on a night when I imagined out loud that we'd disrupted the sleeping patterns of the local wildlife with the violence of our lovemaking, Amanda chuckled softly beside me, not bothering to cover herself with a sheet, and said, "There were so many times, Harley, when I thought I'd never see you again."

"When was that?" My heartbeat had begun to slow, and I wondered if it was too late at night for the outdoor shower, if I'd find a raccoon or skunk taking advantage of the constant drip from the showerhead.

"In school," she said. "You'd come to my room, and we'd have sex, and you'd get up and walk away like you were never coming back."

"But I did," I said.

"Yes," she said, breathing slowly, her chest rising and falling beside me, "you did."

"And we're married," I said.

She lifted up on one elbow, facing me. "Right," she said, "so I guess I can relax."

Every afternoon, I pretended to fish, and usually I fell asleep on the dock, and in dreams I visited with my father and he told me to take care of my mother and Amanda, to floss and take the lawnmower in for a tune-up every February, before the spring rush. Once, he told me to use condoms, and another time, he told me to stop concentrating so much on the things that made me unhappy. I would wake up, feeling not so much that he'd spoken to me from beyond the grave, but that my own memory was taking over, reminding me of the things he would have wanted me to do. And it was comforting to think I had this advice to follow, that I could be the adult I was supposed to be now.

Toward the end of the two weeks, we heard that Gordie and Diane had had twin girls. They'd known for months that Diane was pregnant with twins, but they hadn't told anyone, because, with Diane sick for most of the pregnancy, there was some question about whether they'd have to abort one of the fetuses in the womb. Both babies were underweight and in an incubator, but Gordie told us over the phone that it looked like they'd both pull through.

"It's a miracle," he said. "An honest-to-God miracle."

⌁

"Your wife called," Bernie says without raising his eyes. He sits at his desk, on a chair that always looks too small for him, compiling work orders. He knows I usually go home for lunch, and that I'm a half hour late getting back.

"What'd she say?"

He pushes his chair back from his desk, looks up at me over the rim of the half-glasses he wears for reading. "She said your mom wouldn't get out of bed. She wanted to know if she should call the doctor."

"Jesus. Yes."

He nods. "Well, good," he says. "That's what I told her." He wheels himself closer to the desk, until the front buttons of his shirt make a faint click against the metal edge. "Stop home before you do these," he says, and hands me a stack of three order forms.

"Bernie," I say, "thanks."

He nods, but doesn't look up. "Call me," he says, "from home."

I take the back way home, avoid the lunch traffic on

Main Street near the diner. I leave the supply truck in the driveway, walk around to the front door. I try the handle, but Sonia's got it locked, as usual, and I'm still fishing around for my keys when she comes and lets me in.

She kisses me quickly on the cheek. "The doctor was here," she says. "Now, he went."

"He's gone?" Her lapses in grammar, which I usually find kind of cute, are, at times, nothing short of annoying.

"Yes," she says bashfully, hearing the anger in my voice, "he is gone."

I walk ahead of her into my mother's room, for a minute feeling the embarrassment of the smell that must have hit him once he opened the door. "Ma?" I ask, knowing immediately that although she doesn't answer, she's wide awake. Then my mind catches up with me, and I know it's because of the snoring, because I can't hear the snoring.

"What did the doctor say?" I ask Sonia, who's standing behind me.

She crooks a finger and motions for me to follow her out of the room. "He says it is…," and she searches for the word, flapping a hand in the air, "big sadness."

"Depression?" I ask.

A smile spreads quickly across her face. "Yes. He says that."

"What does he want to do about it?"

She doesn't answer but goes into the kitchen, comes back with a prescription slip. "Pills," she says, handing it to me.

"More pills?" I can't read the name of the drug, but even if I could, I doubt I'd recognize it. No one in my family's ever had depression before, or at least no one's ever been treated for it.

"Happiness pills," Sonia says.

I fold the slip in half and put it in my pocket. "She's already taking too many pills."

Sonia shrugs. "She's old."

I ignore her and walk back to my mother's room, push open the door and go sit on the edge of her bed. The room's dark, even in the middle of the afternoon, because the windows are shaded by the porch roof. The neighbor's dog barks a few times, and an ambulance backs into the garage, beeping shrilly.

"I asked him to let me go," she murmurs from the bed, her face half covered with blanket.

I resist the urge to pull the blanket from her face. "Asked who?"

"Dr. Baldwin."

"To go?" We must have forgotten to wash the windows in this room when we did the rest of the house. Clouds of grime from the street turn what light does come through a dingy gray.

She sighs, as though tired already from the effort of explaining. "Die," she says.

She has a photo of my father, a close-up from his retirement party, on the nightstand next to her bed, and I take a long, slow look at it, noticing the tiny details, like the spots of confetti on his suit jacket and in his hair, the tiny gap between his upper front teeth. I open my curled fists and stretch my fingers until they bend back, away from my palms.

"Why would you want to do that, Ma?" I ask, trying so hard not to be angry.

She sighs again and coughs lightly, shifts in the bed, so that one foot bumps against me. "I used to be a lady," she says.

"You still are."

"Your father liked that about me," she says as if she has-n't heard. "He was proud of me." She coughs again, harder this time, but doesn't bother raising a hand to cover her mouth. "I made my own hats," she says, "with feathers. He liked the ones with feathers and the one..." she stops to cough again, her spasms shaking the bed, "with a veil that dropped over one eye."

"You are a lady," I say.

"No," she says, and the bed shakes beneath her. "I'm an old woman," she says, "who pisses the sheets."

I'm surprised that she even knows the word—though, of course, how could she not after so many years—because I've never heard her use it, never heard her even substitute another word for it. Pissing was a subject she wouldn't have discussed with any terms; if I was sick and she had to ask, she used the words the doctor used, "urinate" and "defecate."

"Ma," I say, and now I do reach up to her face and pull the blanket away, "that's no reason to die."

"Well," she says, and she smiles now, and reaches a hand slowly out from under the blanket, "that's easy for you to say." She holds her hand out, trembling, and feels for where my arm is, then holds me with a grasp that's sur-prisingly strong. "You've never been a lady."

༄

"Well," Bernie says, "I'm going now." He has on his sweater, wrinkled from spending the day in his desk drawer, and his parka, also wrinkled, over the top. He brushes the sweater with his hand where it strains across his stomach. "I must've spilled something," he says. "It's a little wet here."

"She won't notice."

"Maybe it'll dry in the car."

"Sure." I pick up his soft-sided briefcase, which seems to be empty except for a pair of sweat socks and what looks like an unopened juice box, and follow him down the fire stairs to the first floor.

"You ever been ice fishing, Bernie?" I ask, holding the door for him.

"You're still worried about that girl."

"Woman," I say. "She's got kids. Three of 'em."

He nods. "Uh-huh," he says, "and you're worried because she's a friend."

I decide to ignore the tone of his voice, tell myself it's just Bernie making something out of nothing. I follow him outside, and we both step carefully over patches of ice on the gravel. "Would you fish out on the point?"

"No." He takes his keys out of his pocket and presses a button to unlock his doors. "Is that where they found him?"

"Yeah."

"Well," he says and opens the driver's side door, "then I hate to say it, but the idiot got what was coming to him."

"She said she tried to warn him the ice was weak."

"Yeah?" he says and sighs, settling himself onto the leather upholstery. "Well, he should've listened to her."

❧

I stop at the drugstore on the way home and let the check-out girl help me pick out some scented bath powder and a matching hand lotion that're supposed to smell like hyacinths. For Sonia, I buy a bag of red licorice and a bottle of ink for the fountain pen she uses to write letters home. I don't go to the pharmacy counter; I don't even ask about the cost of my mother's latest prescription.

When I walk in the door, my mother's watching TV

with the headphones on. "Boy," she says when I lean to kiss her cheek, "Dan Rather's gotten old."

"I've got a present for you," I say and open the bag from the drugstore, hand her the powder and lotion.

"Oh, Harley, you shouldn't have," she says, shouting to hear herself over the headphones.

Sonia turns and gets up from where she's sitting on the floor, painting. The lamp on the floor next to her is so bright that I have to wait for my eyes to adjust before I can make out the row of tiny houses: red, gray, yellow and white.

"Hello," she says, kisses me and glances toward the bag in my hand. "Oh, good, Harley," she says, looking at the gifts. "Tomorrow, I write to my sister." She sets the ink down on the coffee table and opens the bag of licorice, stuffs a piece in her mouth.

"You'll ruin your dinner," my mother shouts, but Sonia only ignores her.

I lean toward Sonia and say quietly, so that my mother doesn't hear, "I thought after dinner we could go out for dessert, get mom out of the house."

"But the money..." she says.

"It's fine," I say, but already I'm beginning to wonder how much exactly that coat for Sonia will cost, and whether the gutters will last out the winter. I should be setting money aside for these things, I know, but I can't let my mother spend the day in bed, and I don't want her taking any more pills. And a piece of pie every once in a while, some bath powder and hand lotion, seems like the least I can do to prevent it.

ご

I drove to my mother's at least once a month to help her take care of the house. I cleaned the garage, put up storm windows, resealed the driveway, patched the roof, planted rosebushes and unplugged the sewer drain. I didn't know what I was doing, but I asked questions at the hardware store and tried not to make any serious mistakes. In return, my mother cooked huge meals—pot roast, stuffed pork chops or chicken with some kind of fancy sauce—and gave me the leftovers in Tupperware containers I usually polished off on the drive home.

There were times when I was working on the house and I caught her watching, staring up at me from the ground while I replaced roof shingles or pushing aside the kitchen curtain while I was out resealing the driveway. And I knew she was remembering my father, looking for some kind of sign of him in me.

It made me sorry not to be more like him; I knew how much she missed him. I would have given anything to be broader across the shoulders, stronger, quieter, better with a hammer and nails. I would have liked to think I could be the kind of man other men respected and looked up to, the kind who could spot a woman from across a dance floor and know she was the one he'd marry, the kind who could live a life he thought of as quiet and small, never imagining that his death would leave such a wake. But I think my mother and I both knew all along that she was the one I took after the most.

ᖷ

We have to park up the street from the diner, which means wheeling Mom through the snow; if we don't remember to wipe down the wheels before taking her back in the house, she'll leave tracks all over the rugs, two of which Sonia brought from Russia. I turn off the engine, jump out of the truck and run around to open Mom's door. She's trying to slide her way toward me, but she's already managed to wedge the cast under the dashboard, and Sonia has to help her slide back the other way, disentangle the cast from the radio wires and slide back. I try not to think about how the diner will close in twenty minutes and how much trouble this is for a lousy piece of pie.

"Well," my mother says, "this is an adventure."

"True enough, Ma," I say, walking around to the back of the truck to hand down the wheelchair. Sonia gets out of the truck and walks toward me, takes the wheelchair handles and stands waiting. I then lift Ma from the truck seat, bending my legs so I can take the weight of the cast. I carefully step backward, double-checking my traction on the wet sidewalk, and drop her in the chair Sonia wheels behind me.

"Good job," Sonia says, clapping her mittens together.

"Some mighty fine teamwork," I say, deciding to imitate her upbeat mood.

The diner is located in an old trailer, and it's not easy getting my mother through the door, but we manage it and wheel her to the last table, where there's just enough space for the wheelchair. The diner's close to closing and empty except for an old man finishing his coffee at the table next to ours.

"Well," says Vera, the owner's wife, as she walks over to our table and stands behind Ma, "we're all out of the special."

"We just want pie," I say, "and coffee."

"Well," she says and considers this, tapping her pencil, "we got two or three slices of rhubarb left, and I think there's a lemon meringue in the fridge."

"Rhubarb?" Sonia asks me, not understanding the word.

"Three coffees," I say. "Rhubarb, Ma?"

"Rhubarb," she says, but Vera can't hear, because she's standing directly behind her.

"One rhubarb and two lemon meringue," I tell Vera.

She nods and steps backward, knocking her hip on the next table over, where the old man grabs his coffee before it spills. "Be just a minute," she says.

"Uh-oh," my mother says.

"What, Ma?"

"I think I have to go."

"Go?"

"Bathroom," she says and nods her head toward the bathroom door directly behind Sonia's chair.

"Shouldn't you have gone before we left the house?"

Sonia stands up, shooting me a look.

"I'm an old lady," my mother says, too loudly. "I've got an old bladder. I don't always know beforehand."

I stand up, moving chairs out of the way so Sonia can at least try to wheel Ma through the bathroom doorway. I'd have to squeeze around the next table to get behind Ma.

"Would you mind if I moved this back a little bit?" I ask the old man, putting both hands on the edge of his table.

He stands with the help of the cane he had placed on the floor next to him. "Sure," he says, "I've got one of those old bladders, too."

I move the table back about six inches, trying not to knock the old man off his feet. Then I walk around behind Ma and tell Sonia to open the bathroom door. I push Ma forward, and the wheelchair barely fits through the open doorway, scraping the door frame on both sides.

"Phew," the old man says. "That was a close one."

Sonia stands against the far wall of the bathroom, and I

manage to push Ma in so that she can fit inside with the door closed. I sit back down and can hear the two of them negotiating, Sonia asking Ma to try and slide forward onto the toilet seat and Ma asking her how on earth she expects her to do *that.*

"I was in a chair for a while," the old man says. "Broke my hip." He gestures toward his cane, lifting it a couple inches off the floor. "Getting around with that thing was a bitch."

Vera comes over with a tray full of coffee cups and hands the old man his bill.

"Let me get your coffee," I say to the old man.

"Nah," he says. "I had the special. Liver and onions."

Vera sets the coffee mugs down on the table, a small pitcher of milk and a handful of packets of sugar and Sweet 'n Low, then walks away.

"I'll owe you one, then," I say.

The old man shrugs. "Okay, but you better remind me," he says, tapping a bony finger to his temple. "Lord knows I won't remember." He leans toward me, as if about to tell me a secret. "Brain's old, too." He opens his wallet, pulls out two dollar bills and leaves them on the table, waves his hand in my direction and shuffles toward the cash register.

"Harley?" Sonia calls from inside the bathroom. "Can you open the door?"

I get up and open the door, and my mother wheels herself backward, scraping the chair on both sides as she maneuvers through the doorway.

"At least they keep it clean in there," she says.

Vera comes back with our pie, and I make her stand there while I help us all get settled at the table. She sets the two slices of lemon meringue in front of Sonia and me and the rhubarb in front of Ma. "That everything?" she asks, and when I nod, she sets the bill face down in the center of the table, next to the sugar packets.

"Your father used to love the pie here," Ma says, cutting a piece with the side of her fork. "But he said they make the hamburgers too small," she says, dropping her voice as if Vera might still be standing behind her.

"This pie is good," Sonia says, stuffing a forkful of mostly meringue into her mouth.

My piece is still cold from the refrigerator, with tiny ice crystals on top of the meringue, but the lemon filling is good, a little tart and not too sugary.

"Later," Sonia says, wiping her fork clean with her mouth, "we'll get Mama's pills."

Vera comes out of the kitchen with a mop and a pail and starts at the other end of the trailer, mopping the floor.

"Why would we do that?" I say quietly, in case Vera's listening, but she seems to be humming softly under her breath.

"She needs them," Sonia says, confused.

"She just needs to get out more."

"No, Harley..." Sonia says, beginning to look upset.

"Ma?" I say. "You're not depressed are you?"

"What?" she says, wiping a red rhubarb smear off her lips with a napkin.

"Mama," Sonia says, not noticing my mother's frown at the word, "you would like the pills from Dr. Baldwin?"

"He says I need them."

"You're not depressed, are you, Ma?" I ask. I watch her eyes as she takes a sip of coffee, her hand trembling just a little when she sets it on the table.

"I have a right to be," she says quietly. "I'm old." She picks up her fork and presses it against the last few pie crust crumbs on her plate. "We'll see how you feel," she says, "when you get to be my age."

꒚

Amanda begged me to quit my Blimpie's job after the hold-up. "Jesus, Harley," she said, standing in front of me in her nightgown, "the way you're clinging to that minimum-wage job like it means something. What am I supposed to do? Sit here and wait for you to get your head shot off?" And as much as I hated the fact that she sounded more angry than afraid, I had to agree.

At five minutes to ten, Frances had been putting away leftover onions, green peppers and pickles in the back freezer, and the only customer was a kid about fifteen, drinking a bucket-sized pink lemonade, his leg jumping up and down like he had to go to the bathroom. Then his friend walked in, a coffee-colored kid with a short afro, denim jacket and wide-leg jeans over a huge pair of Converse high-tops. He walked up to the counter with a gun held sideways like Chinese mafia members are always doing in the movies. "Gimme it," he said, smiling as if he might be posing for his high school graduation photo.

"What?" I took the piece of Saran Wrap I'd been holding in my hand and twisted it over the far edge of an aluminum bucket full of ketchup, all the while thinking of the phone that was hanging on the wall next to the cash register, and how someone should have thought to put it closer, under the counter, with the police on speed dial. My thinking was sluggish and dangerously off-kilter, and I said to myself: If I live through this, I'll bring it up at the next staff meeting.

"The money, asshole," he said, and his hand jerked the

gun, so that I thought he might actually end up shooting me by accident. "Gimme it."

I opened the cash register drawer by twisting the tiny key, my fingers barely able to keep hold of it for the shaking, and the bell on the cash register was louder than I remembered and seemed to echo, so that I kept hearing it for seconds after, when I was already stuffing tens and twenties into a to-go bag.

His friend was on his feet and sprinted to the door. He stood there, staring nervously at the street, which I thought, more than anything, would draw a cop's notice and possibly get me killed. There are so many ways for me to get killed in this, I thought. The odds are definitely not good.

I filled the bag and handed it to the kid with the gun, and he didn't wait for me to finish emptying the drawer but took it and turned toward the door. I could hear Frances whistling in the back, and I prayed she wouldn't come out of the freezer for a few seconds more. The white kid, the one at the door, went out into the parking lot first and threw his lemonade down on the pavement, where it left a sticky puddle I'd have to clean up later. The kid with the gun followed him, and they both jumped over the guard rail at the side of the parking lot, then ran down a grassy slope to the Pizza Hut below, to their car parked where I wouldn't be able to see it.

I reached for the phone next to my head and dialed the police, in a voice that was jittery and unfamiliar to me, explained the situation to the person who answered the phone, then stood with the cash drawer open at my waist and tried to tell how much money was missing, even though my hands were shaking so badly that I kept losing count of what was left.

Frances came up from the back, saw me shaking and asked in a small voice what was wrong.

"Robbed," I said and cleared my throat. "We were robbed."

"Just now?" She was holding a stack of clean food trays, which she'd wiped with a damp cloth. They dripped onto the front of her uniform where she held them to her chest.

"Kids," I said. "Fifteen, sixteen, maybe."

"Fifteen of them?" She set the trays down on the counter and looked at me, horrified.

"No. Two of them. They were fifteen or sixteen years old."

"Black?" she whispered.

"One black, one white."

"Geez," she said and let out a long, slow breath of air. "I was right in back." She lifted a hand to her face and absently picked at a scab on her cheekbone.

"I wanted you to stay where you were," I said. "I wanted to keep you out of it."

She nodded. "Maybe we should lock the door," she said, nervously looking out at the empty parking lot; she and I had both parked in back, next to the dumpster.

"I have to wait for the police." I turned to her and saw that the scab on her cheek was bleeding and that she was smearing blood on the tips of her fingers. "I'll walk you out to your car, and you can go home."

"I should wash the floors first."

"Leave it."

I closed the cash drawer, pushing it with both hands, and motioned for her to walk ahead of me to the back of the store. She pulled a light blue windbreaker from the coat rack next to the manager's office and held it in her arms, not putting it on, even though it was cold outside.

She looked at me and opened the door, and we both

stood scanning the parking lot before walking toward her car. She bumbled in the pockets of her windbreaker for a key ring with a tiny stuffed Garfield and unlocked the door. I held it and she slid onto the car seat.

"Harley," she said, whispering. "I'm so glad they didn't hurt you."

"Me too," I said. "I'm glad they didn't hurt you either." I let go of the door, and she pulled it closed. She waved before heading out of the parking lot, and I waited until she was safely on the highway before going back inside.

ॐ

I leave the truck running so my mother can stay warm while Sonia and I go into the drug store for her pills. The checkout girl remembers me from a few hours ago, nods hello when I walk past, smiles brightly and says, "You forgot something."

The Valentine's Day displays are up already: bags of candy hearts and boxes of chocolate, stuffed animals and silvery mylar balloons that say, "I love you" and "Be mine." Sonia squeezes the middle of a stuffed gorilla, and it begins gyrating to a recorded version of the macarena. She laughs, grabs me and starts to dance, but I lock eyes with the checkout girl and let go of her, walking away.

I hand the prescription and my mother's Medicare card to the woman at the pharmacy counter. She takes them from me without saying a word, just carries them over to where the prescriptions are filled and lays them on the counter. She then goes back to counting and weighing pills, sliding them into bottles with labels she types herself. Her movements are quick and automatic—her mouth is slack, her eyes are like slits—and I wonder if it's occurred to any of the other customers, the old woman with a huge purse balanced on her lap or the teenage boy with what looks like an inflamed rash over the left side of his face, that she could be sleepwalking.

Sonia's wandered toward the greeting card aisle; I can see her trying to read cards. She tends to pick out the ones with kittens or bunnies on them, because the language is easier for her to understand; she doesn't seem to know or care that they're meant for children.

The pharmacist calls the teenage boy to the counter and, without making eye contact, hands him a bottle of ointment and tells him to use it three times a day, "after washing." He gives her the money, and she takes it, straightening the bills before placing them in the cash register.

I become aware that the Muzak, which had been playing without my noticing it, has stopped, and both the old woman and I have lifted our chins, blinking, searching the store to figure out what's different.

Sonia has a card in her hand, and she walks quickly up the center aisle of the drug store to the cash register. She must be buying a Valentine for me; since she can't drive, she'll have to use this chance to sneak it out of the store.

The pharmacist calls the old woman's name twice, but doesn't walk toward her or motion to her. The old woman seems lost in thought or deafness. I tap her gently on the arm and motion toward the pharmacist. She rises slowly to her feet and walks to the counter, where the pharmacist hands her her a white paper bag with instructions typed on a piece of paper stapled to the front. The old woman sets her purse on the counter and opens the metal clasp along the top. She pulls loose dollar bills from it and holds them in her hand, counting, before handing them in a pile to the pharmacist. The pharmacist takes them and straightens them, turning them so that they face the same direction before setting them in the cash register drawer.

Sonia passes the old woman in the aisle and smiles, nods hello, but the old woman is so intent on not tripping on the recently waxed floor that she doesn't see.

"Harley," Sonia says, "I'm thirsty." The card is nowhere to be seen; she must have tucked it inside her coat.

"Do you want a soda?" I ask.

She thinks for a moment before shaking her head and saying, "No." She gestures for me to follow her over to the refrigerated cases full of soda and milk and beer. "I think tea," she says. "You want something, Harley?" She hands me a bottle of iced tea and stands with the door to the refrigerator case open.

"No," I say. "I'm fine."

The pharmacist calls my mother's name, and Sonia and I walk to the counter. Sonia takes the pills from her, and I pay for them and the iced tea with the rest of the cash in my wallet. Someone must have pressed the gorilla's belly after Sonia; it's still gyrating as we walk past it to the front door.

"Harley," Sonia says, putting an arm around my waist as we walk out to the parking lot, "I'm sorry."

"For what, Sonia?"

"For ..." she says, "fighting."

"It's all right," I say. "It's just...she's always been so strong."

"Yes," Sonia says. "A strong woman." She reaches under my jacket and pats a wool mitten against my bare back.

"She shouldn't need those pills."

Sonia stops a few feet from the truck, pulls away from me and instead holds my arm with both hands. "Maybe so," she says, taking the iced tea bottle from me and twisting the top to open it. "Maybe you are the strong one now."

CHAPTER XIII

I ANSWERED AN AD AND GOT A JOB doing the billing for a local law office. There were five attorneys who did mostly family law: divorces and custody cases, but also the occasional bickering between neighbors over property lines. They gave me a key to the office and said I could come and go whenever I wanted; that way, if I ever figured out what I wanted to be, I could go back to school. I worked mostly at night, when I could play the radio and read old case files.

Some of the cases were shocking because of their frivolity—the guy who claimed an accident at work that dislocated his shoulder caused "extensive psychological trauma" and kept him from having sex with his wife—and some for sheer meanness, like the guy who poisoned his neighbor's dog with antifreeze, because it barked late at night. And there were so many divorces: divorces because of infidelity; divorces that happened after all the money had been spent; divorces that followed years of fighting over the kids.

Reading the files made me feel lucky and smart. It was passion that caused all those problems, too much passion that turned into anger. But Amanda and I didn't have passion. We were friends. We cared about each other. We'd never hurt each other.

I'm up early, and I unhook Sonia's arm from over my shoulder and slip out of bed, listen for a minute to my mother's snoring through the baby monitor, close the nightstand drawer and walk quietly, trying to avoid the squeakier floorboards, to the bathroom. I pee but don't flush, and pull clothes from the hamper: jeans, T-shirt, sweatshirt, socks. I put them on but carry my work boots downstairs. I'm sneaking around in my own house, and it's probably not even necessary; I mean, if I explained to Sonia why I need to go and see Lynette, she'd probably understand—but I just don't have the words yet to tell her. It has something to do with the reason I double-check the door locks and make sure the stove's turned off before going to bed—because I just can't sleep unless I'm sure.

I pass the stair landing window, see ice in the trees and know the sidewalks on both sides of the house will be slippery. Sonia never wears the boots I bought her, and I don't want her breaking her neck, so I'll have to go out there with a can of rock salt. But first I start the coffee and wonder why it is that I never started smoking, because it would be nice, right now, to have something delicious and a little dangerous to do.

I figure I might as well salt while the coffee's brewing, so I get my coat from the closet in the hall, notice that the broken clock doesn't chime 7:30 and head into the garage for the bag of salt I bought on sale last spring.

I open the garage door, startled by how light it is already, sunlight reflecting off the ice in the trees, on telephone lines, on the sidewalks and even on the street. Someone's shoveled and put sand down in front of the ambulance barn. I open the bag of salt, dip in a coffee can and scoop as close to a full can as I'm able. The driveway's slick enough that my work boots ride on the surface without catching hold, and I take small steps and bend my knees, bracing myself for a fall.

I start spreading salt in wide arcs, first holding the can away from my body and swinging it, then dipping in my fingers and throwing handfuls where the salt hasn't reached. It takes a full can to do the driveway to where the sidewalk meets it, and I walk back slowly, fill the can again.

I've got a rhythm now and less area to cover, and I use back-and-forth motions, my boots crunching salt as I move up the walk to the front door. There are pawprints on the inch of fresh snow on the ground, and I think briefly of Whitey, before deciding it's one of the dogs the neighbors are lazy enough to let run loose.

I stop for a minute when I reach the porch, listening for some kind of movement in the house, or the ticking of the hall clock. I believe I can hear the gutters groaning from the weight of icicles, separating themselves by inches or fractions of inches from the porch roof, the furnace kicking in, wind rattling a cracked storm window, and I think again of cigarettes and stealing time for something private and sinful.

Instead, I step carefully down from the porch and head back to the garage for another can of salt. But even while I'm doing it, digging the can into the salt and turning it upright, so that the salt falls heavily against the bottom, I'm thinking about bad habits and the necesssity of them. And I know that before Sonia is awake, before she finds my pee in the toilet bowl or my coffee cup in the sink, I'll have driven the truck away from here, and when she sees that I'm gone, she'll know exactly where I am.

꙾

I've brought the bag of salt, the coffee can and my gloves, and I tell myself I'm here to do a favor. I park the truck on the street and start at the end of her driveway, walking slowly from side to side. Crows pick at the corn stubble in the fields near the house; I turn away and keep moving, because they always seem to me like some kind of omen.

I'm about halfway up the driveway when Whitey comes running from around the back of the house. He sees me and starts barking, all four legs tensed, muscles jumping, but I call him to me and he recognizes my voice, comes over to sniff the legs of my jeans.

"There, boy," I say. "Good job," and I reach a hand out for him to sniff the fingers of my glove.

I see her then, in the window, and I wave and keep moving, a little faster now, throwing salt in wider arcs. Whitey follows me, sniffing at the edges of the driveway, and with my head lowered, from underneath my eyebrows, I'm watching her, watching me.

By the time I've reached the top of her driveway, she's disappeared, and I stand for a minute, petting Whitey, and think I'll go back to my truck, but then she opens the door and calls him to her by whistling with two fingers between her lips. It's something she learned from her father; it was his way of calling her to dinner whenever she was hiding in the orchard, and I remember how she jumped when she heard it, pulling away from me, wiping the back of her hand across her mouth and pulling dead leaves from the back of her hair.

"Harley," she calls to me, "I'm gonna have to start paying you."

"Better be careful," I say, walking toward her, "it's still pretty slick."

She's wearing her bathrobe, a white terry cloth that reaches to her ankles, but her hair's been blown dry and combed; it falls thick around her face, probably still warm from the dryer.

"Awfully early for a visit." She reties the robe tight around her middle and stands with the ends of the terry cloth belt in her hands.

"I guess you don't get up early to run anymore." I'm still walking toward her, conscious of setting each boot on the ice.

"No," she says. "I'm too busy running after my kids."

Whitey sidles past me and leans against Lynette's legs, so that her robe lifts and I can see an inch of bare leg her slipper socks don't cover. She pats him lightly on the back, runs her fingers backwards through his fur.

"What're you doing here, Harley?" she says softly, scratching her fingers through Whitey's fur, and I keep moving, keep setting one foot and another in her direction. Her eyes are so full, like the eyes of a girl, so brimming with a kind of knowledge only girls understand, and I'm left to stare dumbly at my own feet, propelled in slow motion toward her.

"I'm just..." I say as slowly as I'm walking, "looking out for you."

She nods. "I see that." Her voice is still soft, not like I remember it being; it's kind and generous, the voice of a grown woman with small children.

"I can't ..." I say. "Ever since you brought the dog to me..."

"Yes," she says and frowns. "I probably shouldn't have done that."

"No," I say, "no," and I reach toward her without an exact purpose in mind, so that my hand brushes hers, and I grab hold and pull it from the belt of her robe, holding it with gloved fingers and wishing so much for less clumsiness, for having thought first, so that I might have known enough to take off my gloves.

She lets her hand rest lightly in mine. "Harley," she says, "you don't have to…" and the unfinished sentence drops in air gone suddenly still: no wind, no birds, no plastic flowers fluttering near her mailbox.

"I want to," I say, and just as I'm afraid she might, she pulls her hand away and wraps both arms over the opening of her robe.

"Let me," I say, speaking quickly because I know she's about to walk away from me. "Let me do things for you."

She nods, says, "Okay," and looks down, making eye contact with Whitey and motioning for him to go into the house. "Thank you," she says and reaches a hand to the edge of the door, gently pushing it closed.

꒜

At Amanda's insistence, I enrolled in what were called "career enhancement" classes at the local community college: basic computing 101 and GRE preparation. In basic computing, I sat next to a woman named Angelita who chewed fruity-smelling gum and tapped at her computer keyboard with inch-long fingernails painted to coordinate with her outfit, sometimes with curlicues or stripes.

Angelita let it slip during a coffee break that she'd gotten an A on the midterm, so I kept my C+ a secret. But when she heard me cursing at the computer screen, listening to it beep every time I tried to call up a file, she grabbed me with those long-nailed fingers and suggested I go take a walk down the hall, clear my head. "Some people got the right kind of brain for this stuff," she said, tapping a turquoise nail to her temple. "Some people don't," and she smiled and patted me on the arm before turning back to her screen.

In GRE preparation, I shared a book with a guy named Stephan, who looked like he couldn't afford his own. He wore olive-gray Army-issue T-shirts and the kind of pants that have loops on the sides, for hammers. The T-shirts clung to his sunken chest; he said he'd had an operation to correct a birth defect that made his chest too small for his internal organs. He was twenty-two and, in graduate school, he was planning to study French literature. I didn't have the heart to ask him how he was going to make a living. Stephan was brilliant; he aced the practice tests, despite the fact that he always let me take the book home.

Amanda started taking classes, too; she enrolled in elementary education classes at the nearby university. Her study group sometimes met at our apartment: three fat girls who brought cookies they baked themselves and a guy named Gabriel Harrison Burnwell III, who had a sweaty handshake and said his name, all three parts of it, then smiled and said "Gabe to my friends." He was hairier than anyone I'd ever seen; he had five o'clock shadow by mid-afternoon, and I could see that he had to draw a line with his razor to separate his chest hair from the hair on his neck.

Gabe wore torn jeans and big, bulky sweaters; Amanda said he sold them at college campuses and craft markets. He was also a published poet. After their first meeting at our house, one of the fat girls asked him to recite a poem, and he stood up and started shouting something about love and the moon and some kind of bird that mates for life. I was passing through from the bed to the kitchenette, and he was staring at the ceiling, talking much too loud and too slowly, swaying on his feet and stroking his own sideburns. At the end, the three fat girls broke into spontaneous applause.

Amanda was still a favorite at the daycare center; when she was halfway toward her degree she was promoted to teaching four-year-olds and qualified for health insurance. She was especially liked by the kids for her unusual field trips; she shunned the usual fire station tours and walks to the park in favor of art galleries, where she held the children up one at a time in front of gruesome religious paintings and nudes; potter's studios, where the kids came out covered in clay; and Kabuki theatre productions. At the graduation ceremony/talent show at the end of her fifth year at the center, her class performed a dance called "Trees Sway in the Wind," complete with four-year-olds in homemade kimonos, black wigs and white geisha makeup.

༒

I listen to travel advisories over the radio while heading back into town, and I realize this might work for me as a kind of excuse: I can stop at the hardware store for more salt and the grocery store for bread and milk, and Sonia will think that's where I've been, doing errands because of the weather.

The hardware store parking lot is mostly empty, just a police cruiser and three pickups, two of them with snow-plows on front. I pull into a parking space, feeling the truck shimmy when I touch the brakes. Inside, the older woman at the cash register is ringing up the sheriff's deputy's order: a couple of ice scrapers, a bag of salt, some Juicy Fruit and two snow shovels.

"It's slick out there," he says, "and they say there's another front coming in. Three or four inches." He's a young guy; under his parka his gut is flat, and his uniform shirt stretches tight over the muscles in his chest. He's got a wedding ring on; anybody working as a cop in this town would most likely be married. The guys looking for excitement move to the city straight out of the academy.

"Ooooh, boy," the woman says, stuffing the ice scrapers and gum into a brown paper bag. "That's snow on top of ice."

"Yeah, we're likely to get a mess of accidents," he says.

The woman shakes her head and hands him the paper bag, showing the nametag she wears that says "BEVERLY" in magic marker. "There'd be no reason for it," she says, "if folks didn't drive so crazy."

"Well, you're preaching to the choir," he says, "but there's all kinds of stupidity around."

I grab a bag of rock salt from the display near the door and debate whether to add a new pair of glove liners.

"I suppose so," Beverly says. "You want this on the department account?"

I decide against the glove liners and hoist the rock salt onto the counter.

The deputy nods. "I forget the number," he says.

"Oh, that's all right," she says. "We got a list here somewhere," and she starts rooting around next to the cash register until she pulls up a printed list of numbers and names. "Oh–one–six–oh–seven," she says, typing each number with the index finger of her left hand. The computerized cash register beeps and shows a row of asterisks on the screen.

"Talk about stupid," the deputy says. "We lost a guy ice fishing out on the bluff a few weeks back."

"Right," Beverly says. "I think I heard something about that."

"Any fool knows not to fish out there," he says, picking up the snow shovels in his free right hand and tucking them under his arm. "We post a warning in the paper."

"He have a family?" she asks.

The deputy nods. "The wife was with him. She was pretty banged up herself." He leans close to Beverly and lowers his voice. "We didn't recover the body for over a week. It was an awful mess. He must've cracked his head, falling on the ice." He leans back away from her and repositions the paper bag in his arms. "They had to send him to the city for an autopsy."

"Poor woman," Beverly mutters, fascinated by the gory details. "She got any kids?"

I rest a hand on the counter and tap my fingers, trying to look like a guy in a hurry.

"Couple, I think," he says.

"Three," I say, then clear my throat and say again, "Three kids."

The sheriff glances at me, then looks down at the snow shovels he's holding. "Right," he says quickly. "See you later, Bev."

"Sure, Bill," she says. She looks at me, frowning, then back at the deputy. "Don't forget your salt."

The deputy nods. "I'll come back for it," he says, but after Beverly's added up my order and I've walked out to the parking lot, he's still sitting there in his patrol car.

꒳

Throughout my marriage, I dreamed of Lynette. There were nights when I chased her through the orchard, over ground littered with rotting fruit and leaves, following the sound of her laughter, stumbling over tree roots, my own heartbeat pulsing in my ears. I breathed with my mouth open and thought I could taste apples, and the sound of crickets was a rhythm like the flow of blood in my veins.

And in the dream when I saw her, she was leaning

against a tree, her face in shadow, moonlight falling through the branches above her head and resting unevenly on the hair she had left loose to her shoulders, one sleeve of her T-shirt, the wrist of the hand she held to her hip.

Then she would say something. "Took you long enough" or "Where've you been?" But when I walked toward her, slowly and still breathing hard, I'd look again, and the shadows would have rearranged themselves; she would have melted into the trunk of a tree.

On other nights, the two of us were alone on Gordie's rowboat; the waves were high, slapping against the rim of the boat where my hand rested, and Lynette leaned backward, laughing, her arms open wide and the corsage hanging limply from the front of her dress. And when the boat tipped again, I knew what to do, and I swam easily from under the hull over to where she was dog-paddling, with her hair fanned out in the water, and I pulled her to me, swimming backward toward shore, saving her.

༄

They've got five lanes open at the PriceBuster market, but there are still lines, and there's been a run on batteries and toilet paper. I've got a couple of loaves of bread, a six-pack of beer, milk, ice cream sandwiches, the breakfast dough-nuts Sonia likes, paper towels (in case we run out of toilet paper), orange juice, Cheerios and two bags of Doritos: all the essentials. I start unloading my cart onto the conveyer belt, and Bernie walks up behind me with a 24-pack of toi-let paper, two boxes of low-fat chocolate Pop-Tarts and a *Good Housekeeping* magazine.

"Hey there, stranger," he says, setting his stuff down too

close to mine, so the checkout girl won't know where my groceries end and his start.

"How'd you manage to get toilet paper?"

"You gotta be quick," he says, rocking on his heels.

The woman in front of me takes out her checkbook and starts shifting through her wallet for her pre-approval card.

"How was the date?" I ask Bernie.

"Well," he says, as though considering his answer, "I believe it went fine."

"Just fine?" I ask.

"I can't find my card," the woman says, lowering her voice and leaning over the aisle divider. "Can't I just give you my name?"

The checkout girl, Chloe, looks like she's only trying to earn some prom money with as little hassle as possible. She glances at the line of people waiting to check out. "It's okay," she says, looking over her shoulder to make sure the store manager isn't watching. "Just put your phone number on the check."

"A gentleman doesn't kiss and tell," Bernie says stiffly.

"So you kissed her."

"Well," he says, blushing to the tips of his ears. "I might have."

The woman quickly writes a check, circling the phone number printed below her name. "Thanks," she says, breathlessly. "You're a doll." She nods at Chloe and wheels her card toward the front of the store.

Chloe nods woodenly, looking over toward the service desk, and starts checking through my groceries, moving her arm over the scanner, listening for the beep, while her eyes continue to seek out the store manager.

"Is the magazine for Bernice?" I ask Bernie.

"What?" he asks. "Oh. No."

Chloe passes one of the Doritos bags over the scanner, but it doesn't beep, so she does it again three more times, then lifts it and straightens the section of plastic bag with the UPC code, until the scanner finally beeps.

Bernie clears his throat. "It's for the recipes," he says, pointing to the advertisement on the front for easy winter warm-up foods. "I do my own cooking," he says and lowers his voice. "I'm not half bad."

"Maybe you'll cook for Bernice."

"Oh," he says, frowning. "I don't know if I'm ready for that."

༈

I walk in, and Sonia's on the phone, speaking a halting Russian that tells me she's talking long-distance to her sister in St. Petersburg. At the end of each sentence, she stops and waits for the transatlantic echo to sort itself out. Even with the pauses, she's speaking too quickly for me to pick out what she's saying, only the occasional question about what the weather's like and whether Lena received the package full of clothes.

I find my mother in the kitchen, drying tea cups with a dish towel. "We have a dishwasher, Ma," I say.

"These are old. They're too fragile." The dish towel is already damp, and I doubt she's doing much good with it.

"Sonia puts them in the washer."

"She should know better. I took them out."

"There's a dish rack under the sink. You can let them air out."

"Spots," she says.

"What?"

She turns toward me and sighs. "That's how you get spots."

"Oh." I wonder what would be so bad about spots on the teacups, but decide not to ask and instead put the cups she's already run the dish towel over back in the cupboard.

"Harley," she says, handing me the tea cup she's just dried, "what happened to that dog that was here?" Her voice is quiet, conspiratorial, as if she's afraid it's something we told her but that she's forgotten, and she's trying to hide the memory lapse from Sonia.

"Lynette took him back."

She nods and picks a dripping saucer up from the counter. "The Wilson girl."

"Yes," I say. "Hale now."

"Married?" she asks, and I cringe, thinking: She should know this. I've already told her. I took her to Lynette's house. She saw the bruises on Lynette's face.

"Widowed," I say.

"Oh dear," she says, and hands the saucer to me, jutting her hand out from her side. "That's a shame," she says. "Such a nice girl. Your father and I thought you might end up with her someday."

"Dad liked Amanda."

She laughs a little. "Yes," she says. "For himself." She has trouble reaching the tea cup at the back edge of the counter, and I hand it to her. "But not for you." She holds the tea cup by the tiny handle and wipes the dish towel over it. "He didn't think you were in love with her."

"He should have told me."

She hands me the tea cup and smiles. "It was your life."

I hand her the last saucer, and she takes it from me, briskly wipes it and hands it back, pausing a minute to admire the china pattern. "Does she have children?"

Seconds pass, and I'm not sure what she's talking about, but then I remember that she's asked me about Lynette and the dog. "Three," I say.

"Oh dear," she says again. "I hope she's careful."

"You mean the dog?" I ask.

She nods, smoothing the wet dish towel in her lap. "Animals can be a lot like people that way," she says slowly, staring out the kitchen window, at the snow that's started to fall. "Once they learn fear..."

"I tried to warn her."

"Yes," she says, nodding. "That's something you'd do." She's refolded the wet dish towel, and she hands it to me.

"Harley," she says suddenly. "The Wilson girl had a bruise," she says, pointing to the place on her cheek where Lynette had been hit.

"Yes."

"Well," she says and sighs. "That would explain about the dog."

She backs her wheelchair up and swings it around suddenly, so that I have to jump out of the way of the cast. "I miss him," she says.

I think I'm beginning to understand the logic of this conversation. "The dog?" I ask. "I didn't think you liked dogs."

"Well," she says, wheeling herself out of the kitchen, so that she's talking to me over her shoulder. "It was nice having a warm body in bed."

༃

Sonia walks into the kitchen, twisting the cap closed to a glass peanut butter jar with paint in it. She edges past me and carries the jar to the sink, wiping the sides with a wet paper towel. She doesn't say anything, but sniffs and drops the paper towel in the trash, sniffs again.

"Are you crying?" I ask and touch my hand to her shoulder, pulling her toward me. She doesn't turn, but allows her body to collapse against me.

"No," she says, sniffing. "Not so much."

"I'm sorry I went over there."

"What, Harley?" she asks and turns now, reaching with the side of her hand, still with paint splotches, to wipe the tears on her face. She cocks her head to mimic her not hearing me, and I realize that whatever she's crying about, it's got nothing to do with me.

"I'm sorry you're crying."

"Yes," she says and sighs. "It's my sister," she says. "Lena."

"You talked to her on the phone."

"Yes," Sonia says and lets her forehead rest against my breastbone. "Lena is so unhappy."

"Why? What's wrong?"

"She is so unhappy with Volodya," she says, mumbling into my T-shirt.

"Is she leaving him?" I hold both of her arms and gently push her away, so that she'll lift her head, and I can hear her better.

"No," she says, and glances sideways, toward the window. "She cannot afford it."

"You want to send her money?"

She looks up, into my eyes, and the expression on her face is miserable and supplicating. "It's difficult to send money," she says slowly. "You can't be sure.... Volodya drinks. He loses his job. Lena says he is angry all the time."

"Then what are you asking me?"

"I want..." she says, and her glance shifts sideways again. "I want to bring her."

"Here?"

She nods. "To live," she says, whispering. "With me. With us."

"That would take a lot of money," I say and let go of my grasp on her arms, gently stroking her. "Sonia," I say, "we don't have much money."

"I know, Harley," she says quickly, because she can tell I'm about to refuse her. "I will not be wanting anything else," she says, looking into my eyes. "I promise."

ॐ

"We'll figure something out," I tell Sonia later and touch her on the shoulder.

She's swirling paint in a glass jar, two or three shades of green, and without allowing it to mix completely, she dips in a small piece of sponge and dabs it across a stand of trees. The pattern appears random, but when she unbends her knees and rises up off her heels, stepping back, the lighter colors she's dabbed across a green that's almost black give the effect of light, of a forest lit from overhead.

"Thank you, Harley," she says, facing me. "I know it is so much to ask."

"It's a beautiful painting."

She smiles in a way that suggests she knew I'd say that, whether it was true or not. "It is not finished."

In the places that are penciled in, there's the suggestion of a marina, with boats tied to wooden docks, and, in the foreground, a porch railing covered with morning glory and bougainvillea vines.

"Is that the Hampton Hill Inn?"

She smiles and nods. "You remember?" she asks and slides her eyes toward me in a way that's supposed to be coy.

I pull her to me, so that my nose nestles in the ponytail at the back of her head, which smells vaguely of beer and mayonnaise. She's reminding me of her first week in America, when I took her one Friday afternoon to the Hampton Hill Inn for tea. I wore a tie, and we pretended to be rich people, holding our cups with our pinkies in the air, paying far too much for cucumber sandwiches and petit fours, sitting on the porch and marveling at the view of the hills surrounding the lake. Sonia's hair was longer; it blew at her face, sending tendrils across her mouth and eyes, until she reached behind her head with two hands and tied it in a stiff knot, laughing. She wore a dress she said had been her mother's, which seemed to be made of odd pieces of lace patched together. It was wide at the neck, showing her beautiful throat and a portion of her breasts; when she caught me staring, she laughed and crossed her arms, wagged a finger, and said, lightly, "naughty, naughty."

"To your mother," I said, raising my tea cup, and she laughed again solemnly clinked her cup against it, then turned toward the view, showing the back of her head, where the ends of her hair stood out from the knot like chicken feathers. She sighed, happy, and the lace caps covering her shoulders fluttered in the wind.

"You were so beautiful," I say to her now. "You should paint yourself in the picture."

"And you," she says. "You are so beautiful, too." She walks toward the painting and dabs the sponge one more time, in a corner she's missed, steps back again, moves forward and touches just the corner of the sponge to it.

"Do you know, Harley," she says and turns to me, "this painting is revolutionary?" She drops the sponge on the drop cloth at her feet, bends and picks up a brush with brown paint, swirls it in a jar with clean water. "No happy workers," she says. "No slogans. No propaganda," she says, separating the syllables: prop-a–gan–da.

"Just flowers and boats."

"Yes."

"You like painting flowers and boats," I say, pressing my thumb to a drop of paint at the corner of her mouth.

She nods. "And trees and clouds and sky." She takes the paintbrush from the jar of water, presses it to the front of the sweatshirt she's wearing, picks up a jar of lighter brown paint and begins highlighting the trunks of trees. "I know," she says without looking at me, "it is much to ask for me to be here. I know it is even more for Lena."

"We'll find a way," I say. "It may take time."

Sonia continues drawing a thin line of paint down one side of each tree trunk, then smudging it with a tiny piece of paper towel. "She is my sister. It is my duty to ask."

"It's not too much," I say.

She turns with the paintbrush in one hand and the crumpled piece of paper towel in the other, the hand with the paper towel covered with brown paint. "I am so grate-ful," she says. "Harley, I am in so much gratitude to you."

⌁

I woke up one morning with a head cold Amanda said I got from not taking vitamins and decided to stay home from work. I spent most of the morning sleeping and watching game shows. I guessed within a hundred bucks of the price of Bob Barker's showcase showdown and would have won a cabin cruiser, a set of golf clubs, two sets of matching cruise wear and a three–night stay at a resort in the Bahamas. At 11:30, I called Amanda at the daycare center and asked if she would bring me some orange juice and more bread for toast.

In the afternoon, I watched soap operas I'd never seen before and tried to follow the plot lines. I kept sneezing, my eyes felt like they were floating in mucus, and, by accident, I took twice the recommended dosage of night–time cough syrup, so that for a while I was sure that the rich heiress on one soap opera was secretly having an affair with the illegitimate baby in another. I fell asleep again at about two and didn't wake up until Amanda came home from work.

I heard her banging the cupboard doors and got out of bed, wandered over to her and leaned against her, moved her braids aside and kissed her neck.

"You reek," she said and leaned away from me, left me swaying on my feet.

I looked into her face. "You're crying," I said, though I was having a little trouble focusing my eyes.

She shook her head and sniffed. "You look terrible."

"I'm sick."

"Yeah," she said and sniffed again, "so I gathered."

"Why are you crying?"

She shook her head, said nothing. She reached into a paper bag and handed me a gallon of the organic, pesticide–free, no–sugar–added brand of orange juice.

"I like the kind with extra chemicals," I said, thinking I might cheer her up, but she ignored me, opening a package of paper towels and sliding them onto the plastic holder under the sink.

"It's cheaper," I said, "if you let them leave the pesticides in. This stuff is five bucks a gallon."

"It's better for you," she said and didn't turn around. She sniffed again and squared her shoulders.

"What?" I said. "What is it?" and I walked up behind her,

pulled her to me more roughly than I meant to, because I was squinting in the overhead kitchen light and couldn't measure distances.

"No," she said and let me hold her a minute before pulling away. "Not now."

"What?" I said again weakly, falling into the director's chair closest to the kitchenette.

She looked at me, still deciding whether to answer.

"Tell me." I started to cough and thought about raising my hand to cover my mouth, but decided it was a lot of trouble.

Amanda frowned and looked away.

"Tell me," I said again. Each cough brought a new spasm of head pain.

She waited for me to finish coughing, sighed and looked at my face, then down at the dirty socks I'd pulled on that morning when my feet got cold.

"Gabe loves me," she said softly.

It hurt when I moved my head, so I lifted the sleeve of my T-shirt and gently used it to wipe the sweat off my forehead.

"The poet?"

She nodded and started crying harder. Her mouth twitched; tears ran from the corners of her eyes. I wanted to rise up out of the chair and hold her, but knew I didn't have the energy.

"And you?" My voice was thin and strained from the coughing.

She shook her head, slowly. "I don't know."

But I knew she was lying. Because, even with my head like a block of wood on my shoulders, I knew it had been so long—probably not since my father's funeral—since she'd looked at me with that much sympathy.

ᴢ

THE SNOWPLOW CLEARING THE DRIVEWAY to the ambulance barn beeps when it backs up, and wakes me. Sonia's face is close to mine, buried between the two pillows, her breathing deep and raspy, with a slight snore on the exhale. She mumbles in Russian, something about a boat, says her sister's name and mine and something about ice in the boat.

I find a pair of socks at the foot of the bed, where I kicked them last night when I was too warm. I put them on and stumble to the window, see frost on the windowpane, but where the sky shows, it's cloudless and steel gray.

"Get the baby," Sonia says, louder, but when she burrows under the covers, I know she's still asleep.

It must not be much past seven, but I'm too cold and too much awake to go back to sleep now. I pull on the sweatshirt Sonia's been painting in, see that she's stretched the sleeves where she had them rolled up to her elbows. I go quietly downstairs, listening. She's gone back to snoring and says nothing, and I make it down to the front hall without waking her.

The clock says it's 6:45, which could be accurate within twenty minutes either way. From the picture window, I can see snow on the trees, a few inches of it still smooth and white in the street. On a Sunday, three or four inches of snow is a judgment call; I can shovel it or leave it to melt by itself, but I decide, rubbing my belly, that the shoveling is good exercise, so long as there isn't very much of it, and so long as it's not too heavy and wet.

I pad into the kitchen first and turn on the coffee maker, do a quick slide across the linoleum. It feels gritty through my socks, and I wonder how often Sonia washes it. If I tilt my head, I can make out the tracks of my mother's wheelchair over by the trash can and in front of the sink. I might wash the floor myself, but I decide to shovel first and see how it feels.

I almost miss Whitey on a morning like this, miss the sound that barely registers, of his toenails on the floor, following me. I wonder if it's a comfort to Lynette, the presence of another body in the room, or if her house is so full of the clamor of children that she truly doesn't notice. I wonder if she feels his breath on the back of her legs, nudging her toward the cabinet with dog food in it, or his chin resting on her thigh when she sits at the kitchen table. I wonder if there are quiet moments when she's glad not to be quite so alone.

I pick up one foot and see that my socks are already dirty, curse, try to spend more time on the rug as I pass through the living room again to the front hall. My work boots are in the back of the closet; I have to climb almost completely inside before I find them both, each with an extra sock in it. I decide against the extra socks, put the boots on and leave them unlaced. With any luck, I won't be out long, and the work will keep me warm.

I flip on the porch light before heading outside. The sun's up, and there's enough natural light to see by, but it's less gloomy with a little help. I stand on the porch and sniff; it's a habit I picked up from Whitey, and I can see how he thought this was a good vantage point. I think I can detect moisture in the air, a recent drop in temperature, tree limbs sighing with the added weight of the snow. It's bullshit, I know, but I like the thought, like sorting through the possibilities.

The Sunday paper sits in snow that's drifted across the porch rail. The paper's wet across the front, where there's a photo of some kids scrabbling across a snowdrift at the outlet mall in Canasteo. The photo must be a few weeks old; there haven't been snowdrifts that high in weeks.

There are two sets of footprints on the porch, and I think they must both be the paper boy's, but the second pair leads off to the side, near the painted milk jug Sonia bought months ago at the craft market. The milk jugs come from local dairy farms and are painted up for tourists, usually with flowers or the occasional black cow spots against a white background. To own one locally is a sign of stupidity; folks around here know the dairy farmers give the old, rusted ones away for free, and the going price for them at the craft market is somewhere around forty bucks.

Ours is green and says "Cookson" in white letters, making me wonder if Sonia paid extra for the personal touch. I pick it up; the thing weighs a ton, which is probably why neither one of us bothered to move it before the cold weather came. Behind it is a small box without a lid, and inside are a pair of men's work gloves—the expensive kind lined with Thinsulate—and a pair of work boots, two sizes too big for me. Both have been worn, but not much.

I follow the footsteps down the sidewalk, to the driveway, which I now see has been swept clear and salted within the last couple of hours. There's new snow on top, but not enough to worry about, and a half bag of salt's been left in front of the garage door. The tracks of her truck are still visible in the street, leading from the foot of our driveway and heading out of town.

I know this is some kind of message to me, but I don't have any idea what it is. She could be telling me to leave her alone, she can fend for herself, or she could be telling me she wants to see me. And what if she does? What does she mean by *that*?

৵৲

I knew from the smell of paint in the hall that Amanda had finally left me. She'd told me she could repaint the walls in an afternoon, and that's exactly what she did. I came home from work, and they were brilliant white and clean, as unlived-in as a doctor's waiting room. She'd left while the paint was still wet; what furniture she'd left me—the couch and homemade coffee table, the bed and mattress and one of the director's chairs, but not the dresser she'd painted or the curtains she'd made or the dishes she bought—was piled in the middle of the floor, covered with a flowered sheet. Taped to the sheet was a note that said: "I'm sorry, but he loves me more than you do."

I found the phone and sat on the floor with the receiver in my hand. I thought I would call her and tell her she was wrong, that I loved her as much as anyone. But instead, I just sat there with the dial tone buzzing in my hand, until a recorded voice told me to hang up the phone.

And the amazing thing was this: At the moment of not calling her, I did love her. I loved her more than I'd ever realized. And I was sorry, so sorry for not realizing it sooner: that I loved her enough to let her be happy.

৵৲

Whitey comes trotting around the corner of the house, sees me and hunkers down, growling. I stand frozen with my arms at my sides, the palms of my hands facing toward him. I'm debating whether to shout for Lynette, and he runs toward me a few more steps, stops and hunkers down again. But this time I see the tail wagging. "Hi, boy," I say and hold my hands out, and he comes a little closer and goes through the same routine again.

I remember a game between Whitey and Sonia, when she stood in this yard, shaking his snout, and I think maybe he's trying the same thing with me. I move toward him, and he jumps up, gives a quick, excited bark and hunkers down again. "You don't scare me," I say, my voice unconvincingly boisterous. "You big, bad dog." I hold out my hand and reach blindly for him, feel my hand graze his snout, and he barks again, still wagging.

I feel the need to count all my fingers, so I take my hand out of the glove and wiggle them. Whitey comes toward me and nudges my hand with his snout, so I put the glove back on, grab at his nose and shake it back and forth in front of me. I hold him, but not tightly enough that he couldn't get away, and he growls but doesn't release himself from my grasp.

"Whitey, good boy," she says from the porch. "You caught yourself a prowler." She has on a pair of jeans, a black T-shirt and the green sweater with sunflowers on the pockets. She must have colored her hair; it looks blonder—at least two shades lighter than her eyebrows—and dried out, brittle from the chemicals.

"Don't you ever put this dog on a leash?"

"Well," she says and looks off toward the birds in the fields. "I could tell you he stays in the yard, but I guess you know better."

"He could get killed," I say. "There's traffic on this road."

She looks toward him and nods in the direction of the house. "C'mere," she says, and when he runs to her, she leans down and hooks a finger in his collar.

"So," she says to me. "Did you come here to tell me what a bad dog owner I am?"

"I came to ask what's the big idea. Salting my driveway."

She smiles. "Funny," she says. "I could say the same." With her hip she nudges open the door behind her and gives me the same quick nod toward the house that she gave Whitey a minute ago.

The kids are in the living room, sitting on the floor in their pajamas and playing with Doug's blocks. The baby chews on the sanded corner of one of the smaller squares. Tim uses the back of his hand to smash a tower Matty's built, and Matty leans back as though he's about to slug Tim in the mouth.

"Hey," Lynette says in a voice that's more like a bark, and points her finger. "None of that." Matty sits down, and the baby keeps chewing.

"Okay," she says, leading me into the kitchen, where she pours me a cup of coffee without asking if I want one. It's strong coffee, bitter, and I consider asking for sugar, but decide against it. "I thought I'd return the favor."

"And?"

"And insomnia," she says. "My mom's been coming over early in the morning, after I finally fall asleep. She's afraid I won't hear the kids if they need me. But last night, I didn't fall asleep. And this morning I wanted to get out of the house."

"Okay."

"And I did it to let you know I appreciate the favor, but I don't need the help." She adds two sugar packets she must steal from restaurants to a coffee mug with "World's Greatest Mom" printed on it.

"Yes, you do." I pull a chair out from the table and sit down. The kitchen light is on, and when she sits across from me, the light on her hair turns it white and darkens the shadows under her eyes. "And I told you I want to help."

"Your wife...."

"Sonia's all right."

She sighs. "Okay," she says. "How about this?" She waits for me to make eye contact, raises her eyebrows and says, "It doesn't look good, Harley."

She waits for me to say something, but when I don't, she says, "You know how people are. If anybody still had questions about Doug's death...."

"Who would have questions?"

She shrugs and looks down at her coffee. "They're doing an autopsy. They can't believe he was so stupid."

I consider telling her that it's a little hard to believe, but decide that's something she already knows. While she looks at her coffee, I search her face for bruises; I don't find them, but I remember where they were.

"He was hurting you, wasn't he?"

She smiles and says lightly, so lightly I can't believe it, "It's over."

"I should have helped you. I need to help you."

She leans against the back of her chair, shaking her head. "It's not a good idea, Harley."

"Just tell me what to do."

"Go home," she says. "Help your wife," but when I sit there without moving, just drinking my coffee and staring out her kitchen window, she sighs and says, "Okay. You can help me get rid of his things."

∽

"There's some stuff in the closet that might fit you," Lynette says, walking up the stairs ahead of me. The stairs are carpeted, but her footsteps are heavy, and at the top, she grabs the railing and pulls herself forward, pushing off on it and swinging her body onto the upstairs landing. Walking behind her, I can see that she's wider, that her hips have spread in the way of women with children, but the way she hoists her body around seems to have more to do with attitude than anything else, with a feeling of solidity and weight. "We have to keep the one suit to bury him in, but the one we bought for his brother Donny's wedding might be all right."

"We don't have to do this now," I say, following her onto the landing, where one wall is covered with baby pictures of the kids, Matty and Tim wearing the same outfits in different years, posed in front of backdrops with falling leaves and fake logs or fireplace mantles hung with Christmas stockings. The baby is there, too, posed on Santa's lap, beaming into the camera while Santa's looking the other way, with a finger scratching somewhere under his beard.

"Take whatever you want," she says, leading me into the bedroom and gesturing toward the closet. "Donny's gotten too fat."

The bedroom's unfinished. The drywall on one side is fresh; I can still smell the joint compound. On the other three walls, wallpaper that ranges from pink to dusty brown where it's stained with age and tobacco smoke hangs in strips that someone's started peeling, leaving the torn wallpaper in chunks on the floor.

"I've been working on this room," she says, catching me

staring at the pattern of stains along the wall, the lighter patches where pictures must have been hung, "a little at a time. The paper's pretty well stuck. It's making a mess of my hands," she says, showing them to me, the paper cuts and fingernails turned white with gummed-up glue.

"This is what I do," she says, "when I can't sleep."

I clear my throat, feeling it go dry from the stale air and joint compound. "I could help."

She shakes her head and opens the closet doors, where her sweaters and dresses are crammed next to flannel shirts that must be Doug's. There's a smell of soap or perfume, something like cedar and air freshener where a green plastic disk is stuck to the inside wall. She doesn't seem to notice how intimate this is, my standing in her bedroom and staring at her private things, and I begin to be afraid she'll open the dresser drawers next and offer me his undershorts.

She pulls out a navy blue suit and walks toward me with it, pushes the hanger against my chest to check the size. "I think it's a 44 regular," she says, "but maybe not. That was a few years ago."

"I take a 42," I say.

"Well," she says and continues to press the hanger to my chest, "try it and if it doesn't fit, throw it away or give it to Goodwill." She looks up into my eyes, then she steps back and lets go of the hanger, so that I have to reach out to catch it before it falls to the floor.

"You could just give me everything," I say, "and I could sort through it."

She nods and relaxes the muscles in her shoulders. "You want the shoes, too?"

"Sure," I say, though I know I won't have a use for them. She slides a flattened cardboard box from under the bed and hands it to me, then goes back to the closet and digs in the bottom for Doug's shoes. She pulls out one sneaker at a time, some so worn and creased they're more gray than white, and when I have the box put together, she throws them from the closet directly into the box.

When she's finished with the shoes, she stands up, with her knees cracking, grabs a handful of shirts on hangers and lays them flat across the top of the open box.

I walk over to the box and finger the sleeve of a thermal undershirt. "You don't want any of these?"

She shakes her head. "No."

"When my dad died," I say, "my mother kept some things...."

She sits at the foot of the king-sized bed, the mattress sinking a little with her weight. "No," she says. "I'm letting it all go."

⌇

On the weekends, I avoided the empty apartment by driving to my mother's and working on the house. The two of us dressed in my father's rubber hip waders and raked seaweed we burned in a barrel on the beach. She shaded her face from the heat of the barrel and turned, facing the house.

"This may be too much for me."

"What, Ma?"

"This house." She was staring at the roof, where some more shingles had worked loose from one of the dormers.

"It's not that bad," I said. "I'll help."

She let her hand down and shook her head; her hair was damp near the edges, crowding her face, her eyes red from the smoke. "We thought there'd be more time," she said and smiled, leaning her weight against the rake handle. "We thought we'd grow old here, with grandchildren playing on the beach."

I had taken my shoes off to fit inside my father's rubber boots, and I rocked my feet, feeling the sharp stones underneath. "Ma," I said, "Amanda left me."

She nodded. "I was wondering when you'd tell me."

"You knew?"

"Amanda called me." She bent down and picked up a small piece of beach glass, green, most likely from a beer bottle, and reached inside her hip waders, dropping it into her jacket pocket.

"Why?" I could feel a rush of blood to my head. "Why would she do that?"

"Well," she said, and her voice was quiet, a signal to me that I didn't need to shout, "to say goodbye, I guess." She turned her rake, picking up a clump of seaweed we'd dropped on the beach.

"Did she tell you why she left?"

She straightened, turned the rake over, dumping the seaweed into the burning barrel, and stood with her hand on the rake. "Yes."

"Did you tell her," I said and cleared my throat, covering for the unsteadiness of my voice "she shouldn't have done it? Did you say she shouldn't have left me?"

"No," she said softly, shaking her head.

"No? Why not?"

"Because, Harley...." She used the toe of her boot to pick at something, a piece of bark, and sighed. "It's not for me to say, even if..." She turned the piece of bark over, looking at the worm holes underneath.

"Even if what?"

She sighed again and squinted at the sky. "Even if I knew that was true."

I watched the smoke rise, the cinders snapping over the top of the barrel. "You think she should have left me."

"No, Harley."

The wind had changed, smoke billowed toward the house, and I hoped we hadn't set the barrel too close.

"It's just..." she said and stopped short, bit her lip, as though she was still debating whether or not to say anything.

"Say it, Ma," I said.

"It's just..." she said and sighed. "When two people really love each other, Harley, it's like a light goes on inside." She walked toward me and patted me on the arm, her work glove leaving smudges on my sweatshirt. "With you two, I just never saw the light." She smiled at me, shook her head, then went back to raking seaweed farther up the beach.

⚬

Amanda sent divorce papers to the law office; she must have assumed I'd get legal representation for free. One of the secretaries left the envelope from Kotlowitz & Brown on the chair where I usually sat, and Midge Anderson, the lawyer who did most of the family law cases, attached a Post-it to the outside: "Problem? See me."

I walked over to the appointment book and penciled myself in for an appointment at one o'clock on a Wednesday afternoon. (Midge had taped Post-its to the phones, reminding the secretaries not to schedule appointments between eleven and one, when she took her aerobics classes.)

On Wednesday, I sat in Midge's office, on a leather chair with a rip on the seat, counting the number of files on her desk and trying to remember how many of her clients I'd billed.

She came in red-faced and sweaty and dropped her gym bag on the floor. It was wet along the bottom; she must have set it too close to the shower. "Harley," she said, as if making an announcement. "Troubles, Harley?"

"Divorce."

"Okay," she said and nodded, glancing at the clock she kept turned toward her on the desktop. "We can take care of that."

The secretaries kept forgetting to water her ficus plant; the roots were covered with dead leaves. Midge reached under her desk and untied her gym sneakers, rooted in her bottom desk drawer for her pair of brown pumps and slipped them on.

"I don't think it'll be very complicated," I said, conscious of having to raise my eyes from her shoes to her face. She had a run in her stocking, on the underside of her foot, that disappeared when she slid on her shoes. "We don't own anything."

She smiled, dropping her sneakers on top of her gym bag. "Well," she said, "you never know."

"I don't think she wants anything," I said and laughed and wondered what I should do with my hands, "just out."

She crossed her legs under the desk. "That certainly makes things easier." She was still sweating; I could see it on her forehead.

"We don't have much money," I said. "She makes more than I do. I might have to pay over time." I looked down, at my hands in my lap, saw that the toe of her pump was scuffed. She wore big shoes; her ankles were thin and knobby.

"Well," she said and smiled. "I'll have to speak to my billing clerk about that."

"I could pay a little each week, or you could take it out of my check."

She shook her head and held up a hand for me to be quiet. "We'll figure something out," she said and looked toward the clock again. "But tell me, Harley, is she seeing someone?"

I was surprised by the question and didn't say anything for a minute.

"You said she wanted out," Midge said carefully. "Sometimes that's the reason."

"Not this time," I said. I knew Midge Anderson would want to punish Amanda, and as much as I wished Amanda hadn't cheated, I couldn't bring myself to hurt her. I'd already started to believe I might have been at least partially at fault.

"Okay," she said and smiled, checking the clock and standing up from her desk, "I'll look over the papers and get back to you."

I nodded and walked past her, around the corner of her desk, and she walked me to the door and patted me on the back, the first time I could remember her touching me. "Harley," she said, "I *am* sorry." She held the door open and lifted a lipstick-stained Kleenex from the pocket of her suit, dabbing it across her upper lip. "But you're young," she said. "You'll live."

༄

I pull out the stepladder from against the garage wall and set it up so that I can use it to reach the shelf under the eaves, where we keep the porch furniture in winter. The box with Doug's clothes is heavy, but I manage to lift it over my head and slide it into a back corner, where it will stay hidden. I move quickly and unfold the ladder, put it back where I found it, before Sonia will have a chance to come out and ask me what I'm doing.

There must be men who are good at this, who know how to keep secrets from their wives, who can say hello and smile and kiss their wives on the cheek and all the while know there's something they're not saying. But I'm not one of them, and I don't want to be. I should tell Sonia why I keep going to see Lynette. I should tell her it has to do with the past, with setting things right from the past. I should tell her it has nothing to with her or our life together.

In the kitchen, Sonia's leaning over my mother's wheel-chair, pointing to the instructions on the back of a box of Hamburger Helper.

"What is this, to 'brown the meat'?" she asks.

"In a skillet," my mother says, and when Sonia shakes her head, my mother says sharply, "fry-ing pan."

Sonia nods and carries the box over to the stove, sets a frying pan on top and dumps in the hamburger meat. "How much heat?" she asks my mother.

Mom wheels herself to the stove and adjusts the burner temperatures herself, then points to it and says, "That much."

"Oh, Harley," Sonia says, seeing me in the doorway. Her face is flushed as she walks toward me to kiss me on the cheek. "You can set the plates."

"She means you can set the table," my mother says.

"I know," I tell her, step around the wheelchair to the sink and wash my hands quickly, drying them on a dish-towel, before opening the cupboard where the plates are kept and counting three of them.

"She'll never learn if you don't correct her."

"Her English is good," I say, and Sonia catches my eye and smiles.

"It's not that good," my mother says, stabbing the hamburger meat with the edge of a metal spatula.

I count out the silverware, set it on top of the plates and carry the pile over to the table. Sonia follows me with three glasses, sets them on the table and touches me on the shoulder. "Yes, Harley," she says. "You help me talk correct."

"I like the way you talk," I say, and lean an arm around her waist, pulling her toward me.

"No, truly, Harley," she says and nestles her head under my chin, letting her ear rest against the buttons of my shirt. "You must help me."

"Okay," I say and kiss the top of her head, near the bare skin where her hair is parted. "I will help you speak correctly."

She pulls away from me and nods, frowning. "I will speak correctly," she says.

"When does it say to add the sauce?" my mother asks, pretending not to have heard, watching the hamburger meat sizzle in the pan and turning it with the spatula, so that it will cook evenly.

Sonia walks past me, muttering, "correctly, correctly," to where she's left the box on the counter. She carries it to my mother and points again to the instructions.

I distribute the glasses above and to the right of the plates and take napkins from the lazy Susan in the center of the table, fold them and set them under the forks. Then, while my mother and Sonia are adding the sauce, I walk out to the porch to gather up the box with Doug's gloves and work boots.

On my way past the living room, I stop and admire

Sonia's painting. I can see now the outlines of green hills in the distance, the yellows and blues and pinks of the sky just before sunset, the trees that appear to be swaying in the wind. I don't understand the things about painting that Sonia must know, but I can tell this painting is good. Something about the way it pulls me in, makes me think I'm almost there, sitting on that porch, looking out at the sky, and something about the way she's stopped time, so that the trees are caught swaying, the sky is darkening, the birds are in mid–flight and boats are bobbing on the lake. I'm not sure I realized before now that Sonia is a real artist, not a craft-fair artist or Ramada Inn Starving Artist Sale artist, but someone whose paintings should be in museums. And I wonder if she knows it too, that she's traded St. Petersburg and the Hermitage for a small American town where people will buy her paintings to match their sofa cushions.

Sitting on the edge of the coffee table, I can see Sonia in the kitchen, arguing with my mother over Hamburger Helper, and it crosses my mind for possibly the hundredth time that she could have done better. She was beautiful enough and smart enough and, God knows, talented enough to find someone who could help her become the artist she was meant to be. But instead, she spends her days shopping for Hamburger Helper and washing my mother's pissed–on sheets. And the thing is, she doesn't seem that unhappy about it, which means she must love me, and not just in the Ivan Tsarevitch capturing the fire-bird kind of way, but real love, the kind that makes you look forward to dirty sheets and hamburger meat.

So I start counting dollars in my head, how many we could get for the house, how many it would take for an apartment in New York, how many to live near museums and art galleries, for Sonia. And when the numbers are staggering, I promise myself what I've promised her before, that I'll find a way, I'll figure something out.

But for now, I go to the front door, open it and walk out onto the porch, take the box from behind the painted milk jug and carry it upstairs. I set it in the back of my closet where Sonia won't find it, next to my father's old type-writer with a broken space bar that'll cost me eighty-five bucks to fix, and my mother's old photo albums she gave me before moving into the retirement center. Sitting on the edge of the bed, staring into my closet, I'm still adding numbers, wondering what I have that's worth something, and all I can come up with is a broken clock and a broken typewriter and old photos of nobody knows who. I think: These are the things that clutter my life, the useless arti-facts, and I marvel at Lynette's ability to throw it all away, to simply shove it in a box and be done with it.

It makes me wonder if, after all these years, she even remembers those nights in the orchard, when I held her and breathed in the scent of apples and her hair, and was pretty sure I loved her. I wonder if she wakes at night from a dream of rescuing me in cold water, if she leaves the light on and lies in the dark, waiting for her heartbeat to slow toward sleep, or if, like the box with Doug's belongings, she's decided it's better just to leave all that to me.

༈

After dinner, Sonia and I wash the dishes, then Sonia goes back to her painting. My mother sits in her wheelchair with her headphones on in front of the TV, watching a Biography special about Greta Garbo. I sit for a while, pre-tending to read the paper, watching Sonia shade in the outlines of houses in the foreground of her painting. Her ponytail is loose and slumps against her collar; pieces of it fall forward onto her face, so that she has to nudge them out of the way by leaning her face against her shoulder. I set the paper down and walk over to her, pull the cloth-covered rubber band from her hair, smoothing it with my hands, gather the strands and knot them tightly with the rubber band at the back of her head. The ponytail is so tight now that it sticks straight out from her skull and pulls the skin taut at the sides of her face, but it will hold.

"Thank you, Harley," she says, leans her head back and pretends to kiss me from across the room.

I watch her for a while longer, then go into the other room and pull the phone book from the cupboard where it's kept. I turn to the half page of Christensens and look for the name of my lawyer; there are three Edward Christensens, but only one is a lawyer, and his entry has "attorney" written next to it. Ed once explained to me that the Christensens were all related, though most of them don't know exactly how, and that they believe they're distantly related to the Christiansens and the Christensons, but not the Christiansons. Most of the Christensens are scattered on farms around the southern end of the county. There's a part of County Road 18 that's known to the locals as Christensen Place; it's the site of the original farmhouse of Jebediah Christensen and his wife, who had seventeen children sometime in the early 1800s. "We're the kind of people who stay where we're planted," Ed once told me.

"Lawyer Ed," he says when he answers the phone; he must get an awful lot of wrong numbers.

"Ed," I say, "it's Harley Cookson."

"Harley," he says, "how's the Patterson place?" This is a kind of joke; Sonia and I bought the house six months ago from the Pattersons, who lived in it forty years. He's reminding me that it'll be forty more years before the house is known as the "Cookson place."

"Good," I say, "good. It's gonna need a furnace soon, a roof, gutters, storm windows, some paint…."

"Yep," he says. "So you lucked out with the plumbing, then."

"Yeah, I guess so."

In the background, I can hear the same opera music he plays in his office. He says it's the reason he can't keep a secretary; eventually, they all complain. "But it clears out the noggin," he told me once, tapping his head with the end of his pipe. "I can't seem to put two and two together without it."

"So Ed," I say, "you remember my wife, Sonia?"

"Sure," he says, and I can hear him strike a match close to the mouthpiece of the phone. "Beautiful gal."

"She's got a sister she wants to bring over."

He puffs air through the pipe. "To stay or to visit?"

"Stay."

"Well," he says and puffs again, "immigration's not really my area."

"I just need to know how to get started, what sort of application process there is."

"Yep," he says and coughs, covering the receiver with his hand. "I've got a buddy I might call, see what he knows."

"And Ed," I say, "I need to keep an eye on the money."

"Yeah, no kidding," he says, "with that money pit you just bought." He's joking, of course. Ed's cousin Ritchie did the inspection and said the house was worth more than we paid.

"Right," I say. "Especially after what we shelled out in lawyer's fees."

"Whoa, now," he says. "Don't go talkin' crazy." He sucks on the end of his pipe, then says, "hey, can you carry a tune?"

"What's that?"

"We're doing *Guys & Dolls* this year," he says. "We need gangsters." Ed plays the lead in most of the amateur theater company productions. He's only about five-foot-seven, but he's got a loud singing voice, and what he doesn't have in height, he seems to make up for in stage presence. He was Oberon in *Midsummer Night's Dream* and managed to look kingly, despite the fact that Titania was a full head taller.

"I'm pretty busy, Ed."

"The rehearsals are after work for a couple of weeks, and we usually have pizza and either cookies or dough-nuts."

"I don't really sing."

"Can you move?" he asks. "We need male dancers."

"I don't think so."

"You wouldn't need to audition. I could put in a good word."

"It's not really my thing."

"Okay," he says, "okay. I won't push you. But call me if you change your mind."

᠉

I never had a curfew when I was young, never had to sneak out of my parents' house. My mother knew I stayed out with Lynette sometimes until the early morning; she may have even known, from the grass stains and the smell on my clothes, that we chased each other around the orchard, but she told me she trusted me and kept the porch light on for me, and she believed, so long as I didn't get anybody pregnant, that my personal life was my own business. I don't know if it would have been the same for a girl; I never asked, but she was always kind to Lynette in a distant, formal sort of way, always asked after Lynette's mother and sent a card at Christmas.

So this sneaking out of the house is a new thing, and I tell myself it's normal, that everybody does it at one time or another, and I'm not really doing anything wrong. I stand peeing and listening for Sonia in the other room, and I straighten my sweatpants and T-shirt, glance into the mirror and pull a sweatshirt over the top, still listening, and I'm rehearsing what I would say if she woke up now and asked me where I was going: something about not being able to sleep and needing some time to myself, about moonlight drives and empty roads and the soothing feeling of going nowhere, and the whole time I'm listening, holding my breath to hear her better and hoping to God she doesn't wake up.

I make it out to the garage, raise the door as quickly as I can and start the truck, leave the door up, where hopefully, no one will be tempted by our bicycles or my tools. I back slowly out of the driveway, glance toward the darkened upstairs windows and out to the street.

The roads are empty and mostly clear of snow, and I head through town, past shop windows where a single lamp is lit, to the intersection next to the 24-hour Sunoco station. This is new since I've lived here, and the parking lot is full of high-school kids' rusty pickups and twelve-year-old Chevies. Four girls, dressed almost exactly alike in different shades of the Polarfleece pullovers that have to be ordered from catalogs, Levi's and fashion boots not meant for snow, stand in front of the window, eating the pizza the Sunoco station serves all night long, and a group of Mennonite boys, in thin black jackets and black hats, standing on the pavement with their bicycles leaning against their legs, laugh and joke with each other in their German–English dialect and eye the girls from outside the store.

The light turns green, and I take a left onto the road that skirts the east side of the lake, down to the point. I drive past the country club, closed now for the season, and the agency that rents cottages to tourists for thousands of dollars a week. I remember my father once leafing through a rental guide put out by the Chamber of Commerce, reciting the prices and, after each one, letting out a slow, appreciative whistle. "You see that, Margaret?" he said, "we do live in the richest place on earth."

I turn onto the steep, unpaved road that leads down to the point, step on the emergency brake and leave the lights on. I get out and lean against the truck with the headlights behind me. I don't know what I was expecting, but the light doesn't reach far, and I can't even make out the hole in the ice. I walk around to the passenger side, open the glove compartment and take out the flashlight I keep there, shine it on the ice a second to see if that makes it any better, though I know it won't, and it doesn't.

I zip my jacket up to the neck, check that my gloves are tucked inside the cuffs and take a few steps out, listening for cracking ice, lifting each foot and dropping it squarely down, so that there's less shimmy forward or sideways.

The wind pulls at my jacket, and I think I'm used to the slide of my boots, bending my knees and moving quickly, into the beam of my flashlight. This is real craziness now, not the mild craziness of sneaking out of my own house or showing up at Lynette's, but the kind that could get me killed, and still I half walk and half slide, toward moonlight and the middle of the lake.

I'm about fifty yards out, and I stop with my hands on my knees, breathing the frigid wind that whips and howls over the lake, and take a look over each shoulder, scanning, then stand and turn in each direction.

I see it then, about fifteen yards to my left, and walk carefully toward it, knowing the ice there is weak enough for a man to drown and half afraid I might find something I don't want to see, some kind of gory evidence the police overlooked.

I stop a good ten feet from the edge of the hole and feel my stomach lurch, try to concentrate on my feet, holding steady and keeping me upright. The wind pushes my jacket flat against my gut, and I stare at the hole and wait until I can imagine her there, with her knees bent on the ice, surrounded by fishing poles and nets and blankets and a big thermos full of coffee and bourbon, with the hair whipping around her face and her arms in the water, crying and calling to him.

A person could go numb, I think. With the shock, a person could go completely numb and possibly stay that way. And her numbness wouldn't mean anything. It could mean only that, despite everything, she loved him and lost him in a second, saw him fall and flail and wished, immediately, that she could undo it, that she even reached into the water and prayed to undo it, wanting, despite everything, to have him back again.

And it could mean that God, who saw her true heart, knew better.

I hold the flashlight with the glove that's worked loose from the cuff of my jacket, on the ice that surrounds the hole where he died, watch the light jerk while my hand trembles from the cold, and think maybe, maybe, God sent me instead.

I feel the moon above me and the empty miles of ice and my truck on the shore and my wife sleeping in our bed and stare at that patch of ice and see, or maybe just imagine, the drops of blood where his head must have hit. And I think: This is the place where he must have known, finally, that he was about to get exactly what he deserved.

CHAPTER XV

کو

MY MOTHER CALLED to tell me she was putting
the house on the market. It was past midnight;
the understanding between us was that neither
one of us was sleeping much, and she often called me late
while lying in bed with a cup of cocoa, after she'd been
trying a while. I had turned on the TV halfway through an
old Vincent Price movie, and I lay on the bed drinking
beer and reading *Moby Dick*, leaving the empty bottles on
the nightstand. "If you're not doing anything, you might
come up this weekend and clear some of your things out
of the attic."

"Don't sell the house." Simulated lightning flashed
across the TV screen, and I hoped I wasn't sounding as
drunk as I felt.

"Oh, Harley," she said and sighed into the phone.
"You're not going to be difficult, are you? I just don't think
I have the energy."

"For what? For taking care of the house?"

She must have been trying to cool off her cocoa; her
breath whistled into the phone. "For having this conversation."

"Don't sell the house."

"I've already talked to Larry Burger," she said. "Lake
property's gone up so much, he thinks we'll get twice what
we paid."

"Don't, Ma," I said, leaning my head back against the

window over the bed. The glass was cool, and I let my head rest there, even though I had to strain my neck to talk. "Where would you go?"

"There are some new condos out by the college," she said. "Near the beach. All maintained."

"Full of old people."

"Well," she said and blew again into the phone. "I'm an old person."

"Not yet," I said. I straightened my neck and felt the blood rushing into my face.

"Some of them are younger than I am."

"You don't need that yet."

"Harley," she said. "The house needs things. The roof is going, the stucco's peeling off the north side." I heard crunching; she must be eating the salt-free Saltines the doctor made her buy. "Jim Porter says replacing stucco costs a fortune. They have to blow it on with a big machine."

Vincent twisted the tips of his mustache and gazed meanly into the camera.

"I could help you. I could move in. Share costs."

"Well," she said and paused for a sip of cocoa, "I thought of that. But no."

"What do you mean 'no'?"

She sighed. "You have your own life," she said, and there was more crunching.

"I don't," I said. "Amanda left me, remember?"

She made a "tisk" sound with her tongue behind her teeth. "Yes, Harley, she did," and I could hear the impatient tone in her voice. "That part of your life is over. And now you'll have to start again."

"I could find a job. Pay rent. Fix things."

"No," she said again.

"Why not, Ma?" I righted a beer bottle that the phone cord had knocked over.

"Because it's not a good idea, Harley," she said, and the impatient tone was still there. "You have a life to live, and I have one, too."

"You don't want me there?"

She paused and swallowed again. "No," she said flatly. "I don't."

Vincent walked across a stone courtyard. His shoes had pointy toes; they looked shiny and expensive.

"Harley," she said, and the impatient tone was gone, "it's only a house. You can't cling so much to things."

"It could work," I said. "With the two of us."

"It wouldn't be good for you or for me. Mothers and sons don't live together," she said. "Not at our ages."

I had a picture in my head of myself at four or five, sitting on the stairs to the basement, spying on my father at his workbench. He was whistling, making a table for my mother for Christmas, letting his hand glide across the top of the table leg resting on the lathe. "How could you go," I asked, "after so many years?"

My mother sighed and said gently, "Oh, Harley, that's why." She paused, waiting for me to say something, and when I didn't, she said, "He's long gone now. He'll be just as gone somewhere else." I settled under the covers, pulling the comforter to my chin, and imagined her doing the same, in the bedroom she had shared with him, with his dresser and the ashtray where he kept his change. "There just won't be so many reminders."

"I don't want to forget," I said, and she must have felt my giving in to her, because she breathed her relief.

"If you forget," she said, "ask me." She took a sip of her

cocoa, slurping a little from the rim of the mug. "I'll remind you."

∽

I pass my mother's room on my way to make coffee, and she hears me and calls out.

"What's the matter, Ma? Are you wet?" I reach for the light switch, already wondering how long it will take to clean her up and how late it will make me for work.

"No," she says. "I'm not."

"Are you in pain? You need your pills?" I turn on the lamp next to the bed and start picking up bottles from the nightstand, reading the labels.

"No," she says, as if considering. "No, not yet."

"What is it, Ma? You hungry?"

She tries to sit up, but she's pinned by the weight of the cast and only falls back against the pillows. I reach around behind her and grab her under the armpits, pulling her upright.

"Harley," she says. "I heard noises. I thought someone was breaking in."

"What kind of noises?"

She leans toward me and says, "Like the door. On the garage," and her eyes widen, as if she's afraid.

"No, Ma," I say, fixing a pillow behind her back. "That was me."

"In the middle of the night, Harley?"

I go to the blinds and open them, only wishing the windows were cleaner and would let in more light. "I couldn't sleep. I took a drive."

"Oh," she says and leans back against the pillows, as if

resting from the exertion of lifting her body. "Was Sonia sleeping?"

I think about asking her not to say anything to Sonia, but decide she's less likely to remember if I don't make an issue of it. "I didn't see any reason to wake her."

She nods and squirms a little, adjusting her nightgown. "You must be worried," she says, "about the Wilson girl."

I pour a glass of water from the bottle on her nightstand, open the container with her blood pressure pills, shake one into my palm and hold it out to her. "What makes you say that?"

She takes the pill from me and swallows it, without seeming to remember to take a sip of water. She points to another container of pills. "One of those green ones, too," she says, and when I hand it to her, she swallows it, then gulps from the water glass, so that I can see the muscles jump in her throat. "Because you're not sleeping," she says, wiping her mouth with the cuff of her nightgown.

"Yeah," I say, "maybe."

"Yes," she says and nods, staring toward the grimy windows. "Your father hit me once."

"What?" I ask. "What?" I'm remembering my father, running out of the house and jerking me by the arm during a game of neighborhood football, after I'd tackled Shelly Simonson. "Never," he said, under his breath but furious enough to scare me, "never hit a girl. Never."

"Well," she says and turns her gaze from the window back to me. "It was after a party. We were young." She reaches up and smooths the hair at the crown of her head, patting it flat against her skull. "We'd been drinking."

I sit on the edge of the bed, trying not to jostle the cast, and she touches it with her hand, resting her palm against it.

"One of the husbands..." she says, and pats the cast,

curls her fingers and lightly knocks on it with her knuckles. "Marty Culhane. A real jackass..." but when her voice trails off, she's smiling with the memory of it, "got a little fresh when we were dancing."

I look down at my wrist, turn it a little so I can read the time on my watch. I'm supposed to be at work in half an hour.

She tisks her tongue against her teeth and looks apologetic. "I should never have tried to make your father jealous." Her fingers twitch over the satin strings that tie the nightgown at her throat. "You see, Marty was tall, with wavy hair," she says, lifting her hand over her head to show me how high it reached, "and your father, well, you know your father was never..."

I clear my throat and look again at my watch. "What happened?"

She brings her hand to her throat, winds one of the satin strings around her finger and lets it fall. "Your father didn't say anything. He knew Marty was drunk." She turns toward the window, then back to me, smiling. "I was stupid," she says, "and young. I knew your father loved me. I just had to test him, to find out how much."

"What did you do?"

She smiles, sadly, and drops her hands to her lap. "In the car, on the way home, I said he should have defended me. My honor," she says, and laughs once, to show how stupid it all was.

"What did he say?"

"Nothing," she says and reaches a hand to my face, gently brushes my cheek, feeling the smoothness where it's freshly shaven. "But when we got home, he walked into the house ahead of me and plugged in the coffee," she says, mimicking the gesture with her hand. "And when I said again that he should have punched Marty, that it was what a real man would do, he stepped away from the coffee pot and slapped me hard across the face." She gestures to the side of her face, holds her palm against it.

"What did you do?"

"I stomped off to bed alone, and he slept on the couch," she says, and she lifts her hand again to her throat, to the skin that hangs loose at her neck.

"And in the morning?" I ask.

She smiles. "In the morning, he made breakfast. There were two aspirins next to my coffee."

"What did he say?"

"Oh," she says slowly, as if explaining something to me, "nothing. We went on with our lives."

"He never apologized?"

"He didn't have to," she says, still with that explaining tone of voice. "He made breakfast. I knew he was sorry."

"But he never said so?"

"Harley," she says. "We were both sorry," and she reaches out and pats me again on the cheek. "Your father never hit me again," she says, "and I never told him he wasn't a real man."

⌇

Larry Burger managed to sell the house for more than twice what my parents paid, to a retired doctor and his wife from Long Island. They were going to use it as their "summer place."

My mother talked to lawyer Ed, who urged her to spend the money from the house on a new car or a fancy trip, but he told me later she kept shaking her head, saying, "Ed, you know I've got no use for those things." He did persuade her to make a $10,000 gift to me, which I later used toward the house with Sonia, but even so, most of the profit from the house was sucked up by the state two years later, when she was forced to move into the retirement center.

I asked her once, while I was walking behind her into the retirement center lobby, carrying the box with her night creams, if she regretted the decision to sell the house. She turned, shifting her whole body because of the brace holding her collarbone straight; she had fallen in the tub and had lain there for two hours before someone thought to go and turn off the icy water running in her shower.

"Of course," she said and smiled, patting me on the arm. "It would have been lovely." She let her fingers settle, brushing the nap of my shirt with her thumb. "But it would have been wrong for you, Harley," she said. "You were much too young to get stuck with me."

⁓

I go to pick up my work orders from Bernie's desk and notice the small gold picture frame on top, next to the baseball from his Little League no-hitter and the five-by-seven of Sharon. Inside the frame are two of those black-and-white photos from the booth at the movie theater, where you have to drop in your quarters and wait for the flash, two people crowded in on one stool. In both, half of Bernie's face is out of frame, but Bernice is smiling, with her hair curled around her face and a blouse that's open three buttons from the top.

"Nice pictures," I say and pick up the frame. The photos have been pushed in by hand on a background of blue construction paper, and when I pick the frame up, both of them slide to the bottom.

"Sorry, Bernie," I say, handing it back to him.

"Oh," he says, "that's okay," and he opens the back of the frame and readjusts the photos. "Happens all the time."

I pick up the work orders and start sorting them by geography. "So things are going pretty good," I say, "with you two."

"Yeah," he says and picks up the frame, carefully laying it on its back, so the photos won't shift around. "She was shy. She didn't want to have her picture taken," he says, smiling, "but I talked her into it."

"Bernie," I say, "Bernice doesn't strike me as shy."

He dusts off the picture frame, wiping his pinkie across it, and sets it back on his desk. "Well," he says, "it's a different kind of shy."

I decide on the orders I can finish in a day and set the rest in his basket. "Have you told her about Sharon?"

Bernie picks up the five-by-seven of Sharon in her wedding gown, standing with her back to the camera, ready to throw the bouquet over her shoulder. Her head is turned, she's flushed and beaming; through the veil, I can see her bare shoulders and a long row of white buttons. "Sure," he says and pulls a handkerchief from his back pocket, wipes it over the glass. "It's only fair."

"Fair?"

He nods, stuffing the handkerchief back into his pocket. "It'd be a lot to live up to," he says, "for any woman."

"Yeah," I say. "I guess so." I rearrange the orders in my hand, match the corners together and tap them on his desk, so they line up.

Bernie smiles suddenly. "But I told her I didn't think Sharon would mind," he says, still gazing at the photo, "my dating."

"Well," I say, noticing my boot prints on the floor in front of his desk, "it's been a few years."

"Yeah," he says and smiles again. "She would have wanted to pick out the woman, though."

"Oh yeah?"

He laughs. "Sure," he says. "Geez. You kidding? She wouldn't even let me pick out a tie."

↪

For months, my mother pretended she was just passing through, that her stay at the retirement center wasn't permanent. She avoided the nightly sing-a-longs and slide shows of other people's children's vacations, and she ate at a table by herself with a book, usually something literary, Thomas Hardy or Henry James, something other people wouldn't stop and ask questions about.

She sat in her room, alone and overdressed, listening to classical music from the radio on her nightstand and writing chatty letters to relatives, avoiding the subjects of my divorce and where she was living, using the condo as her return address. She wore wool pants and silk blouses, knee-high stockings and pumps she could barely squeeze her swollen feet into, and each weekend, when I drove up to see her, she handed me a pile of clothes for the dry cleaner and gave me instructions about spot-cleaning and starch. Then, for a few weeks after one of her silk blouses ended up in the retirement center laundry and was ruined, she asked me to stop at the laundromat in town and give all her clothes to the woman at the counter, who for three dollars a load, would separate, clean, press and fold them.

She had written her name in her clothing, the matching suits with what I knew she called an Eisenhower jacket, cut short at the waist, the silk blouses and the pumps in different colors. Even her underwear had her writing in black fabric marker on the tags, and I knew what this had cost her, the invasion of her privacy that having strangers reading her name in her bras and panties would be.

She carried it off for a while. Many of the residents assumed she was a visitor, stopping by on her way to somewhere more glamorous to visit a sick neighbor or friend. But then, gradually, it was too painful to shove her swollen feet into matching pumps, and the pantyhose were too binding, even over a girdle. She resorted to elastic-waisted jeans and plaid canvas sneakers, the kind of sweatshirts with flowers stenciled on them that were sold at the Mennonite craft market. She still wore makeup and asked me to bring her favorite, expensive night cream, but she had her hair done at the beauty parlor next to the downstairs lobby, where the order of the day was a too-tight perm that left burn marks around her hairline and made her almost indistinguishable from the other old women in polyester pantsuits or housedresses that zipped up the front.

She had her nails done by the students from the community college who came to the retirement center as part of their cosmetology training, and the seventeen- and eighteen-year-olds chose garish colors, bright red or orange, something called "passion pink" and once, a dark purple that made her fingertips look bruised. It was a shock to see her that way. Until then, I don't think I'd ever thought of her as old. She was older than my friends' parents, but she had never seemed old to me, certainly not the old woman she was now.

Her collarbone was slow to heal, and she winced whenever she moved suddenly; the doctor said her bones were fragile and prescribed hours on the retirement center patio, sitting in the sun, calcium supplements and ten laps a day around the building's carpeted corridors. But even so, the doctor said there were sure to be more breaks, and without someone to watch her constantly, she was better off in the center than she would ever be in a condo by herself.

After three months, when my mother was still wearing the brace that kept her collarbone straight, she gradually dropped the subject of moving back to her condo, and another month later, when the lease on the condo expired, she asked me to go and move her things into storage.

"Keep what you want, Harley," she said. "It'll be no good to me here." She craned her head, making sure the door-way to her room was closed. "You can't keep anything nice," she said. "Some of them *steal*."

After that, she started reading romance novels and joined a bridge club that met every Tuesday in the com-munity room. The eight of them played for pocket change "to add excitement," she said, rolling her eyes. She went on bus trips to Toronto, where she bought postcards she left blank and simply handed to me when she returned, and she waited each week for the woman who owned the ladies boutique to come and sell her more of the silk blouses and wool pantsuits she'd never wear again.

"It's not so terrible," she said to me one day, after the two of us had lunch in the cafeteria and she caught me staring at a man with black sunglasses that wrapped all the way around his head, who was winding his way among the cafeteria tables, tapping with his cane, until an old woman reached out and literally pulled him into a chair. "They haven't all lost their minds," she said, jabbing her thumb in the direction of a woman with some form of dementia, who sang "Don't Worry, Be Happy" over and over, ignoring the song on the radio. "But I miss my things, Harley," she said. "Didn't I used to have lovely things?"

～

My usual supply truck's in the shop; I've got to use a backup and cross an old cabbage field to replace a line on the north end of town. The wind's died down and the air's warmed up a little, and my boots sink an inch into the soil, so that I think I can smell what's left of the cabbage that ripened in the fall. The job goes quickly, and I turn back the cuff of my jacket, checking my watch; it's 5:30, and, after I climb down from the pole and head back to the truck, I call Bernie and tell him I'm done for the day, then I call Sonia and tell her I'll be a while longer.

I head north out of town with the supply truck; we're supposed to keep track of mileage, but Bernie never checks it, just shoves the mileage sheets in the bottom drawer of the file cabinet, in a stack that's been there so long that it's turned yellow around the edges. The truck rumbles and heaves, and the spring in the seat jabs me in the ass, but I'm too lazy to head back the other way for my pickup, so I take country roads, cutting past abandoned produce stands and Mennonite farmhouses, to the entrance to the thruway, where I have to open the door and lean out of the truck to grab the ticket, because the driver's side window doesn't roll down.

The sky's turned dusky already, and I drive the speed limit, checking the sides of the road for deer. The mall is three exits up—at least I always think of north as up—and I stay in the right-hand lane, behind a heating-and-cooling truck, and let my mind drift, thinking of Sonia at her painting, my mother nodding off in front of the TV, Lynette making dinner for her kids and Bernie stopping at the bar for pizza and a glimpse of his girlfriend. I wonder if I were with any one of them now, would I be thinking about the others? If I were with Sonia now, would I be thinking about Lynette, or if I were with Lynette, sitting at the table with her kids, listening to her daughter smack her fist against the metal tray of her highchair, would I be thinking of Sonia? When is it enough to be in one place at one time and not be thinking or worrying about something else?

I see my exit and slow down, turn on my blinker and drift toward the off–ramp, the truck rattling over patches of ice the plow missed. I open the drawer on the dashboard that holds an ashtray with somebody's loose change and sift through it for quarters, pull close enough to the toll booth to hand over the change, but far away enough to get the door open. The toll booth collector is a guy maybe ten years older than I am, with a tattoo of an eagle on his hands, the tips of the wings spreading up to his pinkie and index finger. He takes my change without seeming to look at it or count it, just nods slightly, and I pull away, toward the sign that points to the mall.

It's dinnertime and the mall is quiet, just a few cars with parents parked next to the entrance, waiting for teenagers. I park on the far end, next to the department store, and on my way inside I open my wallet and check for cash. I didn't plan on doing this tonight, and I've only got thirty bucks, but I find the department store credit card in one of the plastic holders where I keep pictures of Sonia. It's in the bottom holder, cracked from age and being sat on, but I hope it's still good and I can use it without any hassle.

I remember this much: that Sonia's an eight, and I find a salesgirl in women's coats and ask her to help me. She's sitting on a stool behind the cash register, and when she slides down, it makes a squeaking noise against her leather miniskirt. She looks embarrassed but decides to ignore it, and I follow her over to a rack of coats.

"Is this for your wife?" she asks adjusting her sweater where it's lifted over the waistband of her skirt.

"Yes," I say. "She's an eight," and already I'm staring at the rack of coats, knowing this is about to get more complicated if she asks me to choose a color or style.

"Eight regular or eight petite?" she asks, and when I don't answer right away, letting my eyes wander over to the sign on the wall announcing dresses and formalwear, she adds, "Is she taller than five-four?"

I nod, and she says, "Okay. Eight regular," and chooses a dark green coat with a wide collar, pushing the coats next to it aside by shoving with all her weight. "This is a nice one," she says, standing and waiting for me to show some kind of approval. "A shawl collar," she says, and I'm staring at the nametag that says "Monica" and guessing that she wears a petite.

"Too much, I think," I say, waving a hand near where the collar would be if I were wearing the coat myself. "She's pretty small," I say, and Monica nods officiously and stands back, staring at the rack, before choosing another one, again shoving the others aside with all her weight.

"How about red?" she asks, showing me one that's double-breasted with buttons almost down to the floor. While she waits for a response, she stares at my feet, at the boots leaving dirt tracks on carpeting she'll have to vacuum.

"I don't know," I say. "There sure are a lot of buttons," and she nods again and pushes the coats back together, so that the rack is a complete circle.

"Well," she says and sighs before turning back toward me, "maybe you should take some time and choose something you like." She points with a red-painted fingernail to the stool where she was sitting before. "I'll be over there," she says, "if you need me," and she bows her head slightly and hurries back to her stool, where she sits staring at the front entrance of the store.

There are five more racks with coats on them, and even though some of them are short—like what my mother called a "car coat"—I could be here a while. I decide to stick close to what Sonia already has, and so I limit myself to gray or black, with a fur collar and a medium number of buttons.

Monica makes a phone call, mumbling into the receiver and looping the phone cord around her fingers. When I come to the desk with my choice, a dark gray with a fur collar and gold buttons I'm not exactly sure about, she says, "Hold on a minute, okay?" and sets the receiver down, lifting the coat over the top of the desk.

"What do you think about those buttons?" I ask, noticing for the first time that they have lion faces on them.

Monica holds a button between her fingers and takes a quick look. "Sure," she says. "Fine."

"They've got lions on them," I say. "I don't know about those lions."

Monica picks up the phone and says into the receiver, "Hold on, okay?" then sets it down and looks at me. "Well," she says, "I don't think they're so bad." She reaches under the desk for a huge shopping bag and starts folding the coat into thirds. "If you keep the receipt," she says, "your wife can always return it."

I nod and she stuffs the coat into the bag, which even I know will wrinkle it. I hand her my credit card, and she looks at it, fingering the crack, and says, "Charge?"

I nod again, and she picks up the phone and says, "I

have to hang up. For a charge." Then she hangs up the phone and passes my card through the machine, swiping it three or four times until it beeps, waiting for the machine to dial the phone and tapping her nails on the desk.

"You should get a new card," she says. "This one's toast."

The machine beeps again, and the cash register spits out a receipt I sign and hand back to her. Then she gives me a copy and smiles. "Good luck," she says, handing me the shopping bag. "I hope she likes it," and then, almost as an afterthought, while I'm walking away from her toward the entrance, she says, calling to me across the store, "Tell her she can return it. So long as she keeps the receipt."

෴

About three years after Midge Anderson finalized our divorce, Amanda sent me an invitation to her wedding to Gabriel Harrison Burnwell III. She had made the invitations herself; in the same calligraphy that announced the wedding would be held in a small chapel near Waneta Lake, she added to the bottom: "I really hope you can come." I had talked to her only a handful of times since we split; we divided our books and records and what little money we had without any real hassle, and Midge Anderson charged me only for the cost of filing the papers. The last time I'd talked to Amanda was about a year before, when I'd gotten drunk and called demanding my Springsteen album. She hung up on me that night, but then about a week later I got it in the mail, in a padded envelope with "fragile" written on the side.

I checked the box marked "respectfully declines" and added a small note to the bottom. It said: "Be happy."

✌

I stash Sonia's birthday present under the eaves of the garage, next to the box with Doug's clothes. I have to jam the box against the far wall; with any more secrets, I'll have to find more hiding places.

Sonia presses the button for the microwave when she sees me walk in the door. My mother's already eating, with leftover Hamburger Helper smeared across her lower lip.

"Harley," Sonia says and kisses me, pulling me toward her and pressing against me, "thank you so much."

"For what?" I wonder for a second if she hasn't already caught sight of the coat.

My mother waves from the table and wipes her mouth with a napkin.

"Lawyer Ed tells me he will send some papers." The microwave beeps and she opens the door, uncovers the Saran Wrap from over my leftover Hamburger Helper, stirs it with a fork and puts it back inside, pressing the button for another two minutes. "For Lena."

"That's good," I say and pour myself a glass of milk, "but Sonia, we don't know what the papers will say."

"I know," she says and hands me a paper towel for the milk I've spilled on the counter, "but Harley, I am so happy."

The microwave goes off again, and she uses pot holders to pull out the plate with Hamburger Helper and stands in front of me, waiting for me to get more pot holders out of the drawer and take the plate from her.

"It could take time, Sonia," I say. "Years. And we don't know what the cost might be."

She hands me the plate and picks up my glass of milk, walks with it over to the table and sets it down in front of my usual place. "But Lena will wait," she says. "She is happy waiting."

"I already told her all that," my mother says. "You're wasting your breath."

I run my fork through the Hamburger Helper, waiting for the steam to escape. Sonia cooks things too long; some of the pasta will be crunchy.

"And Harley," Sonia says, sitting with a glass of water, watching me eat, "I tell Lawyer Ed I will paint scenes for him."

She reaches out and touches the back of my hand. "And maybe he will cut the cost." She makes scissoring motions with her hands, showing me how Lawyer Ed will help us.

༄

I made the decision to move back to my hometown while sitting in the laundromat, waiting for my socks and under-wear to dry and doing the Jumble from a three-month-old newspaper. I figured since I was spending every weekend visiting my mother, I might as well save the gas money and move back to town. My mother was still using the condo as her return address; it was her own fault that no one else came to visit her at the retirement center. But I couldn't stand to think of her in that tiny room alone, so I ripped down the four handwritten apartment ads tacked to the laundromat bulletin board, counted out the change in my coffee can and decided I had enough left over to make a few phone calls.

The third phone number belonged to Bernie's brother's sister-in-law, Margie; she ran a boarding house of sorts on the second and third floors of her huge Victorian on Stiles Road and said she didn't believe in leases. "When a rela-tionship ends," she said, "it ends." She coughed into the phone and told me she was thinking of giving up smoking but said she'd just started on a new diet, "And you can't do both at the same time." Then she said, "Besides, people are gonna leave, lease or no lease, and I don't have the energy to go tracking 'em down."

I explained that I was heading out of town, but that I'd be back the next weekend, and she said, "Well, you'll want to be settled before then," and suggested I stop by on my way to the thruway. "I've got two packages of Weight Watchers spaghetti," she said. "If you close your eyes and use your imagination, it's not all that bad."

I stopped at her house at around 5:30, after folding my laundry in the back seat of the car. Margie opened the screen door and held it open with one arm, laughing at me tripping over the concrete gnomes in her garden.

She wasn't as fat as I'd expected from the talk about Weight Watchers; she was probably only trying to lose twenty or thirty pounds, but she smoked constantly, and I tried not to notice when ashes fell into my packet of diet spaghetti. She stirred the two packages and stuck them into the microwave for another couple of minutes. "You can have the top floor for three hundred. It's got its own shower," she said, unsticking a plastic placemat from the middle of the kitchen table and setting it down next to her own. She pulled two napkins from the brown plastic dispenser shaped like a teapot, folded them in half and set one at each place. "The smaller rooms are two hundred, but you've got to share a bathroom with the Chinese nurses."

"Chinese nurses?"

She nodded and pulled two green drinking glasses off the counter and set them in front of our places. "The nursing school at the college." The microwave beeped, and she pulled out the packets of spaghetti, carried them in a rush to the table because they were hot and set them down without plates. "They live here because they're saving money to send home." She opened her packet and set the lid face-down on the table, then picked up a salt shaker and sprinkled her spaghetti liberally. "Some people don't mind the way they talk," she said and suddenly mimicked the singsong pattern of Chinese, scrunching up her face and making long neee-yaaaa sounds at the back of her throat. "But if I were you I'd save myself the headache and live upstairs."

I finished my spaghetti, cutting it into pieces with the side of my fork and spooning the sauce back on top of the noodles. Margie kept the cigarette in her left hand while she ate, eating one-handed with the fork in her right.

"So," she said impatiently, after I'd eaten my spaghetti but before I'd finished my coffee, "you'll want to see the room."

I followed her upstairs, then over to another flight of rickety stairs at the end of the hall. These led to a large open space with two electric heaters at either end and a ceiling fan in the rafters.

"In summer, I won't lie to you, it's a little warm," Margie said. "But there's an air conditioner you can stick in the window, and I don't charge for utilities, so you can keep it on all night if you want.

"Rent's due the first of the month," she said, pulling the cord to the ceiling fan, so that it came on full blast and kicked up dust along the floor, which somebody had painted mint green. "I don't mind if it's a couple of days late, but no more than that," she said, wagging a finger at me.

"Don't worry."

She smiled and walked over to a door built under one of the eaves, opening it. "I'll confess," she said. "It's not so much that I need the money. My husband left me pretty well off."

She held the door and waited for me to walk through, dropping ashes on the wooden floorboards. Inside was a bathroom that must have been handmade, with rough pine planks surrounding the fiberglass shower stall, a chipped mint green toilet, free-standing sink and walls that stopped a few feet short of the ceiling. "It's more the principle of the thing."

"Three hundred?" I asked, signaling that I was ready to leave the bathroom. With the two of us standing in there, I was already a little claustrophobic.

"Yup," Margie said and waited for me under the ceiling fan while I took another look around.

"Okay," I said, "I'll take it," not so much, I think, because I wanted to live there, but because I was tired and it seemed like the easiest thing to do.

"Good," Margie said. "Move in whenever you want." She turned the ceiling fan off and walked toward the stairs. "I had a feeling about you," she said, "from the phone." She walked down the stairs ahead of me, with her cigarette smoke drifting toward my face. "You've got a nice voice. Not a nice voice like a nice-sounding voice, but a nice voice like the voice of a nice person."

She waited at the bottom until I walked past her and switched off the lights. "My husband," she said, "had a voice like that," and she stood in front of me, smiling, and patted me gently on the arm.

꒰꒱

"Mama is good," Sonia says, sitting on the edge of the bed and pulling off her shoes, "with the pills." She takes the shoes in her hands and slides them, one at a time, under her dresser without getting up from the bed. "She is not so much sad."

"Good." I have "Nick at Nite" on mute; Elizabeth Montgomery is talking to a horse, which may or may not be her husband. "If she starts feeling better, maybe she won't need them."

Sonia stands, frowning at me, and takes off her pants, holding them in her hand. "No, Harley. The doctor says always." Her underwear is pink with flowers; there's an old bloodstain in back, long since washed and bleached a dull brown. She turns and sets her pants on top of her dresser, pulls her sweater over her head.

"That can't be good for her," I say, watching as the static in her hair makes it lift in back, fluttering near her head. "Pills like that can make you addicted."

She looks at me, then turns away again and unhooks her bra. She changes in front of me, shyly, like a girl, and I like the show of it, the brief glimpse of breast before she pulls a nightgown from her drawer and lifts her arms into it.

She turns toward me. "Harley," she says, "you are worried she will be addicted?"

"It's not good for anyone." Elizabeth Montgomery argues with her mother by shouting at the ceiling of her living room. "I'm supposed to look after her."

Sonia pulls back the covers and smooths the bottom sheet with her hands before climbing into the bed. She sets her two pillows flat, a sign to me that she doesn't want to watch television. "She's an old woman, Harley," she says. "If she is addicted..." She shrugs and lets the sentence drop, signaling it's no big deal.

I push back the covers and turn off the TV as Elizabeth Montgomery pleads with her mother, who's wearing too much eye shadow. "I don't want her jacked up on happy pills." The picture tube on the TV is going, and the screen is slow to blacken, with a flicker of blue in the center. "I want her to be the way she is."

"You don't want Mama to be happy?" she asks, pulling back the covers for me.

"I don't want her medicated." I get into bed, wipe a Kleenex over the glass globe of my nightstand lamp, dusting it, and turn it off. Lying on my back, I watch the darkness settle, feel Sonia breathing next to me. "I need her the way she's always been."

"Harley," she says and shifts toward me, settling her breasts against my arm, hooking her leg over mine. "She is an old woman." Her hand hovers over the waistband of my sweatpants, and her toes curl under the elastic near my ankles. "She is sad for the past." She slides her foot up my leg, pulling the sweatpants with her, and rests her hand on my groin. "Let her be happy, Harley," she says. "Let her have this happiness."

᠔

The garage door slides up easily. It's snowing lightly, flurries drifting onto the wet driveway, where they disappear immediately, melting on the pavement. I start the truck, check the clock on the dashboard, which tells me it's past midnight, back into the driveway. I fell asleep dreaming of the coat I bought for Sonia, and the thought that woke me, that made me get out of bed and go downstairs and put my coat on and walk outside to the truck was that I could have bought one for Lynette. Or I could give her money for one. Wind catches the neighbor's screen door, making it bang against the frame, the truck engine rattles and ticks, and I wonder if Lynette would accept an envelope with money, or if I'd have to leave it on her porch or send it through the mail. With a few nice things, she could still be a handsome woman. She could lose the hollow look around her eyes, the puffy, ready-to-bruise texture of her skin.

I wonder if she's sleeping. I can imagine her there, under the quilt with a hole where the stuffing leaks, in that room that looks like it's molting, the walls covered with shredded wallpaper. She would have pulled the baby crib close to the bed, close enough so that if the baby woke, she could reach out in her sleep and rock it over bare floorboards. In half-darkness, her hair and skin would be smooth and washed of color. Her arm with the cast would be curled to her body, and she would be warm under the quilt, and perfectly still, and dreaming.

With ten dollars a week from my paycheck, I could change her life. A few months without beer or Big Macs, and I could buy her a coat that would be a symbol of her new life and of the ragged, dirty, misshapen life she'd left behind. And who, seeing her in the new coat, one that wouldn't make her look older and fatter and uglier than she is, could blame me for wanting to do it? Who could blame me for doing something so charitable?

And if helping her helps me, if it makes me feel a little better about seeing bruises on her legs and on her face and doing nothing about it, then who's to say there's anything wrong with that?

I back the truck into the street, turn in the direction of Temperance Road. But then something stops me from driving to her house. It's the thought that she might be sleeping, and I might wake her from her dream—or maybe it's the thought that she might not be sleeping, and she might wake me from mine.

CHAPTER XVI

"HEY, BERNIE," I say, pulling off my gloves so I can wrap my fingers around the mug of coffee I poured on the way in, "your message light's blinking."

"What?" he asks, setting his coffee down on a pile of truck maintenance reports. He must have just pulled off his knit cap; static makes the hair in front stand at attention. He glances at the phone and says, "Damn. I can never remember the code for that damn thing," sets the cigar he holds between his fingers in the ash tray on his desk and starts rummaging for the manual to the phone system.

I shuffle through work orders while he flips pages, muttering, "Message announcements, message sending, message retrieving," stops at the right page and runs his finger down the middle, creasing the binding so the manual will lie flat. "To retrieve a message sent to you, press star seven two." He looks at me, picks up his cigar and says again, "Star seven two."

"Are these all for today?" I ask, holding up the work orders, and he waves at me to be quiet.

"Star seven two," he says and jabs at the phone buttons with his fingers, then he looks at me still holding up the work orders and shakes his head. "Do the ones on top first," he says, moving his lips around the cigar in his mouth.

The phone clicks and I can hear Bernice's voice through the receiver. I can't make out the words, but Bernie smiles and at the end of the message, holds out the receiver without hanging up. "How do you keep it from getting erased?"

I pick up the phone manual and scan down to the section on saving messages. "Hit the number sign."

He jabs a finger at the number sign and hangs up. "She said something kinda funny," he says. "I wanted to remember."

I nod and leaf through the work orders. "Top ones first?"

"Yup." He taps ash from the cigar, sees that one of the secretaries is headed in our direction, and slides the ash tray with the cigar in his desk drawer. "Hey," he says, "what are you guys doing for dinner?"

I pick out a couple of orders on the south end of town and set the rest back in his "in" basket. "I don't know," I say, "leftovers?"

"I'm cooking," he says, "for Bernice. Stroganoff." He waits for the secretary—Denise? Clarice?—to pass before opening his desk drawer and taking out the cigar. "I got plenty," he says. "You guys want to come over?"

"We can't really leave my mom."

He nods. "Bring her over." He puffs on the cigar, blowing smoke toward the sliver of open window behind him.

"It's tough," I say, "with the wheelchair."

He nods again. "Okay," he says. "It's just, I thought it'd be nice to have other people."

"You two aren't getting along?"

He looks surprised. "Oh no," he says. "We get along great. I just wanted her to see I've got friends." He glances at the photo of Bernice and him on his desk. "You know," he says, "I wanted her to see I'm a stand-up guy."

"You could bring her to our house," I say, already wondering what I'll tell Sonia on the phone.

Bernie puffs on his cigar, turning toward the window.

"Well," he says and nods. "Sure. That might work." He turns back to face me, holding the cigar below the desktop, where the secretaries won't see it. "But I'm cooking," he says. "I'll bring the stuff over and cook before she gets there."

"Let me call Sonia," I say.

"Sure," he says, "good idea. Call the little missus." He takes a sip of coffee with his left hand, still hiding the cigar with his right. "Hey," he says. "She's gonna love Bernice." He sets the mug back down, where it's left a brown stain on the maintenance reports. "Bernice is just crazy for foreigners."

ॐ

I sat in Margie's kitchen, drinking coffee and watching the rings the coffee mug made in her plastic placemats slowly disappear every time I lifted the mug to my lips, while she smoked and talked about food. "Coffee cake with swirled frosting," she said, inhaling deeply and turning to blow the smoke over her shoulder. "Chocolate brownies with walnuts, hot from the pan. Cheesecake with raspberry sauce. Butterscotch sundaes." She exhaled again and looked me in the eye. "That's what I want," she said, jabbing her cigarette in my direction. "And I don't even like butterscotch."

"I need a job."

She nodded and inhaled, turning the tip of her cigarette fiery. "I took up smoking, because they say it makes you eat less," she said, holding the smoke in her mouth before letting it go over her shoulder. "Total bullshit," she said, making a cutting motion with her cigarette. "Now I'm gonna die young and fat."

I finished my coffee and sat picking at the peeling goose decal on the side of the mug. "You know of anything?" I asked. "Jobs?"

She nodded. "Talk to Bernie. My brother's wife's brother." She got up from the table suddenly and took the
mug from me, set it in the sink and turned on the faucet.
"He works at the telephone company. They always need
people. I could call him for you."

"Doing what?"

She turned off the water and leaned against the sink.
"What's that?"

"What does he do there?"

She thought for a minute, letting her eyes drift up
toward the ceiling. "Come to think of it," she said, "I'm not
sure. Something to do with phones."

"Well," I said, pushing my chair back from the table. "I'll
take anything. I need a job."

She nodded and watched her smoke drift toward the
hanging light fixture over the table, with a shade that had
started out white and gone gradually tan and sticky with
tar. "What I need," she said, "is food. Or maybe sex." She
turned and stubbed out her cigarette in the sink, then ran
the water to flush it down the drain. "Possibly both."

"How long ago did your husband die?"

"What?" she asked, turning from the sink. "Oh. No. He
didn't."

"You said he left you pretty well off. I thought..."

"No," she said and laughed, shaking her head. "Gary's
alive and well, living in Boca Raton with his partner, Gerald."

"Partner?" I asked, getting up from the table.

"Business," she said, "and otherwise."

I pushed my chair in, wiped my napkin over a wet spot
on the place mat. "Wow. I'm sorry."

"Yeah, well," she said and shrugged. "You live and learn,
right?"

⟶

"Bernie," Sonia says, holding the door open for him. "Good to meet you." She's met Bernie maybe eight or ten times; she means "good to see you," but Bernie doesn't seem to notice. He hands her a bag of groceries and stands shaking snow off his boots onto the rug she brought over from Russia.

"Stroganoff," he says. "My specialty."

"Bernie?" I ask. "When's Bernice coming?"

"Half an hour," he says. "We better get crackin'." He takes the groceries back from Sonia and heads toward the kitchen, still with his coat on. "Oh," he says as if he's sud-denly remembered, "she's bringing Pammy, too."

Sonia looks at me, then quickly heads to the cupboard and pulls down another plate. I start shifting around the kitchen chairs, making room. The table usually seats six, but my mother's wheelchair and the cast take up a lot of space. Sonia hands me a glass and some silverware, and I set them where someone will have to straddle a table leg.

"Hey," Bernie says to no one in particular, "you got some lettuce for a salad?"

Sonia opens the refrigerator and roots around in the crisper. She pulls out half a head of lettuce and hands it to Bernie.

"You think this'll be enough?" he asks, looking at it doubtfully. Sonia looks at me, and I look back at her, and when neither one of us says anything, Bernie says, "That's okay. We'll just use a lot of this other junk," pulling cucumbers and celery, carrots and green peppers and hardboiled eggs out of his grocery bag.

"You want a beer, Bernie?" I ask, already moving toward the refrigerator.

He smiles. "Good idea," he says. "Calm the nerves."

"Take your coat off," I say, "stay a while," and Sonia moves behind him, ready to take the coat from him and hang it in the closet.

"What?" he says. "Oh, sure." He sets the baggie full of radishes on the counter and starts unzipping his coat, but he doesn't see Sonia behind him, takes a step backward and bumps into her. "Whoa," he says. "Sorry."

"Okay, Bernie," she says and holds her arms out for the coat. He looks uncertain, but hands it to her. Underneath, he's got on a suit jacket I've never seen, creased across the back and along the sleeves, where it was jammed inside his parka. It's a light green color and matches the camel and green plaid of his pants surprisingly well.

"Nice threads," I say, handing him the beer bottle.

"Oh," he says, "well...." He takes the beer from me, reading the label and frowning. It's a Corona; Bernie would have preferred something American, but I didn't have time to go out and buy more beer.

Bernie's got the recipe written on a sheet of paper, and he runs his finger down the list of ingredients, checking to see that he's got them all. "Meat," he says, "flour, sour cream, butter, mushrooms, onion, garlic, noodles...." Bernie's set the recipe down in a puddle of water; the magic marker is already starting to smear. "Hey," he says, "you got bouillon? I forgot the bouillon."

Sonia looks at me uncertainly; this is a word she doesn't recognize. I start rummaging through the kitchen cabinet with baking supplies, and she heads toward my mother's room, to wake her up from her afternoon nap.

"I don't see it, Bernie," I say, pushing aside baking soda and baking powder and the tiny bottle of vanilla. "Can you do without?"

He turns toward me, frowning. "Well," he says slowly, considering, "ordinarily, I might try it, but tonight" he pauses, "I can't afford any screw-ups." He pulls his car keys out of his pants pocket and starts looking around for his coat.

"Front hall closet," I say.

Bernie nods and heads toward the front of the house. "If she comes," he says, "give her a glass of that wine in the bag there. I'll be back as soon as I can." When he walks past the china cabinet, the dishes inside rattle, inching closer to the shelf edges. "Oh," he says, "and there's Mountain Dew for Pammy." He bangs the front door on the way out, and then, after a few minutes, I hear him peeling out of the driveway.

I take the radishes out of the bag and start slicing them, and Sonia wheels my mother into the kitchen, with her hair a little mussed. I kiss Sonia, then lean down to kiss my mother's cheek while patting the back of her head.

"Where's Bernie?" Sonia asks.

"Market."

My mother lifts her chin and sniffs, looking something like Whitey. "What smells?"

"Sirloin, I think, for Bernie's stroganoff."

She nods and wheels herself closer to the table. "Is there wine?" she asks, and Sonia reaches into the bag and pulls out the bottle Bernie brought with him, still with the price tag on, $7.99. She pours a glass of wine for my mother, hands it to her at the table, then looks at the Tupperware container with Bernie's salad, reaches into the cabinet under the counter for a pottery bowl and dumps the salad into it, adding some of my sliced radishes.

Bernice knocks hard on the door with her fist, and Sonia wipes her hands on her pants before going to answer it. "Hello," she says, "good to meet you," and I can hear Bernice's voice loud and clear from the front hall, "Well, hi there, honey."

Somehow, Pammy comes into the kitchen first and stands, bending her ankles to the floor. She's got on a suede jacket with fringe on the sleeves, a T-shirt and jeans stuffed into red cowboy boots. "Hey, Harley," she says, not quite making eye contact.

I introduce her to my mother and tell her Sonia's the lady who answered the door, then offer to take her jacket and hang it in the closet.

"No, thanks," she says and doesn't add anything else about being cold or taking it off later.

I pour a glass of Mountain Dew and hand it to her, and she doesn't seem surprised that I had it on hand especially for her. Bernice comes into the kitchen, sees Pammy with the glass of fluorescent green soda and says, "I keep telling her that stuff'll make her sterile, but she doesn't listen to me."

Pammy, as if to deflect attention from her possible sterility, says, "Where's Bernie?"

"Market," I say. "He'll be back in a minute."

Pammy nods, sipping at her soda, and my mother says in a challenging voice, "How old are you?"

Pammy looks from her mother to my mother to me, and I know she's thinking about the fact that I've seen her serve beer. "Twenty-one."

Bernice looks at Pammy and back at me and shrugs. "It's all right," she says. "She's seventeen." She picks up the bottle of wine from the counter and holds out her hand until I hand her a glass. "We can't afford another waitress," she says, "and if anybody asks, she's got a fake I.D." She pours a glass of wine and takes a long sip from it, then runs her tongue over her upper lip. "I don't let her drink the stuff," she says defensively, "just serve it."

"I think Ma was just curious," I say.

"She's got a nice little figure," Ma says loudly to no one in particular, and Pammy blushes but looks a little pleased.

"Well," Bernice says, looking at the cluster of ingredients on the counter. "I'm starving. Let's get this thing started." She picks up the Tupperware bowl full of noodles and starts checking the ingredients on the counter against the recipe.

"Hey," Bernie says, coming in the front door, "what's the big idea?" He looks at Bernice and smiles, and I get the feeling he might kiss her if we all weren't standing around watching. "Get away from there," he says, shooing her from the counter.

"Okay, then," she says, "but I'm hungry, Bernie. Let's get the show on the road."

"We have crackers," Sonia says and moves to the cupboard, pulls a sleeve of Saltines from the box and hands it to her. Bernice rips open the plastic sleeve and takes out a few crackers, then hands the rest to Pammy.

"Got a boyfriend?" my mother asks, and it takes a minute before anybody realizes she's talking to Pammy.

"No," Pammy says.

"Why not?" She sets her wine glass down unevenly on the table, and wine sloshes up toward the rim.

"I'm a lesbian," Pammy says flatly.

Bernice gives Pammy a hard look and rolls her eyes in my direction. "She is not," she says. "She's just being nasty."

"Okay." Pammy says and turns to my mother. "I don't know. I just don't."

"They say a lot of girls are lesbians," my mother says, "at your age."

"I'm not really," Pammy says, and my mother nods.

"Want some cheese with those?" I ask Pammy, nodding toward the crackers in her hand, and she shakes her head.

Bernie slides a glass baking pan into the oven and sets the temperature. "That runs a little hot," I say, and he twists the knob back toward the left.

"How'd you break your leg?" Pammy asks my mother.

"Skydiving," my mother says and takes a sip of wine. "See? I can do it, too."

Pammy laughs and sits down at the table across from her, and Bernice, watching from the counter and chewing Saltines, says, "What do you know? Best friends."

✧

"So," Bernie says, slurping noodles into his mouth, then wiping the sauce off his chin with a napkin, "how's your friend?" He raises his head, smiles at me and takes a sip of milk from his glass.

"Friend?"

The stroganoff is mushy, but by the time it's cooked, we're all hungry enough to overlook it. Bernice stands guard over the casserole dish in the middle of the table; as soon as my plate's empty, she snatches it from me and adds another scoop of noodles and meat.

"Lynette," Sonia says quietly.

"The one with the husband," Bernie says, ignoring Sonia.

I take the plate from Bernice and set it down on the table, and when I look up, I've locked eyes with Pammy, who seems to be searching my forehead for sweat. "I don't really know," I say and start pushing the noodles around on my plate.

"Poor girl," my mother says, jabbing at her plate with the tines of her fork, trying to spear the last noodle. "We've been worried about her." She manages to pick up the noodle, but with the fork halfway to her mouth, it drops back onto the plate.

"It's a terrible thing," Bernice says. "I can't believe I served him drinks." She shakes her head, tisking her tongue against her teeth, then pulls my mother's plate away from her and fills it. I look at Bernie and see that he's told Bernice everything, and even though I guess I never told him not to, I wish he'd keep at least some things private.

"Well," my mother says, staring at the dollop of food on her plate as though deciding whether or not to eat it, "she'll be all right. Harley's been looking after her."

Sonia turns toward me, raising an eyebrow to signal a kind of bland curiosity that I know is only hiding something more severe.

I clear my throat, turning from Sonia to Bernice. "I went over a few times," I say, noticing that Bernice has dyed her eyebrows the same orangy-blond color as her hair, "to check on the house," and Sonia lowers her eyes from my face and coughs into her napkin.

"I hear," Bernice says, her voice hushed, "they never found the axe."

"The what?" my mother asks. She picks up a forkful of salad and stuffs it into her mouth, still deciding whether she wants any more of the stroganoff on her plate.

"The axe," Bernice says, shouting across the table at my mother. "You know, for cutting the ice."

Sonia stands, scraping her chair across the hardwood floor. "There is ice cream," she says, placing her hands flat on the table, "for dessert."

"Who told you that?" I ask Bernice. She's wearing makeup that's caked into her pores, turning the old acne scars and lines around her mouth a funny pinkish-beige.

"What kind of ice cream?" Bernice asks Sonia, and Sonia

moves toward the kitchen to check the freezer. Bernice turns, sees that I'm still staring at her and says, "I don't know. Somebody in the bar."

"You don't know who?"

Pammy shifts in her seat and finally takes her jacket off, laying it across the back of her chair. She picks up her glass of soda and holds it with her arm pulled in tight, her bent elbow resting on her stomach.

"Well," Bernice says, looking from Pammy to me, "it must have been one of the deputies." She looks quickly at Bernie and back to me. "They're the only ones who'd know about it. There hasn't been anything in the papers."

Sonia walks to the head of the table and stands facing us with the half-gallon of ice cream in her hand. She points to the word *spumoni* and says, "This kind."

Pammy smiles at her and says, "I'll have some."

She turns to Bernice and Bernie, still pointing at the ice cream container. "No thanks, honey," Bernice says, and Bernie shakes his head.

Sonia turns to face me, and I shake my head, too. "Which deputy? Do you remember which one?"

"It doesn't mean anything, Harley," Bernie says. "You know how people talk."

My mother nods and drops her fork onto her plate. "That's right," she says. "They're all busybodies." She pushes her plate toward the center of the table and tries to make eye contact with Sonia. "A scoop of the vanilla, dear," she says.

"You don't remember which one?" I ask again.

Sonia steps back from the table and goes into the kitchen, starts pulling cereal bowls down from the cabinet.

Bernice looks nervously at Bernie. "No, Harley," she says, "I'm afraid I don't."

"I'm sure it doesn't mean anything," Bernie says, looking from Bernice to me.

"That's right, Harley," Bernice says. "Even if…" She lets the sentence drop, smoothing the napkin in her lap. "They wouldn't do anything about it." She looks down, sees a crumb on her blouse and brushes it off. "If she was defending herself…" she says slowly, looking up, and stops.

Sonia comes back to the table with ice cream in three cereal bowls, sets one in front of Pammy, one with just vanilla in front of my mother and takes the last one for herself.

"I'm sorry, Harley," Bernice says. "I shouldn't have said anything."

"That's okay, honey," Bernie says quietly and pats her on the thigh.

I nod agreement, and Bernice smiles and turns to Sonia. "So," she says loudly, "tell us about Russia."

⌒

Bernie, Bernice and Pammy leave without doing the dishes, and when Sonia and I have finished, and my mother's dried the cups by hand, we all head into the living room.

"He reminds me," my mother says, "of the kid who used to deliver my paper."

"He is the kid who delivered your paper," I say, settling onto the couch next to Sonia.

"Well," my mother says, "you see that?" and curls her fingers into a fist, knocking twice on her head. "Pretty sharp," she says.

"They are happy together," Sonia says, sitting beside me and laying her hand on my thigh.

"Seems that way."

"He was lucky to find her," my mother says. "A single woman with her own business."

"She's not much in the beauty department," I say and take Sonia's hand, with it still resting on my thigh. "That hair's the color of circus peanuts."

"I like her," Sonia says quietly.

"Right," my mother says, "and anyway, that Bernie's no Tyrone Power."

"Who?" Sonia asks.

"Mel Gibson," I say. "He's no Mel Gibson."

"Oh," Sonia says and lays her head on my shoulder.

ᴈ

I MET SONIA in the local diner, where she was trying to order a cheeseburger with extra pickles for the fat government official who sat next to her in the wooden booth, forcing her to squeeze against the wall. She couldn't remember the word for pickle, so she was saying, "Not onion, not ketchup. Green," to the waitress, a high school girl named Ginny something who was also the star forward on the basketball team; her picture was in the paper on a near-weekly basis, surrounded by other tall, solid girls with scars on their knees.

"Lettuce?" Ginny asked, ready to turn away from the table, where the fat government official was smiling at her with bad teeth and looking forward to a peek at her rear.

"No," Sonia said doubtfully. "I don't think so."

I had read in the paper that a handful of Russian agriculture ministers were coming to tour the buckwheat mill and the agricultural experiment station in Glennville. The president of the chamber of commerce had called it a coup for the town and spoke of the "increased international tourism" that was sure to follow.

I used a paper napkin to wipe ketchup off my hands and walked up behind Ginny, smiling at Sonia, who was sweating because of the government official's fur coat, which he had chosen to wear in mid-October and which was pressed up against her.

"Pickles?" I asked, holding up the pickle I'd taken off my

own patty melt, then I said it again in Russian. For some strange reason, this was one of a handful of words I remembered from my three college classes in beginning Russian. The humanities college required that everyone take at least three classes in a field other than his major. I had chosen beginning Russian, because it met only twice a week for two hours at a time. The professor was a gay man who'd been a Russian major at a fancier college; at the last class meeting, he made us watch *Dr. Zhivago*, sighing along with the girls every time Omar Sharif's face appeared on the screen.

"Yes," she whispered, then turned and said something in Russian too rapid for me to understand to the government official, who nodded and grunted his approval.

"Thank you very much," she said, turning back to face me. I saw then how pretty she was and wondered if the government official's right arm was purposely lodged against her left breast. "You will tell me the word for blintzes?" she asked then, slowly, and the bald man sitting across from her grinned sheepishly.

"They won't have them here," I said, and she frowned and repeated what I said in Russian to the bald man. He frowned also and asked her something in Russian.

"Something like?" she asked.

I shook my head. "Not really." I glanced down at the menu open in front of her. "Tell him the turkey soup is very, very good."

"It is?"

"I don't know," I said, "but it's the special, and they have a lot of it."

She laughed then and turned back to the bald man, told him the soup was good, and he smiled and nodded his approval. Then the man sitting next to him, a younger man with thick, black glasses, said he would have some, too.

"You will tell her," Sonia asked, pointing to Ginny, who had walked away and was standing behind the lunch counter, "two soups?"

The government official grunted again, leaned toward Sonia until she gasped for air, and said something in Russian, mumbling into her face. Then he leaned back, and she turned to me again.

"Three soups?" she asked.

౩

I pull the covers back slowly, trying to keep the half of the quilt wrapped around Sonia from lifting off her. She giggles and says, "Blue," but doesn't open her eyes, and I step around the creaky floorboards and out the door. Through the dusty mini-blinds in the bathroom, I can see that the streetlight next to the fire station has shown the sky to be a deep, midnight blue, and the stars are brilliant and clear.

The clock at the foot of the stairs says it's twenty past midnight, and I gather my boots from the closet, put on the extra pair of socks this time, since I can tell by the clarity of the sky that it's bitter cold, and huddle into my jacket, shrugging it on over my sweatshirt.

The rest is easy. I walk out the front door, so that I won't have to walk past my mother's bedroom and possibly wake her again, to the garage, slide the garage door up in one quick motion, listen for movement in the house and, when I don't hear it, get into the truck, start it and drive away. And each motion, while I turn the radio on low, barely a whisper above static, and press the button for the defroster, seems predetermined, as if I knew about them before going to bed, and maybe I did.

The wipers do a bad job of clearing the frost from the windshield, but the defroster melts it slowly, and the streets are empty. I keep using my turn signal, not wanting to tempt fate or cops working the night shift, looking for something to do.

I pull into her driveway and wait, listening to the engine tick, for Whitey's barking to wake her. A light goes on in her bedroom, I see her face for just a second in the window, and it takes maybe a full minute more for her to pull on a robe, come downstairs and open the door.

She stands on the porch, hugging herself for warmth, and I get out of my truck and walk toward her, feeling my skin tighten with the cold.

"Harley," she says, "you can't keep doing this," and I listen to Whitey inside the house, barking at the sound of her voice, and stuff my hands in my jacket pockets because I forgot to bring gloves.

"What happened to the axe?" I'm walking toward her, trying not to trip where I can't see the ground.

"What?"

I stand at the edge of her porch, hunching so that the collar of my jacket rises closer to my ears, covering more of my neck. "I heard they haven't found it."

She stands shivering, holding her robe closed across the front. "That's right," she says. "They haven't."

The wind kicks up, blowing strands of hair across her face, her mouth and her eyes, and she reaches up quickly, tucking them behind her ears. "So you came here to ask me where it is."

"Yes," I say, and glance up over my head, to where her wind chimes are swinging from the nail where they're hung, moving in a group and barely sounding. "No." I turn my body, so that my back is to the wind; I can feel it against my jacket, like something solid. "I think I came to warn you."

The light on her porch is so strong that it washes out her features, taking away the lines around her eyes. "To warn me," she says, repeating.

"That people are talking about it." The flannel lining of my jacket pocket has a hole, and I test it with my finger, wondering if this is where my change keeps disappearing.

Lynette sighs, and I see how tired and strung out she is from lack of sleep. "Harley," she says slowly, and I wonder how she can continue to stand there like that, facing into the wind, with just her bathrobe to cover her. "I know people are talking."

With her hair tucked, I can see the tips of her ears, which are pink and probably freezing. She looks into the distance, over my head, and I stand fingering the hole in my pocket, and wait for her to turn back.

"What exactly are you asking me?" Her gaze holds mine for a couple of seconds before sliding away, toward the fields across the road, and I resist the urge to turn and see what she's looking at.

"I need to know what happened." I say it quietly, and I'm not sure she's heard until she turns to face me again, and her expression is sadder, slack at the corners of her mouth.

"You think I might have killed him." When she closes her mouth, her lips tighten and pull inward.

"No."

She sighs and wipes her hand over her mouth, then quickly lowers her arm and holds it over the front of her robe, pulling the fabric tight to her body. "He fell in, and I held out the axe," she says. "I had the end with the blade, but I was holding the blunt end," she says and pauses, looking away. "He couldn't hold on. It slipped through my hands," and she raises her left hand, showing me again the cut on her palm. "The ax is in the lake." She glances at the palm of her hand, at the puckered scar, before pulling her arm in tight to her body.

"Okay."

The cast rests against her stomach, and she flexes her fingers, curling and uncurling them over the plaster that covers half of her hand. "So maybe you can tell me," she says slowly, "why it's your business, Harley." She looks down at her feet, at her bare ankles under the hem of the robe, and away again, off toward the fields.

The wind blows hard against the back of my neck, and I can feel it through the fabric of my sweatpants. I don't say anything, and she stays posed like that, facing away from me.

"Because, Harley, I don't know what you're doing here." She sighs and looks quickly at me before glancing away. "I mean, just because we knew each other a million years ago, and I knew you were a nice guy and I asked you to take care of my dog...." I can hear the tears in her voice and know she's trying to hide them from me. "Are we friends?" she asks. "Because friends don't spy on each other, and friends might have talked to each other once or twice in the last fifteen years."

She still isn't looking at me, and I start counting the lights on in her windows, the upstairs light, the one by the front door, the small one in her kitchen. "I wanted to help."

She finally turns toward me, nodding slowly, and I can see the tears she's holding back. "So this is how you help?" she says. "By accusing me of killing my husband?"

"No," I say. "I didn't mean to," and I take a few steps back, in the direction of my truck.

She sees me walking away from her and steps forward, rests her cast on the porch railing. "Harley," she says, and she would raise her voice, but I know she's keeping quiet because of the children sleeping upstairs, "if you want to help me, don't come here anymore." She leans toward me, over the top of the railing. "If you want to be my friend, just stay away."

෴

I slip back into bed next to Sonia, and she burrows against my body for warmth, curling her legs against my waist, fitting her head against the crook of my neck. "Hmmmm," she says, fluttering her toes against my thighs, and I lie still and wait for her to settle, only moving when the corner of her pillow pokes me in the eye. Her breath is warm and moist against the collar of my T-shirt, and I lift my head a little higher, so that I can lean against her without breathing in her carbon dioxide all night.

I can imagine Lynette holding onto the axe, can even see her holding onto it so tight that it sliced across her palm. But something still bothers me: I can't see the moment when it slid into the lake. I lie in bed next to Sonia, feel her breath on me and the warmth of her body, and I remember the night Lynette clamped an arm around my neck, holding my head out of the water, and swam with me flailing against her. I was afraid, that night, that she would hold me so hard that she'd choke me, and when I knew I was safe, I was afraid she'd carry me from the water like a child and humiliate me. I remember her strength, the tightness of her grip, and I can't for a second imagine the moment when the axe slid away from her and was lost. I can see Doug falling; I can even imagine him falling so fast that he couldn't reach the axe handle. But I can't imagine the axe getting away from her. Because I remember her well enough to know this: that in order for the axe to be lost, she would have had to let go.

♒

The day after I saw Sonia in the diner, Jimmy Weaver, president of the chamber of commerce, called me at work. "Harley," he said, "did you help out a Russian girl at the diner?"

"Yesterday?" I asked stupidly, as if there might be Russian girls at the diner on a regular basis.

"Yeah." Bernie had patched him through to the supply truck, and I had to lean close to the dashboard in order to get decent reception.

"She didn't know how to say 'pickle.'"

"Pickle?"

"Yeah," I said. "Never mind."

There was a pause while I heard nothing but static, then he came on again. "So you know Russian?"

"Yeah," I said. "A little. I took a couple classes."

Bernie's voice suddenly came on the line, talking to one of the other trucks. Jimmy Weaver, who was at least forty-five and was referred to always as "Jimmy," never "Jim," waited until he was sure Bernie was done talking before he came back on the line.

"Listen," he said, "we could really use your help at the Rotary dinner tonight." He waited for me to say something before he went on. "The translator's a little tiny thing. The

Russians keep ignoring her and talking over the top of her, and we can't understand a word she's saying."

The windows on the truck were rolled up, and I started sweating, because I was wearing three shirts and I'd gotten used to being outside in the cold.

"I'm not exactly an expert," I said. "I just took a couple of classes."

"Well," he said and paused again, and there was heavy static, "at this point, we could use any help you can give. Yesterday, there was a whole soybean mix–up."

I leaned forward again, feeling the bottom shirt stick to my back. "I don't think I even know the word for 'soybean,'" I said.

"Yeah," he said, "well, neither did she. She just kept calling them 'the little green ones.' Nobody knew what the hell she was talking about."

↬

Sonia wore a red dress that crossed between her breasts and tied in back. It seemed to have been handed down from someone bustier; the pockets for her breasts, instead of molding to her body, sagged open, and the V–neck slid sideways, showing the white straps of her slip.

"Thank you," she said, "for helping." Her hair was clipped back from her forehead with two barrettes covered in rhinestones, and her shoes were open–toed sandals with such high heels that they pitched her forward, so that she seemed to be leaning toward the floor.

"How did you find me?" I asked, whispering, standing at the front of the room with her, while the Rotarians were getting ready to introduce the Russian agriculture ministers and the spaghetti buffet was being assembled in the back.

"Oh," she said and turned suddenly, unclasping the purse she carried over her shoulder. She pulled out a slip of paper and handed it to me. On it was a small pencil drawing of my face. "I see your truck. I tell the man your company. I say you look like this."

"You drew this?" I asked, and when she nodded, I asked, "Can I keep it?" and she nodded and blushed again.

"It is not so good," she said.

There was clapping, and the fat government official walked to the podium, glaring at Sonia. He gave a short speech, which she translated while staring at the floor, thanking the Rotarians for their hospitality and declaring that the three government ministers had learned "many interesting things about American agriculture and enjoyed very much American sights and kind American people."

Afterward, Sonia and I were seated next to each other, and while she was busy translating questions from the Rotarians, I let my shoulder brush against hers and pretended to be paying close attention to the conversation while I took in the scent of her hair. If I leaned forward, I could just barely see the edge of her slip inside the neck of her dress, so white and old-fashioned, the same kind my mother would let me see her in while getting ready for a night out with my father. Amanda had never worn a slip; she said if anybody was that interested in her underwear, they were welcome to take a look, but seeing it on Sonia made me think she would be the kind of girl who'd expect a peck on the cheek at her door, who would press her dry palm in my hand and let me walk her to the dance floor, who'd apply lipstick at the end of a date by using the rearview mirror of my car, and who would say thank you, and that she'd had a wonderful time.

"You're the prettiest girl in the room," I said, leaning

close to her, and she turned her head so that I took in the perfumed scent of her soap, which reminded me of wild-flowers.

She paused a second, grasped my meaning and laughed. "I am the only girl in the room."

"Not so," I said and pointed to the two waitresses clearing plates and the woman in her fifties working the buffet, in a chef's hat and a white chef's jacket that strained over the rolls of fat at her waist.

"Oh," she said. "Too bad. I think the cook, she likes you."

The fat government official made a joke while patting his stomach, something about taking advantage of the local crops, and Sonia was forced to translate it twice, since he was still laughing at himself too loudly for Jimmy Weaver to hear.

"How did you learn English?" I asked, while Jimmy Weaver pretended to find the joke uproarious.

She smiled. "My sister, Lena," she said, "goes to a special school…." She turned to me and waved her hand in the air, telling me that she was searching for a word. "For gifted?" she asked, making sure she'd said it right, and when I nodded, she added, "She is older. She teaches me."

Talk at the table turned to deer hunting season, which would start in a few weeks, and snow tires. Sonia translated for a while, until coffee was served and the fat government official rested his cup on top of the commemorative plaque he and the other Russians had been awarded, then turned his back to Sonia and started joking with the other Russians at the table.

"What is he saying?" I asked, leaning toward her enough to see that one of her straps had slid off her shoulder, shifting the V-neck of her slip sideways.

"Oh," she said. "He wishes there are more ladies," and

she blushed so that I knew she was editing his remarks. Then she turned and leaned her face close to mine, and I could smell the garlic on her breath. "But he says he likes your girlfriend very much," she said and wagged her eyebrows, looking off in the direction of the cook.

"Should we introduce them?" I asked, and I saw her blink from my breath on her skin.

"I think his wife will not like it," she said, and she didn't pull away from me, and I breathed in sharply and was sure I tasted garlic.

"What does his wife look like?" I asked, lowering my voice to barely above a whisper.

She laughed and covered her mouth, her fingernails painted red like her dress, but shorter than the tips of her fingers, like a child's. "Angry," she said and looked me in the eye, still with her hand over her mouth. "The wife looks very angry," and she scowled, showing me the look on the government official's wife's face.

"Always?" I asked, and she laughed, giggling into her fingers.

"Yes," she said, and scowled again.

❧

I go downstairs and out to the garage, where I climb on a stepladder and pull down the shopping bag with Sonia's new coat. When I've climbed down and put the ladder away, I take it out of the bag and see again the ugly buttons, and I check that the receipt is in the bag, knowing she won't like the coat but wondering if she'll keep it anyway.

Then I climb the back stairs to the attic and find the flat box with rolls of wrapping paper, some of it my mother's, left over from before she sold the house. I find a pattern with flowers, old-fashioned and not too faded, and the kind of ribbon that little girls wear in their hair, that you can tie in a simple bow.

I carry the wrapping paper and the shopping bag into the kitchen and unroll the paper over the tabletop. I take out the unfolded box the girl at the store gave me and reassemble it, set the coat inside, wonder if I need tissue paper and decide it's too much hassle, then measure out what I think will be the right amount of paper and cut it off the roll. The scissors make a funny saw-toothed pattern, and I think these are the fabric kind I'm not supposed to use on paper, but I figure Sonia won't care if I do it just this once.

When I put the box face-down on the middle of the paper, the two ends don't quite meet in the center, but I don't think Sonia will notice the missing paper on the bottom of the box, so I tape the two ends as close as I can get them, flip the box over, tape the sides and tie the ribbon. Then I hide the box in the hall closet for later, after I've come home with a cake.

I plug in the coffee maker, measure the grounds and pour in a pot of water, then I go back upstairs and walk into the bedroom, singing "Happy Birthday," and Sonia rolls onto her back, shields her eyes with her arm and groans.

"Harley," she says, "you go away now."

I sing louder and climb onto the bed, straddling her, and she moves her knees to make room for me but stays with her arm covering her face.

I end the song with a lot of vibrato, wait for her to lower her arm and kiss her hard on the lips.

"You are a terrible singer, Harley," she says, breathing hot air into my face.

"And you," I say, "are a terrible birthday girl."

"No," she says, lowers her arm and shakes her head with her eyes closed, then opens them again. "You will see. When the cake comes, I am very happy."

I lift off her and roll onto my side to face her. "Who said there was going to be cake?"

"Oh, Harley," she says and pouts, pushing her lips out, "no cake for me?"

I kiss her, grabbing her pouty lower lip with my teeth and gently biting, then roll onto my back and pretend to consider. "Mmmmm. Well," I say, "maybe."

She smiles and rolls toward me, starts kissing me with her eyes closed, sometimes missing my mouth and kissing my cheek, rubbing her face against my beard stubble, and when she presses against me and nudges my erection with her hip, she mumbles, "Pretty please, Harley?" and giggles, with her breath buzzing against my lips.

⌁

After the Rotary dinner, I led Sonia to the coat rack and helped her on with her coat, lifting the heavy wool fabric onto her shoulders. "You've lost a button," I said, pointing to the loose threads where it was missing.

Sonia smiled, buttoning the collar, said, "I am not taking good care with things," and shrugged. "Lena tells me," and she looked into my eyes with the strap of her purse hanging from her elbow.

I leaned toward her and raised her purse to her shoulder. "I could drive you home," I said, conscious that I was standing too close to her again, that I had a habit around her of standing too close.

"Home?" she asked. "You will take me to St. Petersburg?"

I laughed. "If you want."

She looked behind me, at the rack of coats next to the door, and pointed to the fur coat belonging to the fat gov-ernment official. "It smells like goat," she said.

I turned back to face her, feeling the hair on my arms rise. "Do they make them from goat hair?"

She laughed and shook her head, slowly. "I don't think so."

I zipped my jacket, wondering if anyone else could see how I was leaning toward her, how my skin tingled wher-ever it was closest to her. I searched my mind, trying to remember the details of a newspaper article I had only scanned once. "You'll be here another week?"

She smiled and lowered her eyes. "Yes," she said. "You may take me home." She reached into her pocket and pulled out a room key, dropping lint. "To the Relax Inn."

"Another week?" I asked.

She nodded, letting her eyes drift up toward mine.

I looked over to where the fat government official was walking toward us, searching for his coat. He moved slowly, shaking hands randomly with whoever appeared ready to say something to him.

"You'll tell them I'm taking you?"

Sonia turned and looked over her shoulder at the two other officials, standing by themselves at the door. "Yes."

"You won't be in trouble?"

She opened her mouth to say something but stopped and turned to the fat government official, who reached behind me for his coat, pulling it from the hanger in one motion and saying something angrily in Russian. I didn't recognize the words but knew he was calling her something disparaging.

Sonia looked at me and said quietly, "I am in trouble already," and when the fat government official walked away, huffing toward the door, she turned to me, rolled her eyes and shrugged. "With the goat man," she said and giggled, raising a hand to her mouth.

She walked to the door and said something quickly to the government officials, who turned toward me, surprised. Then she came back, the two of us nodded good-bye to Jimmy Weaver, and I held the door open, watching her pass through, smelling something fertile like eggs in her hair. Her rhinestone barrettes sparkled in the street-light, and I walked her to my car and held the door and breathed in sharply when she stepped past me. She smiled and climbed onto the truck seat, rearranging her dress, and when I walked around the back of the truck, I saw her reach inside the neck and straighten the strap of her slip.

At the entrance to the thruway, we pulled into the Relax Inn parking lot, and Sonia had me stop at the gas station convenience store. "One moment, Harley," she said, and the way she said my name, so that it seemed to come from somewhere soft at the back of her throat, made me wish she would keep saying it, adding it to the end of every sentence.

I waited while she went to the counter, and she came out a few minutes later with a full grocery bag. She tipped the bag toward me, so that I could see the six-pack of beer and the bags of pork rinds and Doritos. "For the goat man and his friends," she said, handing it to me.

Inside the motel, she told me to wait while she went with the grocery bag to the two adjoining rooms shared by the government officials. While she was gone, I walked around the room, looking into her suitcase, spread open on a luggage rack, at her shampoo in the bathroom and her small bag of makeup, at the tweezers and the silver compact with her face powder.

When she came back to the room, I was staring at the Kandinsky postcard wedged into the frame of the vanity mirror, and she smiled and told me the story of Ivan Tsarevitch and Jelena, riding back to Ivan's father's kingdom with the gray wolf, the firebird and the horse with the golden mane. She spoke of Ivan's efforts to capture the firebird for his father, his friendship with the gray wolf, his love for the princess Jelena, and her voice when she recited the story had the same softness from when she said my name, and I knew I could kiss her if I wanted to, and I did.

We stood in the middle of the room, between the mirror and the bed, and I kissed her and felt the jolt of it not just at my lips, but at the back of my neck and in my stomach and knees and feet and, God, my groin. She leaned toward me, and I could see the crease in her eyelids, the powdery eye shadow and her lashes brushing the skin under her eyes, and I tilted my head and reached for her, closing my eyes, and found her lips that were soft and full and able to conduct this strange electricity.

I kissed her lips swollen, kissed the lipstick and powder from her mouth and cheek, brushed my nose past her ear and smelled her hair near the roots, where it was darkest and most fragrant. She touched my arm and I felt her hand at my back, gently stroking the fabric of my shirt, and I reached behind her and pulled her to me, held her until she had both arms around me, her fingers brushing my neck. She kissed my cheek, breathing through her nose, and I felt her breath in my ear.

I took a step backward, and she said, "Harley?" and I stood looking into her eyes, stroking the side of her face with my hand, imagining that if she hadn't been going back to Russia in a week, the two of us might have had an old-fashioned courtship. I would have taken her to dinners and movies, and at the end of the evening, we would have sat in my truck, kissing and longing for each other, and it would have been sweet and innocent and romantic.

But there was no time for that now. Instead, I would fumble with her clothes and there would be the risk that my body would betray me, that I would be flabby or smelly or needy or slow or too quick. I had slept with two women since Amanda, and in both cases, the sex had been loveless and unsatisfying. So I stood there, stroking the side of Sonia's face, with her head leaning into the palm of my hand, and her eyes, when she looked up at me, so open and trusting, so gentle and full of light, and I said softly, "I should go."

She stepped away from my hand, worry and confusion passing across her face in a rush. "You are married?" she asked.

"No."

She frowned. "You love someone?"

I shook my head. "No," I said, and I stepped toward her, tilted my head and kissed her again, reaching a hand to her shoulder and holding it there, firmly. "I'll see you tomorrow?" I asked, and she was still looking at me with that light in her eyes.

"Yes, Harley," she said, and I looked quickly in the mirror, saw where she'd ruffled my hair and saw her begin to straighten the front of her dress where her slip showed. I ran a hand through my hair, turned and walked away from her to the door.

"Tomorrow?" I asked, and she nodded again.

"What time?" I asked, and she said "seven," raising the correct number of fingers.

"You will come for me, Harley?" she asked, and I nodded and opened the door, felt the rush of cold air where it touched the skin she'd been kissing, brought the door closed behind me and walked to my truck, already memorizing the feeling of the moment for later when I would have to remember.

I drove home, having to keep my foot off the gas to avoid speeding because I was so full of energy and the desire to see her again. I could still feel her fingers in my hair, see that look of love on her face, and I knew I would sleep with her the next time I saw her, and that it might not be perfect. But it wouldn't matter. Because that evening, when I replayed it in my mind, was.

༃

"Hey," Bernie says, waving me over to his desk. "I'm sorry about last night."

I take my coat off and throw it on the desk next to his. "It was fine," I say. "What are you talking about?"

He shrugs, tapping cigar ashes into his desk drawer. "Bernice shouldn't have said that stuff," he says, "about your friend who died," and he checks for secretaries before raising the cigar to his lips.

"He wasn't my friend," I say stiffly. I see the secretary coming whose name I have so much trouble remembering—Cherise, I think—and move to the side of Bernie's desk, blocking her view.

"Right," he says, "right," and drops his cigar into the ashtray, closing the drawer and waving his hand over the top. "You're friends with the wife."

I shrug and wait for Cherise to pass, then move back around to the other side of his desk. "That's okay, Bernie," I say. "She didn't bother me."

He nods and fiddles with the handle to his coffee mug, picking at a chip. "She shouldn't shoot her mouth off like that," he says, letting flecks of ceramic glaze drop onto his desktop. "She says so herself."

"It's okay," I say. "Really."

He takes a look around and opens his desk drawer, letting the smoke curl out of the top. "Don't worry," he says. "She won't say anything about it to anybody else." He lifts the cigar and holds it in his fingers, balancing his wrist on the top edge of the drawer. "I told her she should keep it quiet."

I take the orders from his desk and pick up my jacket. "Really," I say. "It's okay."

He nods. "Yeah," he says. "She's a good woman."

"Yup," I say. "Seems that way."

He brings the cigar to his lips, turns and sees that the window behind him isn't open and bangs on it with his hand before raising the sash. He blows the smoke out the window and turns toward me, taking a furtive look around. "Bit pushy sometimes," he says.

"Well," I say, holding my jacket folded over my arm, "we all have our faults."

"Yup," he says, "a good woman," and glances up at me from under his eyebrows.

"So," I say, "you're pretty serious."

"Well," he says and coughs into his fist, "could be."

I nod and step back. "Good for you."

"Yup," he says, nodding, and when I turn to walk away, he adds, "anyway, she said to tell you she was sorry."

"No problem."

"She didn't mean anything."

I nod again. "Right, Bernie. I know."

He takes another drag from his cigar and sets it back into the ashtray in his desk drawer. "She really liked your wife."

"We liked her, too."

"She said..." he says and looks at me again, then glances toward the photo of his dead wife turned face down on his desk. "She said she didn't understand why you were bothering with this other woman, the one whose husband got killed." He doesn't look at me, but starts chipping again at his mug.

"Bernice said that?"

Bernie nods sheepishly. "She said your wife loves you, and you should spend your time thinking about her."

"Hmmmm," I say and start putting my coat back on. "That's interesting."

He nods and looks relieved that I'm not going to get mad. "Well," he says, "like I said. She's got a habit of shooting off her mouth."

꒳

CHAPTER XVIII

SONIA TURNED HER BACK TO ME and set the alarm clock next to her bed for four o'clock, an hour before Jimmy Weaver would come to drive the Russian agriculture ministers and her to the airport in the new chamber of commerce minivan. Then she lay back with one arm curled under her head and asked, "When you are a boy, Harley, what do you wish?"

Her voice was soft and murmuring, floating over me while I lay breathing and sweating, already wondering when, if ever, I might make love to her again.

"I don't know." I thought about getting up for a glass of water, decided I didn't want to get out of bed. "I wanted to be a pitcher for the Yankees."

She rolled onto her side and kissed my shoulder. I could feel her breasts pressed to my side. "I wish for love."

I didn't know what to say and lay still, letting her playfully bite my shoulder. A part of my brain was busy telling me a week wasn't enough for these feelings, that after she left for Russia, I'd never see her again.

"My parents," she said slowly, "are unhappy. My father is drinking, my mama is crying. But I am reading romantic stories…hoping."

"And now?" She had her head leaning against my arm, and I hoped I didn't smell too much like sweat.

"And now," she said, lifting her head to look at me, "I am so happy for this week."

"I don't want you to go." It was the closest I thought I could come, after a week, to telling her I loved her.

She smiled. "It's okay," she said and leaned to kiss me. "Tonight I am happy. My wish is answered."

༄

My mother's blowing up balloons when I walk in the door, but Sonia comes toward me, holds out her arms and says, "Surprise."

I set the cake on the table, take her in my arms and say, nuzzling her ear, "It's not my birthday. It's yours."

"Surprise," she says and kisses my cheek. "Happy birthday to me."

My mother blows a last puff of air into a red balloon and holds it closed by pinching it with her fingers. I kiss Sonia and let go of her, and my mother holds the balloon out to me.

"There's no sense in singing to her, either," my mother says.

I tie the balloon off, and Sonia takes it from me, climbs on a chair and Scotch tapes the balloon to the overhead lamp, where a ring of them turns the lamplight strange colors and makes shadows on the tabletop.

"We can have cake before dinner, Harley?" Sonia asks, still standing on the chair.

My mother laughs. "She's just like a kid," she says, taking another balloon from the bag and stretching it between her fingers. "I told her it's against the rules."

I shake my head and step behind Sonia, because the chair is old and tends to wobble. "No cake before dinner."

"But Harley," she says, mock serious and frowning, turning her toes carefully so that she faces in my direction, staring down at the top of my head, "It is an old Russian custom," and my mother laughs again, harder this time.

"Sure," she says, laughing. "Sure. I wonder how many times she's gotten away with *that.*"

⌇

For her birthday dinner, Sonia's made hamburgers and frozen french fries, and waits until we're all seated before she goes to the refrigerator and brings me a jar of pickles.

"You would like some pickles?" she asks, holding the jar out to me. "You would like some extra pickles?"

"Yes, please," I say. "I would like some extra pickles," and she hands me the jar before sitting down.

"I'll have some of those," my mother says, and Sonia smiles wide, showing the metal cap at the back of her mouth.

"To the goat man," I say, holding up my glass of leftover Mountain Dew.

Sonia holds up her glass, tipping it toward mine. "And his great goat coat."

My mother lifts her coffee cup in her trembling hand. "And to my lunatic son," she says, "and his even crazier wife," and we all clink glasses, laughing and spilling coffee and green soda on my mother's antique tablecloth.

⌇

The local telephone company was understaffed; I volunteered for extra shifts, working evenings and weekends for months, and when that still wasn't enough, I asked my mother to let me use some of the money she'd given me after selling the house.

Sonia was waiting for me at the airport in St. Peters-burg, and she put her arm in mine and guided me onto and off of a maze of buses, all of them smelling of beef and sweat and something slightly rancid, all of them deafening with talk in that strange, guttural language. We got off the last bus behind an old woman who nearly ran the five blocks to Sonia's apartment building hugging a loaf of bread to her chest, hurrying home in time to make dinner.

The walls of the apartment Sonia shared with her sister and brother-in-law were covered with paintings from baseboard to crown molding, some close enough together for their frames to touch. After Sonia pushed me into an old, overstuffed chair, I could see that there was a kind of scheme to the paintings by color, so that whole sections were predominantly blue or green or white or red or gold. I was dizzy with jet lag, and the walls, while I stared at them, undulated like something in a dream.

Sonia's brother-in-law came in the door and dropped his coat on what looked to be the kitchen table, though there was no kitchen in the apartment that I could see, muttered hello to me in Russian and stepped behind a fabric curtain, giving me a glimpse of a bed and a dresser with its drawers open, showing stacks of folded clothing spilling out of the drawers.

Lena came in soon after, said hello while blushing and staring at the floor, then stepped behind the same curtain and mumbled something to her husband before kissing him on the cheek. She was dark-haired like Sonia but shorter and heavier, like most of the Russian women I'd seen since I arrived, and her skin was flushed and raw-looking from the cold. It made me wonder about Sonia's beauty, what kept her skin so light and smooth, her hair so thick, her eyes so full of color.

Volodya came and sat beside me on the matching overstuffed chair, which was missing a piece of wood from its
frame. The springs groaned and seemed to shift underneath him, so that he had to adjust his rear end to a comfortable position. He wasn't overweight so much as barrel-
chested, with an overgrown mustache that seemed to want
to climb back up his nose. He was already half-drunk, and
he laughed often without needing a reason, as if he
thought everything I did was hilariously funny.

Sonia came back into the apartment with a stack of
sliced bread on a plate and a small dish of butter, saw
Volodya reaching into a cabinet next to the wall and automatically set two glasses on the teetering side table next to
his chair. He pulled a bottle of vodka from the cabinet, saw
the glasses and said, brusquely, "good girl." Then he poured
us both a double vodka, tipped the bottle toward me as if
in a toast, leaned his head back and poured the liquid
straight into his throat. I took a small sip and set my glass
down, and he laughed until I thought he might choke.

Lena came out from behind the fabric curtain and pulled
it closed behind her. She had changed into what my mother
would call a "shirtwaist dress," made of something shiny
like polyester, with an all-over red and purple pattern and a
belt covered with the same material. The belt was wide; it
sat on her hips and seemed to cut into her waist and the
underside of her breasts, but she had combed her hair, and
it fell into a glossy halo around her head that showed how
she had once been a beauty like Sonia.

"I am so happy to meet you," she said slowly and carefully in English, standing in front of my chair, and when I
stood and shook her hand, she nodded and blushed. Then
Volodya mumbled something about his dinner, and she

smiled and walked out of the apartment, and I could hear the heels of her shoes clicking down the hall.

"So," Volodya said in Russian and took another swig of vodka, so that his skin flushed and his eyes began to water, "you like Sonia?"

"Yes," I said and took another small sip from my glass. I was afraid if I drank the whole glass in an hour, the combination of vodka and jet lag would make me pass out, and I still had some hope of making love to Sonia.

"You want to marry her?" His eyes were full of tears, and I wondered if he could even see my face.

"I don't know," I said, and he leaned back his head and laughed loudly, as if surprised.

"Good thinking," he said. "You fuck her first, then decide."

"No," I said, but then Sonia and Lena came back into the apartment with what turned out to be meat stuffed into something like dumplings. There was a salad, too, with bits of fish sprinkled on top, and a bitter-tasting tea, which Sonia and Lena and I drank instead of vodka. Sonia lit candles, which threw shadows over her paintings and smelled like beeswax, and we ate quietly, with our forks clicking against the plates.

"These plates," Sonia said suddenly in English, "come from our mama."

"You mean she died?" There were so many things I still didn't know about her. I poured myself more tea, hoping it would keep me awake.

"Yes," Lena said and offered me the bowl with salad.

"She is dead twelve years," Sonia said, looking at Lena, as if checking her math. "In birth."

"She died in childbirth?" I asked.

"Yes," Lena said. "Also the baby."

The fish made the salad salty, and I ate more bread, trying to cut the taste, but the combination of potatoes and the thick, starchy sauce over the meat dumplings made me feel tired and bloated, and I was still fighting off sleep.

"Your paintings," I said to Sonia, "are beautiful."

"Thank you," she said, holding a napkin to her lips.

Lena saw that my cup was empty, stood and poured me more tea, and I began to wonder where the bathroom was.

"Do you sell them?" I asked.

Sonia nodded. "Sometimes," she said, "and sometimes…" She looked at Lena, searching for the word for what she meant. "Trade."

Lena nodded and sat down. "The meat for this dinner…."

"You traded a painting for it?"

Volodya saw the look of concern on my face and turned to his wife, demanding that she translate what we were saying back into Russian.

"Yes," Sonia said, blushing into her napkin.

ॐ

After dinner, I followed Sonia and Lena into the hallway, where Sonia showed me to the bathroom and the two of them carried the dirty dishes to the kitchen. When I finished, I took a wrong turn and ended up with Sonia and Lena and the old woman from the bus. Sonia and Lena washed dishes, while the old woman stirred something on the stove and stared at me openly. Neither Sonia nor Lena introduced me, so I decided to ignore her, but when I stepped toward the sink to offer help, Lena swatted me away with a dish towel, and the old woman said something quickly in Russian that made the other two women blush.

Sonia set down the dishes she was holding, took my

arm and said, "That woman is a big talker," while guiding me back to the apartment.

She ignored Volodya, who was finishing off my glass of vodka, and took the candles from the table, pushing aside a second fabric curtain into her own sleeping area. She set the two candles on her nightstand and motioned for me to sit on her bed while she took the elastic band from her hair and shook it loose.

"You are tired?" she asked softly.

I fingered the curtain dividing her bed from Volodya and Lena's. "You sleep so close?"

She nodded. "When they argue, I make tea in the kitchen."

"But what about…?" I asked, and she simply nodded again and began to unbutton her blouse. She watched me carefully, while my eyes traveled from her face to her fingers and then to her breasts.

"Sonia," I said, "I don't know if I can…"

"You are tired?" she asked.

I shook my head. "With people so close…."

She stopped before lifting the blouse from her shoulders. "Volodya is drunk," she said, whispering, and tilted her head in the direction of his snoring. "And Lena will be happy for me."

I reached for her and pulled her closer to me by grabbing the waist of her skirt, touching the skin at her waist and feeling again the softness of it, before reaching up toward her breasts.

She pulled away from me to unzip her skirt, took off her blouse and stepped quickly out of her underwear, so that she was standing in front of me completely naked, laughing nervously at my sudden intake of breath while I gazed at her. Then she bent down to pull out the rug that was

half under her bed, stood and took my hand, and gently
pulled me down onto the rug with her.

"We are quiet," she said and, with her back against the
wall, began to unbutton my shirt, running her hand over
my chest and kissing me softly, lips parted.

I covered her hand with my own and held it, watching
her in the candlelight, the way it turned her hair darker,
her lips redder, the way it smoothed the imperfections of
her skin into something more sculpted.

"I should have asked you for a painting of this," I said,
holding her hand and warming it with my own.

"This?"

"You."

She smiled and took her hand from mine, reached behind
me and lifted a painting from the wall next to her bed. She
looked at it before handing it to me. It wasn't more than a
few inches across, in a homemade wooden frame. It was a
portrait of me, in the sweater I wore the night of the Rotary
dinner, with a grin I didn't remember having, with my face
half in shadow from standing next to a darkened window.

"I paint this one not to sell." She took it from me and
reached behind me to slide it back onto its nail. "For me,"
she said, holding her hand flat, over her heart.

ॐ

We were married in a civil ceremony in a government
office building; over the sound of Lena's sniffling, I tried to
decipher what passed as a service, but the sound of someone approaching with clattering heels down the long, tile
corridor outside sent me into a kind of panic left over from
air raid drills as a child, crouching under our desks for fear
of Russian bombs. I had to lengthen my stay in St. Peters-

burg by a week, which Sonia and I spent huddled over paperwork in both Russian and English and standing in line at the consulate. We met other Russian brides, some of them prostitutes, marrying fat or ugly American men for their money, and afterwards, Sonia would be tight-lipped and scornful, complaining that the lines were slow, that her feet hurt and that the government offices were stifling.

She left the paintings for Lena to sell for money to live on, rent or food or the dresses Volodya would never buy, and took only her mother's dresser, which now sits at the bottom of our stairs, and a few small rugs, including the one that we'd been making love on, burning our knees and elbows on the wool fibers. We had them shipped, and I knew Sonia worried for them, that the boat would sink and she'd have nothing left of her mother.

By the time I bought our plane tickets, we'd spent thousands from my mother's gift to me, and I had nothing to offer while Sonia and Lena clung to each other weeping their goodbyes, no regular visits or even phone calls between the two of them. "You will care for her," Lena said, wiping the mascara from her eyes with a cloth handkerchief, and I nodded dumbly and promised I would. "You will send pictures of your children," she said, standing in the main terminal of the airport, in her plain brown shoes and that same blinding red and purple dress, and I took her hand for just a second, felt the roughness of her fingers in mine, and told her not to worry.

༩

"Thank you, Mama," Sonia says, slipping the chain with my mother's gold locket over her head. She takes the locket between two fingers and holds it for a moment before letting it lie flat against her breasts.

"Inside," my mother says, reaching for the locket, and Sonia leans forward, letting her take it in her hands, "you put a picture of you and a picture of your husband." She touches the clasp on the side of the locket, making it spring open to show one of my baby pictures cut to fit inside the tiny oval. She points to the other side, which is still empty. "The one of you goes there," she says, tapping it with her fingernail. "Or someday, you can put in pictures of your children."

"It's beautiful, Ma," I say.

My mother lets go of the locket and sits back in her wheelchair. "It was a present from your father," she says, "after you were born." She reaches into her pocket, pulls out the photo of my father that once fit into the other side, and hands it to me. "I've had it almost forty years."

Sonia walks around the table to my mother, kneels in front of the wheelchair and leans her head against my mother's shoulder. "Thank you so much, Mama."

My mother nods and reaches a hand to pat Sonia's cheek. "You're welcome, dear," she says, gently patting.

꒰꒱

We had been married less than a month when I found Sonia in the bathtub, crying. She was holding a letter from Russia; the ink had smeared where her fingers touched the thin sheets of paper.

"What's the matter, Sonia?" I asked and she sniffled and said, "Nothing." She was sitting with her knees bent and only a few inches of water still in the tub, because the drain cover leaked and the water wouldn't hold.

"I am okay," she said. "I am only missing Lena."

I bent with my knees on the bathroom rug and touched her shoulder, felt the skin that was wet and clammy, goose-pimply.

"I'm sorry," I said, and she nodded, and the tips of her hair were wet where they'd dragged in the water when the tub was full.

"Maybe next year," I said, "you can visit. Or she can come here."

She smiled and handed me the letter, and I put it on top of the hamper, where it would stay dry. "Okay, Harley. That would be so nice."

I came back to the side of the tub and stroked her hair, saw that she was shivering a little. "Sonia," I said, "you don't have to sit in the bathtub to cry."

She shrugged. "In Russia, it is the only way to be alone."

We were so newly married that it actually hurt my feelings a little to think that she wanted to get away from me, but instead of saying anything about it, I asked, "Does Lena want you to go back?"

Sonia shook her head. "No. She wants a good life for me. She says to have fat American babies," and she blushed a little at the thought of telling me Americans were fat.

"Lena reminds me," she said, and sadness crossed her face, "of what my mother says. That Sonia is very brave."

ॐ

When I come upstairs, Sonia is lying on top of the bed, naked under her new coat. She has her hair loose, and she's posed with her arm flung out over the pillow.

"If you wear it like that, you can't return it," I say, dropping my wallet and keys on the dresser.

She sits up and swings her legs over the side of the bed. "Why do I return it?"

I kick off my shoes and leave them under the dresser. "You don't mind those buttons?"

She looks down at the buttons and shrugs. "Lions," she says and growls, swatting at me with imaginary claws. "Sexy," she says and wags her eyebrows.

"How about that collar?"

She rubs her face against the imitation fur. "I like it, Harley," she said. "You choose it for me."

"You could get something better." I pull off my flannel shirt and lay it on the dresser, so I can wear it again tomorrow with a different T-shirt underneath.

She shrugs again. "No," she says. "This is good." She gets up and stands next to the bed, unbuttons the coat and holds it open one side at a time, like a guy selling imitation watches.

"Why, Harley?" she asks. "You don't like it?"

～ろ～

I wake with the sheet and comforter twisted around my waist and know I've been dreaming, and the sound in my dream of crying is only the wind against the wooden window frames, and the sound of waves is the dripping of the humidifier. Sonia is sleeping naked beside me, and I get up carefully and go to the window, looking down onto the quiet street.

Sometimes in dreams I can still hear my father's voice, and I listen for him now, shivering next to the window, and hear only the wind howling and an eighteen-wheeler revving its engine a block away, heading toward the main highway that will take it south and east.

I'm only half-awake, but, if possible, more alert than in daylight, and I go to Sonia's side of the bed, lift the quilt where it's fallen from her bare shoulders, and breathe, taking in the musky scent of her sleeping skin. Her beauty is in her eyes; with them closed, she's a child again, small under the covers, and I brush hair from the side of her face before slipping out the door.

Downstairs, my mother is asleep with her door open, and while I stand listening, I believe I hear her say "Frank," softly, murmuring into the sheets, and I try to imagine her dreams, wondering if she's dancing with the ghost of my dead father, before I remember that this is an image from my own dreams, the two of them gliding vaporous and sepia-toned, like a scene from an old movie. "Frank," my mother says, more clearly this time, and I stand in her doorway with my boots in my hand, feeling like a ghost myself—not the frightening kind, but the kind that stand silent over sleeping people, offering their protection.

Outside, the air is frigid, but the truck starts easily, and I leave it running while raising the garage door, looking up to where Doug's clothes are hidden behind flower pots and porch rockers. I may burn them later, or let Sonia cut them into rags or quilt pieces for my mother's old sewing machine, but I know I'll never wear them; I can't even imagine wanting them next to my skin.

The truck is slow to heat up, and as I come over the crest of the hill, the wind shimmies it sideways, so that I have to move the wheel to fight off a slide into the ditch. Whitey barks when I turn into her driveway and keeps barking in sudden bursts. A golden light in a downstairs window surprises me, and there's movement behind the curtain, and then she's opening the door, wrapped in a yellow afghan, in her stocking feet.

I cross her lawn, stopping to stand the plastic child's sled upright against her porch rail, and she waits, shuffling her feet against the icy floorboards.

"I was waiting for you. In case..." she says, and she reaches for the doorknob behind her and waves me inside. "I didn't know if you'd come," she says, waiting for me to step past her so she can close the door behind me, "but it's not like I'd be sleeping, anyway." She gives a shove against the door, making sure it's shut tight.

"But you told me not to...."

Whitey trots over, sniffing my pant legs, and I stand immobile until he turns away and settles on the landing of her stairs.

She nods. "I'm sorry I said that," not entirely sounding like she means it, and motions for me to sit down. The room is dimly lit and cold, and I keep my coat on, falling onto the couch. Lynette sits in a chair with the same all-over orange and brown pattern and the same enormous wood frame, and I wonder how she and Doug ever managed to get the two pieces of furniture through the door.

"I don't know why I did come," I say, and she nods again, as though she's waiting for me to recite a list of possible reasons, but I only stare at her shag carpet and the book on her coffee table, a discarded library copy of *Dubliners*, with a brittle plastic cover and a broken spine.

The couch has a dip in the middle I've sunk into, mashing the cushions flat against the springs. A blanket at one end, covered in short white hairs, must be where Whitey sometimes sleeps.

"I saw your wife today," she says and tilts her head, watching me carefully.

"What?" The afghan is hand-knitted with a fringe that

brushes the floor. She has a sweatshirt on underneath it, and a pair of blue sweatpants, but she still looks cold.

"Sonia," she says, as if to prove she knows her name, "called me."

"When?"

"This afternoon." She stands up, regathering the afghan around her. "I can reheat some coffee."

I shake my head, but she goes into the kitchen anyway, with me following, and flips the switch to her Mr. Coffee. I still have my boots on; my toes tingle as they unthaw, with tiny shards of pain, and I've left watermarks in her hallway and on her kitchen floor.

"Why?"

She stands for a second with her hand on the coffeemaker, squaring her shoulders before she turns toward me and says, "She wanted to have lunch. In town." She pulls two coffee mugs down from the cabinet over her head and sets them on the counter, lining them up so that they're square to each other and the edge of the countertop.

"What?" I sit at her kitchen table, under the oval of light from the lamp overhead, feeling the warmth of it on my neck and head.

She comes over to the table, pulls a chair out and sits carefully, making room for the afghan. "I dropped the kids at the sitter's. I drove to your house. She got into my car, and we drove to the diner, and she bought me lunch."

"Why?"

She looks down at the front of her sweatshirt and picks at a piece of lint from the afghan, dropping it onto the floor. It must be at least a 100-watt bulb in the lamp over our heads; I can see every gray hair along her part, every wrinkle and scar on her hands.

She sighs. "Because she wanted to know if we were having an affair."

I lean back toward the wall, knocking my head against the swinging pendulum of the clock that squeaks, with the chair legs creaking under my weight. I can feel panic rising, taste saliva flooding my mouth, and I swallow quickly, three or four times, hoping she'll bring coffee to me before I throw up. "Jesus," I say softly. "What did you say?"

She raises her eyes to mine, squinting because of the light. "I said no." She glances at the clock above my head, sees that the pendulum is still swinging, and it's still keeping time. "I said I'd never slept with you, not now and not twenty years ago."

I nod and keep nodding, in a motion that keeps time with the squeaking clock, because my mind is racing, and it seems to help. "Good," I say. "That's good."

She gets up and walks over to the coffeemaker, lets go of the afghan long enough to put both hands on the coffeepot, checking to see that it's warm enough, then fills the mugs and, holding them in one hand and with the other clutching the afghan, carries them to the table. "She knows you've been sneaking over here," she says, setting the mugs down, and I pull mine from the edge of the table, sliding it in front of me. "She woke up in the middle of the night, and you weren't there." She takes a sip from her mug and holds it close to her face, letting the steam rise. The expression on her face is curious; she wants me to tell her why I've been coming to see her, but she won't come straight out and ask me.

"She never said anything."

Whitey comes into the kitchen and settles himself at Lynette's feet. She reaches out her foot and gently massages his rear with it, rubbing his fur in the wrong direction, and he yawns and smacks his gums.

"She loves you," Lynette says flatly.

"I know." I wait for her to look at me, and then I say, "I'm sorry," and when she nods and sets down her coffee mug, I know she thinks I'm apologizing to Sonia, so I say, "I came over here to tell you I'm sorry."

"For what, Harley?" She lifts her eyes, with the harsh light magnifying the tiny red capillaries, the flecks of gold in her irises, the creases at the corners of her lids and the pouches underneath.

The wind blows against the storm window, rattling the outside frame. "For not helping," I say, staring at her curtains as if I might see through them, to the empty fields and Doug's brother's trailer. "For not trying to help sooner."

Her expression changes, as if she might say something, but then she shakes her head and only stares at me.

I can feel tears coming, and I don't think it's just because my eyelashes are beginning to unfreeze. "You were right. I should have tried to be your friend."

She shakes her head. "I shouldn't have said that." She looks toward the window, away from the light, and a shadow crosses over her face.

Her curtains are homemade; the tiny white stitches are uneven, wavering back and forth from the ruffled edge. "I saw the bruises on your legs," I say, holding up my hands, "like fingerprints."

She's startled; she shakes her head slowly and closes her eyes. "When?"

"In high school."

She nods and puts a hand to her forehead, pushes her hair back so that it stands up in front and slowly resettles itself. It must be a nervous habit.

"I should have done something," I say, and I know she's about to pull away from me, and I wish suddenly that the table weren't so wide, that I could simply reach across it to hold her hand. "I've made so many mistakes. If I lined them up, I couldn't see to the end of them."

She smiles slowly, and there are tears in her eyes. "We were seventeen," she says. "Remember seventeen? The kids who work at the Dairy Queen, and the ones whose pictures are in the paper for 4-H are seventeen. Babies."

"But I loved you," and I reach my hands out anyway, letting them rest on the glass tabletop.

She nods. "I loved you, too." She gets up slowly, pulling the afghan tight to her body, with her hand on the back of her chair, and Whitey jumps to his feet, leaning his body against her leg. "But things happen, Harley," she says, patting Whitey, massaging him along his spine so that he leans into her hand, "and three months after you left, I was screwing Doug."

I stand, shocked by the sudden pain in my feet, from resting my weight on unthawed toes. "It doesn't matter."

She nods and pushes hair away from her cheek, staticky where it's brushed against the afghan. "Right," she says and smiles. "Maybe none of it does."

I take a step forward, careful to avoid Whitey, and pull her to me, and I rock her gently in my arms, my fingers warming themselves against the soft yarn of the afghan. I feel suddenly lighter, as though I've finally gotten what I needed from her most, this forgiveness. "Just tell me," I say. "The bruises...." She stiffens, I rub her back in wide circles, and Whitey stands with his body wedged to her side. "Did Doug's hands leave those?"

She drops her shoulders, relaxing them, and doesn't pull away. "No."

I hold her to me, and I don't know what kind of trick of memory this is, but I would swear I smell apples. "I'm sorry."

"Right," she says, nodding her head against my shoulder. "Me, too."

She pulls away from me, wiping a hand under her eyes, smiling in a way I'll always associate with her, full of sadness and defeat.

"It's Sonia's birthday," I say for I don't know what reason. "She was so happy tonight."

Lynette takes the hand from her face, still smiling. "If I had told her we were having an affair, Harley, I think she would have forgiven you. I think she would have understood." She stoops and pats Whitey gently on the back before leading him into the hall.

She walks to the door with Whitey behind her, and when she reaches it, she stops and turns. "I told her if she thought you were cheating on her, she didn't know you very well." She hooks a finger inside Whitey's collar, so that he won't follow me outside. "I said you loved her." She takes the doorknob in her hand and turns it, opening the door just enough to let in a blast of cold air.

"I said I was sure you loved her," she says, "but what I didn't say was, I would have done it anyway." She swings the door open wide, stepping behind it to where it isn't so cold. "I haven't known very many nice guys, Harley," she says, leaning her head against the edge of the door, "and if you'd asked me, I would have done anything for you."

༄

"Oh, Harley," my mother said, opening the door to her room at the retirement center. She had dressed up for us, in a pink silk blouse and gray pants, but she'd been unable to shove her feet in pumps, and she was still wearing her canvas sneakers. "There aren't enough girls in America?"

"Ma," I said, leading Sonia into the room my mother had taken pains to decorate with gold-framed paintings from her living room and large plants blocking the view of the bed. The paintings were too big and too close together for the room, as if she'd had trouble choosing among them, but the center's staff had put my mother on the tour they gave for prospective residents to show them how much like home the tiny, medicinal-smelling rooms could seem. The plants looked dried-out, brown at the edges, from the heat that came full-blast through the register next to the bed, and although my mother had draped the hospital chairs that came with the room in oversized throws and velvet pillows, she couldn't hide the orange vinyl seats or the legs covered with pecan veneer. "This is my wife, Sonia," I said, pulling her forward, and my mother stiffly held out her hand, but Sonia ignored it and drew her into a hug that made her struggle to keep her balance.

"Mama," she said, "I am so glad to meet you."

My mother smiled and looked at me. "Well," she said, reaching up a hand to rub her collarbone. "How nice." She held out an arm, motioning for us to sit in the hospital chairs, and when Sonia knocked a velvet pillow onto the floor, my mother said, "Don't worry, dear," picked it up and placed it on top of her dresser.

"Harley speaks of you," Sonia said. "I am knowing you already."

My mother nodded and said suddenly, turning toward me. "I've got that hot-pot plugged in by the bed, and some tea bags." Then she turned to Sonia and began almost shouting. "But it's difficult to pour with the arthritis in these fingers," she said and turned back to me. "Will you pour, honey?"

I got up, straightening the throw where it had pulled forward onto the chair seat. "Aren't hot–pots against the rules?"

She shrugged and stepped aside for me to pass. "What they don't know won't hurt them," she said and followed me over to where the hot–pot sat on the indoor–outdoor carpet.

I poured water into two of the styrofoam cups she'd stolen from the cafeteria, emptying the hot–pot, thinking about the trouble she'd gone to just to serve us tea, because she would never in a million years allow herself to have guests without offering them some kind of refreshment.

"We can fill this again," I said, and my mother took the hot–pot from me, holding it by the handle, so that she could refill it in the bathroom.

She came back with it, and I plugged it in and carried the two cups of boiling water over to the dresser, where we dropped in the tea bags to steep.

"Well," she said. "She's a pretty little thing, I'll say that much."

"Ma," I said, dunking one of the tea bags. "She speaks English, and this is a small room."

My mother grimaced and waved me away. "So what?" she said. "I'm not allowed to say she's pretty?"

Sonia reached into the pocket of her coat and pulled out the frame with the portrait of me, the one she'd carried with her from Russia. "Mama," she said, standing up to hand it to her. "I bring this for you."

My mother took it from her, peering through the bottom half of her glasses at the tiny portrait. "Oh," she said, "that's very nice," and she scanned the walls, with their oversized sofa paintings and the wide gold frames. "I'll have to find a place to put it."

⌒

Sonia's waiting for me; from the driveway, I glance up and see the light by her side of the bed. I come in through the kitchen and take my boots off, wondering how long Lynette's coffee and whatever Sonia has to say to me will keep me awake, listening for sounds from my mother's room and thinking about my father and what he'd say to me now, if he'd accuse me of screwing up my own life, of deliberately making myself unhappy.

I drop my boots on the floor of the front closet and climb our wooden stairs, with my feet flat and solid, still half-frozen and aching. Sonia smiles when she sees me and puts down the Russian–language newspaper she has sent to her from New York, folding it in half and creasing it so that it lies flat on the covers. She's put on her flannel nightgown and banded her hair into a ponytail.

"You speak to her, Harley?" she asks.

I take my wallet and keys from my pants and drop them on the dresser. "Yes."

Sonia waits for me to pull off my jacket and the flannel shirt, to lay them over my wallet and keys and come to the other side of the bed.

"Lynette," she says, garbling the name so badly that I realize it's maybe the second or third time I've heard her say it, "is a kind woman," she says, and she pulls back the quilt from my side of the bed, inviting me to sit or lie down next to her. "She is kind to me."

I drop my weight on the edge of the mattress and take her hand. "You didn't have to worry."

"Oh," she says, and she laces her fingers between mine, pulling them into the same fist. "Yes," she says, "I worry."

I let go of her and take a look around the room, at the humidifier in the corner and my dresser with its drawers half open and our wedding picture in a frame on top and Sonia's favorite postcard.

"I wasn't sleeping with her," I say.

Sonia nods, raises her bent knees and rests her chin on them.

"I was trying to help her."

She has a small piece of dryer sheet stuck to the shoulder of her nightgown. "But Harley," she says, "if you are only helping, why do you hide? Why do you go to her in the night?"

I pick off the piece of dryer sheet and drop it on the floor next to the bed, where there are clumps of dust next to the radiator and clumps of Whitey's fur. "I don't love her," I say carefully. "I love you."

Sonia nods her chin against her knees; I've said it to her a thousand times, and I probably shouldn't even expect her to respond anymore, but the truth of it is just beginning to settle on me, right now, staring at her new coat hanging on a hook attached to the back of the door, and I wish there were a new way to say it that would clarify the difference.

Because it's dawned on me, finally, that all this time, I've been seeking forgiveness from the wrong person—that Sonia's the one whose forgiveness I need, every day, for being no more and no less than the person I am: weak, confused, and slow to grasp the most basic meaning of life: to know love when you find it, to be willing to fight for it, to never let it go.

"You, Sonia," I say, and she nods again, bumping her chin bone on her kneecap.

"I love you so much, Harley," she says, with that sad smile she must have learned from Lynette.

I pull her hand from around her knees and hold it again, looking down at her chewed nails and the knobs of bone at her knuckles.

"You ask her," Sonia says quietly, "if she kills him?"

I curl my fingers over her hand, kneading her knuckles with my thumb. "I don't want to know."

She leans forward so that she can see my face. "But you think, Harley. You think she does."

I face her, smiling, and shake my head. "No."

⌇

During a visit home from college after my father retired, I asked him what had made him decide to stay at the mill all those years, because I had begun to be afraid, first that I wouldn't find a job, and second that I would find one and be stuck with it forever.

"Oh," he said, and he rubbed his hand through his hair, like he used to do, when my mother complained that he left buckwheat dust on her kitchen table, "people don't decide things as often as you think." He picked up my mother's creamer and splashed milk into his coffee, swirling it with the handle of the sugar spoon, then wiping the spoon on his bathrobe and sticking it back in the sugar. "A lot of times," he said, lifting the coffee cup to blow across it, "things like that, even important things, choose you."

He took a sip of his coffee and laughed when he saw the look on my face. "No," he said, "it's not like that." He looked around him as if he might be expecting my mother, then dumped a spoonful of sugar into his cup without bothering to stir it this time. "Sometimes it's the best thing."

I stared at the pocket of his robe, where the sugar spoon had already left streaks, and I knew my mother would complain, like she always did, about how he managed to get his clothes so dirty, and I, like always, wouldn't say a thing.

"Sometimes God," he said, and it was the only time I could remember him speaking to me about God, "gives you a shove in the right direction. Sometimes the right job is the one you overhear somebody talking about at the diner. Sometimes you go to a dance because you're bored, and you meet the girl of your dreams."

"Is that what happened to you?"

He lifted his cup, wiping his sleeve across the ring of coffee it left on the table. "Listen, Harley," he said, "it's not all that complicated. I stayed at my job because I liked it, and because we had you, and you needed stuff."

"So how do you choose?" I fingered the edge of my mother's lazy Susan and spun it a half turn, and my father reached out and stopped it, before my mother's antique salt and pepper shakers could fall off and get broken.

"Sometimes," he said, "you just gotta pick something." He took a paper napkin finally from the lazy Susan and used it to wipe his mouth. "Life is mostly trial-and-error," he said, crumpling the napkin and dropping it onto the tabletop. "You make mistakes, and if you're smart, you learn from them." He looked down at the front of his robe and dusted off some of the sugar that clung to the pocket. "That's the challenge," he said. "Believe it or not, that's the adventure."

ॐ

I show up ten minutes late for work, and when Bernie sees me, he taps the face of his watch with his index finger and tisks his tongue against his teeth. "Sheesh," he says, shaking his head. "Newlyweds."

"Sorry," I say, not bothering to take my jacket off, and he waves me away.

"Forget about it."

I take my glove off and hold it between my teeth while I go through the orders on his desk. It looks like a light day, and I'm hoping maybe it'll stay that way and I can do something nice for Sonia and my mother, take them to the kind of fancy dinner they deserve.

"So listen," Bernie says, leaning toward me across his desk, "what if I tell her I love her?" and he opens his eyes wide, forming his eyebrows into two furry triangles.

"You mean Bernice?"

He rolls his eyes. "Yeah, yeah, sure. Bernice."

I take the glove out of my mouth. "Wow. I don't know. Isn't it a little soon for that?"

He leans forward again, bunching his stomach against the edge of the desktop. "Well..." he says, tilting his head as if to signal he's gathering his thoughts.

He leans back in his chair, letting out a puff of air. "Okay," he says. "Okay. You think I should wait."

I put my glove back on, watching the cigar smoke coming from his top desk drawer. "Look," I say, and I'm starting to sweat already under the flannel lining of my jacket, "I thought you were just looking for a nice lady to spend time with. Because Bernie," I say, watching the smoke drift over his unfinished maintenance report, "there are a lot of nice ladies...."

He nods. "Yeah," he says, "I know," and he pulls hard on the drawer, so that the ashtray slams against the front of it, picks up his cigar and takes a puff. "But sometimes you get lucky," he says. "You get more than you asked for."

I lean close to his desk, and my boot, where my toes are a little numb, knocks into the bottom of the desk with a loud, hollow bang. "You love her?" I ask.

Bernie nods and looks at the back of his dead wife's photo. "Not like Sharon," he says, "but yeah."

I nod and step back from his desk. "Okay, then," I say. "Okay." I have the order sheets in my glove, and I switch them to my left hand so I can shake hands with my right. "Go to it, then," I say, giving a congratulatory pump up and down of the handshake. "Go get her."

༰

On the way home from the Land Lubber, Sonia switches the radio to the classical station "for when we are being classy." My mother shivers and puts her hands to the heat register, and I tell her it'll take a minute for the truck to warm up.

As we head into town, coming down into the valley, the station flickers half in static, but when I reach for the knob, Sonia sends me a disappointed look that stops me. I can just make out the word "Berlioz" as we head into the intersection next to the house, and I see Doug Hale's truck in the driveway.

"Whose truck is that?" my mother asks, and I park in the driveway next to Lynette and get out, leaving the motor running. I thought Sonia would stay with my mother, but she follows me out of the truck and over to Lynette's driver's side window.

She's leaning against the seatback with her eyes closed, but she doesn't seem startled when I knock lightly on the glass, only opens her eyes and reaches for the handle to lower the window enough to talk.

"Hi," she says, and she looks at Sonia standing behind me. "This is the last visit, I promise."

"Something is wrong?" Sonia asks and touches a hand to the back of my jacket.

Lynette shakes her head. "Nothing." She smiles and lowers the window some more, then leans on it with her fingers. "I need to ask you a favor," she says, and she looks from me to Sonia. "I wouldn't ask if I didn't have to."

I clear my throat, picking at a patch of ice with the toe of my boot. "What do you need?"

She smiles, and I can see that she's got a different cast, a lighter one that lets her move her fingers more. "I put Whitey in your yard," she says, nodding in the direction of our back fence. She looks behind me at Sonia. "I need you to keep him for me."

"For how long?" I ask, and she shakes her head.

"To keep."

My mother's rubbing her hands in front of the heater, and somebody's shoveling the driveway to the ambulance barn by hand, scraping a metal shovel across the pavement.

"Where are you going?"

She's turned at the sound of the shoveling, too, and she faces me again, still smiling. "I'm tired," she says. "I haven't slept in..." and she shakes her head to say she doesn't even know how long. "I'm gonna give up," she says, and she flexes her fingers in the lighter cast. "I'm gonna turn myself in."

"Oh, no," Sonia says, and she raises her mittened hand to the ledge of the window, covering Lynette's fingers.

Lynette holds still under Sonia's hand and looks down at

her, still with that eerie smile. "He nearly killed me so many times," she says softly. "And he was standing there, leaning over the hole he'd made too big, and he said, 'You stupid bitch, you made me drop the thermos.'" She looks down at Sonia's red mitten and laughs and I can see now that she's been crying, and her words comes in bursts. "And I was so tired," she says, "and angry. And I picked up the axe, and…" She pulls the cast out from under Sonia's hand and mimics swinging the axe, then begins crying harder.

"No," Sonia says, and Lynette turns to look at my face, and the tears are running now, and I want to wipe them away, because I know how cold her skin must be.

"But it was the wrong thing," she says. "It was the wrong thing, Harley. Because I was so angry…."

I look into her eyes that she can't even focus because of the tears. "Did he fall in when you hit him?"

Lynette nods and looks from me to Sonia. "Yes."

"And he was dead?"

Sonia tugs at the back of my jacket. "No, Harley," she says.

Lynette turns to me, with the tears clouding her eyes, and shakes her head no, slowly, still hiccuping, breathing in and out with those short, shuddering gasps.

"And you didn't help him," I say, and she shakes her head again, just as slowly.

"I hit him again," she says in a whisper.

Sonia steps forward, putting both hands on the window ledge now. "No," she says.

"And then you cut yourself and threw the axe in the lake," I say, and this time Lynette nods, still not saying a word.

"And when they do the autopsy, they'll know," and Lynette nods again.

"I think so," she whispers.

"Oh," Sonia says, and she's crying now, too, and the two of them hold each other's hands like that.

I take a long, last look at her, at her hair that's brittle and broken and the lines etched into her skin, at her eyes which I can almost remember full of light. "We'll do anything to help," I say. "Anything," and Lynette nods again and looks from me to my wife.

"Thank you," she says, and wipes her eyes and starts the truck, and I stand watching her for a moment before I step away from her truck and kiss Sonia on the back of her head. Then I walk over to my own truck, so I can carry my mother inside.

I have my mother in my arms, and I take her to the porch and wait for Sonia, and Sonia's still crying when she comes up behind me to open the door. Her hands shake with the key, and I wait for her with the weight of my mother's cast in my arms, and somehow my mother knows to be quiet, simply leaning against me and letting me carry her.

ༀ

Flurries were predicted; they're falling now, drifting past the streetlights, and I listen, straining for the sound of them—a hush—on the roof. Tomorrow, I think, I could buy Sonia some skates and take her out on the lake, put an arm around her and glide. But for now, she fills the humidifier in the bathtub. Whitey waits for her in the hall, his toenails clicking on the hardwood, and my mother's asleep downstairs with her memories, her voice murmuring my father's name from the monitor in my nightstand drawer. This is the sound of quiet in our home—of peace—and I wish the same for Lynette, say a prayer for it. I ask God to forgive her more than she's asking for, possibly even more than she deserves, and I push aside Sonia's curtains, look down at the ambulance barn, which is quiet now, for the moment, and before I climb into bed with the wife I love so absolutely, I say to God: Thank you, thank you, thank you for sending Lynette to save me.

ACKNOWLEDGEMENTS

This novel, like any novel, was an act of faith—not just for me, but for those who believed in me and supported me along the way. I'd like to thank my agent, Julie Barer, and my editor, Rob Grover, for their enthusiasm and the work that was far above and beyond the call of duty. For technical expertise, I'd like to thank Jody Taylor, Rudy Guerrero and Melanie Harris; Jack Nichiporuk of Empire Telephone, for giving me the basics about what telephone line repairmen do; Jesse Bond, for a discussion about ice fishing; and Tamara and Grigoriy Levin, for their descriptions of Russian economics and culture. I'd also like to thank my many teachers, both in the MFA program at the University of Michigan and in the writing program at Northwestern University: Nick Delbanco, Charles Baxter, Alyson Hagy, Janet Desaulniers, Sheila Schwartz and Robert Boswell—also Andrea Beauchamp, who was as much a teacher as any of the others. I'd like to thank my colleagues at Keuka College for their moral support. I'd also like to thank my family and the many friends who bolstered my faith at times when it faltered: Tananarive Due, Jeanne Lokar, Ronna Grimes, Craig and Stephanie Shemin, Jennifer and David Reynolds, and Michael Brothers.